Cyberstrike: DC

James Barrington is a trained military pilot who has worked in covert operations and espionage. He has subsequently built a reputation as a writer of high-class, authentic and action-packed thrillers. He lives in Andorra, but travels widely. He also writes conspiracy thrillers under the pseudonym James Becker.

Richard Benham is best known globally as a pioneer in the world of Cyber Security, Artificial Intelligence and Cyber Warfare. As an academic in 2014 he created the first MBA in Cyber Security that was launched at a cross party event at The House of Commons and received the personal support of the Prime Minster. In 2016 he formed the charity The Cyber Trust to help protect vulnerable groups using technology. In 2017 he was nominated for the UK Digital Leader of the Year for his Cyber4Schools initiatives which has been adopted nationally by the National Police Chiefs Council. He is a council member of The Winston Churchill Memorial Trust, an Ambassador for The Diana Awards and the co-author of the Cyberstrike series.

Also by James Barrington and Richard Benham

The Ben Morgan Thrillers

Cyberstrike: London
Cyberstrike: DC

CYBERSTRIKE:
DC

JAMES BARRINGTON
WITH PROFESSOR RICHARD BENHAM

CANELO

First published in the United Kingdom in 2021 by

Canelo
31 Helen Road
Oxford OX2 0DF
United Kingdom

A CIP catalogue record for this book is available from the British Library.

Print ISBN 978 1 80032 394 0
Ebook ISBN 978 1 78863 957 6

This book is a work of fiction. Names, characters, businesses, organizations, places and events are either the product of the author's imagination or are used fictitiously. Any resemblance to actual persons, living or dead, events or locales is entirely coincidental.

Look for more great books at www.canelo.co

Printed and bound in Great Britain by Clays Ltd, Elcograf S.p.A.

Prologue

It's not easy to kill a man who doesn't exist, but Captain Nick Montana and the Allied soldiers under his command were going to try.

The name Abū Omar al-Baghdadi had drifted in and out of reality in Iraq for most of the previous decade. Sometimes he was acknowledged as a real and active flesh and blood terrorist, but at other times he seemed to be something more akin to a mythical Robin Hood character, an insubstantial holy warrior-like image created to inspire and rally the forces of radical Islam.

But whatever the truth about this elusive figure, the previous day the coalition forces surrounding the isolated ISI – Islamic State of Iraq – safe house about six miles outside Tikrit had received solid intelligence that stated the man – or a man the informant had claimed to be Abū Omar al-Baghdadi, which wasn't precisely the same thing – was somewhere inside the building. And the chance of either killing him or laying his ghost to rest was too good to miss.

Attacking a compound comprising a large house inside a stone boundary wall, a house that was known to be occupied by heavily armed ISI fighters, was a potential recipe for suicide, so the American and Iraqi soldiers surrounding the building weren't going to just amble over and knock on the door. Or even strafe it with machine-gun fire. They had an entirely different plan in place.

The two senior officers of the coalition force were lying side by side under cover just over two hundred yards away, studying the building through binoculars.

The word 'desert' reached the English language – late Middle English, to be precise – either from the French word *deserter*, which was itself derived from *desertare* in late Latin and originally from *desertus*, or possibly direct from the ecclesiastical Latin *dēsertum*, a participle of the verb *dēserere*, meaning 'to abandon'. Originally, the word meant 'an abandoned place' in the sense that it was not occupied by people, hence 'deserted', but over the last century or so it has acquired its present meaning: an arid and usually sandy expanse of land.

And that was precisely what the two military officers, and all the soldiers under their command, were looking at. The terrain in front of their position was virtually devoid of vegetation, just the occasional stunted tree or bush that was somehow clinging on to life in the harsh environment. The ground was a mixture of sand and rock, the latter fortunately providing numerous places where the soldiers had been able to conceal themselves before the attack commenced, and which would provide a bare minimum of cover when they began their advance.

Beyond that area of largely level ground a large solid stone house, flat roofed and with small windows and two wooden doors visible from the vantage point chosen by the officers, sat inside a stone boundary wall about five feet high which entirely enclosed it. There were at least two gates that pierced the wall but the coalition troops had no intention of using them until most of the resistance had been suppressed. The stone of the building and the wall were the same whitish-grey colour as the rocky outcrops in the vicinity, and no doubt the building had originally been constructed from stones cut from the bedrock in that area. It looked completely solid and was by any sensible definition a hard target, which was why the coalition force was waiting for one particular event to take place.

About five feet behind the two officers, one of the US Army soldiers was listening to transmissions on his SINCGARS combat net radio, waiting for a specific report. He was a JTAC, a Joint Terminal Attack Controller. That meant he was authorised to control combat aircraft being used in close air support in battle, effectively using the aircraft as a lethal addition to the weapons he already had to hand.

He'd already provided the 'talk on' to the pilot to precisely identify both the target and the weapons to be used. Now he was just waiting for one thing.

He stiffened as he listened to a message, then leaned forward very slightly and in a voice that was little more than a loud whisper said a single word.

'Inbound.'

The American captain glanced at his Iraqi Army opposite number, who nodded. Then he turned back to face the soldier.

'Clear it,' he said.

'Roger, sir.' The soldier pressed the transmit key and spoke quietly into his microphone. 'Boar Three One, you're cleared hot. I say again, you're cleared hot.'

He listened to the reply, then spoke again to the officer.

'Ninety seconds, sir.'

'Good. Pass it on.'

The soldier nodded and spoke just as quietly into the second radio he carried, the AN/PRC-148 MBITR handheld unit. All the soldiers in the combined force carried identical sets.

A minute later they all heard it.

The AGM-65 Maverick air-to-surface missile is just subsonic, travelling at 0.93 Mach or 713 miles per hour, which meant they saw it at virtually the same instant that they heard it. There was a deafening roar from the Thiokol solid propellant rocket motor as the stubby white missile streaked over their heads and smashed into the side wall of the target property. The impact was followed instantly by the shattering explosion as the WDU-20/B shaped-charge detonated.

Lost in the sound of the explosion, they didn't hear the roar as the second Maverick overflew them, but there was no mistaking the sight and sound of the missile hitting the target about a dozen feet to the right of the first impact.

But that, really, was only the prologue, the hors d'oeuvre that preceded the main course.

With a sound like some kind of massive fabric being torn apart, a steam of 30mm high-explosive shells screamed over the dusty ground at around half a mile a second to smash into the wall of the building, detonating in bursts of yellow flame accompanied by a noise like constant rolling thunder as the charges exploded. Windows blew inwards and stones shattered or simply disintegrated, shards flying in all directions.

An instant later, what looked like an old-fashioned light-grey aircraft with straight wings swept over the ground troops, its twin tail-mounted General Electric turbofan engines emitting a deafening scream. The nose of the plane was clouded in smoke as each salvo of shells was fired by the Avenger rotary cannon.

Abruptly, the firing stopped and the aircraft banked hard to the left, turned away from the target and pulled up into a steep climb, releasing a cluster of flares as a countermeasure against possible heat-seeking missiles, though no intelligence reports had suggested the ISI fighters in the safe house had access to Stingers or similar weapons. But it was SOP – Standard Operating Procedure – to always assume that your enemy was better armed and equipped and more competent and dedicated than you believed or expected. That way you didn't get caught out.

Even before the A-10 Thunderbolt, affectionately known to the American troops as the Warthog, had vanished from sight, Montana was checking the target. The safe house was still standing, though obviously battered, and the second Maverick had blown a hole straight through the side wall.

'Target as briefed,' he said to the signaller. 'Immediate execute.'

The soldier relayed the command and coalition soldiers stood up from their concealed positions and began to advance on the property, using overwatch or fire-and-cover tactics, one group dispersing and moving swiftly from one position to another while their comrades stayed in place to provide covering fire if required.

But there was no movement from inside the safe house. No resistance and no sign of any of the ISI fighters they had been told to expect. Or anyone else.

And then, suddenly, there was.

As the first wave of coalition soldiers reached around a hundred yards from the building they heard the unmistakable clatter of an

4

AK-47 firing on full auto, which was perhaps slightly better news than the same weapon firing single shots. The Kalashnikov is the weapon of choice for insurgents and terrorists around the world because it is so rugged and reliable, but it's not the most accurate assault rifle, and especially not when firing on full auto, as the barrel lifts uncontrollably.

The low stone walls and rocky outcrops around the advancing soldiers sparked and rang from the impacts of the 7.62mm bullets, but most of the rounds went high, completely missing their targets. The soldiers dived into cover and returned fire with their Colt M4A1 carbines, but the ISI fighter was hidden behind a broken section of wall and almost invisible from ground level.

But then the unseen defender switched his weapon to semi-automatic mode, pinning down the advancing soldiers. He could see them, but he himself remained almost invisible, only the muzzle of his Kalashnikov showing. All the coalition soldiers could do was concentrate their fire on the section of wall behind which he was standing, their bullets ricocheting off the old stones.

'Take him out,' Montana ordered.

The terse reply came almost immediately.

'Already on it.'

The combined force didn't include a dedicated sniper because they were expecting to carry out what amounted to a house clearance rather than engaging the enemy at long range, but two of the American soldiers had been detailed to take up static positions to provide covering fire. They had established themselves on slightly higher ground, one to the south of the building and the other over to the east, choosing locations that offered the best possible views of the target property.

One of them had no shot, because from his location the ISI fighter was shielded and invisible behind the boundary wall, but the other man could see him – just. To be exact, he could see the end of the muzzle of the AK-47 projecting towards the advancing troops, and he could both see and hear the weapon firing, the barrel moving as the unseen man altered his aim. Every time the ISI fighter fired a round, the recoil forced his upper body backwards and just into view from behind a section of the wall, but never far enough or long enough for the American to take a shot.

Then the Kalashnikov fell silent as the magazine was exhausted, and that was the best chance the coalition marksman had.

The ISI fighter took a half step backwards as he dropped the magazine out of his AK-47 and grabbed another one from a pouch strapped around his chest. As he did so, he also stepped back into the sights of the American's Colt carbine.

Immediately the soldier squeezed the trigger. And then fired a second time. The first round missed the ISI fighter by a few inches, ricocheting off the stone wall beside him, but the second took him on the left-hand side of his chest and he dropped sideways and out of sight.

From his location Montana saw a bearded figure stumble into view and then collapse, a Kalashnikov falling from his hands. But he knew that wouldn't be the end of the resistance.

As if on cue, about a dozen male figures, all with a similar appearance – bearded and wearing predominantly white and grey dishdashas, abas and keffiyehs – swarmed out of the building. Each man was carrying one of the ubiquitous Kalashnikov AK-47 assault rifles and each had a magazine pouch strapped around his upper body.

Despite the damage to the house and the casualties that would inevitably have been caused by the Warthog's strike, the terrorists still had teeth.

A heavy barrage of shots rang out, the firing coming from both sides. The coalition troops were more exposed but they were all experienced in this kind of combat and were taking full advantage of what cover they could find. And they weren't wasting their ammunition, only firing when they could acquire definite targets.

The ISI fighters, in contrast, were much less disciplined, many firing long bursts that sent bullets screaming into the air well above their targets, but they were also better protected by the stone wall surrounding the house and, probably, had far more ammunition at their disposal than the coalition soldiers.

The operation briefing had included all possible contingencies – or at least all those that Montana had been able to think of – and this kind of stand-off had been entirely predictable. No new orders were necessary.

Almost as soon as the ISI insurgents began firing, three of the coalition troops loaded M406 high-explosive rounds into their M203 under-barrel grenade launchers and fired them into the compound almost simultaneously, the clunk of these weapons firing completely inaudible against the rapid, hammering fire of the assault rifles.

Grenades are at their most devastating in a confined space. Three heavy explosions crashed out and instantly the small compound turned into a killing ground. The ISI fighters had nowhere to hide or take cover as the grenades, each with a kill radius of 5 metres and capable of causing injuries within 130 metres, detonated inside the boundary wall.

Screams of pain followed the explosions and, significantly, the firing from inside the compound stopped.

The coalition troops advanced in stages, still using fire-and-cover tactics, towards the target. The first of them checked what was waiting for them on the other side of the boundary wall, then scrambled over it.

About half of the ISI defenders were clearly either dead or badly wounded, but the coalition troops took no chances, eliminating every man who still showed signs of life, just in case any of them had decided that wearing a suicide vest made sense.

Then another two Kalashnikovs opened up, firing from a couple of broken windows on the ground floor of the house itself.

The coalition soldiers ducked into what cover they could find and returned fire. They were too close to the building to use grenades because the weapons wouldn't arm in such a short distance, and in any case the M203 wasn't accurate enough to fire a grenade through such small openings. So they were going to have to do it the hard way.

The soldiers inside the compound were pinned down and unable to do more than concentrate their fire through the windows and an open door of the house, to prevent the ISI fighters from accurately targeting them. But not all the coalition soldiers were inside the compound.

The NCO, a master sergeant, knew exactly what he had to do. With two other soldiers dogging his footsteps he ran along the outside of the compound wall, crouching down so as to be immune to the fire from the house. As soon as they got abeam the wall of the building, the NCO shouldered his Colt assault rifle, clambered over the wall and ran across to the left-hand side window. The besieging soldiers altered their aim to make sure none of their bullets went anywhere near him. He stopped a few feet short and pulled a small brownish spherical object from his utility belt.

Timing is important in life, but crucial in conflict.

The NCO removed the safety clip from the M67 grenade, changed his grip to remove the pull ring and almost immediately released the lever. That type of grenade explodes between four and five seconds after the lever is released, so the NCO counted to three before lobbing it through the open window and over the muzzles of the two Kalashnikovs that were still firing into the compound. He couldn't allow time for one of the insurgents to grab the grenade and throw it back, because that would ruin the master sergeant's whole day. And probably kill him.

He took a couple of paces back, knelt down and covered his ears. As he did so, he heard a shrill yell of alarm from inside the room, followed immediately by the crashing explosion as six and a half ounces of Composition B detonated. A mixture of RDX and TNT, Comp B is the workhorse explosive of the American military, used in everything from land mines to artillery shells.

The master sergeant jogged forward a few feet to the second window, priming another M67 as he did so, and repeated the treatment.

The moment the second grenade detonated, the coalition troops surged forward, streaming in through the half-open door between the two windows, clearing each room as they advanced. It was a case of overwhelming force meeting disorganised and demoralised defenders, many of them already wounded by the Warthog's strafing run. It was more or less a mopping-up operation.

Ten minutes later Nick Montana and his Iraqi counterpart strode around the compound, Montana comparing the faces of the dead insurgents with printed images on half a dozen sheets of paper. Unlike the major players in the invasion of Iraq, who had merited their names and faces being included in the packs of playing cards issued to front-line soldiers to identify them, Abū Omar al-Baghdadi's face had just been provided as a monochrome image on a page spat out by a laser printer.

'Nothing here,' Montana said, using the toe of his boot to turn the head of the last corpse so that he could see the man's face.

'He was supposed to be at a meeting here,' the Iraqi lieutenant replied in good English. 'If he was, he'll be somewhere inside the house.'

The master sergeant stepped out of the door of the property as Montana approached.

'The building's secure, sir,' he said. 'We've got sixteen men in cuffs, some of them wounded, plus a couple of women. All the others in the house are dead.'

Montana nodded and walked inside. The two women had been locked in one room and the surviving men assembled in another. The building reeked of cordite and he stepped over sprawled bodies and crunched over empty shell cases as he made his way from room to room.

None of the prisoners looked anything like Abū Omar al-Baghdadi, but Montana thought he recognised one of the corpses, one of two dead men lying sprawled on the floor in one of the smaller upstairs rooms. It looked as if the other man had been killed by shells from the Warthog's Avenger cannon because of his appalling injuries, but the man whose face was familiar to the American officer had died from small-arms fire. He was also wearing a suicide vest.

'I know your orders were to take as many of them alive as we could,' the master sergeant said, as Montana looked at the body, 'but when my men kicked down this door and they saw what he was wearing they took him down straight away.'

'Good decision.' Montana was looking at a different piece of paper and comparing the image printed on it with what he was seeing.

'That's not al-Baghdadi,' the Iraqi lieutenant said. 'He's a much younger man, but he does look familiar.'

9

'He should. Unless he's got a double, that's Abū Ayyub al-Masri. Until about ten minutes ago, he was ISI's Minister of War and the leader of al-Qaeda in Iraq. He's been on the wanted list for months, so this is a real good result.'

Montana led the way into the other upstairs room, where another dead terrorist lay in an untidy heap on the dusty floor. He hooked the toe of his boot under the shoulder of the corpse and flipped the dead man onto his back.

'And I'm sure this is Abū Omar al-Baghdadi,' he said, holding the sheet of paper next to the face of the corpse, 'or at least this is the man in this photograph.'

Montana was right on both counts. Ten minutes later he called for extraction of his men and also a couple of trucks to haul away some of the stuff they'd discovered inside the property.

–

The raid was considered a massive success by the coalition forces. At a subsequent press conference in Baghdad the deaths of Abū Omar al-Baghdadi and Abū Ayyub al-Masri were hailed as a 'most significant blow' to the insurgency. As well as the two high-value targets, al-Baghdadi's son had also been killed in the attack and one of the two women who had survived was al-Masri's wife. Even more significantly, the coalition forces seized computers that had been used to communicate with Osama bin Laden and his deputy Ayman al-Zawahiri by email, producing an intelligence windfall of massive importance in combating the rebels.

But the mood of the press conference was tainted by the knowledge that in the hours after the raid at Tikrit, a series of reprisal bombings orchestrated by the ISI had taken place in the Shi'ite areas of Baghdad and had killed almost sixty people.

Iraq

Early on the following Sunday morning, the Sharia Minister of the ISI, Abū al-Walid Abd al-Wahhab al-Mashadani, admitted on a militant website that the two leaders had been killed by enemy forces, but did his best to downplay the damage this had done to the organisation, claiming it was nothing more than an 'illusory victory', though he did not trouble to explain what that expression was supposed to mean.

What al-Mashadani didn't say was that shockwaves had been driven through the whole of the ISI by the attack on the safe house, a house that had proved to be anything but safe. And while the insurgents believed themselves more than capable of facing the coalition forces in ground combat, the total air superiority enjoyed by the Americans was something they had no way of combating.

What they really needed to do, the ISI leaders admitted to themselves after the statement on the website had gone live, was to hit back at the Americans – and at the British, who had left the country almost exactly a year earlier – in a way that could not be countered by their military hardware. In short, they needed to move the battleground from the war-torn deserts of Iraq and Syria and away from the military superiority possessed by the West and into the heartlands of the countries of their enemies, which meant onto the streets of New York, Washington and London. They needed to change both the location of the battlefield and the type of combat, the glorious success of the World Trade Center attacks and individual acts of violence on the streets of Europe now almost forgotten. Instead of facing aircraft and tanks, the forces of radical Islam would cut a swathe through the soft underbelly of the enemy and hit the weakest and easiest of all targets, a target that was completely unprepared and utterly unable to defend itself: the unarmed civilian population.

And there was one very obvious way they could do that. It wasn't even a new idea.

In November 1980, during the Iran–Iraq War, a thirteen-year-old Iranian boy named Mohammad Hossein Fahmideh lashed RPGs

– rocket propelled grenades – to his body and detonated them and himself under the belly of an Iraqi tank. Fahmideh was hailed by the Iranian leadership as both a national hero and an inspiration for others to emulate.

That was considered to be the first *istishhad* attack in the modern era, the Arabic word translating as 'martyrdom' or the 'death of a martyr'. Originally the word implied that the martyr was a victim, a person killed because of his or her religious beliefs or, quite often, a refusal to change to or to accept a different religion, but increasingly the term is now used to suggest an act of heroism and self-sacrifice. A martyr who kills himself in this way, by inflicting damage upon his perceived enemy as a consequence of his own death, is given the honorific title *shahid*.

In the West such actions are commonly referred to as suicide bombings, but in Arabic they are known as *al-amaliyat al-istishhadiya*, or 'martyrdom operations', because classical Islamic law forbids Muslims to commit suicide. Perhaps surprisingly to most non-Muslims, there is a body of Islamic law that governs the conduct of *istishhad* actions and operations and other aspects of warfare and *jihad*. In fact, embarking upon a *jihad* – the word translating literally as a 'struggle', though it is normally thought in the West to mean a 'holy war' – is not just an option for Muslims: it is both a religious requirement and an obligation. If a Muslim community of any size, from the smallest group up to an entire nation, faces danger or hostility, the members are required to resist. That is enshrined in Islamic law, and that is the basis of what radical Muslims consider to be their holy duty, to fight any and all oppressors by any and every means at their disposal.

However, those same Islamic laws are very specific with respect to how any such conflict is to be conducted. In particular, it is forbidden for women, children and non-combatants to be targeted, and residential areas and property are not to be attacked: the struggle is supposed to only be between the members of the Muslim community and those troops or forces that are seen to be actively oppressing or otherwise threatening them. Radical Islam has thoroughly embraced the concept of *jihad* but has clearly decided to ignore the other Islamic laws and rules of the struggle, preferring to direct most of their operations against the softest possible targets, the civilian populations of the countries with which they are in dispute or which they see as their oppressors.

The ISI leadership knew that finding people willing to make the ultimate sacrifice in support of their cause would not be particularly difficult. Recent history has clearly shown that disaffected young men in many Western nations were prepared to concoct their own plans and strike at the heart of their adopted country, which in some cases was also the country of their birth. So providing the appropriate guidance, finance and equipment would ensure that devastating attacks could be launched comparatively easily. It would just be a matter of identifying suitable 'volunteers' and then executing the operation. And the elders planning and directing the ISI had every intention of doing exactly that.

Such terrorist attacks were easy enough to plan and, given the proper degree of commitment by the selected *shahids*, would always be successful. Attacks like these, mounted with no warning given and always aiming for the highest possible level of casualties, would be devastating. Every British and American death would be a cause for celebration and they would relish the chaos and carnage the attacks inflicted.

But the other thing the ISI leadership needed was a very different attack strategy. They wanted something as utterly devastating as possible and a lot more inventive than a *shahid* detonating a suicide vest on a crowded street or driving a truck into a mass of pedestrians.

At a hastily convened meeting held in the remaining ground-floor room of a ruined building – a building ruined by American bombing – the ruling council debated the options open to them. The air was dense with harsh and angry exchanges in Arabic, and made visibly thicker by what looked like cigarette smoke, though it was actually dust raised from the floor and the scattered tables by thumping fists and stamping feet. Although many Iraqis enjoy cigarettes, smoking had always been seen by the ISI leadership as un-Islamic and had been banned, with severe penalties meted out to transgressors. Many of the council members still smoked, but always in private locations where they knew they could not be observed. Most of them also preferred American cigarettes to any of the local brands like Sumer, Eridu or Baghdad, making their secret vice doubly anti-Islamic, and the avoidance of detection therefore doubly important.

They needed an entirely new direction and, after spending much of the day in heated discussions, they finally thought they had one. In fact, they had two. Two very different targets and attack methods in their two principal target countries.

It was the youngest member of the council, a thick-set and heavily built man whose intimidating physical appearance belied his keen brain, who came up with the idea for the bigger attack, based upon an article he had read in an American magazine. Mahdi Sadir was no poet, but he was very well aware of the meaning of the expression 'poetic justice'. It seemed to him to be entirely appropriate that the Americans would experience death raining down upon them in a very similar fashion to the carnage inflicted upon ISI soldiers at the hands of the Americans in Iraq with their armed drones and ground attack aircraft. A war waged by technology had given the infidels the upper hand, and ISI had been slow to respond.

He also knew that the elders would wish to see a game-changing attack on London as well as the much more complex and devastating assault on the second and more significant target, and accordingly he came up with ideas for two very different attack strategies. The first was easy for him to explain because it was simply an enhanced version of the kind of retribution attacks that had been launched against the West over the last few years, and he knew that the elders would grasp its inherent simplicity and potential effects almost immediately.

The second phase of the operation he was proposing was a more difficult sell for a variety of reasons, but mainly because Sadir frankly understood very little of the science behind the method of attack, and the elders he was talking to understood even less.

The concept was simple enough, though it would be anything but simple to implement because there were massive technical challenges and obstacles that would have to be overcome. But the idea was so apposite that everybody on the council agreed it was well worth pursuing, even though Sadir explained to them, several times over, that it might take years before the plan could be implemented. There would be several separate components to the final strategy, and to make it work they would have to enlist or recruit specialist helpers in at least two very different disciplines: electrical engineering and computer science. They would also need to find somebody who was employed in an organisation that represented everything they were fighting against. They would need to consort with their deadliest enemy.

But he was both enthusiastic and persuasive and after a further three hours of talking – a comparatively short time for any decision involving a group of Arabs, who liked to explore every possible angle of every possible subject in every possible way, repeatedly – he was given permission to investigate the second proposed attack and, if it appeared to be feasible, to implement it.

Sadir was surprised to have been given so much responsibility, but as well as his clear ability to think laterally, he had one other vitally important attribute that made the elders decide he was the ideal man for the job: he was a cleanskin. A man who had never come to the attention of the authorities in Iraq or anywhere else, his face and description would be completely unknown in the West. He also spoke fluent English, which was perhaps the clinching argument, and when he was recalled before the council once they had come to their final decision, he was told that the entire operation, both the bombing that would mark its beginning and the much more devastating attack on the other side of the Atlantic that would signal its conclusion, would now be his responsibility.

'And there is another consideration that needs to be addressed,' the leader of the council, an elder named Rashid, said. 'We have no doubt that the best principal target is the one you have suggested, but the secondary target, the one that will be attacked first, is equally important to us. We need both countries to feel the full force of our anger and resolve. You will have to recruit several *shahids* in order to carry out that attack, but it is essential that they have no usable information about the second attack, or about you. Never use your real name unless it is unavoidable. Decide on a *nom de guerre* and always use that. And you must ensure that there is no possibility of them surviving the attack if it should fail.'

'It will not fail,' Sadir replied confidently. 'I will make sure of that.'

'Nevertheless,' Rashid insisted, 'you are to devise a way of guaranteeing their deaths. Once they are outside your direct control you must ensure that they will not live long enough to betray our *jihad*. Whatever method you choose must be foolproof.'

Sadir nodded. That was something he had not factored into his initial calculations, but it made sense. And he did have one idea that might well work, again based upon something he had read about in an American journal. It could also, he realised, be used in an entirely different scenario.

'This will be a long game,' Rashid told him as the meeting drew to a close. 'You have much to research and investigate, and you must first ensure that you can deliver what we have discussed. If you cannot, then we will need to devise an alternative strategy to achieve our aims. For our security, you must sever all connections with your family here in Iraq until you have completed the mission.

'You will need substantial funds, which we will provide when you require them. When possible, we will make use of *hawaladars* to transfer money, but once you reach your two principal targets we will have to rely on Western Union.' Rashid smiled slightly at the idea of funding terror attacks upon the West by making use of a Western money transfer system. 'When you leave here to begin your mission you must assume that you will be watched, so on no account are you to proceed directly to your objective. Travel slowly, watch everyone and trust no one outside the brotherhood.'

Rashid was not referring to the Muslim Brotherhood organisation but to the concept enshrined in the Hadith, the record of the sayings of the Prophet Mohammed and second only in Islamic religious authority to the Koran, that 'the Muslim is a brother to another Muslim. He does not wrong him, nor surrender him.' In that sense, every Muslim in every nation is a brother to every other Muslim in the world.

'Your journey will be long. Take care and ensure you keep us fully informed through the usual channels. If we do not know where you are or what you need we will not be able to help you. And remember that this is a part of the most important *jihad* we have ever embarked on, so when the moment comes to strike do not hesitate.'

Mahdi Sadir left Iraq three weeks later and began a journey that would take him to places he had never even dreamed of visiting.

Chapter 1

Ten years later

Vektor, Koltsovo Naukograd, Novosibirsk Oblast, Siberia, Russia

Koltsovo is a *naukograd*, a Russian term meaning a 'science city', located in the Novosibirsk Oblast, roughly 1,800 miles due east of Moscow on the eastern outskirts of the city of Novosibirsk itself, the largest city in Siberia.

In the heyday of the USSR some *naukograds* were also designated as closed cities or ZATOs, meaning that specific permission was required before they could be visited by outsiders, but Vektor, as a relatively new institute established in 1974 and which only became a *naukograd* in 2003, twelve years after the collapse of the Soviet Union, was never a ZATO. Vektor is the core around which Koltsovo, originally the village of Novoborsk, grew. It's a group of nondescript buildings, dominated by a main six-storey structure and all located within a boundary road. Despite its proximity to the city of Novosibirsk it's fairly secluded, though probably not secluded enough bearing in mind what its vaults and freezers contain. Vektor holds samples of virtually all of the species-killer bugs found on the planet, including the deadliest of them all, the Filoviridae family, which includes the Ebola and Marburg filoviruses, as well as the less lethal but still profoundly unpleasant and sometimes fatal dengue, Lassa and yellow fever viruses.

Russian authorities are not big on identifying buildings, and particularly not those where activities of a classified or covert nature take place, but one fairly obvious clue that the buildings at Koltsovo contain something unusual is the permanent garrison of Russian Army soldiers who ensure that all visitors are both legitimate and expected.

The man who approached the Vektor complex that afternoon was very obviously, from his appearance alone, not a local.

The CIS, the Commonwealth of Independent States, is far and away the biggest national unit on the planet, covering well over 20 million square kilometres and bigger than the combined landmasses of North America and Canada. The population is equally massive, numbering about 240 million people speaking ten officially recognised regional languages and a host of minority tongues and dialects. With the freedom of movement that gradually became possible following the collapse of the Soviet Union in 1991 a certain degree of population mixing has occurred, creating something of an international flavour in the bigger cities. But even in the most cosmopolitan and crowded of environments, the visitor to Koltsovo would have stood out.

Physically, he was about half a head taller than the average Russian male, and noticeably broad across the shoulders, but his build alone did not mark him out from the crowd. The complexions of the citizens of the CIS vary considerably with genetics and location, with people living in the north of the huge landmass tending to have a lighter skin colour than those from the south; there is also a kind of folk-belief in Russia that people hailing from the north of the country tend to be tall, white-skinned, lacking body hair, of good character, kind and pure. In contrast, those from the south are supposed to be the precise opposite, with dark complexions, lots of hair, short of stature and generally speaking of a bad or evil character. And it is certainly true that many Russian women, perhaps even a majority of them, tend to wear cosmetics that make their skin look a few shades lighter than its natural colour. In the West, of course, using spray tan to achieve precisely the opposite effect is more common.

But the one skin type that is rarely seen in Russia is an olive complexion, especially a dark olive complexion, and that was probably the defining characteristic of the visitor. Coupled with his imposing build, the combination meant that he was particularly noticeable. It also meant that when Mahdi Sadir had approached the Vektor buildings at Koltsovo on his first planned visit, almost a decade earlier, he had been immediately stopped at gunpoint by a Russian Army patrol and held for nearly half an hour while his documentation was scrutinised and his reason for being there questioned and checked. It was only when a senior member of the Vektor management had been contacted that he had been permitted to be escorted into the complex. That embarrassment had only occurred on his first trip to Koltsovo: the documentation he had carried with him after that had ensured his access to the building with a minimum of fuss on each of his later visits.

Sadir's first visit to the complex had set the tone for his subsequent meetings, and the request he had made of the management and two of the scientists, in tandem with the financial package he was offering, had taken Vektor in an entirely new direction, into a field they had never explored before. It was new technology, with exciting and almost limitless potential, and the scientists at Koltsovo had embraced it. They were helped initially by the considerable amount of information they found published openly on the Internet, but quite quickly they had moved beyond that and begun carving their own paths and developing their own techniques and methods. And all of it had been funded by that single and effectively anonymous investor client who had told the Vektor management exactly what he wanted, what he needed it to do and when he wanted it.

And the Vektor scientists had risen to the challenge.

They had developed the product Sadir had wanted on time. It had been a relatively simple device and had proved comparatively easy to fabricate, 'easy' in this sense meaning that it was only required to do one thing, while the actual manufacturing process had been complex and detailed, involving manipulation at the smallest possible scale. It had also been complicated by the need to use external substances to achieve the required result.

But they had done it, and a slightly modified version of the product had been live-tested on an anonymous subject in front of the client in a suite of sealed rooms located deep inside the complex.

Sadir had declared himself happy with the result and had handed over the balance of the agreed fee in cash – in American dollars, in fact – and then left Koltsovo. That test had been performed on his second visit, when he had also authorised the manufacture of specific variants of the product in the quantities he required, to be collected the next time he visited Russia.

Delivery of the product had been the easiest part of the entire process. For each of his visits Sadir had followed exactly the same routine. He had arrived in Russia with a tourist visa, flying in to the Tolmachevo Airport in Novosibirsk on an internal flight from Saint Petersburg. He'd booked into the Marriott hotel in the city centre and then spent about a week acting as a tourist in the third most populous city in Russia. On one day that week he'd taken a taxi to Koltsovo, ostensibly to visit the railway museum, the park and the churches. The day after that he'd flown back to Saint Petersburg's Pulkovo Airport and from there to Rome by Alitalia, and from Italy onwards to his final destination.

Each of his visits to Koltsovo had only lasted half a day, but that had been easily long enough for him to visit Vektor. On his third and final visit to the laboratory, when Sadir collected the products he had ordered, there had been ample time for him to pick up the goods in an isothermal cool pack. This was a grey fabric bag that looked something like a small washbag with two compartments secured by zips, which had been prepared for him by the staff at the laboratory. In fact, very little preparation had been needed because the bag and its contents – which in the larger compartment included a meter, testing equipment and other peripherals and in the second compartment space for a number of vials, needles and syringes as well as a pouch of cooling gel to keep the contents at the appropriate temperature – was an absolutely standard off-the-shelf item. Because of the quantity of the product he had ordered, he was also given a second isothermal pack that only contained vials.

There had been remarkably little chance of Sadir being stopped or searched anywhere along his route – the Russian authorities were always very wary of targeting or interfering with any tourist spending the hard currency that the country desperately needed – but the reality was that even if his bags were to be opened and searched by some inquisitive customs officer, and even if the isothermal pack was handled and examined, it would make no difference. Nobody would interfere with it and he would be allowed to continue his journey.

The product was only a single weapon in Sadir's armoury, and it wasn't even a particularly important part of his plan. It was just a device that would allow him to snip off one specific loose end that would inevitably be created because of what he was going to do, and it represented the only method of achieving the result he needed in the way he needed it to be done. And he had already decided that he would make additional use of the product ahead of the operation itself. It would be a useful test of its functionality, not to mention acting as a small payment towards a debt that in his opinion was long overdue.

More importantly, the first phase of his operation would begin in less than a month, and his preparations for it had already started, albeit from a distance. Now that Sadir had the product from Vektor he could make his final preparations and then begin the journey that he had planned for so long.

Chapter 2

Six months ago

Lewisham Central, 43 Lewisham High Street, London

According to the Internet, the greatest single repository of information, misinformation and disinformation in the world, the smallest police station in London is concealed inside a stubby lamp standard in the south-east corner of Trafalgar Square. It's just about big enough to accommodate two standing adults who, if they weren't close friends when they entered the structure, probably would be by the time they stepped out of it.

On this occasion the Internet is almost, but not quite, correct. The decorative lamp standard *is* a police building, but it is not, and never has been, a police station. In fact, it's an observation post constructed to allow a police officer to be hidden from view and at the same time to be able to observe demonstrations or other activities taking place in Trafalgar Square. The lamp post was initially equipped with a direct telephone line to Scotland Yard – the headquarters of the Metropolitan Police when the observation post was in use – to allow the observing officer to summon reinforcements if needed.

In reality, the smallest police station in London is almost certainly what looks like a substantial but generally unremarkable detached house at 1 Waxwell Lane in Pinner, Middlesex, unremarkable that is apart from the word 'POLICE' carved in block capitals into the stone lintel above the main door. That, unsurprisingly in view of its location, is Pinner Police Station.

One fact the Internet does get right is at the other end of the scale. The largest police station in London is, by a very substantial margin,

Lewisham Central in Lewisham High Street. It's a fairly new build, constructed on the site of the old Army & Navy Store. Building work started in November 2001 and it was officially opened in April 2004. Not only is it the biggest police station in London, it's actually the biggest purpose-built police station anywhere in Europe, and as well as containing a large car park it also has stables for three dozen police horses and the biggest custody suite in London.

Perhaps the number crunchers and the pointy heads in the Met decided at the beginning of the twenty-first century that Lewisham was for some reason going to become a hotbed of crime, and to combat this predicted future wave of lawlessness they would need to construct the biggest and most modern police station it was possible to build right there in the borough. Or maybe it was just a big site and they needed a big building to fill it.

Assistant Chief Constable Richard Boston had no idea about any of this and wouldn't have cared if he had known. He had other things on his mind and was at Lewisham Central purely because it was a convenient location for the meeting he had planned. It had the space and the facilities, it was only a short walk from the railway station and there were plenty of spaces in the multi-storey car park on site. Parking was not his personal concern, because although he would be arriving by car he had a driver, but it was always good to know that it wouldn't be a problem.

The room he'd been allocated was more like a biggish office than a conference room, but that didn't matter because there would only be three other people attending the meeting. A civilian staff member escorted him to the door, pointed out where the nearest lavatories were located and checked that the refreshments (two large Thermos flasks, one of black coffee and the other filled with tea, several individual cartons of milk and wrapped sugar cubes along with a predictably uninspiring selection of biscuits in cellophane packets) had been delivered and then left him to it. The room was fully equipped with the usual visual and audio aids, a projection screen, speakers, whiteboards, cork boards and so on, but without any of the normal posters, notices, pictures and notes that would have suggested the room was in regular use. Maybe it had been cleaned out in preparation for his meeting.

Boston had deliberately arrived about fifteen minutes early to give him time to make sure his laptop would talk to whatever projection system the room contained. He was by any standards a computer expert, but just because he knew what he was doing didn't mean some kind of electronic gremlin wouldn't strike and simply refuse to allow him to connect to the system, so he always liked to have a little time in hand.

He was a solidly built man, standing just over six feet three inches tall, his dark hair cut short, perhaps to minimise the onset of typical male pattern baldness. Or maybe he just liked it that way. His square jaw and determined expression suggested he was a man who knew what he was doing, where he was going and how he was going to get there, an impression confirmed by the impressive speed with which he had ascended the ranks to the position he now held.

In the event, it only took him about five minutes to hitch up his lightweight Dell and by the time the first attendees arrived the title slide of his presentation was ready to be displayed on the screen at one end of the room, and Boston was sitting at the head of the table sipping coffee from a chipped china mug and nibbling on a shortbread biscuit.

He heard a brisk double tap on the door and two men walked in. Boston already knew Chief Inspector Tim Inskip, having worked with him before, and he knew the second man's name but not his face.

'Good to see you again, Tim,' he said, shaking hands with the burly, fair-haired officer who was a couple of inches shorter but quite a few kilos heavier than him. Inskip's face was dominated by his large and crooked nose, a legacy of his rugby-playing past and specifically of one memorable match when the scrum had collapsed with him at the bottom of it and the boot of one of the opposition front row forwards had made violent contact with his face. It had taken three operations to fix his nose so that he could breathe through it again, but the surgeons had never been able to get it completely straight. It wasn't pretty but it did work, and that was all that mattered.

'Afternoon, Richard,' Inskip said, his voice as usual sounding slightly nasal. 'It's been a while. Now, I don't think you know Ian Mitchell,' he added, turning slightly to introduce the man beside him. 'Ian, this is Assistant Chief Constable Richard Boston, who's organised this little soirée.'

'I know your name, Ian,' Boston said, 'but we've never met.'

The two police officers were wearing civilian clothes, but they both wore them as if they carried badges of rank while Mitchell, who was also in civvies, held himself in an indefinably different way, a kind of casually relaxed poise that suggested he had never worn a uniform. His fair hair was also just a shade too long and there was more than a hint of five o'clock shadow on his chin, as if he had shaved the previous night rather than that morning. He had piercing blue eyes deep-set below a wide forehead and he looked quite athletic, as if he was the kind of man who would enjoy a game of tennis or who perhaps went jogging each morning before work, an impression that was entirely erroneous in every single respect. Mitchell loathed all sport and subscribed to the view that hard physical activity as a young man led inevitably to a broken and crippled middle and old age. And he possessed an almost encyclopedic mental database of facts and figures and anecdotes to demolish the arguments of anybody who disagreed with this point of view.

'Commander,' Mitchell said, extending his hand.

'I'm not in the Met or the City forces,' Boston said, 'and I prefer to keep it informal. Just "Richard" will do nicely.'

In both the Metropolitan and City of London police forces, the rank of commander is equivalent to assistant chief constable, and much less of a conversational mouthful.

'Is anyone else coming?' Inskip asked.

'Yes,' Boston nodded. 'Superintendent Simpson should be here any minute. She called me to say her train was running about five minutes late.'

'Ah, the Nutcracker,' Inskip murmured, just loud enough to be heard.

Mitchell looked puzzled.

'What? Is she a fan of the ballet?'

Inskip shook his head and Boston just smiled.

'Nope, and she doesn't look like the Sugar Plum Fairy either,' Inskip replied. 'She's a very impressive woman who takes no crap from anyone, at any time or for any reason. She acquired the nickname because it's slightly more polite than ball-breaker, but that's what she is. On the other hand, she believes in equal opportunities, which means she frightens her superiors almost as much as she terrifies her subordinates.'

As he finished speaking there was a single knock on the door, and then a statuesque and attractive black woman, her appearance dominated by a halo of curly black hair styled as a kind of restrained afro, stepped into the office and looked, without any particular appearance of pleasure or even interest, at the three men standing there.

'Richard, Tim,' she said shortly by way of greeting, with a Geordie accent, then pointed a long and elegant forefinger at Ian Mitchell. 'You I don't know,' she added, 'so who are you?'

'Good afternoon, Barbara,' Boston said smoothly. 'Come and take a seat, pour yourself a coffee and I'll do the introductions.'

When the four of them were seated around the table, he began.

'Mainly for the benefit of Ian here, I'll just explain who we are and why we're here. My name is Richard Boston and I'm currently the Head of Cyber Criminal Operations for the United Kingdom based within the Home Office. I also wear a couple of international hats as the cybercrime liaison officer between UK law enforcement, Interpol, the United Nations and – most relevant today – the CIA and FBI.'

He shifted his gaze to look at Barbara Simpson.

'Superintendent Simpson and I have worked on covert operations in the past. Her unique skills have led to a very interesting career, if "interesting" really is the right word to describe it. She was awarded the Queen's Police Medal and a couple of Home Secretary's commendations and has spent most of the last two decades working undercover, much of that time down in South America. You don't, obviously, need to be a detective to work out that she was helping to combat the drugs trade.'

'Which, as I've said before, on every committee I've ever sat on,' Barbara Simpson interjected, 'was, is, and always will be a total and complete waste of time and effort. Trying to stop the supply of illegal drugs is about as sensible and as likely to work as passing a law that would make it illegal for it to rain at the weekend. As long as there's a demand for narcotics there will be criminal gangs out there doing their very best to meet that demand. The only way to stop it happening is to legalise the whole lot of them so that your local neighbourhood jakies can pop into Boots and buy what they need for the weekend with their dole money.'

'Jakies?' Mitchell asked.

'Junkies. Or druggies or addicts if you prefer. If we did that, they wouldn't have to break into your house or your car to steal something to get enough cash to score their next fix. The number of street crimes and burglaries that are positively linked to jakies is massive. Most of them need to steal goods worth about a grand every single day, which means stuff like your computer, your phone or your watch or jewellery, so they can sell them for about a hundred quid and buy a few wraps of whatever they need from their local dealer. Drugs that, in reality, probably cost well under a fiver to produce. Ten years ago street crime and burglary directly attributed to drug addicts cost the economy about thirteen billion pounds every year. Today it's a twenty-billion-pound industry, so the real cost has nearly doubled.'

Ian Mitchell raised his eyebrows slightly at the obvious passion and vehemence in the superintendent's words.

'As you might have gathered, Barbara has quite strong views about this,' Richard Boston said, stating the obvious and directing his remarks towards Mitchell, 'but she has both the experience and the knowledge to back up her argument. As she frequently tells me, the American DEA, the Drug Enforcement Administration, has an annual budget of over two billion dollars and at no point since its formation have its activities had any measurable effect on the supply of illegal drugs on the streets of America.'

'But I thought the DEA seized hundreds of tons of drugs from dealers every year,' Mitchell said.

'It does,' Simpson replied, 'and they pat themselves on the back and tell the American public that they're winning the fight against drugs and driving the dealers off the streets. But it's all PR and spin. The only criterion that actually matters when you're assessing the success of an organisation charged with stopping the supply of illegal narcotics is the availability of drugs, and nothing the DEA has ever done has had any effect on that. For every ton of cocaine or whatever that the organisation manages to seize, the cartels in Colombia and Mexico manage to deliver ten or a hundred times as much. The reality is that for the narco-economies of South America the DEA is nothing more than a minor inconvenience, just another business expense, something they need to budget for in the shipping costs incurred by their incredibly lucrative business.'

'Quite,' Boston said. 'But interesting though it might be to explore this, we're not here to talk about drugs.' He looked across the table. 'Tim Inskip here is a chief inspector, and for the last decade he's been working at the sharp end of Britain's counterterrorism operations and he's heavily involved with both the Home Office and MI5, the Security Service, based at Millbank.'

Boston shifted his attention to Mitchell.

'Which brings us to the last member of this group, Ian Mitchell. He's the UK's top official legal hacker. Right, that's who we all are, so the next matter is why we're here.'

Boston woke up his laptop and pressed a key. Immediately, the projection screen mounted on the wall at one end of the room sprang into life. The information it conveyed was neither comprehensive nor readily intelligible: all the screen showed were the words 'Operation Leif' in block capitals and the word 'Confidential' in red at the top and bottom of the screen, the first slide of a PowerPoint presentation.

'Looks like you've got a small typo there, Richard,' Barbara Simpson said, pointing at the screen.

'I might have guessed that you'd be the one to pick that up,' Boston replied, 'but actually that *is* the correct spelling, because you're thinking about the wrong kind of leaf. This is a reference to a man named Leif Erikson, who was almost certainly the first European to discover America, half a millennium before Christopher Columbus started his first westbound voyage. And of course Erikson actually found America, which Columbus comprehensively failed to do. I was going to call it Operation Cabot after John Cabot – Giovanni Caboto – who was probably the first European to set foot in North America after the Vikings, but I couldn't do that because Operation Cabot had already been bagged by the Surrey police for an anti-drugs operation they ran in 2015.'

'I know you love your history, Richard,' Inskip commented. 'Anyone else would have just picked a name at random. And that would have been quicker. And easier.'

'Now I may not be the sharpest tool in this particular shed,' Barbara Simpson said, 'but would I be right in assuming that this has something to do with America?'

Boston grinned at her.

'Obviously,' he said. 'In fact, it's probably going to end up as something of a joint operation between us and the Americans, because what we think we're seeing is the beginning of a widespread, coordinated and sophisticated case of cyber terrorism. And that,' he finished, 'is why we're all sitting here in this room.'

'Before we get too deeply into this,' Barbara Simpson said, as Boston opened the second slide of his presentation, 'can I just remind you that I know sod all about cyber. I can barely even spell the word.'

'That's not why you're here,' Boston replied. 'You've got other talents and abilities that will be vitally important to this operation.' He shifted his attention to the rest of his audience. 'Now, as I'm sure you're aware, GCHQ out at Cheltenham works very closely with the American National Security Agency. In fact, you could almost say that their functions are identical, and between them they provide invaluable intelligence about potential terrorist and criminal activities on both sides of the Pond. What you may not know is that we have a separate and dedicated small counterterrorism unit right here in London with links to Cheltenham, Westminster, Hereford and other places. Basically, if there's a joint national problem that no single agency or department can handle and no one knows where to place it, this lot pick it up.'

'You mean C-TAC,' Ian Mitchell stated. 'The Counter-Terrorism Advisory Committee. I know it's supposed to be covert, but these days not a hell of a lot really is. And I know Ben Morgan very well. He's one of the wheels in C-TAC, and the cyber world is quite small when you get down to it. Rumour has it he was instrumental in saving the UK banking system last year from some kind of a meltdown.'

'I expected you to be well informed, Ian,' Boston said, displaying another slide on the screen, 'but perhaps not quite *that* well informed. All that is still classified. You're right, but officially he's simply an academic working on cyber stuff. Now, we have a problem. It's not really made the papers or the media generally, but there's been a worrying increase in the number of determined hacking attempts directed against the UK's infrastructure, the gas, electricity and water suppliers, companies like that. You don't need me to tell you that the effects of a successful hack that shut down electric power to Greater London, say, for anything more than a few hours would be utterly catastrophic, because not every company or building has backup power supplies. But what's really concerning us is that utility companies in America have also been targeted. According to my opposite number in the FBI, they're not seeing weekly or monthly attacks, but daily and sometimes hourly attempts to breach their firewalls and enter their systems. And because most of these attacks use the same suites of hacking tools and tend to follow the same pattern, the uncomfortable conclusion is that we may have a single group of hackers out there aiming to cause massive disruption in both America and here in the UK, possibly at the same time. It looks like it's all coordinated, and the frequency of the attacks is increasing. And there's one further conclusion that we can tentatively draw about this.'

Boston paused and looked round expectantly at the attendees.

Once again, it was Mitchell who replied. 'You think it's a national actor, not some bunch of spotty teenagers living on pizza and Coke and benefits?'

'What the hell's a national actor?' Simpson demanded. 'You don't mean somebody who's appeared on the stage at the Old Vic, presumably.'

'No,' Boston said. 'He means a group of hackers directed by a nation or a nation-state, like the bloody Chinese. The Red Army – the Chinese People's Liberation Army, I mean – has employed vast platoons of hackers over the last couple of decades to spy on the West, and more importantly to steal technical and other data to save Chinese scientists from having to bother to invent or develop stuff themselves. Pretty much every major advance in the Chinese military and industrial complex since the start of this century has been entirely or largely based on data stolen from the West. But what the Chinese hackers don't normally do is cause any damage, because their agenda is entirely different. They work their way in to somewhere like NASA or Berkeley or MIT or Boeing and steal what they can and then they do their best to get out without leaving any traces. These people are nothing like that. EDF and British Gas don't have any secrets worth stealing. Their computer networks are primarily used just to make sure their electricity and gas supply systems are working properly, so almost by definition any attack on them has to be intended to disrupt or interfere with the operations of the companies. These hackers don't care about leaving a trail and it's fairly obvious that causing damage is precisely what they intend to do.'

'So who are the players this time?' Tim Inskip asked. 'Are you looking at Russia, or North Korea, or where?'

'This is where things get slightly murky,' Boston replied, 'or rather murkier. The feedback I've had from GCHQ and the FBI, and from C-TAC in fact, suggests that most of the attacks have been domestic. As usual, the locations of the attempted intrusions have been carefully concealed, the origin of the attack bounced around the world from one nation to another before reaching the target, but the one place they always seem to come back to is America. Even those attacks mounted here in Britain seem to have the same path, which is another reason why we think we're looking at a single group rather than a bunch of individuals.'

'I'm sure all this is fascinating to those of a geeky persuasion,' Barbara Simpson said, 'like the three of you for example, but what I do is undercover work, and I have no clue what useful skill or knowledge I'm supposed to be bringing to this particular table.'

'Patience, Barbara, patience. I promise you all will become clear.'

For the next half hour or so Richard Boston displayed a series of PowerPoint slides that explained what was known about the attempted intrusions on both sides of the Atlantic Ocean. Everything he said and every image he showed was eminently comprehensible to Inskip and Mitchell and meant the square root of sod all to Barbara Simpson, and when he finally stopped talking she pointed this out to him.

'Geekery upon geekery,' she announced. 'And I suppose this is where you tell me about the shitty little job you've got lined up for me to do.'

'Perspicacious as ever,' Boston replied. 'Right, the purpose of this briefing has mainly been to bring Ian and Tim up to speed on the situation so that they know what we're up against and have a good idea of what to look for in their jobs. And what to do about any incidents or attempted intrusions that they encounter. They're also in the loop to back you up, Barbara, if you need specialist advice later on.' Boston glanced at Inskip and Mitchell and nodded. 'Unless either of you have any questions, that's about it as far as you're concerned.'

'I've got nothing,' Inskip said.

Boston nodded briskly. 'Okay. You both know where to reach me if anything crops up, and I'll be Barbara's conduit to you if necessary. Keep me in the loop about anything that you think could be relevant. Now, Barbara's tasking is classified and on a need-to-know basis, so I need to brief her in private.'

Inskip and Mitchell gathered their notes and mobile phones and other stuff together, said their goodbyes and left the room.

'Now you've really got me worried,' Simpson said. 'Is this where you issue me with a packet of suicide pills and a silenced revolver and send me out hacker hunting?'

'Not exactly. We don't do suicide pills and you can't silence a revolver, no matter what you may see on television or read in bad novels. But I do want you to go hacker hunting, or at least terrorist hunting, because blending into the kind of environment where we think they're hiding is something I believe you would do well. We think these cyberattacks are building up to something that could be catastrophic in its effects and could affect us as well as the Americans.'

'But surely the FBI—'

Boston interrupted her. 'Make no mistake,' he said, 'I have the greatest possible respect for the CIA and the FBI and American law enforcement generally, but they have their own problems with potential sleepers, and I don't mean people too lazy to get out of bed. What they need and I want is somebody on the ground over there able to watch, listen and report. And that, really, is more or less what your CV says you do.'

'Where? Where exactly are you sending me?'

'Near your old hunting grounds on the other side of the Atlantic, but a long way further north.'

'Let me take a wild stab in the dark here, based upon what we've been talking about for the last hour. Washington D.C., maybe? Because perhaps you *do* think there's a link between these hackers and home-grown suicide bombers?'

'You're right about the location,' Boston agreed, 'though we have no definite intelligence to suggest a link. But it occurred to me that the people who are mounting these attacks are clearly aiming at causing destruction or at least disruption, just like a terrorist wearing a suicide vest, so at least they have the same kind of mindset. So you're right: it wouldn't surprise me if they were connected in some way.'

'So what do you want me to do in the land of the free?'

'In fact, it's not so much me as they. While you were down in Colombia you were working for the National Police, but ultimately you were working on behalf of your favourite organisation, the DEA, which was coordinating operations between the two countries and, at least by implication, for the American government. What you did has been noted and been commented on at the highest level, and that's not me using the usual bullshit to try to pebbledash your ego or boost your career. You really did make a difference, and your services have been officially requested again by the Americans. And as I said, I think this tasking is tailor-made for you. You have a kind of sixth sense for spotting people or things that are in the wrong place at the wrong time, and that's what we need from you again.'

Barbara Simpson looked anything but flattered.

'I say again, I know nothing about cyber. Whatever the Yanks think, am I really the right person for this job? Whatever it is.'

'Down in Colombia, according to reports I've read, one of the biggest challenges you faced was trying to decide which of the police officers and other officials you were working with *wasn't* also working for one of the cartels, and the problem Stateside is similar but different. As I said, the Americans are really concerned about the number of sleepers there might be in law enforcement over there, people who appear to be loyal Americans but who are actually nothing of the sort, people who've been radicalised.

'People like Nidal Hasan, that guy at Fort Hood just over a decade ago. American born and bred, he reached the rank of major in the US Army and then flipped and killed thirteen people because he'd basically self-radicalised. He'd worked out that the best way to save his mother's soul – she'd committed the appalling sin of allowing alcohol to be sold in her corner shop, which in his twisted interpretation of the Koran meant she was destined to burn in hell for all eternity – was to slaughter as many unarmed American soldiers as he could.'

'He was a psychiatrist,' Simpson pointed out, 'which means he was halfway loony already, in my opinion, like most shrinks.'

'Maybe. He certainly wasn't completely sane. Anyway, the problem they have in DC is that they don't really know who to trust, so they need somebody like you, untainted and preferably not an American citizen, to burrow down into the underworld, the same as you did in South America, to try to find out what's actually going on and who's involved.'

'How do you know I haven't been radicalised?'

'Anyone who calls a spade a bloody shovel and drinks Newcastle Brown for fun is too far gone to be converted, I'd say. I know you, Barbara. I can't think of anybody less likely to suddenly decide that radical Islam and Sharia law are what the world really needs. Frankly, I'd be more likely to believe you if you told me you'd become a devil worshipper.'

'Well I follow neither Mohammed nor the horned goat, Richard, so you can relax. I presume there's a briefing document somewhere for all this, and somebody I can actually trust on the other side of the Pond?'

Boston slid a thick sealed A3 size package across the table towards her and followed it up with a much smaller but quite bulky envelope.

'The briefing document is in the big envelope and you need to start reading through it right now, because you can't take it with you to the States. You fly out on BA at five tomorrow, which means getting to Heathrow by early afternoon. For tonight we've booked you a room at the Marriott at Canary Wharf so at least you'll be comfortable. A uniformed officer will meet you at the reception desk tomorrow at one thirty to collect the large envelope from you, and he'll drive you to Heathrow for your flight. There's a mobile phone inside the small envelope, with all the contacts from the briefing document already loaded in, plus a memory stick holding all the information, that's the contacts and the briefing data. The phone and the memory stick are both password protected and the password is also in the envelope. Memorise it and then burn the slip of paper. Get the password wrong three times in a row and both devices will lock you out.'

'Cattle class across the Pond, presumably?'

'Regrettably, yes. Your cover, such as it is, is that you're a tourist doing the world on a budget, so you can hardly step off the aircraft from the first-class section smelling of Bollinger and caviar. There's five thousand US in cash in the envelope as well, plus a credit card that doesn't have a limit. But we will need receipts for anything other than food, drink, transport and accommodation, and the bean-counters will be looking closely at meals in Michelin-starred restaurants, champagne, limousines and five-star hotels. You know the rules.'

Simpson nodded. 'I do. Luckily I'm used to burgers, beer, buses and budget flophouses, so I'm sure I'll feel right at home. Are you sure you don't want me to go all the way and live as a street person?'

For a moment Boston seemed to give her question serious consideration. 'Not unless you think it's absolutely necessary, no. Though you could perhaps think about slipping into that persona when you start doing surveillance. Being invisible to almost everybody could be a useful tactic to employ.'

She nodded again.

'So it's back to the streets and the shit and the spying,' she said.

'It's what you do best, Barbara.'

Simpson stared at him with a baleful expression on her face. 'I think I'll take that as a compliment,' she replied, then tore open the large envelope and tipped the contents onto the table in front of her.

Chapter 3

Six days ago

Above Oxfordshire

It's a truism that anybody can be taught to fly an aircraft, just as anybody can be taught to drive a car: the only variable is the length of the training process. Most people with some degree of natural flying ability can reach basic solo standard after about ten to fifteen hours in the air in a fixed-wing aircraft, though reaching the same level of competence in a helicopter will take a bit longer because learning how to drive an egg-beater without adding to the annual aviation accident statistics is a rather more complex process. But the majority of people can achieve a reasonable standard of proficiency in about forty-five to fifty hours.

The military doesn't do it quite that way, as might be expected, and they take a hell of a lot longer. In the British Armed Forces, the usual route is to put wannabe pilots through a flying grading to see if there's any chance of them making it out of the other end of the process in one piece. Then they get them up to a reasonable standard in a fixed-wing aircraft. That's usually called something like elementary or basic flying training, and the embryo pilots emerge from that phase with just enough skill and knowledge to be dangerous to themselves and to anybody and anything else in the air. Even birds.

At that point they're introduced to the bafflingly complex and unlikely flying machine that is the modern helicopter. Just like the bumblebee, it doesn't look as if it should be able to fly. It's probably also at about this point in their training that pilots are reminded that nobody actually knows how or why aircraft stay in the air. There are at least two different and mutually contradictory theories of flight, neither of which provides a complete explanation for the phenomenon.

Assuming their nerves can stand it, they then begin basic rotary wing training, intended to transition them from an aircraft with large and solid visible wings to keep it in the air to a bulbous object possessing no obvious means of support or lift apart from a rotor disk characterised by a small number of remarkably slender blades. If they get through that part of the process they move on to advanced rotary wing training and follow that up with operational training and finally conversion to type. That will familiarise them with whatever kind of helicopter is operated by their designated flight or squadron. And then they go front line, their training over.

Just as there are good drivers and bad drivers, the skill and ability of whoever is sitting at the controls in the cockpit of a military helicopter can vary from – hopefully at the very least – competent up to excellent. And just a handful of the very best of the very best chopper pilots are recruited to serve in various specialised units like the Queen's Helicopter Flight and the JSFAW, the Joint Special Forces Aviation Wing.

Major David Charles North, late of the Special Air Service and currently something of a wheel in the Special Reconnaissance Regiment, was sitting in one of the passenger seats of a dark blue Eurocopter AS365N3 Dauphin II helicopter being flown by a warrant officer from 658 Squadron Army Air Corps and taking remarkably little notice of where he was or what was happening outside the aircraft. He had spent a significant proportion of his working life sitting in aircraft of one kind or another, most of them helicopters, and the experience of entrusting his life to an aluminium box carried aloft by a rotor disk powered by some kind of jet engine had ceased to either bother or interest him. He knew that the JSFAW pilots were among the best in the business, and that the aircraft were maintained to military standards, so he normally just relaxed and let the pilot get on with the job of flying the thing.

The SRR was a kind of SAS lite, meaning its tasks involved identifying, observing and following potential terrorists and other undesirable threats to the people of the United Kingdom rather than tracking them down and then shooting them, though the SRR personnel were perfectly happy to do that as well if the situation demanded it. Right then, North was en route from Stirling Lines, the SAS headquarters at Credenhill near Hereford, to Brize Norton in Oxfordshire to attend a classified briefing in one of the hardened underground rooms at the RAF station.

The pilot was flying VFR – visual flight rules – which meant he was self-navigating and taking his own avoiding action against other aircraft in the area, but he had also been in contact with the Brize Norton air traffic control LARS, the lower airspace advisory radar service, on 124.275 MHz. He'd been passed a weather update – fine with clear skies and light winds – and given the controller his ETA.

It was near the end of a routine, no pressure flight of the kind that North had made countless times in the past.

The pilot slowed and descended the aircraft, aiming towards the hardstanding where the local controller had given him clearance to land, and North felt the slightly increased noise level as he lowered the landing gear.

And then, suddenly and utterly comprehensively, the flight turned to worms.

The warrant officer emitted a kind of gasp that was just audible over the noise of the engines and rotor blades and his head slumped forwards, his arms dropping limply to his sides.

Dave North had been looking forward through the cockpit windows towards the hardstanding and immediately saw what had just happened.

The Eurocopter was single-crewed, with only North and the pilot on board, and the warrant officer had had manual control of the aircraft as it approached for landing. It was probably at an altitude of about five hundred feet and suddenly the ground appeared to be rushing upwards at considerable speed. It looked as if the pilot's left hand had pushed the collective down as he lost consciousness.

'Oh, fuck, fuck, fuck,' North muttered, ripping off his headset and wincing at the sudden increase in noise level. He unclipped his seat belt and scrambled forwards to clamber clumsily into the left-hand seat of the helicopter.

On civilian versions of the AS365 there's a partition between the cockpit and the passenger cabin, which is typically equipped with about half a dozen comfortable leather seats suitable for the large and wide backsides of corporate heavyweights, heavyweights in both senses of the word. The military version dispenses with such niceties and crams in more than twice that number of very basic seats to accommodate a clump of hairy-arsed soldiers and also dispenses with the partition, which was just as well, because if it had been fitted North's life expectancy would have been measured in seconds.

At the rate the Eurocopter was going down he might still be dead in seconds, but at least he had a chance. Vanishingly small, but still a chance.

He dropped into the seat and immediately reached down and to his left, pulling firmly up on the collective, the lever that controlled the angle of attack of the main rotor blades and hence the lift generated by them. North didn't know much about helicopters but he did know that it was the collective that kept the aircraft in the air.

The helicopter shuddered and lurched, the aircraft reacting badly to his clumsy action, but at least it had stopped dropping like a large, heavy, extremely expensive and very fragile stone.

North glanced to his right, hoping that the warrant officer would have recovered his senses, but the man was clearly still out cold.

He looked ahead and grabbed hold of the second control, the cyclic, with his right hand. That was equivalent to the control column in a fixed wing aircraft. The collective kept the helicopter in the air and the cyclic pointed it where the pilot wanted it to go. That was about all North knew. Right then he also knew that he needed to get the helicopter on terra firma. And he didn't much care where.

The ground below him was typical of almost every airfield he'd ever seen, a mixture of runways, taxiways, hardstandings and grassed areas.

North could feel himself starting to sweat.

The Eurocopter was designed to be flown from the right-hand seat and almost all the instruments and controls were either in front of that seat or in the horizontal panel between the two seats. The left-hand seat just had a scattering of essential flight instruments in front of it, and the helicopter's navigation kit sat in the centre of the wide instrument panel, an incomprehensibly complex – to a non-pilot – mix of flat panel colour screens and analogue instruments.

North ignored even the cut-down panel in front of him because none of the displayed information meant anything to him and none of it would help him in his present predicament. He didn't need to know things like airspeed or altitude because he could see all he needed to through the helicopter's windscreen.

And what he could see was that it was in more or less level flight. If it was still going down the rate of descent had slowed, and it didn't seem to be moving forward very quickly, so he guessed the Eurocopter was almost hovering. That at least gave him a bit of breathing space to sort out what to do next. Like how to get it down.

There were numerous buttons and controls on both the collective and the cyclic, he noticed, and he guessed that one of them probably worked the radio, but he had no idea which one. And talking to somebody on the ground wouldn't help him very much at that moment. If he was going to walk away from this he'd have to land the helicopter himself.

North kept a firm grip on the collective and moved the cyclic very gently forward. The Eurocopter responded by moving ahead. He pulled back and moved it to the left. He knew what the helicopter would do, but he was just trying to get a feel for the way it responded, to gauge how much pressure he needed to exert to achieve a certain degree of movement. It felt controllable in a somewhat uncontrolled way.

He put his feet on the two rudder pedals and applied gentle force to the left-hand one as he turned the aircraft. That made the turn smoother, but right then he wasn't interested in smoothness, only in getting the thing on the ground.

Next, he lowered the collective lever very slightly and felt more than saw that the aircraft was starting to lose height.

'You can do this,' he murmured to himself, though he was way out of his depth and he knew it.

North knew that the way helicopters landed wasn't to descend vertically from height but to fly towards the designated landing area, losing height all the time, making an approach not unlike that of a fixed-wing aircraft, and then air-taxi before coming to a hover over the landing spot and vertically descend the last few feet to the ground. He was going to have to try to do that, but on his own terms.

He couldn't risk maintaining the present heading because that was taking him towards a hangar and other buildings, so he put a little more pressure on the collective to stop his slow descent and moved the cyclic and the rudder pedal so that the aircraft was pointing towards one of the runways. If he cocked up his landing out there in the wide-open space of the airfield, at least he wouldn't end up crashing into one of the buildings and taking anyone else with him.

North gently released some of the pressure on the collective to re-start his descent and held the cyclic as straight as he could. He picked a space a few hundred yards away, more or less in the middle of the runway, and aimed the helicopter straight for it. He kept the speed down, still trying to get a feel for the aircraft's handling.

He felt the Eurocopter yaw to the left and corrected the movement as gently as he could but ended up swinging it to the right. He was being careful with the controls but guessed that he was repeatedly over-correcting, so he tried to relax and let the aircraft stabilise itself.

North remembered hearing a pilot tell him years earlier that if you went hands-off in a fixed-wing aircraft nothing would happen: it would just keep on flying at the same height and in the same direction at the same speed. But if you did the same thing in a helicopter, absolutely anything could, and probably would, happen and you needed to fly hands-on all the time. Not a particularly encouraging thought in his present situation.

He adjusted the position of the collective when it looked to him as if he was going down too slowly. He didn't want to overshoot the runway and end up on the grass, though he assumed it was probably stabilised to cope with additional weight in case an aircraft ran off the edge of the asphalt.

He guessed he was only about one hundred feet above the ground, and still descending. His entire attention was focused on what he was doing.

Without his headset, the noise in the cockpit was uncomfortably loud, but there was nothing he could do about that. The runway stretched out below him, getting closer all the time as he tried coordinating the movements of the cyclic and the rudder pedals to keep the aircraft pointing straight ahead while still gently lowering the collective.

The runway surface seemed to rush towards him as he covered the last few feet in descent.

At the last second he pulled up on the collective to reduce the aircraft's downward movement. That caused the helicopter to lurch to one side – probably because he'd applied too much force – and for an instant he feared it was going to topple over, though the logical part of his brain told him it couldn't do that because the rotor was on top of the fuselage and mechanically that couldn't happen.

North had been holding the helicopter in a slightly nose-down position and the nosewheel of the Eurocopter hit the runway first. The aircraft bounced back up into the air, the lurch causing the two mainwheels to bounce off the runway as well.

But that was good enough, and he was near enough, so North lowered the collective lever all the way down. With another bump the helicopter settled onto all three wheels of the undercarriage more or less in the middle of the runway. He slumped back in the seat, his relief palpable.

The rotors were still turning and he had no idea how to stop them or kill the power. And he needed urgent help for the warrant officer, who was still obviously unconscious – or worse – in the right-hand seat.

North looked around the cockpit, wondering which of the myriad buttons operated the radio. Then he glanced through the windscreen and guessed help was already on its way. He could see a couple of fire engines, one a kind of Land Rover conversion and the other a full-size prime mover, lights flashing and heading in his general direction, preceded by what he guessed was a small van used by air traffic control, headlights on and amber rooflight flashing, driving at speed towards him.

The driver stopped the van on the runway directly in front of the Eurocopter and about fifty yards away, well clear of the rotor disk, and an angry-looking man got out. He stared at the aircraft and, apparently when he was sure North had seen him, he walked quickly over to the left-hand side of the aircraft.

North opened the door on his side and waited for him.

The noise of the engines and rotors made normal conversation impossible, but it didn't look as if conversation was what the new arrival wanted. In what was clearly a parade-ground voice he bellowed at North.

'What the fuck are you playing at? This is the main fucking runway.'

North grabbed him by the front of the woolly-pully the man was wearing, pointed at the warrant officer and shouted in the man's ear.

'Get out of my fucking face and get a medic for him.'

Then he shoved him away.

–

Just under half an hour later, North was sitting in a fairly uncomfortable chair in what he guessed was an air traffic control briefing room, a mug of obviously instant coffee in his hand and looking at an RAF squadron leader who had pulled another chair round to sit opposite him. The name-plate on the left-hand side of the officer's light blue pullover bore the name Gerard.

'You were bloody lucky,' he said.

'Tell me about it,' North responded. 'If the pilot had collapsed ten minutes earlier you'd have been pulling my mangled dead body out of a flaming wreck somewhere out in the bundu.'

The Eurocopter had been shut down on the runway by an RAF helicopter pilot who was familiar with the aircraft type, and it had then been towed to the hardstanding on which it had been supposed to land. In the process, the warrant officer pilot had been taken out of the aircraft and rushed by ambulance to the station medical centre. His condition, according to what Squadron Leader Gerard had told North when he entered the briefing room, and which had been passed on by the ambulance crew, was unchanged: he was unconscious and completely unresponsive.

Gerard nodded.

'The local controller told me what he saw from the VCP – the visual control position in the tower – but what happened in the aircraft?'

'I was sitting in the cabin and looking through the windscreen and the guy just collapsed. No warning signs, no prior indication, and we were chatting away over the intercom for pretty much the whole flight. When he collapsed, he pushed the collective all the way down, which was why the chopper lost height so quickly. I got into the left-hand seat, pulled the collective up again and hoped for the best.'

'Have you ever flown a helicopter before?'

North shook his head firmly.

'Never,' he replied. 'I've flown *in* them dozens of times and I've seen how the pilots take off and land, but that was the first time I've ever sat at the controls of any kind of aircraft. And I'd be quite pleased if it was the last time as well. I just tried to get the thing on the ground as quickly as I could without killing anyone, myself included. Is it damaged?'

'It'll need a full check because that was quite a hard landing. In fact, according to the local controller it looked like three hard landings, one after the other.'

'Sounds about right. Look, I need to get to this briefing I'm here for. That should take no more than two or three hours. Any chance of getting a lift back to Hereford when it's finished?'

'We can probably arrange that,' Gerard replied. 'Helicopter or—'

'No bloody chance,' North snapped. 'I want something with four wheels, all of them on the ground, plus a steering wheel and a competent and qualified driver sitting behind it.'

'I'll see what we can do.'

Chapter 4

Secret Intelligence Service Headquarters, Vauxhall Cross, London

Professor Ben Morgan looked across the table at Dave North.

'So I suppose you're going to take some flying lessons now, Dave?' he asked. 'I mean, you've already got one landing to put in your logbook. Or technically a barely controlled crash, but at least you walked away from it.'

North shook his head.

'No way,' he said, 'but I promise you that from now on I'm going to pay even more attention to the people who drive me around the sky, because the only reason I walked away from that was because I had a vague idea about how a helicopter flew. If I'd never watched somebody flying a chopper before, right now I'd be dead.'

'We're delighted you're not,' Dame Janet Marcham-Coutts, the head of C-TAC, the Counter-Terrorism Advisory Committee, said from her normal seat at the head of the table. 'Apart from anything else it would take far too long to house-train another ex-SAS officer.'

Unusually for a meeting of the group, that day the men were outnumbered, Dame Janet being flanked by Angela Evans, a long-time member of C-TAC, and on the other side by Natasha Black, the group's newest recruit, albeit on a part-time basis. She worked at GCHQ out at Cheltenham and had joined C-TAC on Ben Morgan's personal recommendation. Every member of C-TAC brought some-thing different to the table, and Natasha Black – a strikingly unusual figure with a broad pink streak running through her otherwise natural

47

black hair – was not only a mathematical genius, but because of her position at GCHQ she could also provide immediate access to a wide range of surveillance data and other secret stuff should the need arise.

'Agreed,' Angela Evans said. 'You're much too valuable to lose. So what happened to the pilot? Was it a heart attack or a stroke or something? And is he okay now?'

Dave North shook his head.

'He didn't make it. He was an Army warrant officer named Bob O'Brien and he died in the medical centre at Brize Norton. It's that I want to talk to you about. It wasn't a heart attack or a stroke that knocked him out, and really I'd have been amazed if it had been. All pilots go through regular aircrew medicals to make sure that this kind of thing doesn't happen, and those medicals are really thorough.'

'The old idea of an Army medical,' Morgan interrupted, 'was that the doctor made you strip off, grabbed your testicles – sorry, ladies – and told you to cough. I'm still not entirely sure what that was supposed to check. But if that bit was okay he'd tell you to stop smoking and cut down on the booze and chips and burgers and then pass you as fit. I'm assuming aircrew are treated rather differently.'

'Damn right they are,' North replied. 'They go through a whole battery of tests and get pulled off flying duties if there's any serious anomaly, and O'Brien had sailed through his annual medical only a couple of months ago. More to the point, he was given a full autopsy because of what had happened and that revealed no signs at all of heart disease or any other conditions that could have caused his death.'

Morgan looked at him, narrowing his eyes slightly.

'You didn't come here just to tell us how you cheated death by doing a barely controlled crash in a chopper,' he said. 'They did find something, didn't they?'

North nodded.

'I don't understand the technicalities of it, but their first assumption was that the blood supply to his brain through the carotid artery had been interrupted. Some kind of a stroke, in other words. But that would probably have caused damage to the brain, and they couldn't find any indication of that. They also couldn't find any evidence of furring of the arteries or excessive amounts of cholesterol in his blood. And they checked for the presence of plaque in his bloodstream and especially in the coronary arteries, and that result was negative as well, or at least well within safe limits.'

'But,' Morgan said.

North nodded.

'You're right, Ben. There is a biggish but coming. Because they could find no obvious signs of damage to O'Brien's veins and arteries, or to his heart, to the transport system if you like, the docs decided to check his blood, the stuff actually flowing through his circulatory system. At that stage, all they knew for certain was that his heart had stopped beating, but they didn't know why. Again, they did the obvious, like checking for the presence of alcohol or drugs, but he was clear on both counts. SAS personnel are subject to random blood tests anyway, and if there's any trace of a non-prescribed drug in their system they get RTU'd – returned to unit – immediately, so the result was no surprise. SAS personnel drink booze, often quite a lot of booze, but they don't take drugs. Everything seemed correct and normal, but they knew *something* had happened because he was dead, so they decided to do a deeper analysis of the blood samples they'd taken.'

North paused and glanced around the table.

'I don't know how much any of you know about human blood but—'

'Enough to know I don't particularly like looking at it, especially if it's my own,' Angela Evans said.

'Right. Anyway, blood isn't just one thing. It isn't just a thick red liquid. There's all sorts of different stuff in it, and there's a process called blood fractionation that allows doctors, or rather laboratory technicians, to separate out the different components because they have different weights. So they spin the blood in a small glass tube in a centrifuge and they end up with three separate components.

'The largest volume of a sample and the lightest stuff is the blood plasma, which is a clear liquid, and that's what everything else is suspended in. The heaviest part of the blood is the erythrocytes or red blood cells, so when blood has been fractionated they form a dark red layer at the bottom of the tube. Between the two is what's called the buffy coat, and I've no idea why it's called that. It's a—'

'It's called the buffy coat because it often looks buff in colour. That's a kind of light yellowy brown,' Natasha Black interrupted, and they all turned to look at her. She gave a wide smile and nodded. 'That's me,' she said. 'I'm a snapper-up of unconsidered trifles, especially where useless information is concerned. I'm a demon at cocktail parties, not that I often get invited. Or not more than once, anyway.'

'Thanks,' Morgan said, and nodded at North to carry on.

'Right. So the buffy coat is a very thin layer made up of a small quantity of white blood cells called leucocytes mixed with platelets. The leucocytes are responsible for fighting disease, intruders and other foreign bodies, and the platelets are what make blood clot if you cut yourself or suffer an injury. Again, nothing looked out of place and the analyses came back negative or within normal limits.'

'But,' Morgan said again.

'But then one of the technicians noticed a sort of discolouration right at the top of the plasma layer. As I said, that's a clear liquid, but he thought that at the very top there was a slight grey tinge, barely noticeable. Whatever it was, it had to be lighter than the plasma because it was sitting on top of it. He used a magnifying glass and it looked to him like a very, very thin grey film lying on the plasma, but using a hand lens he couldn't see any details. He prepped a microscope slide with some of the film, but even under the highest magnification he had on the optical microscope it was still just a greyish smear, with no indication what it was made of. But whatever it was, it shouldn't have been there, so the technicians decided to take the next obvious step.'

'A SEM,' Natasha Black suggested. 'Or maybe even a STEM, if they had access to one.'

Dame Janet looked at her blankly, not sure whether to be impressed or irritated. 'A SEM?' she asked.

'Scanning electron microscope. Digs down into the stuff that optical devices can't see. The problem with trying to see anything really small is light itself. The wavelength of visible light is between

0.4 and 0.7 micrometres and you can't see anything smaller than half that wavelength, so 0.2 micrometres. A micrometre used to be called a micron, and it's one millionth of a metre. To give you an idea of the scale we're talking about, a human hair is about fifty micrometres in diameter. There's stuff you can do to get higher resolution, like sub-diffraction microscopy, but they're just workarounds. To see atoms and molecules you have to forget the optical stuff and use electrons, because they have a smaller wavelength. That gives you a resolution of between one and twenty nanometres, and a nanometre is a billionth of a metre, so really sodding small.'

'You mentioned a STEM?' Morgan said.

'Yup. A STEM – an STM – is a scanning tunnelling microscope, and that makes the SEM look kind of clunky. The STM works at the atomic level, so the resolution's between about a tenth and a hundredth of a nanometre. And there are a few other high-tech gadgets in the same field like the AFM and the TEM, the atomic force microscope and the transmission electron microscope. They've both got about the same level of resolution as the STEM.'

North looked at her and nodded.

'Yes,' he said. 'You're right. It was an anomaly and they decided to take it to the next level. The next level down, I mean. They took a sample to UCL, University College London, and used the scanning electron microscope they have there.'

'Don't keep us in suspense,' Dame Janet instructed. 'Presumably this SEM thing identified whatever it was.'

North nodded.

'It did, yes,' he replied, 'but that's really where our problems start, not where they finish.' He paused again. 'Do any of you know what a fullerene is?' he asked. 'Or a buckyball?'

Chapter 5

River Thames, London

What had taken most of the time had been working out the delivery mechanism. The target, in the context of the campaign, was both very ambitious and perfectly obvious, and it wasn't even the first time that somebody had tried to destroy it, though that much earlier attempt had been a complete failure. The problem they had faced was that, precisely because the target was so obvious and so important, it was also extremely well protected. They knew from the very start that getting close enough to it to do any significant damage, at least using the easiest approach and one of their normal, tried and tested methods of attack, would never work.

There was one approach path to the target that was essentially unguarded but presented an extremely high degree of difficulty and would have required at least one of the volunteer *shahids* to learn to fly an aircraft, and they really hadn't got time for that. And in any case, after 9/11 the rules and precautions involving powered flights near cities in the United Kingdom, and especially near London, had been tightened up so much that they knew a successful attack from the air could not be guaranteed. It might not even be possible because of the large number of military bases near London from which a fighter aircraft could be scrambled. So they looked again at the other unguarded avenue of approach and decided that was their best option, but using a slightly different and hopefully unexpected method.

They knew more or less what they needed to do, and after about a week spent wandering around in the boatyards and marinas that were dotted about the upper reaches of the Thames, they'd found three vessels that would suit their purposes. They covertly watched to see how often the owners of these boats appeared and then settled on the oldest one, which looked as if it had almost been abandoned.

In the late evening of the day after they had made their choice, Hassan and Tariq, whose combined skill sets included opening locked doors and a certain facility with key-operated systems of all kinds, had entered the small marina after watching it for over an hour to make sure they would be the only people there. That had required picking the padlock securing the pedestrian access gate, which they'd then carefully locked behind them – they would be leaving by a different route – before heading for the office building on which they knew two security cameras were mounted. The most expensive things in the marina were the boats berthed there, not the office buildings, and that was where the cameras had been pointed.

Tariq had found a sturdy wooden box that would give him the height he needed to reach the camera. He stood on it and, taking care to keep his face well away from the lens, he had sprayed a thick coating of black paint onto it. He'd repeated the treatment with the second camera, checked to make sure there were no other monitoring devices, and then they'd made their way through the marina to the berth where the cabin cruiser was located.

The lock on the stern door had given them no trouble at all, and nor had the ignition lock. About five minutes after stepping on board the boat, Tariq had released the mooring ropes and begun keeping a sharp lookout in the darkness of the river as Hassan, keeping the engine running at low revolutions, had carefully edged the boat away from its berth.

It had taken them another hour to travel along the Thames to the almost derelict boathouse that they had discovered during their initial surveillance, and where the cabin cruiser would remain while they prepared it for its short final voyage. That didn't take too long, because while the search for a suitable boat had been underway, the remaining two members of the gang had been sourcing the other components that they would need, principally ammonium nitrate fertiliser.

This they couldn't buy in the quantities they needed because that would attract unwelcome attention to them, but by visiting a number of farms located to the west and north-west of London they had been able to steal bags of the substance, taking just two or three from each farm they visited after dark, reasoning that most farmers wouldn't notice that the fifty-four bags of fertiliser they had owned on Wednesday had become fifty-one or fifty-two bags by Thursday.

Ammonium nitrate is a high-nitrogen fertiliser and is comparatively stable in most circumstances – warehouses in Beirut excluded, obviously – and when mixed with diesel oil in the ratio of about 94 per cent ammonium nitrate to 6 per cent diesel fuel it forms a compound known as ANFO, four letters which rather unimaginatively stand for 'ammonium nitrate fuel oil', which is more stable than ammonium nitrate by itself and is classed as a tertiary explosive, meaning that it can't be detonated by shock or something like a blasting cap. To cook off ANFO a secondary explosive known as a booster or a primer has to be used. The explosive yield of the mixture can be improved by as much as 30 per cent by the addition of about 15 per cent powdered aluminium by weight.

Tariq and his companions had already sourced the aluminium powder and Abū Tadmir, the name adopted by Mahdi Sadir, the leader of their group but a man who was not literally a part of it, had had both the funds and more importantly the contacts to produce a half-kilo block of Semtex and a detonator which together would act as the booster for the ANFO. He had also, at one of their meetings held at random locations outside London, supplied a long canvas bag, the contents of which had clanked mechanically when he handed it over.

That, Sadir had said in reply to the obvious question from Tariq, was their insurance policy. He'd opened the bag and produced a Kalashnikov AK-47 assault rifle, a box of ammunition and two spare magazines.

'This,' he'd said, 'will ensure that the boat will not be stopped on the river by anybody.'

Ten days after they'd stolen the cabin cruiser, it was ready. The very first thing they'd done was to change the name painted on the stern to try to disguise the fact that it had been stolen. That was easy because the original name was made up of six letters and was a palindrome, and by painting over the first and last they'd produced a name that was still a palindrome but quite different to the original.

Then they'd stripped out virtually everything from the interior of the saloon and dumped it. There wasn't much finesse involved in the removal, though they took great care to make sure that the hull wasn't damaged by their actions. Acting on Sadir's specific instructions, they'd then packed all the ANFO into watertight bags and stacked them on the floor of the saloon in a single thick layer wrapped in heavy-duty waterproof plastic sheeting and sealed with copious amounts of tape. Both ammonium nitrate and ANFO were highly hygroscopic and it was essential to keep the mixture as dry as possible to maximise its explosive power.

More or less in the centre of the improvised explosive was the chunk of Semtex into which the electrically powered detonator had been inserted, attached to a simple circuit that included a battery. That would form the booster that would initiate the explosion.

They had known from the start that the mission would require sacrifice because Sadir had made it very clear that the only way it was going to work was if they were directly involved in the delivery of the improvised weapon. And by that he meant one of them would have to stand in the cabin cruiser beside the explosive, steer the vessel to its destination and then trigger the booster charge when the boat was in precisely the optimum position.

That was the reality of the situation. They did not have the technology to even attempt to control the boat remotely, and the strong currents and powerful tidal flow along the Thames meant that any remote-control system would be cumbersome and probably unworkable.

The second relevant factor was timing, and the same argument applied. This was not something that could be initiated remotely. Only a man actually on board the vessel would know when both the time and the position were right, and at that point he would initiate the detonation.

So martyrdom was a given, but that was not a problem. All the members of the group were utterly committed and perfectly prepared to die for their beliefs. They knew beyond any doubt that dying as a martyr was an absolute guarantee that they would enjoy an eternity of paradise in the afterlife.

But that wasn't all. Because of the importance of the operation to Sadir and, more significantly, to his comrades and the elders back in Iraq who were funding it, he had decided that there needed to be two men on the boat. One would have to steer it, to get it into the correct position, and the second one would act as a guard and protect the vessel in the event that it was detected and an attempt made to stop it or board it.

And, though Sadir did not labour the point and none of them would ever say it out loud, having a second man on board, a man just as committed to the mission as the first, would ensure that there would be no hesitation at the crucial moment. Not all martyrs were always prepared to go all the way, as evidenced by the number of truck bombers whose ultimate commitment and sacrifice were known to have been guaranteed by a set of handcuffs linking them securely to the steering wheel of their vehicle and a detonation system that could be triggered remotely.

It was important that the explosion should take place during the day, to ensure the maximum number of casualties and the greatest possible disruption to the centre of London. Accordingly, the two men who had volunteered to accept martyrdom for the cause – Hassan and Khalid – had set off from their requisitioned boathouse in mid-morning when they expected the volume of river traffic to be high. Their intention was to reach the target early that afternoon when most of the occupants of the building should be back from lunch.

Chapter 6

'A what?' Angela Evans demanded.

Natasha Black held up her hand, but North shook his head.

'I know you know, Natasha,' he said, 'because you seem to know quite a lot about almost everything. Okay, for the benefit of everybody else in the room, we're talking about nanotechnology, another subject I'd never even heard of before this thing happened. This past week has been a bloody steep learning curve for me, let me tell you.

'Nanotechnology is basically the manipulation of atoms and molecules, and what I also didn't know is that it's not a new technique. It's been going on for centuries, and to see a really good example of it all you have to do is visit a medieval church and take a look at the stained-glass windows. The artists in that period mixed gold and silver particles to create the different colours in the glass, and that process actually changed the composition of the materials. That was a form of nanotechnology, though obviously nobody realised what it was until modern times.'

'But you're not talking about some accidental process, I assume,' Morgan said. 'It wasn't something he could have picked up out walking his dog or mowing his lawn. From what you've described the grey substance found in O'Brien's blood is presumably artificial.'

'Yes, and definitely a form of enemy action. Anyway, the background is that the element carbon has the ability to catenate, to form long chains or rings of atoms and to have other elements attached to it, and the entire science of organic chemistry is the study of carbon and its compounds. A fullerene is another form of carbon molecule called an allotrope, and it's different because it forms a closed mesh. It comes in a wide variety of shapes, including balls and tubes and flat sheets. The balls are known as buckyballs and all the various kinds of meshes are called fullerenes.

'Both those names come from a man named Buckminster Fuller who, strangely enough, had nothing to do with nanotechnology. His connection is that he made the geodesic dome structure popular in his lifetime – he died in 1983 – and that's pretty much an identical structure to one particular buckyball, C60, which somebody named buckminsterfullerene. The geodesic dome is just a hell of a lot bigger. The scientists needed names to call these things, and fullerene and bucky just kind of stuck. And there are bucky onions and bucky tubes and similar names for other structures.

'Anyway, the point is that what the electron microscope showed was that the grey smear recovered from O'Brien's blood sample consisted entirely of buckyballs, and that's what I meant when I said it was enemy action. That's the commonest fullerene that occurs naturally. It's in things like soot and it's even been detected in deep space, the space between the stars, but there's no way O'Brien could have ingested it in its natural form. It had to have been administered to him, somehow.'

'Empty or full?' Natasha Black asked. 'The buckyballs, I mean.'

'Sorry, I should have explained that better. What the technicians working the electron microscope saw weren't buckyballs as such, but the *remains* of buckyballs.'

'There you go, then. That's your smoking gun.'

North noticed the slightly blank expressions on the faces of everybody else in the room and decided to clarify what he'd been told.

'One of the ways scientists expect to be able to use nanotechnology is to deliver precise dosages of drugs to specific locations in the body. The shape of the buckyball means that a drug can be carried inside it, or chemicals can be attached on the outside and then released. What Natasha means is that because all the buckyballs that the technicians could see with the electron microscope had broken apart, the payload, whatever was inside the balls, must have been released.'

'And you think that was what killed him?' Morgan suggested.

North nodded.

'That's what the medics think. By a process of elimination they ruled out everything except the foreign bodies, the buckyballs, so the only conclusion they could come to is that whatever they carried was the cause. So then they did another check for drugs. Initially, they'd been looking for so-called recreational drugs – heroin, cocaine, crack, that kind of thing – but then they did a broad-spectrum analysis, and that produced something really unexpected.' He paused and looked at Natasha Black before he continued. 'His blood contained traces of sodium thiopental and potassium chloride.'

'That's two-thirds of a lethal injection,' she said immediately. 'Sodium thiopental is a barbiturate normally used as a first step in general anaesthesia for patients undergoing operations and it's really fast acting at very low doses. Potassium chloride shuts down the heart by cocking up the electrical conductivity of the muscles. The other drug usually included in a lethal injection is pancuronium bromide, which works like curare. It's a muscle relaxant that blocks the action of acetylcholine and paralyses the respiratory system.'

'So we're looking at a murder,' Dave North said flatly.

Chapter 7

Neither Hassan nor Khalid knew much about boat handling or had had much experience on the water, and the heavily laden cabin cruiser, the mass of improvised explosives causing it to ride much lower in the water than it should have done, was something of a handful on the fairly choppy waters of the Thames. Hassan worked the throttle to keep the speed high enough to more or less match that of the other traffic on the river, but slow enough that he remained in control of the vessel.

Khalid sat beside him in the stern cockpit, the fully loaded Kalashnikov AK-47, the weapon intended to ensure their mission was neither interfered with nor compromised, resting on the seat beside him and covered by a blanket.

In the event, they seemed to have attracted no unwelcome attention at all, and at just after two o'clock in the afternoon the cabin cruiser passed under Battersea Bridge. As it did so, Hassan picked up the mobile phone from the dashboard in front of him and dialled a mobile number from memory. Just like the phone he was using, the number he called belonged to a burner, an unregistered mobile.

His call was answered almost immediately.

'*As-salamu alaykum*, Hassan,' Mahdi Sadir said, the Arabic greeting meaning 'peace be upon you.' He knew exactly who was calling him because only Hassan knew that number. The other two cell members had a different number to contact him on.

'*Ma'a salama*, Abū Tadmir,' Hassan replied: 'go in peace,' a standard response. 'We are on track and on time. We have just passed Battersea Bridge. River traffic is light, and we do not expect any delays.'

'You have done well, my brother,' Sadir said. 'I do not expect to hear from you again. *Allāhu akbar.*'

'*Allāhu akbar,*' Hassan echoed, his voice rising in fervour as he said the words and ended the call.

'We now have,' he said to Khalid, putting down the mobile and again looking at the chart of the river he had mounted in front of him, 'just over one mile to go. We have three more bridges to pass underneath before the river straightens up to take us direct to our target. Then there is the last bridge, Lambeth Bridge, and we must make our preparations and say our final prayers before we reach it. When we pass under that bridge we will be able to see our target coming into view ahead of us, and by then we must be ready. Completely prepared in all respects.'

'Nothing can stop us now,' Khalid said confidently. 'Our action will bring London to its knees and send an unmistakable message of defiance to the Great Satan.'

'We will prevail,' Hassan concurred. 'But we are not in position yet and there is still some distance to go. Keep alert and be prepared to react at a moment's notice.'

Khalid nodded and reached down to rest his hand on the blanket concealing the Kalashnikov.

'You can rely on me, my brother.'

Chapter 8

'There's no doubt about that,' Morgan agreed. 'But that does pose a lot of questions, beginning with how and who and why. Like how did he get infected – if that's the right word in this case – and how was he able to fly the helicopter as far as he did? Why didn't the drugs take effect a hell of a lot sooner? And that's only the start.'

'I might be able to help about the timing,' North said. 'If what the medical people found so far is accurate, then the payload was this lethal chemical cocktail and it was carried in the buckyballs. One of the medics suggested they must have been constructed so that they would dissolve a certain number of hours or even days or weeks after being administered, or maybe even because of some trigger.'

'If there had been a trigger,' Natasha Black pointed out, 'the medics would probably have found it. We're talking about something like a spike in one element of blood chemistry, something to start a reaction. For example, there's a new treatment for diabetics involving nano-particles that hold insulin but also a glucose-specific enzyme. When the level of glucose in the blood reaches a certain level, the enzyme starts to dissolve, which releases the insulin. The glucose level drops, the enzyme stops dissolving and the release of insulin stops, so it's self-regulating. That's the kind of trigger I mean. There are changes in blood chemistry at different altitudes, but these are quite slow and mild and you need to be a lot higher than most helicopters fly to even notice them. So I doubt there was a trigger. I think this was a timed release that just happened to take place while he was in the air.'

'The nanoparticles can be made to dissolve with that accurate a degree of timing?' Dame Janet asked.

'According to what I've read,' Natasha replied, 'they can be prepped to dissolve anything from a few seconds to months after being administered. But I don't know too much about this subject.'

'Yeah, right,' North said. 'Anyway, at least we now know what killed O'Brien and how. Because this is such a new field, nobody really knows what can be done and what can't, but that looks the most likely explanation.'

'If you're right about this,' Dame Janet observed, 'it sounds like there's somebody out there who's managed to turn nanotechnology into a weapon. But as far as I can see it's nothing to do with C-TAC. Or do you know something we don't?'

'Probably not,' North admitted, 'but it is weird. And whoever did it nearly killed me, so it's become kind of personal. But there's nothing much I can do about it. I'm a soldier, of a sort, and I have this limitation: if it's not big enough for me to shoot I kind of run out of ideas about how to deal with it.'

'Hang on a minute,' Morgan said. 'What you've told us about Bob O'Brien is really weird – you're right about that – and I've no reason to doubt what you've said. So we know what happened and you've come up with a possible method for how it happened, but what we don't know is *why* it happened. Why was O'Brien targeted? Or were you the target and he just happened to be the means for somebody to try to kill you?'

North laughed shortly.

'I've pissed off a lot of people in my career, such as it is, but if somebody wanted to kill me they could take me out with a bullet or a knife or even drive a car into me. And the same applies to O'Brien. There are much easier ways to kill somebody than to do something like this, and using any kind of nanotechnology is *really* expensive. Scanning electron microscopes are sodding pricey to hire, and lottery money to buy, like over a million quid a pop, and you can't do anything in this field unless you have access to one of them. A bullet costs a few pence, so that doesn't make sense.'

'So how do you think some person unknown did this, then? And more to the point, why did they do it?'

'Buggered if I know,' North said.

'This is an obvious question,' Angela Evans said, 'but was Bob O'Brien the only man up at Hereford who was affected?'

'I was getting to that,' Dave North said, 'because that's the really bad news.'

He reached into his jacket pocket and pulled out a folded copy of the *Hereford Times*, a weekly tabloid newspaper. He unfolded it, smoothed it out and showed them the headline on the front page – 'MYSTERY ILLNESS KILLS FOUR AT CREDENHILL BARRACKS' – and passed the newspaper over to Ben Morgan.

'We don't know what's going on or why it's happening,' North admitted, 'and I've no idea if there are any other people at Stirling Lines who are still affected by this thing. The Credenhill Ruperts are running further checks and they'll let me know if anything pops out of the woodwork.'

Chapter 9

River Thames, London

The oldest police force in England is not, as many people erroneously assume, the Metropolitan Police Service, established by Sir Robert Peel in 1829 with a staff of 1,000 constables and based at 4 Whitehall Place in London. The building had a back door in Great Scotland Yard that was used as the entrance to the police station and eventually the shortened form 'Scotland Yard' entered common usage as a synonym for the Metropolitan force. The 'peelers', as they quickly became known – the name a nod to the surname of the founder – were modelled on a law enforcement organisation created in Ireland in 1814, again by Sir Robert Peel, a force that morphed into the Irish Constabulary in 1836. Peel is known as the founder of modern policing, and it's probable that the later nickname 'Bobbies' for police officers is derived from his Christian name. But to discover the earliest organised police force in England it's necessary to look back over thirty years before, to the end of the previous century.

What became known as the golden age of piracy began, broadly speaking, in about 1650 and lasted until the 1730s with pirates and privateers – essentially licensed pirates carrying a 'letter of marque and reprisal' issued on behalf of their monarch to authorise their lawless activities against the ships and ports of countries perceived to be enemy states – plying their brutal trade first in the Atlantic and Caribbean and later in the Pacific and Indian oceans. But by the end of the eighteenth century arguably the richest pickings for pirates were to be found a lot closer to the British Isles than the Caribbean Sea, and in many cases there was no need to even bother boarding a boat in order to participate in the trade.

It's been reliably estimated that in the 1790s the value of the cargoes held on the thousands of merchant ships moored or anchored in the River Thames at any one time typically exceeded £80 million when converted to today's currency. And, equally typically, river pirates and gangs of dockyard thieves were known to make off with around £50 million worth of that cargo in an average year.

Such massive losses were obviously unsustainable, and in 1798 the Marine Police Force was formed on the instigation of three men – a Scottish magistrate named Patrick Colquhoun, an Essex-based mariner and Justice of the Peace called John Harriott and, as a somewhat unexpected participant, the philosopher Jeremy Bentham – initially with a staff of just fifty officers to police an estimated thirty thousand river and dockside workers.

Against the odds the organisation, based in Wapping High Street, was effective and two years later an act of Parliament – the Marine Police Bill – converted this private police force into a public entity and in so doing created the first uniformed police force anywhere in the world. Almost forty years later, in 1839, it merged with the fledgling Metropolitan Police Force to form Thames Division.

Today, it's still based in Wapping High Street and is now known as the Marine Policing Unit, or MPU. It's an elite division within the Met, responsible for the safety and security of about forty-seven miles of the tidal Thames within Greater London between Hampton Court to the west and Dartford Creek to the east. Like all British police forces, the MPU is on duty 24 hours a day and 365 days a year, operating boats of various types from RIBs – rigid inflatable boats – up to 31-foot Fast Response Targa vessels in its patrols of the river.

Just like police officers on land, the crews of the MPU boats are keenly attuned to the traffic they see in their patch, and do not hesitate to intervene when they think it's necessary, stopping and questioning the crew of any vessel that raises a red flag in their minds. And the old and somewhat battered cabin cruiser that had just passed under Lambeth Bridge had raised at least two of them.

First, it was heading north along the river towards the open sea at the mouth of the Thames, several miles distant to the east. That didn't mean the people on board were planning on going that far, obviously, but in the opinion of the MPU officers what they were looking at was strictly a river craft, and an old one at that, entirely unsuited to tackling the rough water conditions that might be found even in the Thames estuary.

The second point was related to the first, because it appeared to be very heavily laden. Most boats have a colour change at the waterline, often a white hull above the water while the lower section of the hull is painted a much darker shade. On the cabin cruiser *Anna* – the name, inscribed in capital letters on the stern of the vessel, was visible to the skipper of the Targa launch through his binoculars – no part of the darker lower hull could be seen, and the boat appeared to be wallowing slightly, as if it was either unbalanced because it was overloaded or because the man standing in the rear cockpit was very inexperienced. Or possibly both.

It could all of course be entirely innocent, but it never hurt to make sure and to ask the appropriate questions. And Sergeant Paul Carter, the Targa's skipper, had several. He also thought it was worth running a preliminary check. All boats on the Thames are required to be licensed with the Environment Agency, though it didn't look to Carter as if the owner of such an old vessel would necessarily be interested in complying with all the rules.

'Get someone to check the registry, Bob,' he instructed the constable standing beside him, 'and find out who owns that wreck.'

At the same time Carter goosed the throttle slightly to start closing in on the suspect vessel from behind.

'I think there's a problem,' Constable Fisher said a couple of minutes later, having done Carter's bidding. 'There are three boats registered on the Thames with the name *Anna*, but none of them are anything like that.' He pointed ahead. 'But about a fortnight ago a cabin cruiser named *Hannah* was reported stolen from a mooring up at Walton-on-Thames and the description of the missing boat is pretty much a match for what we're looking at. I reckon the aquatic tea leaf who did the job just painted over the first and last letters of the name and figured that would fool us.'

'I'm not certain,' Carter replied, 'that I'd be particularly enthusiastic about getting it back if I owned that boat. I think I'd prefer the insurance payout, but that's another story. Okay, Bob. We'll go alongside and get this sorted.'

As well as Carter and Fisher, there was another constable, Mark Crichton, making up the crew of the patrol boat, and as they headed towards the vessel he suspected was stolen, Carter issued the appropriate orders.

'We're going to come alongside the cabin cruiser ahead of us, starboard side to. As soon as we're next to it you two get on board, arrest the guy driving it and anyone else and give them the usual warning about it being a suspected stolen vessel. Get cuffs on them as soon as you can and each of you take a spare pair as well in case there are other bodies inside the cabin. Take over the controls and obviously keep it running until our lords and masters decide where they want us to park it, and we'll sort it out from there. Any questions?'

It was the kind of operation that the team had carried out dozens of times before, and Carter was completely unsurprised when both constables shook their heads.

He looked ahead, estimating the distance to the cabin cruiser by eye rather than using the radar because the two vessels were now quite close together.

'Three minutes, maybe four,' he said. 'Get ready.'

Just like marked police patrol cars on land, the MPU's Targa launches have sirens and blue lights as attention-getters in case anyone should fail to recognise the word 'POLICE' in large white capital letters on either side of the dark blue hull, or didn't notice the bright blue and yellow Battenberg-pattern paint on the superstructure.

As the Targa closed to within about a hundred and fifty yards of the cabin cruiser, Carter switched on the blue lights and gave a brief whoop of the siren.

Immediately, the man standing in the stern of the cabin cruiser turned round and stared at the approaching police boat. But, conspicuously, he failed to reduce speed. In fact, it looked to Carter as if he had actually opened the throttle still further.

'Possible failure to stop,' Carter reported, his voice untroubled. There was no possibility the probably stolen vessel could outrun him, and there was also nowhere on that stretch of the river where it could hide.

It was all standard and routine, though stopping a stolen boat was actually something of a rarity, and Carter guessed that his men would have control of the cabin cruiser within a matter of minutes and shortly after that they would know whether or not the vessel was the stolen *Hannah*.

And then, as the police boat closed to within about eighty yards of the cabin cruiser, the incident stopped being routine in any sense of the word.

Chapter 10

'So what's next?' Morgan asked, into the silence that followed North's final comment and looking along the table towards Dame Janet. 'We didn't all pitch up here just to hear about Dave North's aerial adventures.'

'Correct,' she said. 'Keep us in the loop about this, Dave, and especially if there are any other deaths. Now, the Prime Minister is worried. The Home Secretary is worried, and so is the Foreign Secretary. And just for a change they're not all worried about the next election, because it's too far away. What's caused this particular high-level angst-fest is the bloody French. And the bloody Germans, in fact.'

'Not planning to invade, are they?' North asked.

'What do you mean "invade?" The buggers are already here, but that wasn't what I was driving at. Here's a quick general knowledge quiz for you. Who owns British Gas?'

'That's something of a non sequitur,' Angela Evans said, 'but I'll take a wild stab in the dark and say we do. The British, hence the name.'

'Correct. It's a subsidiary of Centrica. How about EDF?'

'I think you'll find the clue there is also in the name,' Morgan said. 'EDF – Électricité de France. Which means it's ultimately owned by the French government, because that's the biggest shareholder in EDF.'

Dame Janet nodded.

'What about E.ON and Npower?' she asked. Nobody replied as she looked around the table. 'Both German. Here's an easy one, or rather an easy two. ScottishPower and Manweb. You should know about Manweb, Dave. It supplies North Wales, not that far from your usual stamping ground up around Hereford.'

'Not a clue,' North replied. 'Presumably not British, so maybe they're French?'

'Nearly right. Spanish, both of them.'

'Is there a point to this?' Morgan asked.

'There's a point to everything I say or do, Ben,' Dame Janet replied. 'You should know that by now. Now, I personally happen to believe that every nation should have control of its essential utility companies, but of course decisions about ownership are taken by politicians whose only interest is in getting elected and keeping their seats and who are, by definition, totally unqualified to govern and in most cases have about the same level of intelligence and attention span as a fruit fly. And to save any of you asking, yes I have had something of a run-in with a couple of members of our alleged government in the House, both of whom demonstrated a lack of knowledge about the dangers this country faces that would have been frankly embarrassing if they'd been expressed on a street corner by a homeless wino.'

Nobody responded. Dame Janet's critical and somewhat strident views on politicians in general were well known to all the members of C-TAC.

'The short version is that over the last ten days both EDF and Npower have suffered attacks on their corporate networks.'

Ben Morgan immediately looked interested. Cybersecurity and cyber warfare were his speciality.

'In fact, not so much attacks as intrusions,' Dame Janet continued. 'But however you describe or define what happened, a third party managed to get inside one supposedly secure system, and neither of the two idiots I spoke to today in Westminster seemed to think that was much of a problem.'

'Which it certainly is,' Natasha Black said.

'Obviously. One of the two MPs kept wittering on about zombie servers and—'

'Zombie servers?' Morgan interrupted. 'Really?'

'Yes. Hang on, Ben, I'm getting there. He talked about zombie servers and Tor and the dark web, so he'd obviously picked up a few buzzwords from somewhere. Eventually I played the "I'm just a simple woman and I don't know what you're talking about so please explain it all to me in words of one syllable" card and it turned out he knew some words and names but not what they meant. As you all know, I'm not an IT expert, but when he told me what a zombie server was he was actually describing a proxy server, and he knew that Tor was a browser but he had no idea what the name stood for. I even gave him a clue. I asked him if he'd ever heard of The Onion Router and he just shook his head. That should give you some idea of the calibre and level of ignorance of the sort of people I have to deal with at Westminster.'

Dame Janet slumped back in her chair and shook her head.

'I'm more interested in these attacks or intrusions than I am about what a couple of typically completely clueless politicians think,' Morgan said. 'What happened? What was the source?'

'I had a conference call with the security people at both companies. The ostensible source of both attacks was Vietnam, and you know as well as I do that means about the only place they couldn't have originated was that country. They'd have bounced the origin around the world before using the software.'

'Did they crack a legitimate password or hack into the system using some vulnerability?'

'You'll need to talk to their security people for chapter and verse, Ben, because this stuff is well outside my comfort zone. But I gather that in both cases the hackers first tried cracking passwords using tools called JTR and Cain. I suppose you know what they are?'

Morgan nodded.

'John The Ripper and Cain and Abel,' he replied. 'They're both password crackers often used by White Hat hackers doing pen testing.'

'Pen testing?' Angela Evans asked.

'Sorry, shorthand. Penetration testing, to see if a system is vulnerable. I presume that's not how they got in?'

'No. Then they looked for system vulnerabilities,' Dame Janet confirmed.

'They probably used something like Nessus or Metasploit,' Morgan suggested.

'Yes to both of those, and also something called Sniper.'

'The program's actually spelt Sn1per, with a number "1" rather than a letter "i", and it's often used with Metasploit. And they found a way inside?'

'Oddly enough, no.'

'No?' Morgan echoed. 'But I thought you said—'

'As I said, Ben, I'm getting there. The attacks weren't simultaneous but consecutive and repetitive, and because of the hacking tools that were used, and the way that they were used, it looks as if the same person or group of people were involved. I understand that most hackers have preferred suites of tools they're familiar with and that do the job, and they tend to use them in much the same way each time.'

'Just like anyone who uses a computer,' Morgan agreed. 'Or like any other tradesman, in fact, would use a tool.'

'Right. What I didn't tell you was that both these attacks failed to breach the firewalls and counter-intrusion systems and get inside the servers. The hackers tried for several days, first on the EDF and then on the Npower servers, and when they got nowhere with Npower they went back to EDF and vice versa. They were quite determined. The security people were pleased with the way legitimate users were able to access the system while the alleged Vietnamese attackers couldn't get inside.'

'Until,' Morgan prompted.

'Exactly. Until the people at EDF noticed one apparently legitimate user on their system who was behaving oddly while the attack was still going on. They knew his identity from his log-in details, obviously, but he wasn't doing what they would have expected, which was accessing the modules that his job required him to use. Instead, he was cruising around the system, looking at completely unrelated material, and at one point it seemed as if he was trying to get access to the encrypted password files and other low-level stuff.'

'Presumably they kicked him off? And checked that he wasn't a legitimate user just being a bit too curious?'

'Yes, and then they started an internal investigation, which didn't help. They realised only an idiot would use his own log-in credentials to snoop around the system like that, but they checked anyway and ruled him out, for one unarguable reason.'

'Which was?'

'He was in hospital. He'd contracted Covid-19 and was in intensive care with barrier nursing and no access even to his mobile phone, far less to a computer, when the intrusion occurred. Whoever it was, it wasn't him. The EDF security people were cagey about how far the intruder had got, and said no damage was done. No ransomware installed, no data stolen or website pages defaced, nothing like that.'

Morgan shook his head.

'Hackers don't normally breach a system just to show that they can,' he said, 'and it worries me if this one apparently did nothing apart from take a look around. He might have been trying to install a backdoor so he could access the system in the future, or maybe he was just copying the log-in details of other users. The best place to find a system vulnerability is when you're inside it, so perhaps that was what he was after. It's an obvious concern.'

'I agree with you, so get yourself over to see these security bods at EDF and find out exactly what happened and what they've done about it.'

'Will do. What I don't quite follow is why you also talked to a couple of politicians about this.'

'Only because I couldn't get in to see the Home Secretary or the Foreign Secretary. They were tied up in meetings, so I had to make do with a couple of their minions. And they're both involved, along with the PM, because of the foreign ownership of these two companies and the possible impact a hacking attack could have on the parts of the UK served by EDF and Npower. I asked the idiot MP who'd been telling me about zombie servers how comfortable his home would be if the mains electricity and gas went offline for a couple of weeks with no backup power supplies available and he actually went white. Best part of my day, that was.

'Anyway, C-TAC is in the loop now, so off you go and check it out, just in case there's more to this than meets the eye.'

Chapter 11

North of Lambeth Bridge, London

As Carter steered the launch on an intercept course with the cabin cruiser and continued to close the distance between the two vessels he saw a second man appear in the stern of the boat. He couldn't tell if he'd just stepped out of the saloon or if he'd been sitting down at the stern of the boat and out of sight.

'There are at least two of them on board, Bob,' he said, 'so don't forget to take a spare pair of cuffs.'

The attention of all three men in the Targa patrol boat was focused on the cabin cruiser, but it was Crichton who saw the threat first.

'Is that a boat hook?' he murmured, almost to himself. Then he recognised the object for what it was and immediately shouted out a warning. 'Rifle! He's got a rifle.'

Carter slammed the throttles forward and at the same moment turned the wheel hard to port, trying to drive the patrol boat clear of the sudden and completely unexpected danger.

In fact, Mark Crichton was wrong. Or at least not entirely right.

The word 'rifle' in the minds of most people, certainly members of the almost entirely unarmed population of the United Kingdom, conjures up an image of a bolt action weapon, probably in .22 or another fairly small calibre, the kind of thing a farmer would have to hand to take care of rats and rabbits and other small animals. But place the word 'assault' before the word 'rifle' and the image instantly changes.

What Crichton had seen was the long barrel of a weapon in the hands of the second man on the boat they were pursuing, but at a distance and from a bouncing and unstable platform. If they'd been a little closer, he might have seen the distinctive gas cylinder mounted above the barrel which, along with the forward-curved magazine, are the two most obvious identification features of the Kalashnikov AK-47 and its variants.

But even though Crichton hadn't immediately realised the exact type of weapon they were facing, it became blindingly obvious in the next few seconds as Carter took evasive action.

As the Targa heeled over, the three police officers heard the yammering sound as the unidentified man on the cabin cruiser fired the assault rifle towards them, the slamming noise echoing off the buildings and river walls on both sides of them.

Carter reckoned they were about a hundred yards away from the gunman, well within the lethal range of the assault rifle, which he guessed was a Kalashnikov because it was the obvious weapon of choice for terrorists around the world. He didn't know exactly how many shots had been fired in that first burst, but he thought he had felt the impacts of at least two rounds hitting the starboard side of his boat.

'Fucking hell,' he yelled as he steered the launch back the way they'd come, swinging it from side to side so as not to present a static target and keeping the speed up to produce a curtain of spray behind the boat to further confuse the gunman's aim. 'Anybody hurt?'

A pair of answering shouts told him that his men were uninjured, and as far as he could tell the bullets hadn't done anything terminal or even serious to his vessel.

MPU boats do not normally carry weapons, and when they do they are usually in the experienced hands of members of SCO19, the Metropolitan Police's armed division, which includes roaming ARVs – Armed Response Vehicles – and groups such as the Specialist Rifle Officers, or SROs, all highly trained marksmen, and the Tactical Support Teams that provide armed backup for police raids when the suspects are known or believed to be in possession of weapons. But in that boat on that day, the three officers hadn't even got a pistol between them.

Bob Fisher was already on the radio, calling in the incident, but unlike a situation on dry land, when the driver of a police car can request the help of other units to apprehend a vehicle that has failed to stop, out on the river there were no other units. Or at least none close enough to lend a hand. And for obvious reasons roadblocks and spike strips or stingers were never going to work. Ultimately, the boat could be stopped by the Thames Barrier out at the London City Airport, but Carter had no intention of letting it get that far east.

He turned the boat through a half-circle as quickly as possible so that the bow of his vessel was aiming back towards the cabin cruiser, now about two hundred yards distant. That put most of the Targa between the three officers and the man with the assault rifle, which would hopefully provide at least some measure of protection, but they were still well within range of the Kalashnikov and they all knew it. But at that distance, using the notoriously inaccurate assault rifle from a moving platform – the cabin cruiser – to hit another moving target would be difficult at best.

'There's another Targa heading our way,' Fisher reported, 'but he's down by the Isle of Dogs and he'll be stopping to pick up a couple of SROs from Wapping so it's going to be a while getting here. There are a couple of ARVs heading for the river to get in position to try to take out these two comedians. And they've scrambled India 99 but they estimate it'll be at least fifteen minutes before he's on task.'

That was the callsign of one of three Eurocopter EC 145 helicopters of the ASU, the Air Support Unit, that provide airborne surveillance and other assistance to the Metropolitan Police. They're based at North Weald Airfield, about twenty miles from the centre of London, a distance the EC 145 could cover in a little under eight minutes at its maximum speed of 153 miles per hour. If it was already airborne over the airfield. The extra time quoted was the inevitable delay caused by the crew getting from their ready room, out to the aircraft, doing pre-flight checks, pre-start, post-start and pre-take-off checks, and actually launching the helicopter into the air. Obviously most of these were pre-done to allow as fast a take-off as possible, but no sensible pilot would ever even think about getting into the air without running through these checks. As the old adage has it, there are old pilots and there are bold pilots, but there are no old, bold pilots.

'It'd be a big help to us,' Carter said, staring towards the cabin cruiser, which was still heading north along the eastern, the right-hand, side of the river, 'if that chopper was fitted with a fucking great machine gun as well as cameras and lights. Then we could just back away and watch chummy being blown out of the water.'

The man with the assault rifle had only fired that one initial burst of maybe six or eight rounds, but all four officers knew that the standard magazine for a Kalashnikov AK-47 held thirty cartridges, and most terrorists – because that was very obviously what they were dealing with – who managed to obtain an assault rifle also managed to obtain more than one magazine for it. The expression 'outgunned' covered the situation perfectly.

'So what the hell's this guy up to?' Crichton asked. 'It's not much of a terrorist attack if all he does is shoot up a police launch.'

Carter didn't respond for a few seconds, mentally trying to put the pieces together. Then he shook his head.

'They'd only be carrying an assault rifle and be prepared to use it if they're planning an attack right now,' he said. 'Think about it. We had truck bombs over here when the IRA was playing around, and at Oklahoma in the States as well, and the Americans have had aircraft bombs when planes were used as weapons on 9/11. I think we could be looking at the first boat bomb in Britain.'

Bob Fisher didn't look entirely convinced.

'So what's their target, down here on the river?' he asked, then glanced up towards the western bank of the Thames at one of the most recognisable buildings not just in Britain but in the entire world: the Palace of Westminster, home of the House of Commons and the House of Lords. 'Oh, shit. Not Parliament?'

'Think about it,' Carter said again. 'If what we're looking at is part of an active branch of some radical Islamic organisation they'll be aiming for either the maximum possible loss of civilian lives or the maximum possible embarrassment to the British government. Or both. There's not a big enough civilian presence anywhere on the river to form a target. If all they wanted to do was mow down a few civilians they could have used that assault rifle to shoot up a London bus, no problem. But this is different. I think their target is almost certainly either Parliament or the MI6 headquarters at Vauxhall Cross, but that's a hardened facility, not to mention the fact that they've already gone past it. Unless you can think of something else, that means they must be heading for Parliament.'

As Carter spoke, the three police officers watched as the cabin cruiser started angling over to port, heading for the wrong side of the river – traffic on the Thames, as on almost every waterway, always keeps right – and Westminster. That was a clear and unmistakable confirmation of what he had suspected.

'It's wallowing,' Fisher said. 'It could be stuffed full of Semtex or C4 and you can get a hell of a lot of explosive inside a boat that size.'

'I doubt if they'd have access to that much plastic,' Carter said, 'but a fertiliser bomb would be bloody nearly as dangerous.'

'So what are we going to do? They're heading for Parliament right now.'

'We're going to stop them. Buggered if I know how, but that's what we're going to do.'

Chapter 12

Ben Morgan was standing up ready to leave when the phone beside Dame Janet rang. There were standing orders in place to ensure that that particular number was only known to certain high-level officials and government ministers, the intelligence services, the military and the police, along with very specific instructions about who could call it and under what circumstances. So when it rang it meant that one of two things had happened. Either a confirmed terrorist attack, or an incident that was most likely the work of a group of terrorists, had taken place or was then in progress.

Morgan sat down again as Dame Janet picked up the phone and announced herself crisply just as 'C-TAC' and then listened. About ten seconds into the conversation she told the caller to wait.

'It's the duty officer at the Marine Policing Unit – the river police – out at Wapping,' she said, and switched on the loudspeaker. 'Tell me that again.'

'We have a developing situation on the Thames near Lambeth Bridge,' a male voice said, speaking urgently. 'There's a cabin cruiser out there that failed to stop. It was approached by one of our patrol boats because it looked as if it was overloaded, and a registry check showed that it was possibly stolen. But when our launch started to close with it, one of the two men visible on board opened fire with an assault rifle.'

'Bloody hell,' Dave North muttered.

'Any injuries?' Dame Janet asked.

'None reported.'

'Which side of Lambeth Bridge?' Ben Morgan interjected, and Dame Janet repeated his question to the duty officer.

'North, near the—'

'Houses of Parliament,' Morgan finished for him, walking up to Dame Janet so that the duty officer would hear his voice. 'Put it together: an overloaded boat, a man with an assault weapon and the Houses of Parliament. It has to be a bomb attack. Are the officers on the police launch armed?'

'Negative. We have armed officers preparing to board a second patrol boat but it will be at least half an hour before they can reach that location. You're on my list of people to call.'

'There's not much we can do from here,' Morgan said, 'apart from shut down the cell phone network in central London in case the weapon is intended to be remotely triggered by a mobile.'

'I'll do that right now,' Angela Evans said, reaching for her own phone.

Dame Janet nodded her approval.

'Keep us in the loop,' she told the police officer, and ended the call.

'I really hope,' Natasha Black said, glancing in the general direction of the River Thames, 'that we don't hear a sodding great bang in the next five minutes.'

'Amen to that.'

Chapter 13

North of Lambeth Bridge, London

The obviously laden cabin cruiser was wallowing its way across the river, now aiming directly towards the centre of the Palace of Westminster, the vast and elegant building glowing golden in the afternoon sun, the roofline marked by spires and scaffolding in equal measure, a necessary part of the refurbishment work that had been going on for some time on the fabric of the structure.

'We need to keep him in the middle of the river,' Carter said urgently, 'where the effects of the blast will be minimised.' He pushed the throttles forward and started to accelerate. The target vessel was still about two hundred yards in front of them. 'Get on to Wapping and make sure they've warned the PaDP at the House. They'll need to evacuate Parliament and get everyone into the Old Palace Yard or at least outside and somewhere on the west side of the building. And then they need to send as many armed officers as they can to the wall by the river. Make sure they know that we've been fired on, and what we think the people in that cabin cruiser are planning. It'd be a really good idea if they forgot about their stupid bloody rules of engagement and loosed off a few rounds to persuade the people in that boat to back off, or at least to show them that we've got teeth.'

The PaDP was the Parliamentary and Diplomatic Protection branch of the Met's Specialist Operations directorate, with responsibility for guarding Parliament, 10 Downing Street and other government buildings and politicians, and while on duty they were invariably armed, usually carrying both a Glock 17 semi-automatic pistol and a Heckler & Koch MP5 submachinegun. Neither of those weapons would have been Carter's choice to try to stop the cabin cruiser, but he was hoping that a few carefully aimed volleys of 9mm bullets from the riverbank beside the Palace of Westminster would be enough to try to deflect or disrupt the bomb attack that he was now sure was in progress. He also knew that it was almost certainly too late to get a sniper in position anywhere close enough to the scene to be able to take out the men in the cabin cruiser.

So he was going to try and do his bit to resolve the situation. He had no access to a firearm, but he was sitting at the controls of several tons of powerboat, and in the right hands that could be a very effective weapon.

'Don't forget that fucking assault rifle,' Fisher said, glancing at him.

'Don't worry – I won't. Hang on, all of you. This is going to get very bouncy, very quickly.'

Carter ran the Targa launch up to full power, getting it on the plane, and steered it not towards the cabin cruiser but north down the eastern side of the Thames.

'You have a plan?' Fisher asked.

'Sort of. More of a gamble, really. The gunman's in the stern of the cabin cruiser, so if we're in front of his vessel he'll have to shoot around or over the cabin, which hopefully will make it more difficult for him to aim. Plus, if we're going at speed we'll be a fast-moving target, not a static object. And the wake that we're producing right now is going to make the cabin cruiser even more unstable as a shooting platform. So when we get beyond him I'm going to do a U-turn and head straight for him. That'll also put some of the hull and superstructure of this launch between us and him. That won't make us bulletproof, but it'll sure as hell help.'

–

'Shall I shoot at it?' Khalid asked as he watched the police boat start accelerating, but north down the river, not towards them.

Hassan shook his head. 'Save your ammunition,' he instructed. 'When we get closer to the building you'll need it in case there are any police in the grounds. If there are, they'll be armed.'

At that location, the Thames was roughly two hundred yards wide, which meant the cabin cruiser had to cover a distance of about three hundred yards on its diagonal course from the eastern side of the river to reach the optimum point for the detonation of the explosives. Hassan didn't want to get too close to the solid stone wall that marked the edge of the river and which would provide a measure of protection for the building. Instead, he intended to initiate the detonation when he believed the vessel was in the most advantageous position, close enough to the palace to inflict catastrophic damage, but not so close that the river wall would deflect most of the blast.

He had a minute, perhaps two, before the cabin cruiser would reach the ideal detonation point, so he picked up his mobile to tell Abū Tadmir that they had been detected at the last moment, but that they would still complete the mission. But when he looked at the screen there was no signal at all, and in disgust he tossed the phone onto the control panel in front of him.

Angela Evans's instruction from C-TAC had been implemented almost immediately, and the network would stay down until the situation had been resolved.

Khalid switched his attention from the police launch, which was still heading away from them down the river, to the building in front. He saw perhaps half a dozen black clad figures appearing at the top of the wall and had no doubt at all who they were.

Hassan pointed at them and nodded. 'Armed police,' he said. 'Give them something to think about.'

Immediately, Khalid aimed his Kalashnikov at one of the men, his aim uncertain because the boat was now rocking in the wake caused by the police launch – which at least explained why it had accelerated away so rapidly – and fired a volley of three shots towards his selected target. He had no idea where his bullets went and switched his aim to the next man along and repeated his action. While Hassan tried to keep the boat on a steady course, he continued firing.

'Why aren't they firing back?' he asked, slotting a new magazine in place and again picking a target.

'Because they only have small calibre weapons, ideal for taking down a target in the street but useless for trying to stop a boat at a hundred yards. They'll probably start firing when we get closer.'

—

The Targa patrol boat powered past the other vessel, staying close to the eastern bank for maximum separation from it because distance was their only real defence against the assault rifle.

Carter was switching his attention between the cabin cruiser and the water ahead of him. When the vessel was about a hundred yards north of the laden boat, he called out 'Brace!' and swung the wheel hard round, trying to keep up the speed in the turn. Then he headed due south at full throttle, directly towards the target vessel.

—

Khalid was standing on the right of the cockpit, his entire attention focused on the police officers positioned behind the river wall in front of them, some of whom were now firing short bursts towards the cabin cruiser, most of the small-calibre bullets either missing their target or falling short.

Hassan was standing on the left-hand side, the wheel, single throttle and other engine instruments and controls right in front of him. His view to the right, to starboard, was partially obscured by the superstructure of the boat and by his companion, which is why he didn't immediately react when the police launch made its sharp turn to port further down the river, simply because he didn't see what was happening.

In fact, neither man saw it until the launch was already established southbound, at speed, and was only about fifty yards away.

'Stop it,' Hassan yelled in sudden panic, pointing at the oncoming vessel. 'Stop it right now.'

Khalid reacted slowly, but he did react, turning to his right and switching his aim. Because the patrol boat was travelling almost flat out on the plane, the bow was lifted out of the water. The occupants were invisible from the cabin cruiser and all that he could see was the white foam and spray of the wave underlining the dark shape of the bow, aiming straight at them.

He switched the Kalashnikov to full auto, the mid position on the weapon's selector, braced himself against the side of the cockpit and pulled the trigger.

—

The sound of the assault rifle firing was unmistakable and audible even above the roar of the launch's engines and the thumping as the bow cut through the waves, and Carter thought he felt the impact of a handful of bullets, though he couldn't be certain.

His original plan had been to pass as close as possible to the cabin cruiser so that the wake from the launch would swamp it and cause the probably inexperienced helmsman to lose control of the vessel. If he timed it right, the really close pass might even be enough to topple the gunman with the assault rifle out of the boat and into the dark and unwelcoming waters of the Thames.

But as he took another glance ahead, measuring angles and distances, he realised that that wasn't going to work. The cabin cruiser was too close to the Palace of Westminster, and in a matter seconds or perhaps a minute at the most it would be in what he thought would be the optimum position for the explosive charges to be detonated. And then there would be nothing that he could do about it.

He would also be signing his own death warrant and those of the two other officers on board with him, because they would be so close to the epicentre of the detonation that his launch would be reduced to matchsticks, or whatever the fibreglass equivalent was, and they'd be obliterated with it. But he was going to do his best to make sure that that didn't happen.

'Time for Plan B,' Carter said, taking a firmer grip on the wheel and glancing at the two men with him. 'Hang on tight.'

'You didn't mention a Plan B,' Fisher objected, though it was perfectly obvious to him what Carter was going to do.

He altered the position of the wheel very slightly and pushed the throttle levers to confirm that they were already in the fully forward position, meaning the engines were delivering maximum power.

'Brace for impact,' he ordered.

Eight seconds later, the bow of the Targa launch smashed into the side of the cabin cruiser, more or less amidships.

--

The cruiser was old and built of wood. It hadn't been properly maintained for much of its life and was comparatively flimsy. The patrol boat didn't so much hit it as cut it in half, splintering the timbers of the midsection. The Targa surged forward, the power of its engines and its momentum reducing the centre of the cabin cruiser to little more than a collection of shattered timbers. The impact utterly destroyed the vessel.

The stern section lurched down as the patrol boat powered over it and then tipped backwards as the two craft separated, knocking both Hassan and Khalid off their feet, drenching them with cold river water.

Khalid screamed as the dark blue bow of the patrol boat, an unstoppable force despite now being riddled with bullets from the Kalashnikov, powered into and then steamrollered over the cabin cruiser. The impact was so massive that he lost his grip on the assault rifle. It bounced on the tilting side of the cockpit, then tumbled over the gunwale and immediately vanished below the surface.

Khalid was a long way from being an expert user of the Kalashnikov, or of any other weapon, come to that.

He'd received very rudimentary instruction on the assault rifle from Sadir, who had spent countless hours on the ranges in the various Al-Badr training camps in the Azad Kashmir region near Islamabad, close to Pakistan's eastern border, but in the time they'd had available Khalid had learnt only the basics: how to aim and fire it, remembering to squeeze rather than pull the trigger, to only use the weapon in semi-automatic mode both to conserve ammunition and to increase accuracy, how to load and change a magazine and so on. What he hadn't been able to do under Sadir's direction was actually fire it for real, there being almost nowhere in the English countryside, and certainly nowhere within fifty miles of the centre of London, where the sound of automatic rifle fire wouldn't attract unwelcome attention. And of course they also had only a very limited stock of ammunition.

But one of the basics that Sadir had emphasised was the importance of fitting a sling to the weapon, particularly as Khalid would be using the Kalashnikov on a boat on the often choppy waters of the River Thames. The standard two-point tactical sling for the AK-47 uses an attachment point where the barrel emerges from the fore-end of the weapon and another near the end of the buttstock.

No sling had been supplied along with the assault rifle, and so Sadir had constructed one using a long leather belt, the ends of it secured to the attachment points on the Kalashnikov with heavy-duty wire. And as well as the belt, for additional security he had also provided a length of strong cord to be knotted around the sling and the other end attached to one of the grab handles in the cockpit of the cabin cruiser.

Khalid had followed his instructions to the letter, and as soon as the Kalashnikov bounced out of his grip and he was back on his feet he seized the grab handle and began pulling on the cord to recover the weapon, which emerged muzzle first from the black waters of the river.

As the heavily waterlogged cockpit more or less stabilised he once again aimed the weapon at the police launch, now turning towards him and towering above his location more or less on the surface of the river. He made sure that the fire selector was still on fully automatic and aimed roughly, because at that distance he couldn't possibly miss. Then he squeezed the trigger.

–

When the raked bow of the patrol boat impacted the side of the cabin cruiser, the entire vessel rode up out of the water and for the briefest of instants it felt almost as if the Targa had become airborne. And then it crashed back down again, sending a massive cloud of spray and a large wave surging across the surface of the river. It didn't land completely flat, the collision having knocked it slightly to one side due to the angle

88

at which it had struck the other vessel, but it righted itself immediately and rocked from side to side as it stabilised.

The three MPU officers on board had seen the impact coming and had not only braced themselves for it but also ensured that their harnesses were properly attached so that when the collision was over they would still be on board the boat rather than swimming for the shore.

Paul Carter had pulled back the twin throttles at the moment when the Targa had hit the cabin cruiser and checked that his two colleagues were uninjured as soon as the boat landed.

'You both okay?'

He had no doubt that all three of them would develop impressive bruises over the next few days, but there were no broken bones, which was all that mattered.

'We're still afloat then,' Bob Fisher pointed out.

'Somewhat to my surprise, yes,' Carter responded.

The Targa launch seemed to be handling somewhat sluggishly, probably because it had taken some water into the hull through the bullet holes from the Kalashnikov, and from the inevitable damage caused by the impact, but it *was* handling and didn't seem to be in any immediate danger of sinking.

Cautiously, he turned the wheel to head back to the expanding area of floating wreckage which was all that remained of the cabin cruiser.

He and Bob Fisher saw the threat at precisely the same moment as the bearded man in the shattered remains of the cockpit of the destroyed boat aimed his assault rifle directly at them and at point-blank range.

Neither of them said a word, just threw themselves down flat on the deck of the Targa to try to avoid the fusillade of bullets that they knew was coming their way.

–

The Kalashnikov is arguably the most robust and reliable assault rifle ever made, and it can and will operate even if it's been dug up out of the ground or pulled out of a body of water. But most people on retrieving such a weapon will at least remove most of the debris before attempting to fire it.

That thought never occurred to Khalid because of his inexperience. He also failed to register the fairly obvious fact that he had pulled the weapon muzzle first out of the river, and was then aiming it upwards. So when he pulled the trigger and the round in the chamber fired it was an instance of an unstoppable force – this time a 7.62mm bullet – meeting a largely immovable object, in this case the barrel of an old and very well used assault rifle almost full of murky and incompressible water and debris from the Thames.

The result was predictable and utterly catastrophic for the man holding the assault rifle.

The breech and barrel of the weapon blew apart, and because Khalid was the person holding it and his face was just a couple of inches from the breech, most of his head blew apart as well.

He slumped down in the right-hand side of the cockpit, dead before his legs had even started to give way.

–

Carter heard the bang, which sounded louder than a rifle shot and nothing like the barrage of rounds he'd been expecting, a volley of shots that he was quite certain would be the last sounds he would ever hear because nobody, not even the most comprehensively untrained and manifestly incompetent person ever to have been given a weapon, could possibly miss him and the two other officers with an AK-47 at that range.

But what he didn't hear was a second shot, assuming that the bang was the first round of a volley. He eased himself up cautiously into a crouch and stared warily at the wrecked cabin cruiser. He was just in time to see the body of the man with the assault rifle collapse bonelessly into the remains of the cockpit like a puppet the instant the strings have been cut. His face and head appeared curiously misshapen and Carter guessed that either something had gone wrong with his weapon – a catastrophic blowback or something of that sort – or against the odds the Met police had managed to get a sniper in place in time. That seemed less likely because no sniper would go for a headshot unless it was unavoidable. But either way, it was clear that he would be taking no further part in the proceedings.

But the other man, the one who had been driving the boat, was still on board and could quite literally have his finger on the trigger, so the danger was still absolutely immediate and very real.

Carter pushed the throttles forward and turned the wheel to point the bow of the Targa launch directly at what was left of the cockpit and the figure of the second man standing there. The boat was the only weapon he had and there was no way he wasn't going to use it. The last time he'd aimed at the midships section of the cabin cruiser. Now his target was going to be what was left of the flooded cockpit at the stern.

Perhaps twenty or thirty yards separated the two vessels and he knew that it would still take precious seconds to cover even that short distance from a standing start on the river. But Carter had no other options.

He had to go for it. There was nothing else they could do.

–

Despite having been knocked off his feet, Hassan had managed to hang on to the wheel with one hand. And although the cabin cruiser had been comprehensively wrecked and the cockpit was already knee-deep in ice-cold water that was getting deeper by the second, it was still afloat. And, more importantly, so was their improvised explosive charge in what remained of the cabin, at least as far as he could see.

When Khalid pulled the trigger of the Kalashnikov Hassan immediately knew that something had gone very wrong with the weapon. He glanced sideways just in time to see the terminally damaged assault rifle fall from his companion's hands at the same moment as Khalid collapsed. He didn't know what had happened, but the sight of the limp body beside him confirmed that he was on his own. However Khalid had died was irrelevant.

He looked up the river towards the police launch. At that moment it was virtually stationary in the water, the skipper just starting to manoeuvre it towards him.

Hassan knew – as long as the detonation circuit still worked after the collision – that he could still do it. And the police launch, the vessel that had interfered with their carefully laid plan at quite literally the eleventh hour, was so close to him that he knew he would take the police officers with him when he detonated the charge. He also knew that he had to initiate the detonation right then, otherwise all would be lost and his and Khalid's lives would have been forfeited for nothing.

He released the wheel as the cabin cruiser lurched sideways again and scrambled forwards into the entrance to the saloon to reach the simple trigger they had constructed. It was a cheap electric toggle switch that would do nothing complicated when it was activated, just complete the circuit between the battery they'd fitted and the electric blasting cap embedded in the block of Semtex. They'd waterproofed the switch to avoid the circuit being completed before they were ready in case of spray splashing into the cockpit. That would trigger the plastic explosive and that detonation would provide the booster to ignite the combination of ANFO and powdered aluminium, the mass of improvised explosive that had virtually filled the saloon of the vessel.

But as he reached for it, his world spun crazily around him as the cabin cruiser disintegrated further. The forward and aft sections of the vessel started to separate and the boat's engine, wrenched free of its mountings in the collision, began a one-way journey down to the bottom of the river.

The thing about wooden boats is that they're made of wood, and wood floats, so although the cabin cruiser had been comprehensively wrecked by the impact, both sections of it were still floating, albeit separated, as was the solid mass of the bags of explosive within their waterproof covering. And Hassan could still see the switch, screwed to what was left of the aft bulkhead of the saloon.

Stumbling clumsily forwards, half-swimming through the water that had engulfed the cockpit, he hauled himself towards his objective.

He grabbed hold of what was left of the saloon door, pulled himself the final couple of feet and rested his finger on the switch.

For perhaps a second or two he didn't move, just stared across the few yards of water that separated the wrecked boat from one of the most hated symbols of Western oppression. He glanced back towards the Targa launch, which was again accelerating towards him, closed his eyes and muttered a very short final prayer.

He tensed every muscle in his body in the knowledge of what was to come. And then he flicked the switch into the 'on' position.

Chapter 14

The phone in front of Dame Janet rang again. She answered it immediately and switched it to loudspeaker.

'C-TAC. What's happened?'

As everyone in the room had guessed, the caller was again the MPU duty officer out at Wapping.

'Right at this moment we don't know. We had a radio message from the sergeant who's skippering the Targa launch. He said he was convinced the cabin cruiser was a floating bomb and that he was going to try to ram it. Since then nothing.'

'If it was stuffed full of explosives,' Dave North interjected, 'a massive impact like ramming the boat might be enough to spark the detonation. But if he hit it out in the middle of the Thames that would mean the effects of the blast would be less than if the cabin cruiser was right next to Parliament. So that might have been a good decision.'

'Are your skippers expected to ram vessels that don't stop?' Dame Janet asked.

They could almost see the duty officer shaking his head.

'No. That's much too dangerous and usually unnecessary. But in the circumstances the sergeant might have felt he had no other choice. He was suspicious about the appearance of the vessel, and when one of the two men in it opened fire at him with an assault rifle it was obvious that they were terrorists of some kind. And then when they started steering the boat straight towards Parliament, he probably thought his suspicions were justified. And in the absence of any other way of bringing the vessel to a halt, ramming was about the only option he had left.'

'But you've had no reports about an explosion near Parliament?' Morgan asked.

'Not yet, but the radio network has almost gone into meltdown and the mobile network's crashed. As soon I have anything definite I'll give you a call. Look, I have to go now. I've got three different phones ringing.'

Chapter 15

As Hassan's fingers flicked the bulkhead-mounted switch, he heard a sudden sharp crack audible even over the roaring of the engines of the patrol boat and a flash of light right in front of him. But what he didn't feel was any sense of being instantly transported to paradise, only the numbing cold as the dark waters of the Thames soaked more of his clothing.

All around him floated scattered timbers that had, just a matter of a minute or two earlier, formed part of the hull of the cabin cruiser. In front of him the plastic-wrapped mass of improvised explosive charges was very clearly still in one piece, presumably being kept on the surface by the air trapped within it.

And as he looked around him in shocked desperation, he realised what must have happened. The crack he had heard could only have been the sound of the blasting cap firing. But because the ANFO hadn't exploded, that meant the detonator must have been pulled out of the lump of Semtex plastic explosive when the cabin cruiser was torn apart. They had only had a single blasting cap, so there was no possible way that he could still initiate the explosion.

That in turn meant that their mission had failed. They – he and Khalid – had failed. And that was the bitterest pill of them all.

Even as this realisation dawned on him, the battered bow of the Targa smashed into what was left of the cockpit, flinging him bodily to one side as the police launch completed the job of demolition that it had started.

Hassan's body was driven underwater by the impact and for a few seconds he could see nothing, visibility underwater in the Thames being very poor even at the best of times. Then he saw light, or rather a lightening of the darkness, and his survival instinct took over as he struggled towards the surface of the river.

–

Carter hauled the Targa around in a tight port turn and throttled back to survey the wreckage. In the midst of the shattered timbers he could see one figure face down, clearly either dead or unconscious, and if he was just unconscious he would be dead within a couple of minutes from drowning. As he looked, the second man broke the surface just a few yards away and began swimming desperately away from the wreckage.

Carter moved the wheel slightly and applied a little throttle to close with the two figures in the water.

'Call Wapping and tell them we've neutralised the threat,' he ordered, 'and we'll be picking up two suspects. Or maybe one suspect and a body. We'll need some other boats out here as well sharpish to recover all this wreckage.'

'Or we could just run both of them down,' Fisher suggested. 'Save the cost of the trial, all that kind of thing. Help the struggling British economy.'

'I assume you're joking,' Carter said. 'And in any case, this doesn't look to me like it was an amateur effort, and that means Five will want to sit down with the survivor at Millbank or somewhere and find out what they can about whatever terrorist network they belong to. Right, stand by to grab the live one. Handcuff his wrists behind his back and see if you can get a second pair of cuffs around his ankles as well. But before you haul him on board make sure he's not wearing a suicide vest. If he is, I might just decide to opt for the Bob Fisher solution for dealing with swimming terrorists.'

Two minutes later, the man trying to swim away from the wrecked cabin cruiser had been dragged on board the police launch, none too gently, and slammed face first onto the decking while he was secured. Once he'd been immobilised, Carter told his men to leave him right where he was, and that if he tried to get up they could use whatever force they thought was appropriate to make him lie down again, up to and including clubbing him senseless.

Carter had never been the most politically correct officer employed by the Maritime Policing Unit, and he was irritated by the damage caused to his boat.

Recovery of what Carter knew by then to be a dead man took a little longer, but finally Crichton managed to pull the body to the side of the police launch with a boathook and then he and Fisher hauled the limp corpse onto the deck.

'Bloody hell,' Crichton said as he saw the extensive damage to the man's head for the first time.

'No point in trying mouth-to-mouth on that,' Fisher said, 'because he hasn't actually got one any more.'

'I'll get a body bag.'

The recovery of corpses from the River Thames was another one of the duties of the MPU, and not one that any officer looked forward to carrying out, 'floaters' being almost always badly disfigured thanks to the action of marine life and decomposition, and usually extremely smelly.

They'd just got the corpse zipped up when a small civilian vessel, somewhat like a half-size version of the Targa, hove to alongside them and the man at the wheel asked if they needed help.

'We've got to head back to Wapping,' Carter said, 'but if you could give us a hand to haul whatever's wrapped in that plastic sheeting onto our vessel we'd appreciate it.' He pointed at the object he was describing.

'If that's a bloody great IED,' Fisher said, 'do you think it's a good idea letting a couple of Thames boatmen fiddle about with it?'

'If it was going to explode,' Carter retorted, 'it would have done when contestant number one pressed that switch. I watched him do it, and nothing happened, so whatever's wrapped up in that sheeting must be pretty much inert. Go and give them a hand.'

Chapter 16

Secret Intelligence Service Headquarters, Vauxhall Cross, London

'Panic over.' The relief in the MPU duty officer's voice was quite obvious through the loudspeaker. 'The suspect boat has now been converted into firewood. Our patrol boat is a bit battered but it's still afloat and our officers picked up one suspect and one dead body, both of Middle Eastern appearance but neither carrying any form of identification.'

'Was it full of explosives?' Dame Janet asked.

'We'll have to wait for forensics, but that's the way it looks. Part of the aft section of the cabin cruiser is intact and afloat and according to the Targa's skipper he can see a battery and a switch and some lengths of wire inside it. There's also a semi-submerged plastic-wrapped object that could be an IED, which they're trying to recover. But as I say, we need the forensic people to tell us one way or the other.'

'Where are you taking the suspect?' Dave North asked.

'Initially they'll bring him here to Wapping so we can process him, but I've already had Five on the line so I guess he'll be transferred to Millbank or maybe to Paddington Green for questioning. But that decision is above my pay grade.'

Dame Janet ended the call and glanced around the table. 'Assuming this isn't a case of hopelessly mistaken identity and some waterborne rozzer seeing something that quite literally wasn't there, I think we can say that we've been lucky. More importantly, Parliament has been lucky, and that doesn't happen very often. Dave, this is more your department than anybody else's, so get yourself out to Wapping, take a look at this character and whatever evidence the MPU manages to drag out of the Thames and then let me have your assessment.'

North nodded. 'There may not be all that much to find,' he said, 'because if that was an IED that these two managed to cobble together, the most likely explosive for them to have used would be ammonium nitrate and that's highly hygroscopic, meaning it attracts water. If you put it in enough water, and I promise you there's definitely enough in the Thames, it can turn to liquid. Can you call back the guy at Wapping and tell him to make sure that the people on the scene recover at least a sample of whatever was inside that plastic if they can't get the whole thing out of the water?'

'No problem,' Dame Janet replied. 'Now get on your way. I want to know what's going on as soon as possible. And why are you still here, Ben?' she asked, swivelling her attention to Morgan. 'Cyber stuff and cyberattacks are potentially a much bigger problem than a couple of terrorists in a stolen cabin cruiser, so get moving.'

Chapter 17

London

Like almost all the great cities of the world London is built on a river but, unlike most other cities, it is also to some extent divided by the tidal waterway that runs through its heart. With few exceptions, the 'best' districts in the capital city, areas with names like Belgravia, Chelsea, Knightsbridge, Mayfair and of course Westminster, the seat of the government of the United Kingdom, are all located on the northern side of the river. In this half of London, property prices are higher, the buildings are more elegant and the streets always seem to be wider and cleaner and prowled by more expensive cars.

To the south, the names resonate less well: districts like Brixton, Clapham, Croydon and Peckham, the last achieving enduring fame as the location of a perennially popular television comedy series that seemed to encapsulate the hand to mouth, cash-based, quasi-legal economy of one of the poorer sectors of the capital's population. And many of these areas enjoy less than savoury reputations. In the past cab drivers were known to demand a higher fare if they had to venture 'south of the river' and especially if it was a late evening or night-time journey.

Those organisations and businesses that did, for whatever reason, establish themselves on the southern side of the Thames seemed almost unwilling to venture too far away from the river, clustering as close as they could to the waterway. The headquarters of the Secret Intelligence Service, popularly and incorrectly known as MI6, the building commonly referred to throughout the intelligence community as 'Legoland' and by certain other less polite epithets, demonstrates this perfectly. It's located at the south-eastern end of Vauxhall Bridge and if it was any closer to the river it would actually be in the water.

But not everywhere north of the river enjoys the wealth and kudos of a district like Mayfair, and a good example is the north-east London suburb of Stratford, part of the old parish of West Ham. It's been inhabited for the better part of a thousand years; the name Strætforda, a compound place name deriving from the Old English *stræt* or 'street' and 'ford' and referring to a river crossing, its exact location unknown but somewhere north of the present Stratford High Street, being recorded as early as 1067. The area began the twentieth century in a state of economic decline that continued to worsen with every passing decade. De-industrialisation had ended the district's importance as a manufacturing centre, as a major railway hub and as London's principal commercial dock area.

Then, on 6 July 2005, London was announced as the venue for the 2012 Summer Olympics, and what happened after that changed Stratford permanently. Because of the need to not only create world-class sporting facilities in the area but also to improve and update roads and transport links, and in some cases to create brand new ones, Stratford received an astonishing level of expenditure, totalling almost £10 billion, making the London Olympics the third most expensive games ever held after Beijing 2008 and Sochi 2014.

Leyton Grange Estate isn't a part of Stratford but of the much larger borough of Waltham Forest. It lies north-west of the A12 that forms the northern boundary of Stratford, and north-east of Hackney Marshes, and is a primarily residential London suburb. The modernisation and gentrification of Stratford inevitably had an effect upon the surrounding areas, and despite the sometimes unfortunate connotations of the word 'estate' when applied to urban housing, the Leyton Grange Estate is a popular area to live for both owners and renters. Most of the older properties are solidly built mainly Victorian terraced houses, originally intended for single family occupation but in some cases now divided up into two or three flats to maximise their rental potential and overall property value, or converted into HMOs, houses in multiple occupation, where people rent single rooms, often with shared facilities.

Radlix Road, between Leyton Jubilee Park and Leyton County Cricket Ground, is fairly typical of the area. Quiet and prosperous looking, with newish cars parked on the street in the 'permit holder only' bays, it looks like the kind of area likely to be occupied by people in decent jobs who need fast and reliable access to London, and certainly not the kind of area most people would expect to find a terrorist cell.

Which, of course, was exactly why Mahdi Sadir, the Iraqi man who was calling himself Abū Tadmir, had chosen that location.

To protect his own security he had never visited the property, which was occupied by the four volunteers he had recruited soon after he had arrived in London, and he only ever met them in neutral locations at least two miles away from the house and never used the same place twice. Most of the recruitment had been done in advance by other people who were involved in some capacity with the large number of mosques in the vicinity of Stratford.

It was the usual routine. People sympathetic to the cause of radical Islam were asked to keep their eyes and ears open and be on the lookout for young men, and possibly young women as well, who might be aggrieved enough with the way that Muslims were being treated in the Middle East by the various occupying forces and who were sufficiently dissatisfied with their lives in the West that they could be persuaded to exchange their earthly existence for a guaranteed afterlife in paradise through the medium of an explosion or other act of terminal and murderous defiance. By becoming, in other words, a *shahid*, or a *shahida* if female, and taking an active part in the *jihad*, radical Islam's war against the West. Once a suitable 'volunteer' had been identified, he or she would be singled out for special treatment, for their general dissatisfaction to be discussed and escalated and honed and eventually for their hate and resentment to be pointed in whatever very specific direction had been selected by the people who'd recruited them.

And for all that, for that ability to develop and nurture a home-grown terrorist presence, Sadir knew that the organisation he had to thank was – bizarrely enough – the British government, and two factors that had enabled domestic terrorism to take root and flourish: freedom of movement and political correctness.

Freedom of movement allowed students from around the world to enrol in courses at schools and universities in the United Kingdom. This was not in itself a bad thing, obviously, but what had worried British intelligence from the start were the students who vanished below the radar at some point after their arrival. The concern was that some of these now invisible students might be following their own agendas and could become either radicalised or function as sleepers. And political correctness and the even more insidious Woke movement made it difficult or impossible to get people in authority to listen to questions or allegations about individuals in case they were perceived as being racist or sexist or some other kind of politically unacceptable -ist.

The result was probably inevitable and entirely predictable. It has been reliably estimated by the British intelligence services that by 2020 there were at least two hundred sleepers in the United Kingdom and in the United States the situation was even worse. There, it was estimated some four thousand sleepers had taken positions in the core industries driving the American economy, places like MIT and Silicon Valley, and in the organisations supposedly working to keep the country safe, the CIA, FBI, Homeland Security, the police and the NSA.

Many of the sleepers were involved in one way or another with the computer industry because what they and their distant masters directing their operations had realised was that although conventional warfare was still going on in the perennially troubled Middle East and other hotspots around the world, the new battlefield involved mice, keyboards and screens rather than aircraft, armies and naval task forces. It was much easier to destroy an enemy's capability to wage war by simply denying essential services like electricity or fuel rather than physically planting explosives to try to do the same job.

And for exactly the same reason, the vast majority of the sleepers had not the slightest intention of becoming *shahids* themselves – that was reserved for the cannon fodder, the lowest of the low in the struggle against the West – but many of the sleepers were extremely adroit at persuading other people that blowing themselves up or performing some other kind of violent action was the best way forward in their short and bitter lives.

When Sadir had arrived in the United Kingdom after following a complicated and erratic route from Iraq, a route that had included almost a year on the other side of the Atlantic carrying out the necessary preparations for the principal part of his planned operations, the Islamic recruiter working in the Stratford area already had six potential martyrs largely primed and ready to go. Sadir had sat behind the recruiter as each man's commitment and motives were discussed and had selected the four men he believed were the most committed for the operation he had come to Britain to implement, the first strike, before continuing his journey to his ultimate destination.

Sadir had arrived with a fully developed plan to cause massive loss of life and catastrophic destruction to the centre of London, as well as the contacts and sources they needed and effectively unlimited funds to ensure that it would all work. He'd rented the property in Leyton Grange Estate to provide a secure base for his four volunteers. Then he'd briefed them collectively in a secure location and explained exactly what he needed each of them to do and when and how they were to do it.

He had kept his orders simple, easy to understand, and unambiguous. He had begun by specifying the target – the Houses of Parliament – and the means by which the attack was to be carried out: a powerboat of some description. He had set two of them to work combing the boatyards and looking for a suitable craft to steal, while the other two men sourced enough ammonium nitrate fertiliser to turn whatever boat they chose into a powerful floating bomb. While that was going on, he had taken personal delivery of a metre-long box made of heavy-duty cardboard from a man who had been vouched for by Rashid, the most senior elder back in Iraq, and who had introduced himself simply as a friend and a brother. Inside the box Sadir had found a somewhat battered but still perfectly serviceable Kalashnikov AK-47 assault rifle with two spare magazines and a box of a hundred rounds of 7.62mm ammunition, a lump of Semtex wrapped in brown paper and, in a separate bag for security, a blasting cap to act as a detonator.

Sadir had been puzzled by the fact that the two wires on the blasting cap had been twisted together and asked the man who had supplied the equipment the reason for this.

'Surely they need to be separated to allow them to be connected to the battery?'

'They do,' the 'brother' had replied, 'but only when you assemble the weapon. If you leave the wires separate there is a possibility – very slim but nevertheless real – that they could act as an aerial for some of the radiation that surrounds all of us all of the time from things like digital broadcasts, radios and mobile phones. That could allow a current to flow down the wires and trigger the blasting cap. That's why we twist the wires together until you mount the detonator in the circuit. Linking the two makes a short circuit and prevents them acting as an aerial.'

The blasting cap had come with a page of printed instructions that explained it was to be triggered electrically in accordance with the wiring diagram on the page, and that it was a short period delay – SPD – detonator. Despite the name, which to a layman could have implied a wait of seconds or even minutes, the 'SPD' meant it would detonate only a few milliseconds after being triggered. The instructions also included directions for safely turning the ammonium nitrate fertiliser into a viable explosive and where the Semtex booster charge should be positioned within the IED for maximum effectiveness.

And the four men had done well. They'd managed to steal the boat they'd identified without – at least as far as Sadir knew – triggering any alarms at the marina, though undoubtedly the theft would have been detected within a few days, and the combining of the ammonium nitrate with diesel fuel and aluminium powder in a rented garage had been completed without a hitch.

Sadir had checked everything on the vessel before Hassan had steered it away from the derelict boathouse, including the assault rifle and, most importantly, the commitment of the two men who would be aboard it for its final destructive voyage. He had joined them for the *salat al-zuhr*, the second mandatory prayer performed daily by devout Muslims.

Prayers comprise the second Pillar of Islam, one of the five obligatory actions that Muslims are required to perform according to the conditions and teaching of their religion. The pillars are *shahadah*, the recitation of the Islamic profession of faith; *salat*, the five daily ritual prayers; *zakat*, the giving of an alms tax for the benefit of the poor; *sawm*, the requirement to fast during Ramadan, and finally the *hajj*, the pilgrimage to Mecca.

All five of the men had already performed the first prayer of the day, the *salat al-fajr*, which is required to be completed before the sun rises. The second obligatory prayer is the *salat al-zuhr*, performed after the sun has reached the highest point in the sky at midday, and although when the five of them knelt on their prayer mats it was actually late morning rather than early afternoon they all believed this minor deviation from their daily routine was unimportant to Allah within the scale of the operation they were engaged upon.

As soon as the purloined cabin cruiser had begun its journey towards the heart of London, Sadir had left the other two members of the group to clear up any last traces of their occupation of the boathouse, while he had climbed back into his hire car and driven to West London and one of the airport hotels near Heathrow where he had already booked a room for the night.

He would remain there until it was time to report for his flight to America the next morning. He only expected to receive a single call from Hassan shortly before the culmination of the attack, a final confirmation that the mission was proceeding correctly. After that, he knew he would be able to obtain all the information he needed direct from the news media that would swarm all over London as soon as the explosion had taken place.

He would enjoy a quiet celebration in his hotel room that evening as he watched the events unfold on television. He would also be able to confirm the success of the first part of his mission to the elders in Iraq, though he had no doubt that they would also be watching the news media and expecting to see the results of the detonation and, bearing in mind the proliferation of security cameras throughout the British capital, very probably be able to watch the explosion itself being endlessly replayed and commented on by grim-faced newscasters.

He was certain it was going to be a particularly good evening.

Chapter 18

'And you are who, exactly?'

Dave North opened his wallet, extracted his Army ID card, MOD Form 90, and held it up right in front of the police sergeant's face.

'As it says, David Charles North, Major, British Army,' he said. 'And before you ask your next obvious question, I'm here because I'm a part of C-TAC. You have heard of that, I hope.'

The desk sergeant looked only very slightly less puzzled. And no friendlier or more welcoming.

'I've heard the acronym, yes, because C-TAC is on our Tier One contact list in case of a terrorist incident, along with a bunch of other initials of various secret squirrel outfits dotted about the capital and elsewhere. But I have no clue who you are, apart from your name. I still have no idea what C-TAC stands for, or what you're doing here. As far as I can see, we've arrested an alleged terrorist buggering about on the Thames, which makes this a police matter until somebody in my command structure tells me differently.'

'Right. C-TAC is the Counter-Terrorism Advisory Committee, and the reason we're on your Tier One notification list is because terrorism, or rather stopping it, is our job. And from my point of view this is still a police matter and I'm not here to interfere with what you're doing. What I *am* here for is to get answers to a few urgent questions, so I'll need to talk to the skipper of the launch that stopped these comedians and maybe the other crew members of the boat as well.'

The sergeant looked doubtful.

'He's pretty busy right now answering questions from some of our brass.'

'Here's a news flash,' North said, leaning forward slightly to emphasise his words. 'Oddly enough, I'm pretty busy as well, and I'm not going to hang around here like a spare prick at a wedding. I need to speak to this guy right now, and if you don't want to be on the receiving end of an extremely high-level and potentially career-terminating bollocking I suggest you talk to whoever you need to call and make sure that happens. I'll give you three minutes. And I like my coffee white with one sugar.'

It took four minutes, not that North was actually counting.

When he walked into the interview room, escorted by a somewhat nervous-looking constable, he found another man wearing sergeants' stripes standing behind the table, clearly waiting for him.

'I'm Paul Carter,' the sergeant said, extending his right hand. 'I was the skipper of the Targa.'

North shook hands and introduced himself, but before he had even sat down there was a knock at the door and another uniformed constable appeared carrying a tray on which were two disposable cardboard cups, both steaming, a couple of plastic spoons and a selection of individual milk cartons and packets of sugar.

'Take your life in your hands drinking this stuff,' Carter said, picking up one of the cups of coffee.

North nodded, peered doubtfully at the contents of his cup, and added sugar and a couple of cartons of milk to try and tone it down a bit and help disguise the taste.

'I'm military,' he replied. 'We're used to hot brown stuff in cups. Sometimes it's so bloody awful you can't tell whether it's coffee, tea or soup. Now, tell me what happened on the river.'

Carter took him through the events of the afternoon, from spotting the apparently overloaded cabin cruiser to capturing and securing the surviving terrorist.

'And you've no doubt that the boat was filled with explosive?' North asked. 'And that their target was the Palace of Westminster?'

Carter nodded. 'The man driving it steered it directly across the river from the east bank towards the Houses of Parliament. That was very clearly a deliberate act and as far as I could see at the time there could only be one reason for him doing so. And after we'd rammed the cabin cruiser I saw him lean forward into the entrance to the saloon and flick a wall-mounted switch that didn't look to me like it was part of the boat's original wiring. And then I heard the crack as the blasting cap or whatever it was detonated. So the short answer is I'm certain it was a floating bomb and that the target was Parliament. And we were bloody lucky it didn't go off. If it had, you'd have needed to find a fucking good medium to be having this conversation.'

North nodded in his turn. 'I can't pick holes in any of that. Where's the surviving terrorist right now?'

'As far as I know he's still here. A couple of guys wearing sharp suits and not saying a lot turned up a few minutes before you did and they've been having a few quiet words with chummy ever since. I assume they're from Millbank.'

'The men with the sharpest suits usually seem to me to be from Six rather than Five, but you're probably right. Okay. No doubt my section will get fed whatever intelligence they managed to extract from him.'

'He might well clam up,' Carter pointed out. 'I gather he asked for a solicitor as soon as he arrived here and he said nothing while he was on my launch.'

'One thing he won't be getting is a solicitor,' North replied. 'There are rules governing how suspects are handled, but for suspected terrorists we tend to be flexible, shall I say, and some rules might well get bent or possibly even broken along the way. Right, I'll get out of your hair. And well done for what you did on the river. I'll feed a note about your and your crew's conduct up the line and make sure that the right people hear the right things about you.'

North was on his way back down the corridor towards the front desk when he was aware of a sudden commotion behind him.

A door slammed open and a man who from his appearance was one of the 'sharp suited' guys Carter had mentioned stepped into the corridor and shouted a single word: 'Medic!'

Like many of the soldiers who ended up in the Special Air Service, North had qualified in field medicine. He wasn't exactly in any kind of a field at that moment, but a medical emergency was a medical emergency and so he pushed past the besuited man and stepped into the room.

An unmoving figure was lying on the floor, his wrists secured with handcuffs, and another man wearing a suit was crouching over him. As North appeared beside him, he turned, the distress in his face obvious.

'We never touched him,' he said. 'He was just sitting there and then he kind of fell over sideways.'

North unceremoniously shoved him out of the way and bent to see what he could do. The man was wearing a lightweight one-piece disposable garment, presumably supplied by the police as his own clothing would have been soaking wet after his immersion in the Thames, and would have been taken from him in any case for forensic examination as part of standard procedure. Carter had told him that the man had been wearing casual Western-style clothing on the cabin cruiser, but his thick black beard and dark complexion suggested a Middle Eastern or Asian origin.

North manhandled him into the recovery position, lying him on his side to ensure that his airway remained clear and then immediately felt the side of his neck, searching for a pulse in the carotid artery. But he found nothing, and when he placed the back of his hand in front of the man's mouth he could detect no sign of breathing.

The next step was obvious: CPR, cardiopulmonary resuscitation.

North laid the man flat on his back, straddled his body, inter-locked his hands, positioned them in the centre of the man's chest and began regular compressions, aiming to depress the chest a couple of inches and then release, and counting to achieve about one hundred compressions a minute. He knew that as long as CPR was started within about five minutes of a person's heart stopping and them losing consciousness, it was possible to keep the patient alive until proper medical aid arrived, and he guessed he was well within that timescale.

When he reached thirty compressions he stopped and leaned forward, intending to try rescue breathing, to force air into the man's lungs before resuming chest compressions. But before he could do so two police officers ran through the doorway and into the interview room, one holding what North recognised immediately as a defibrillator and the other carrying a medical bag. They had the equipment and very probably better knowledge and medical ability than he had and so he stood up, stepped back, and left them to it.

The room filled quickly. One of the new arrivals was the doctor who'd been called in to assess the suspect's condition because of the circumstances of his arrest. He immediately took over. He worked on the collapsed man for several minutes but without any response, and finally had to admit that he was completely unresponsive. Dead, in short.

That wasn't the result North had been hoping for, and clearly the two men he assumed were from Millbank felt the same way. He buttonholed one of them in the corridor outside the interview room.

'You're from Five, right?' he began, and the man nodded. 'Okay, I'm C-TAC, so we have a high-level interest in this. To save us having to hack our way through a jungle of red tape while our lords and masters decide exactly where the buck is going to stop and how best they can cover their arses, just tell me what happened in that room.'

'Let me see some ID.'

North obliged him by again producing his MOD Form 90 and his C-TAC pass that allowed him access to SIS headquarters at Vauxhall Cross.

'Okay. We'd hardly even started with the suspect, just organised coffee and were trying to empathise with him. You know, softly, softly to get him to start talking, but he just asked for a solicitor and then clammed up. No response at all, even if we were well off subject, like asking him if he took sugar in his coffee and if he would want to eat halal meals while he was in custody. We kept on trying but we really weren't getting anywhere. He hadn't been carrying any kind of ID or anything else that would identify him, and the same went for the stiff with half his head blown off, so we didn't even have his name or the name of the man in the boat with him. What we did know was that he was clearly really upset that they hadn't managed to pull off the attack. That was quite obvious, but non-verbal.

'The only thing he did say didn't make too much sense, and that was clearly deliberate. He kept checking the time on the wall clock as if he was expecting something, or maybe somebody, to walk into the interview room. Then he seemed almost to relax, but he still didn't say anything. But a couple of minutes before he collapsed he came up with what sounded like a memorised and prepared short statement, almost like the kind of videos that *shahids* make before they carry out their attacks as justification for what they're about to do. But his statement was really short. He just said the West was going to pay – so nothing much new there – and the next attack would be much bigger and on a much bigger target.'

'Did you note down exactly what he said?' North asked.

The man from Millbank nodded. 'Yes, and both of us had digital recorders running from the moment the interview started.'

'Right. I'd like audio copies of both those recordings sent to C-TAC please, so we can do our own transcription. Then what happened?'

'He just sat there looking at us across the table as if he was expecting us to react to what he'd said, but of course we didn't. And then he keeled over, just fell sideways out of the chair. No warning, no indication that he was sick. He just collapsed. I'm not a medical man, but I don't think it was a heart attack. I mean, he didn't gasp for breath or clutch his chest or do anything like that.'

'So what do you think killed him?'

The man from Five shook his head. 'You know that their boat was rammed? Well, perhaps he hit his head on something when that happened. That could have caused bleeding inside his skull, but the doctor didn't find any evidence of head injuries when he gave him the once-over, so maybe it was something else. I don't know.'

North was experiencing something akin to déjà vu. What the man from the Security Service was describing seemed to him to be remarkably similar to what he had personally experienced in the helicopter above Brize Norton: a person apparently acting normally and then suddenly totally losing consciousness and with death supervening seconds or minutes later. But that suggested links and motives that appeared to dramatically increase the seriousness of the situation. And it could of course all be some kind of bizarre coincidence, though

North really wasn't a fan of that kind of explanation. It was certainly worth investigating, to get an answer to the obvious question.

'You've probably got more top weight around here than I have, so let me suggest something for you to follow up. When they do the autopsy make sure they pay particular attention to the composition of his blood. What they're looking for is a couple of unusual chemicals, but more importantly they need to fractionate a blood sample and check for a discolouration above the plasma layer.'

'I have no idea what you're talking about.'

'This was all new to me until a few days ago,' North replied, 'and I haven't got time to explain it to you. Just remember what I've said and make sure that the pathologist who does the autopsy is made aware of this. I'll submit a formal request to Millbank as soon as I get back to Vauxhall Cross to get it all in writing. But if what I suspect is true we – all of us – are looking at a much bigger problem than a couple of nasty bastards trying to blow up the Houses of Parliament using a sodding great IED.'

'I still have no bloody clue what you're talking about, but I will pass it on.'

Chapter 19

Heathrow, West London

Mahdi Sadir knew that something must have gone wrong, simply because all the news broadcasts he watched that evening on the wall-mounted flatscreen television in his hotel room just north of Heathrow Airport were mainlining on yet another government crisis. When they weren't interviewing a couple of MPs or officials or alleged experts with diametrically opposed views, the newsreaders did their best to dissect the half-truths and rumours that passed for investigative journalism in British newspapers or banged on about sporting events about which Sadir knew nothing and cared less. But what they didn't mention was an explosion, or indeed any other sort of an incident, on the River Thames.

So Sadir knew that the carefully planned attack must have failed, but what he didn't know was how or why. The last mobile phone call he'd received from Hassan had suggested that the cabin cruiser had been on track and on time and that the vessel had attracted no attention whatsoever on its voyage. About the only thing he could deduce, from the lack of any further contact from the *shahid*, was that there hadn't been a malfunction of the IED because in that case Hassan had been told to abort the attack and return to the boathouse, and to immediately call and explain the situation. If the blasting cap had been faulty, for example, it was possible that Sadir's contact would be able to supply another one to allow the attack to be attempted again over the next few days. This probably meant that somehow the two *shahids* had been intercepted and stopped before they could detonate the explosives, and also that this had happened so quickly that Hassan had been unable to make a call to explain what was going on.

The only news item that appeared in any way relevant was one of those little filler pieces, tucked in to quite literally fill the time before the next ad break. It just stated that the sittings in both Houses at Westminster had been disrupted for about twenty minutes that afternoon because of a suspected gas leak. The building had been cleared as a precaution while the matter was investigated, and it turned out to be a false alarm. Most of the newsreaders made some kind of a weak joke about a gas leak in a building where people went to gas – to talk – and where leaks of one sort or another were all a part of normal government procedure.

Sadir did not find any part of this news item amusing in any way but it did peripherally confirm that the attack must have been detected and the building evacuated while Hassan and Khalid were either captured or killed.

Perhaps the only surprising thing was that there was also nothing on any of the social media sites that he visited about an incident on the Thames, and he was quite certain that somebody on one side or other of the river must have seen what happened. But he was also aware of the power of the British intelligence services and assumed that pressure had been brought to bear on the providers to ensure that nothing was promulgated. And of course if the press had got wind of it they could well have been told the incident was subject to a D-notice to prevent any publication.

Later that evening Sadir did find a couple of social media posts referring to what one person described as a collision on the water quite near the Palace of Westminster, the man who'd written the post suggesting it might have been a part of a film, a staged event. But after that, nothing.

Just before midnight, having spent the last five hours channel hopping on the television system and looking for any further inform-ation on the Internet, Sadir finally opened his laptop and began preparing a very different email from the one that he had hoped to be composing. In it, he explained that the major attack he had been supposed to carry out in London, the precursor strike directly targeting the British government and intended to be almost as devastating as the main strike against the American administration, had completely failed. He had to conclude that the boat loaded with explosives had been intercepted just before the detonation was supposed to take place.

He apologised for the lack of any definitive information and explained why he had nothing else to tell Rashid and the elders back in Iraq. But he was able to reassure them that even if the two *shahids* had been captured alive by the British authorities, they would not be able to compromise the second, and much more important, part of the mission. First because, although all four members of the cell knew there was going to be a second and much bigger attack in America, only Hassan and Khalid had been told any of the details, and only enough to convince them of the vital importance of their sacrifice. So they had no critical information they could divulge. And second, Sadir had taken his own precautions to ensure the permanent silence of the two *shahids*.

The sealed vials he carried in his luggage had been designed by the scientists at Vektor for precisely this kind of situation. Before Hassan and Khalid had set off that day, Sadir had given each of them a drink of water. Both men had remarked that it was somewhat cloudy, and Sadir had then explained that each glass contained a substance that would ensure they would enter paradise at a particular time that very day in an entirely painless manner even if something went wrong with the attack.

It was, in its own way, something of a final test of the commitment of the two *shahids*, and both men had swallowed the drink without even a pause. Sadir had calculated that the detonation of the IED would take place in mid-afternoon, and the chemicals in the drink would only be released, through the magic of nanotechnology, after five o'clock, around two hours later. So all the two men had to do if they were captured was to tell the authorities nothing at all in the certain knowledge that the gates of paradise would be standing open to welcome them before nightfall.

He didn't explain this in his email, but simply said that he had ensured the silence of the two volunteers. He had absolutely no doubt that the two *shahids* in the cabin cruiser were dead, because as well as the live demonstration that the Vektor management had arranged for him to see in Koltsovo, he had also spent a little over a week in the Hereford area visiting local pubs and looking out for two things: the right group of people and the opportunity he needed.

Although he knew that the hated British SAS – Special Air Service – had left Iraq in 2009, the year before the disastrous assault on the safe house at Tikrit, he also knew the soldiers from that unit of the British Army had been responsible for killing dozens, perhaps hundreds, of his Muslim brothers. And just as he knew that the SAS liked to move in darkness, like ghosts, the ability to exact a form of revenge upon them by employing an invisible killer had seemed too good an opportunity to waste. He had eventually found himself sharing the bar of a public house with a group of about a dozen young men that he had been certain were soldiers.

He'd picked his moments with care, ensuring he was standing at the bar ordering a drink at the same time as a couple of the men from the group were buying a round. He'd slipped a prepared syringe out of his pocket and ejected the contents – a long-delay dose of the product he'd obtained from Vektor – into one of the pints of beer waiting on the bar, then repeated his action with a second syringe in another pint. Half an hour later, he'd done exactly the same thing with two more pints. Then he'd left the pub and returned to his hotel, certain that he had enacted some form of revenge. The headline in the local newspaper had been an unexpected but welcome confirmation.

So he had no doubt Hassan and Khalid were dead, and the other two members of the cell knew none of the details of the American component of the plan, only that an attack was going to happen. Sadir had made sure of that.

He was using a web-based email client, and he read his message through several times before saving it as a draft. Rashid or one of the other elders would log on to the same email account before the morning and read and probably copy the message before deleting it. In that way, there was no possibility of the message being intercepted by any law enforcement agency, because it had never been sent. If it was never on the system it was, by definition, impossible for Echelon or any of the other national and international monitoring systems to detect it. It was a very basic but extremely effective way of communicating important information with complete security.

Chapter 20

'I have no idea why you're even in the building.'

It was almost lunchtime the following day and Nigel Foster was clearly irritated at what he perhaps saw as an unjustifiable and unnecessary interference in his domain. He was, Morgan guessed, in his late forties, though he looked older, the brown-tinted frameless glasses, obvious comb-over and wispy beard evidence of his desire to retain at least the appearance of youth. If that was the reason for his trichological uncertainty and inadequate and ill-advised growth of facial hair, it wasn't working.

'As I told you before,' Morgan replied, his patience slipping away by the minute. 'There are two ways of doing this. We can work together so I can find out what's happened and what you've done about it, and then I'll be on my way. Or, if you prefer, you can shout and scream and kick and throw all your toys out of your pram and at the end of it I'll still be here, if necessary with a ministerial directive or a court order, whichever I think will cause you the most personal aggravation and EDF the most adverse publicity. And I can have either of them delivered right here by courier within the hour. Frankly, I don't give a shit either way, so it's up to you, Nige.'

'Don't call me that.'

'Sorry,' Morgan said with blatant insincerity.

Then he sat quietly and waited. Silence can be quite intimidating, as he remembered one of his SAS instructors telling him. The corporal had been talking about interrogation – or rather how to resist interrogation and avoid telling whoever was questioning you anything that he wanted to know – but he guessed the same tactic would work in this kind of situation. Human beings are social animals, and social animals communicate. Silence – the absence of communication – can be difficult to cope with, and some people feel compelled to fill it. He guessed that Nigel Foster might be one of that type.

After a minute or so he took out his mobile phone, placed it flat on the desk in front of him, opened up the Kindle ebook reader and picked up where he'd left off reading the previous evening, making quite sure that the other man could see what he was doing.

He'd only read a couple of pages before Foster, clearly recognising that he'd been out-manoeuvred and essentially backed into a corner, broke the silence.

'Oh, very well. What do you want to know?'

Morgan switched off his phone and put it away before he replied.

'Thank you,' he said. 'You had a security breach. My organisation has a brief from the British government to monitor events of that type so I need to know three things. First, how it happened. Second, what damage was done in terms of data loss or anything else. And third, what you've done about it.'

'Don't tell me your lot investigate every single hacking event,' Foster said, a distinct sneer in his voice. 'You'd need a massive staff and it would be a full-time job.'

'I didn't say we did that,' Morgan responded quietly. 'But we do investigate attacks on mission-critical organisations, which obviously includes banks and financial institutions of all sorts, government websites and the utility companies, because a major hack of any of those could cause catastrophic damage to what's left of Britain's economy after the Covid-19 shutdown, and could also cause loss of life in certain circumstances. And that's why I'm here. So what happened?'

'We weren't hacked. That's the first thing,' Foster said, starting to open up. 'We could see the attack developing as they looked for vulnerabilities in the systems. They ran Firewalk to check for open ports in the firewall but didn't find any, then used a mixed selection of hacking tools like Metasploit and Sn1per to look for weaknesses and finally ran John and Cain to try to break a password. We backtracked the origin of the attack through a whole chain of proxy servers. It supposedly started in Vietnam, but we're fairly sure it actually began in America. I can supply you with the audit trail if you want it.'

Foster looked at Morgan, apparently checking that he understood the shorthand.

'Pretty much standard,' Morgan said, nodding. 'I would like to see any data you obtained, so I'll give you my email address. But I gather they didn't get anywhere?'

'Nope. Not with the system we've got here. I presume you don't want to know how we've configured the firewall or the security monitoring and analysis software we use? Stuff like that?'

'No. I'm sure you know what you're doing or you wouldn't be in the job. I'm only interested in what happened and the results. But I do have a question. You watched the attack take place. It doesn't sound to me like it was part of an APT but more like a brute-force attack. Was that your impression as well?'

An APT is an advanced persistent threat, one of the most dangerous types of hack because it's a group effort and it's patient, organised, complex and intelligent, and usually directed at major corporations to steal data or trade secrets. It's particularly favoured by Chinese government-directed teams of hackers trying to steal technology from the West. Planning and execution can take months as the website is studied and probed for weaknesses – a phase known as 'target development' – before attempts are made to breach it, often using apparently legitimate emails or social media link requests sent to employees.

These typically contain a malware attachment that will provide an access channel once activated, and it only takes one employee to click on the embedded link for the damage to be done. Some APTs have only been detected months after the initial intrusion when huge amounts of sensitive data are picked up leaving the system. By which time, of course, it's much too late to stop it. Completely cleaning a system after an APT can be difficult. Months after one American company had cleared its network, a printer was found to still be sending messages to a server located in China.

Foster shook his head firmly.

'This wasn't an APT,' he replied. 'This was the barbarians banging on the gates of Rome. It was crude, basic and short-lived. I think it was just an opportunist attack. These hackers were just seeing if they could force their way inside the system.'

'Okay. Then you detected a user acting suspiciously. Do you think that intrusion was orchestrated by the same group that tried the brute-force attack?'

'Good question. Possibly, maybe probably. I wondered if the unsuccessful attack was a kind of diversionary tactic to make us concentrate on them trying to breach the firewall while another hacker used the log-in credentials they'd obtained to get inside. While the attack was still going on, one legitimate employee – a man named Simons – logged on as usual, but then didn't visit the parts of the system he normally did, which the monitoring software flagged up. Everybody on this system, with just a few exceptions, is restricted to the areas relevant to the job they do, as you'd expect. This user started by typing the command prompt, CMD.EXE, and then began inputting low-level DOS commands to try to change the directory, view the directory structure, copy sections of the drive, things like that. We didn't shut him down immediately because there are internal barriers and restrictions so we knew he couldn't do any damage, and just watched him.

'At the same time we checked his user credentials and permissions. We assumed he was just bored or nosy, but when we found out he was incommunicado in hospital we knew we had a third-party intrusion. We recorded the inputs he was using for a few more minutes, and then locked him out. We blocked the user's log-in credentials and his password, and as far as we were concerned that was the end of the matter, at least in terms of the breach. We reported it up the line because that's our standard operating procedure and wrote it up.'

'So how did your unknown hacker get this man's credentials?' Morgan asked.

'We don't know, and obviously we'll be interviewing Simons when he gets back. We've already done a thorough check of his computer terminal and working space, just in case he was stupid enough to write his password down on a post-it note and stick it on his monitor or in a drawer or somewhere, but we didn't find anything like that. We have rules against that kind of thing, obviously, but you'd be amazed how many otherwise sensible and intelligent people think that for some reason those rules don't apply to them.'

'So I suppose you'll be looking at social engineering, something like that?'

'That'll be one of our first questions when Simons gets back. Again, it's staggering how many people will answer the phone, and if the bloke at the other end tells them he's from technical support and sounds convincing enough they'll tell him their password or PIN or almost anything else. I've talked to a few people who've told me they never gave away their entire PIN and have then admitted there was a problem on the line and when the caller asked for the first and third digits he apparently didn't hear them and then asked for their second and fourth characters, which they cheerfully gave him. It's just incredible how stupid some people are.'

Morgan nodded.

'Sometimes it's not simple stupidity, just that the person doing the social engineering is really good at it. I was involved in bank security in a former life and I remember dealing with one woman, a shop manager so presumably reasonably bright, who'd been contacted by somebody pretending to be from the local branch of her bank. He told her there was a major problem with her account and her credit card and said the matter was so serious and so urgent that they would send a courier round immediately to take her credit card and arrange for a replacement. They also asked her to write down all her personal details – not just her name and address but also her credit card PIN and the numbers of all her bank accounts and the numbers and PINs of all her other credit and debit cards – and give all that information, with the card, to the courier. Twenty minutes later a scruffy man wearing jeans and a leather jacket and riding a battered old motorbike turned up at her door. She handed everything over to him and it was only when he rode away that she even started to have any doubts. They took her for five or six grand, if I remember correctly. And, as I said, she was an intelligent woman, but the caller was so convincing on the phone that she believed the whole story. They're really clever, these people.'

'I know,' Foster agreed. 'I think that's probably the most likely explanation for the misuse of Simons's log-in details, and obviously we will find out what happened in this case. But we have blocked his account, so we won't see anybody else coming in that way, and he didn't have anything like the access he would need to set up a backdoor or create a superuser account, so we're happy that the system wasn't compromised.'

'Good,' Morgan said, standing up ready to leave, 'but keep your eyes on it. This could be just the start. Npower had an attempted hack as well over the last few days, and the last thing we want is for any of our utility providers to be compromised.'

'Before you go,' Foster said, 'I've got a question for you. You told me your outfit, this C-TAC group, is full of anti-terrorism specialists.'

Morgan nodded and sat down again.

'So I presume you're not just interested in investigating cyberattacks?'

Morgan nodded again.

'So let me ask you about the fairly obvious elephant that may or may not be standing in the corner of the room.'

Morgan already had a good idea where this particular conversational thread was likely to be heading.

'Did you hear about the gas leak that wasn't in the Palace of Westminster? Or about a collision on the Thames between a police launch and a cabin cruiser?' Foster asked. 'There were a few social media posts about it last night and this morning and even a couple of not very clear pictures. Do either of those events have anything to do with the cyberattacks on the utility companies?'

'Those are good questions,' Morgan replied, then paused. 'Before I say something I shouldn't, I presume you were vetted before you took up this post, so what security clearance do you hold?'

Foster didn't look surprised by the question. Most people in sensitive positions in either the military or civilian life are frequently asked to confirm this information.

'I'm BPSS and CTC. That's Baseline Personnel Security Standard and the Counter Terrorist Check.'

'I do know what the initials mean,' Morgan said. He'd already checked Foster's background. The man had served in the Royal Air Force with distinction, a career path slightly at odds with the man in front of him. He looked bored and Morgan suspected he missed past glories stuck in EDF's IT department. His answer was more or less what Morgan had expected.

'Okay, and for your ears only, although no doubt the media will eventually get hold of it, the gas leak was a cover story, and the reason the cabin cruiser was rammed by the police launch was because the two Middle Eastern gentlemen on board were about to try and do a Guy Fawkes on the Houses of Parliament with a sodding great IED. But as far as we know at the moment, based on what little information and analysis I've seen, there's no direct link between that failed attack and the cyber stuff.

'However, the one terrorist who survived the collision did give a kind of warning that whichever outfit he worked for had something much bigger planned than blowing up the Houses of Parliament. And because the attack he was involved in was aimed at destroying the Palace of Westminster, the initial analysis from MI5 at Millbank is that they may be going after Western governments. If that's correct, the next obvious target after Westminster is most likely Washington D.C. Because we know that cyberattacks have been launched in both America and here, it's possible that there may be a link between destructive hackers on the Internet and physically destructive terrorists on the streets, or in this case on the water. But we don't know for sure if there is a link, or what that link might be if there is one, because the two worlds are really entirely separate.'

'If that bomb had gone off,' Foster asked, 'would it have destroyed the Palace of Westminster?'

'It probably wouldn't have flattened the building, because the epicentre of the explosion would have been too far away, but it would've done substantial damage to the structure. We're talking about collapsing walls here, not just a few bits of broken glass. Millbank and everybody else in the loop thinks they probably had three separate but linked aims. They wanted to cause a massive loss of life, because that's the hallmark of a radical Islamic attack, which we're pretty certain this was. But they also wanted to kill as many members of the government as they could, because they would certainly create far more of a national and international sensation by slaughtering a hundred Members of Parliament than by killing a hundred assorted citizens of London. So those two aims kind of morphed into one.

'The obvious way for them to achieve this would have been to cause massive damage to the Palace of Westminster while Parliament was sitting, and wrecking the building that's home to the British government was their third aim. We were lucky that the crew of one of the river police boats spotted the cabin cruiser and worked out what the two terrorists were trying to do. That gave us time to evacuate the building so that even if the bomb had exploded the loss of life would have been minimal. If the attack had worked, it would have sent an unmistakable message to what was left of the British government, and you probably know how these terrorist groups like their messages. I'm slightly surprised they weren't videoing it.'

'Maybe they were,' Foster suggested, 'but they wouldn't have wanted to broadcast a film of a failed attack.'

'True enough. Anyway, I think the papers will have it on the front pages by the end of week, but until it's in the public domain please keep all this to yourself.'

Chapter 21

Dave North collected a pint of bitter from the bar and walked over to a wooden table on one side of the lounge bar of a pub called the Gloucester Old Spot located at Piff's Elm on the A4019, just north-west of junction 10 of the M5 motorway. The slightly strange name of the location dated from the mid-eighteenth century when the pub, then known as the White Swan, was owned by a member of the Piff family and referred to a vast elm tree, reputedly with a girth of over twenty feet. The name lasted longer than the tree, which was felled in 1845, the process taking a team of nine men two weeks to complete.

It was a typical village pub, with uneven white plastered walls decorated with hunting prints and framed by wooden beams blackened by paint and age and smoke. At one end of the lounge bar was a fireplace that wasn't quite an inglenook but which certainly had aspirations in that direction, and where a fire had been laid ready for lighting in the early evening.

North sat down opposite Ben Morgan, who already had a drink in front of him, having arrived a few minutes earlier.

Morgan stood up to shake hands, then lifted his glass a foot or so above the table in greeting. 'Cheers. Good to see you again, Dave. Is this purely social, or was there something else?'

'Both, really. I wanted to pass something by you before I raised it with the rest of C-TAC at Legoland, just in case I'm tilting at windmills and seeing something that really isn't there.'

'Go on,' Morgan replied, replacing his glass on the table and leaning forward slightly. 'I assume this is something to do with what happened to your helicopter pilot?'

North nodded.

'It is. I told you the Ruperts up at Credenhill were going to run checks. They took blood samples from everybody there, from the CO downwards and including me. They had them analysed just in case any of us had the same buckyballs in our bloodstreams, but thankfully none of us had either intact or broken up fullerenes, so we obviously hadn't been infected. Autopsies on the other three men – the local paper had included Bob O'Brien in the headline figure – showed that they all had broken and empty fullerenes in their blood and traces of the same chemical compounds as O'Brien, so the cause of their deaths was the same.'

'I assume your officers did an investigation to try to identify the source?' Morgan suggested.

'They did. None of the people who died had any unusual habits or hobbies or anything like that, so it was all a bit inconclusive. Eventually the Head Shed came to the conclusion that the most likely source was a local pub, because that was about the only place where any hostile agents could actually get into close contact with SAS personnel. When the SAS hit a boozer they tend to go as a group, nobody usually bothers to keep count and it can get quite noisy. On a typical evening some third party might be able to drop something into a few of the drinks as they were being ferried from the bar to wherever the members of the Regiment were standing or sitting. In each drinking session the troopers talked about, it was just a typical night out on the town, and none of them thought any more about it.'

'Until you almost ended up in a smoking hole in the ground somewhere in Wiltshire and three other men dropped dead.'

'Exactly. And then the Ruperts did the obvious. They checked to see if there was any link between the four men apart from a certain fondness for alcoholic beverages.'

'And?'

'And there was one link. Or a sort of link, anyway, but it's a bit tenuous. Have you ever heard of Task Force Black?'

Morgan shook his head.

'Okay. It was a Sabre Squadron that operated from 2004 to 2008 on a six-month rotation in Iraq after Saddam Hussein was forced to find a hole to hide in. It was based inside the Green Zone in Baghdad in a building known as "the Station" and it was mainly tasked with hunting down and eliminating senior members of al-Qaeda. As it turned out, two of the four men from the Regiment who died had been members of Task Force Black.'

'So do you think it was a targeted attack?'

'Possibly, but I'm not convinced for several reasons. First, people in the Regiment try to remain anonymous as much as possible because of the kind of work they do.'

Morgan nodded and grinned.

'You've told me before that most of the people who claim to have been in the SAS almost certainly have never been within fifty miles of Stirling Lines.'

'Exactly. Mind you, you don't need to be a rocket scientist to work out that if you walk into a pub somewhere within staggering distance of Credenhill and see a dozen or so young, fit and healthy men talking and drinking together as a group they might very possibly be members of the Regiment. But none of them is ever going to confirm that, and even if somebody did manage to identify a particular soldier as a member of the SAS, finding out what missions and operations he'd been involved in would be impossible. So the chances of some hostile force identifying Task Force Black personnel are somewhere between nil and nil.'

'But you've just told me that two members of that particular op had been targeted,' Morgan pointed out.

'That was the only link the Head Shed found, but it's a long way from being conclusive. And the third man, and Bob O'Brien for that matter, hadn't been a part of that op, and they were infected as well. And you have to remember that a Sabre Squadron typically numbers about sixty people, so I think this Task Force Black link is nothing of the sort. It's just a coincidence. If you randomly picked fifty men from Stirling Lines and checked their operational history you'd find that many of them would have been together on missions in the past, because the SAS is still a small unit. I think what probably happened was a hostile agent identified a group of men in a pub as probably being from the Regiment and somehow managed to spike some of their drinks. And as I said, take any group of men from the SAS and the chances are that some of them would have been involved in one particular operation.'

'And would that work? Spiking their drinks, I mean?'

'Not my field,' North replied, 'so I don't know. Nor do the medics, come to that, because nanotechnology is such a new field. But from what Natasha Black was saying, it might be possible to prepare fullerenes that wouldn't be broken down by stomach acids and would pass into the bloodstream intact and activate later. The bottom line is that nobody knows, but what does seem clear is that those four men all had to have been infected at about the same time. I can't think of any way that could have happened inside Stirling Lines, so assuming it was down at a local pub or at some other social event does make sense.'

Morgan took another sip of his drink and nodded.

'So if you're right and it was nothing to do with Task Force Black, who do you think did it?'

'It could still have been the Iraqis or other al-Qaeda sympathisers,' North said. 'Bearing in mind that the joint operation with the Americans killed hundreds of al-Qaeda personnel and took about three and a half thousand of them off the streets for the loss of just six Regiment soldiers. Maybe al-Qaeda decided to strike back in an unusual way, administering a lethal poison to people they believed to be members of the SAS.'

'That really doesn't work for me,' Morgan said, after a moment, shaking his head. 'Developing nanotechnology to produce a weapon like that would be incredibly expensive. Logically, if it had been al-Qaeda and their intention was to take revenge for what happened in Iraq, why didn't they just knock up an IED, identify a pub where troopers went for a drink and position it there? They would probably take out a lot of innocent bystanders as well as the targets, but al-Qaeda has never been bothered about collateral damage. That would have been far more obvious and devastating, and would have made the national media rather than just a headline about an unusual illness in a local paper, and most terrorist organisations actively seek publicity whenever they can get it. So for me that idea really doesn't make sense.'

'I know, and I agree. Anyway, there's nothing much more we can do about it here in the UK, unless you've got some brilliant idea. What I have done, though, is pass on what we know to the Americans, to Delta Force and DEVGRU – SEAL Team Six – because they were working with the SAS out of Baghdad during Operation Crichton. That was the codename for the combined op. It'll be interesting to see if any of their personnel were also targeted by anything like this.'

Morgan finished his drink and leaned back in the wooden wheel-back chair.

'I don't often have brilliant ideas,' he said, 'and I haven't got one now, as a matter of fact. But I do have a suggestion based on the facts as we know them. We've established that a lethal cocktail of drugs was administered to a handful of SAS personnel by persons unknown, and we also know that whatever delivery system was used worked and did its job. And we know that this would have been a really, really expensive way of killing somebody.'

'I don't see where you're going with this, Ben.'

'I'm not sure I do, really,' Morgan replied, 'but I can only think of one halfway sensible reason why whoever did this decided to use nanotechnology as a weapon rather than a couple of assault rifles or a few kilos of Semtex or C4, which would have been a hell of a lot cheaper as a revenge attack.'

'I'm listening,' North said, leaning a little closer.

'I wonder if it was maybe just a test run. A way of proving that the delivery system worked, and that they could deliver the chemicals and have them released at a predetermined time by the fullerenes. Then maybe targeting members of the SAS was just convenient and nothing to do with Task Force Black or any other operations carried out by the British military. If that were the case then perhaps the perpetrators were nothing to do with al-Qaeda or ISIS or any other group of regular terrorists. They could be entirely unknown to us, and that worries me.'

North nodded.

'I get it,' he said. 'If you know the bad guys are al-Qaeda or some other known group you can make a pretty good guess at their likely targets. But if you don't know who's doing it, then you have no idea who their target might be. You're right. That is a concern.'

North's mobile rang at that moment, and a few seconds later so did Morgan's.

'Did you initiate that, Dave?' Morgan asked a couple of minutes later as he ended the call. 'The test on the terrorist's blood, I mean?'

North nodded. 'According to the man from Five, what he saw at Wapping was so similar to what I experienced in that bloody chopper that I thought it was worth suggesting they ran a check.'

'Good call. So we have the mixture as before: sodium thiopental and potassium chloride.'

'But if the Five guy was right in his interpretation of the interview, I think the terrorist knew that he was going to die, and more or less when it was going to happen.'

Morgan's expression changed. 'You need to explain that,' he said.

'According to him, the terrorist kept on looking at the clock in the interview room but refused to say anything except that he wanted to see a solicitor. He seemed quite tense, which is what you'd expect bearing in mind where he was and what had happened. And then he seemed to relax, made that statement about "The West will pay" and a few minutes later he was dead. Unless the man from Millbank was completely misinterpreting what he was seeing, it looks to me as if the terrorist knew the fullerenes and their lethal payload would be activated after a particular time that day. Five o'clock, in fact.

'And that,' North finished, 'gives us some answers – but it also poses a hell of a lot more questions.'

Chapter 22

Mahdi Sadir had landed in America and walked through passport control and US Customs with no problem at all, although both his briefcase and carry-on bag had been opened and searched. The customs officer had stopped short when he saw a packet of syringes and what looked like a grey fabric washbag in the briefcase and had told the Iraqi to open it.

'What's this?' he had demanded, pointing at the bag.

'Is cool bag,' Sadir had replied briefly, thickening his accent and stumbling slightly over the words to disguise his fluency in the language. 'For medication.' Then he'd reached into his jacket pocket, taken out an envelope and passed it to the customs officer.

The man had read the sheet of paper that it contained, nodded, handed it back and told Sadir that he could proceed.

He'd had no trouble at any border crossing, carrying the sealed vials obtained from Vektor quite openly because the name printed on the side of each one was a word that almost anyone would recognise, and the letter and prescription that he carried with him was all the justification he needed for possession of the medication. The only time a problem could possibly occur would be if somebody decided to run a comprehensive test on the liquid contained within the vials, and he was confident even that wouldn't matter.

Realistically, Sadir thought the chances of such a test being carried out were extremely remote: it would take a notably brave or a very foolish customs officer to start analysing a collection of obviously factory sealed vials of insulin belonging to a man confirmed by the letter he was carrying to be a diabetic. But even if they were analysed, the customs people would be looking for the usual suspects – the so-called recreational drugs like heroin and cocaine – and that would be all that their basic testing equipment would be capable of detecting. The nanoparticles and their lethal contents would be undetectable to anyone performing that level of analysis. That had been a part of his brief to Vektor from the very start. And the insulin was exactly that – insulin – as any test would confirm.

Sadir, of course, was not a diabetic, and nor was he suffering from any other form of illness. He had ordered several different activation periods from Vektor and anticipated having to use only two of the remaining vials in America because the attacks there would not be martyrdom operations, or *al-amaliyat al-istishhadiya*, and he and the other *jihadists* had every intention of walking away afterwards. But there would be three exceptions to that. There were two people who would become involuntary *shahids* and who would have to imbibe the nanobot cocktail unwittingly – that was an integral and essential part of his plan. And there was one volunteer who would certainly not survive the encounter Sadir had planned for him, and so there would be no need to provide him with the lethal fluid.

A well-placed contact in Riyadh, a man known to Rashid and who was sympathetic to ISIS and its aims, had come up with several helpful ideas and, more importantly, the contact details of several people in America, dedicated and committed volunteers for the cause, who would be glad to provide material assistance. They were, the man in Riyadh had told Sadir the first time they met, all on the same side and all facing the same enemy, the Great Satan. And the beating heart of that hated beast was Washington D.C.

The city itself is something of an anomaly.

It's located within the geographical boundaries of the United States of America but it's not a part of any of the fifty states. The Residence Act, signed in July 1790, mandated the creation of a capital and federal district beside the Potomac River to form the seat of government for the newly independent fledgling nation, and the City of Washington was founded the following year. Today, the federal district extends to just over sixty-eight square miles in total, seven square miles of which are a part of the Potomac River so the land area is only sixty-one square miles, meaning that in global terms Washington D.C. is very slightly smaller than Lichtenstein. It encompasses the original settlements of Alexandria and Georgetown as well as land donated by the neighbouring state of Maryland. The original district also included a part of Virginia, but Congress returned this land, including the city of Alexandria, to the state in 1846.

With a population of over 700,000 residents, a number that swells to more than one million people every day of the working week, it can get extremely crowded, which was just one of the reasons why Sadir had chosen it as his base for the American operation. The other reasons were rather more compelling.

He had guessed that he, and almost anyone he associated with, would be likely to attract attention in America because of the colour of their skin and, more importantly, because of the identity of the nation that had issued his passport. Although the events of 9/11 were no longer fresh in the minds of most Americans, their memories were long and the identities of the perpetrators of that astonishingly successful attack had cast an almost permanent suspicion over the activities of anyone born in the Middle East or carrying a passport from that part of the world.

He would undeniably have been more noticeable had he selected somewhere in small-town America as his residence, and so Sadir had decided from the start that the best place for him to hide was in one of the most crowded cities in the country, on the same basis that the best place to hide a tree is in a forest.

What he did not know was whether or not he had managed to escape detection, but because he always took precautions when on the move and when meeting other people and had never seen the slightest sign of anybody following him or apparently taking any interest at all in what he was doing, he assumed he was still some way below the radar.

Which at that moment he was, but that was about to change.

Chapter 23

Cheltenham, Gloucestershire

'Is this line secure?'

Ben Morgan had no idea who the man was, but because he had called his work mobile rather than his personal phone, he assumed it was an official call, not least because that number wasn't published anywhere outside the various classified directories. So at least he was reasonably certain that he wasn't about to be told that the caller understood he had had an accident that wasn't his fault. In fact, Morgan had discounted that possibility as soon as he had heard the man's voice: most of the desperate ambulance-chasing solicitors who resorted to that kind of pointless cold-calling employed young girls to read from a carefully prepared script at irritated people who had far better things to do than listen to such rubbish.

But whoever the caller was, what he had asked wasn't a sensible question.

'These days,' Morgan replied, quite sharply, 'no mobile phone call is secure unless both the caller and the recipient are using encrypted phones like the Enigma, Blackphone or Blackview. This phone was given to me by the government, so it's just a plain vanilla mobile, because encrypted phones and the encryption service cost money and the government, as usual, won't pay for anything unless it absolutely has to. So the short snappy answer to your question is no, of course it's not secure. Who are you, and what do you want?'

'I'm calling from London and I've been told you need to return to Vauxhall Bridge as soon as possible, with clothes for a week and your passport.'

For 'Vauxhall Bridge' Morgan read 'Vauxhall Cross' and for 'Vauxhall Cross' he read 'C-TAC' and wondered why he hadn't been called by Dame Janet or maybe Angela.

'Why?' Morgan asked, which seemed to stump the man who had called him.

'I have no idea. I'm just delivering the message. You've got it, so it's up to you. What's your estimate for London?'

Although Morgan frequently travelled by train to the capital, he didn't retain an up-to-date timetable in his head and he certainly didn't know the time of the next train. Plus he needed to sort out his bag, secure the house if he was going to be away for a week – and in his experience it would probably turn out to be longer than that – and get a cab to the station.

'Three hours,' he replied. 'Maybe four. It all depends on the trains.'

He heard the caller hold a muffled conversation with somebody else in the background, then the line cleared again.

'You'll need to get your skates on then. You're booked on the 1700 British Airways flight out of Heathrow to Dulles. Your ticket will be waiting for you at Terminal Five.'

'Why am I going to Texas?' Morgan demanded, looking at his watch.

There was a brief pause while the caller digested his question. 'Not Dallas,' he replied. 'Dulles Airport, in Washington.' And with that he rang off.

Morgan stared at his silent mobile for a couple of seconds as if daring it to emit any kind of sound, then put it in his pocket and walked into his study, where he kept a bag ready packed for short notice journeys. Living on his own had some advantages, and he was used to not having to explain his actions to any dependants and being able to act and react as he wanted and needed to. The downsides were the evenings usually spent alone, and not much of a social life.

He picked up his landline phone, speed dialled the number of the local taxi company he normally used to book a ride and organised a cab, then opened the bag to quickly check its contents. Then he took a leather briefcase and put in it his Panasonic Toughbook – he liked travelling with a laptop that was heavy enough to use as a weapon – one of his backup hard drives that contained additional software that he found useful, the connecting leads, mains charger and a couple of travel adapters so that he could plug it in when he reached whichever hotel he would be using in the States. He added his phone charger, checked that he had his mobile in his jacket pocket along with his passport and credit cards, then walked quickly around the house, checking the security of the doors and windows before setting the alarm and stepping outside. As he locked his front door he heard a brief toot from the road and saw his taxi just pulling up. The timing had worked perfectly and he hoped that might be an omen for the rest of the journey.

Or perhaps not, he wondered less than ten minutes later as the taxi joined the end of a seemingly unmoving queue of cars at an extensive length of carriageway repairs controlled by a set of traffic lights. Traffic lights that had clearly been programmed by an idiot, because the green period in each direction lasted only long enough to allow half a dozen vehicles to drive through, providing they were already in first gear and ready to move, followed by an unnecessary long wait while the lights at both end were obviously showing red. The queues in both directions were lengthening by the minute.

'This is nothing,' the taxi driver commented when Morgan expressed his understandable irritation in words consisting largely of four letters and single syllables. 'You should see it in the morning rush hour. It's like the biggest car park outside the bloody M25.'

But eventually they were through that particular jam and a few minutes later the taxi turned into Queen's Road and stopped outside the white painted building that was Cheltenham Spa station, a structure that Morgan always thought looked more like a provincial cinema than a railway station.

In the ticket hall he offered his credit card to exchange what seemed like an excessively large amount of money for a small piece of cardboard that would give him the right to – probably – stand all the way to London's Paddington Station, then changed his mind and spent twice as much to buy a first-class ticket, on the grounds that he could probably reclaim the money through C-TAC. And at least then he would get a seat.

Almost the first person he saw when he stepped onto the platform was Natasha Black.

'I assume you also had the urgent summons from above?' she asked as Morgan walked over to her. 'And I'm not talking about a message from the divine ruler and creator of the universe, just some irritating and anonymous little oik in London issuing orders on behalf of somebody else.'

Morgan nodded. 'You're going to Washington as well?'

Natasha nodded in her turn. 'I am, and I don't know why. I find that irritating, and when I'm irritated I tend to get quite snappy, so I apologise in advance for anything I say that you don't like. What ticket have you got?'

'I splashed out on first class,' Morgan said. 'It seemed like a good idea at the time.'

'So did I. I worked on the basis that if I'm going to be irritated for the next few hours at least I can be irritated in comfort, or at least in something marginally more comfortable than standing up in Great Western Railway's usual cattle class accommodation.'

The train departed Cheltenham Spa just over nine minutes late, which probably counted as being bang on time to a twenty-first-century railway company, and Morgan spent nearly twenty minutes talking to Angela Evans on his mobile once they'd found their seats. He ended the call and glanced at Natasha, sitting opposite him.

'Well?' she demanded.

'If I said I knew what was going on I'd be lying,' Morgan replied. 'Angela was able to provide some information, but the situation is still unfolding.'

'Don't fanny about,' Natasha ordered. 'Give me the alligator sandwich version – make it short and snappy.'

Morgan grinned at her, then glanced round to ensure that nobody else was within earshot. 'I'll do my best,' he said. 'I don't know how they managed it, but a team from Millbank was able to retrace the route the cabin cruiser took when it travelled to Westminster and discovered a derelict boathouse where they think it was prepared for the operation. They obviously found some usable clues either there or on what was left of the boat, most probably fingerprints, and that led them to a terrorist cell in north-east London. Apparently one of the men involved was already on the MI5 radar and they analysed the street camera images to pin down his address.

'They went knocking with a team of armed officers from the Met carrying a big red key. They smashed open the door and grabbed the two occupants who were getting ready to clear out. Under interrogation, they were persuaded to reveal what they knew, which wasn't much. The short version is that they were proud of the London attack and clearly very upset that it hadn't been successful. They both used the same expression – "The West will pay" – which is exactly what the terrorist who briefly survived the Thames attack had told the two men from Five, and both said that the main attack was going to be in America. According to Angela, the Millbank interrogators said they were arrogant and totally convinced that the American attack would not and could not fail, which is obviously a bit alarming. But they had no idea of the details of it. Or so they claimed.'

Natasha nodded in a somewhat distracted fashion, then leaned forward.

'Some obvious questions,' she said. 'First, those two numpties were obviously foot-soldiers, just there to fulfil their warped destiny by strapping a few kilos of Semtex around them and then lighting the blue touchpaper in some suitably crowded place. When the men from Five with the rack and thumbscrews persuaded them to open up, did they find out anything about the puppet-master, the man pulling these idiots' strings? Like a name or a description, I mean? Something we can scan for at GCHQ?'

'I think interrogation techniques these days are a little more subtle than that,' Morgan pointed out. 'Perhaps some sleep deprivation and maybe a touch of chemical coercion if the subject is particularly reluctant to talk. But I gather from Angela that these two were reasonably willing to open up, almost as if they knew that they held the moral high ground. That's something we've seen before with *shahids*.

And as I said, they were both convinced that the American attack would be successful. To answer your question, neither man supplied any description of the person who organised the attack, and so far there's no CCTV footage of anybody entering the house they rented in Waltham Forest apart from the two men now in custody and the two who were on the cabin cruiser. But they did both come up with a name for their leader – Abū Tadmir – so Millbank will be running that through their databases to see if it raises any red flags.'

Natasha laughed shortly. 'I suppose they can waste their time doing that if they want to, but I can guarantee that they won't learn anything that would help identify him.'

Morgan asked the obvious question. 'How do you know that?'

'You know me, Ben. I'm like a sponge. I just soak up useless information, but maybe some of the time it's not entirely useless. I'm sure Millbank will get hits, but they won't learn his identity, because Abū Tadmir isn't an Arabic proper name. It's a *kunya*. In fact it's a corrupted *kunya*, and it's quite obvious to me that it's an assumed name, a *nom de guerre*.'

Not for the first time, Ben Morgan was somewhat awestruck by the depth, and especially by the breadth, of Natasha Black's knowledge. 'A *kunya*?' he asked weakly. 'What's that?'

'It's a teknonym, a name assumed by a man or woman that incorporates the name of their eldest child. So a male might adopt the *kunya* Abū Hussein, meaning "the father of Hussein", while his wife could call herself Umm Hussein, meaning she was Hussein's mother. It's quite a common practice.'

'So this man is calling himself "the father of Tadmir"?'

She shook her head. 'Not quite. *Tadmir* isn't an Arab name. It's an Arabic noun, and it translates as "destruction" or "devastation", so our shadowy master terrorist has adopted a name, an invented *nom de guerre*, that means "father of destruction". I don't know about you, but I don't much like the sound of that.'

'Well,' Morgan suggested, 'I suppose the good news is that if this terror campaign is concentrating on America, at least the citizens of Britain should be reasonably safe. We of course won't be, because we'll be flying into what might turn out to be the epicentre of the attacks across the Pond.'

'That's why they pay you so much.'

Morgan gave a hollow laugh. 'If only,' he said. 'Any other thoughts about this?'

'Obviously the one that I'm sure has occurred to you as well.'

Morgan had no idea what she was talking about, and the expression on his face confirmed his obvious bewilderment.

'The expression they used,' Natasha said, sounding slightly exasperated. 'Come on, Ben, do try and keep up. This is more your world than mine. All three of them said "The West will pay", which is an obvious threat, albeit non-specific. But it's also ambiguous.'

'Is it?'

'Of course it is. It could mean something like "We're going to make the West pay for the damage caused to Iraq or Syria or somewhere" and off they trot with their Semtex or whatever and blow up the White House or the Capitol Building or just cause a massive loss of life in New York or somewhere. Eye for an eye stuff. Biblical, or rather Koranic, revenge. But it could also mean that the West will quite literally pay in hard currency for what's happened, and I don't mean that ISIS is planning on sending the American president a sodding great bill. I think it'll be much easier than that.'

It had taken Morgan a few moments to catch on, but he was finally on the same page as Natasha.

'I see what you mean. Stock markets around the world hate uncertainty and tend to panic when anything unexpected happens. If you know when a major terrorist attack is going to take place you can buy a huge number of well out-of-the-money put options and clean up when the market falls through the floor. The gains these terrorists could make would potentially net them millions.'

'So what are you going to do about it?'

Morgan picked up his mobile and opened up his contact list.

'I'm going to give Cam the Man a heads-up and ask him to check the London Stock Exchange records to see if there was any unusual trading in the few days before the failed attack using the cabin cruiser.

And I'll ask him to talk to his opposite number in New York and get some tripwires set. If you're right, as soon as there's an unusually high level of that sort of trading on the options market we need to know about it, because it could tell us that whatever's going to happen is going to happen soon. It wouldn't tell us what or exactly when, but it would be some kind of an early warning.'

Cameron Riley was another member of the C-TAC team, a former Royal Navy and Special Boat Squadron officer currently employed by the Bank of England in the most senior position within the security apparatus. He and the Governor apparently almost never saw eye to eye on anything, but because Riley was the keeper of the secrets and knew where the bodies were buried, not necessarily only in a metaphorical sense, his position was secure.

He and Morgan had successfully exposed a personal blackmail conspiracy generated from China that had sought to manipulate leading banking executives guilty of less than acceptable behaviour. Monthly fees had been demanded from the executives and their exposure would have destroyed market confidence. The sheer number of compromised people, their status and the depth of the plot, had shaken the UK government to its core.

Morgan ended the call a few minutes later and nodded to Natasha.

'Any other suggestions or questions or snippets?' he asked.

She nodded. 'Yes. What are we doing?'

'You mean why are we being sent out to Washington, and what are we supposed to do when we get there?'

'Exactly. America is crawling with alphabet soup agencies – CIA, FBI, NSA, DHS and all the rest of them – and everybody involved in law enforcement and a hell of a lot of people who aren't carrying weapons at all times. So exactly what they're expecting a GCHQ analyst and a slightly overweight professor of cybersecurity, both unarmed and largely uninformed, to do in Washington is somewhat beyond me.'

'What do you mean "overweight"?' Morgan asked. 'I'm in my physical prime.'

'Whatever you say, Chubby.'

Chapter 24

When Barbara Simpson had arrived in Washington she'd done things in what seemed to her to be a logical sequence. Her most immediate concern was accommodation, so the first thing she'd done was to find a seat in a cafe at Dulles, order a coffee and a sandwich and use her mobile to identify what she hoped was the cheapest hotel room in or near DC, though the price was still eye-wateringly expensive. She'd booked it for two nights, then taken a cab to the hotel, checked in, dumped her bags in the room and called the private mobile number of the FBI officer known personally to, and vouched for by, Richard Boston.

It wasn't a long conversation, and just over forty minutes later Simpson had walked into the coffee shop of a completely different, and clearly much more expensive, hotel near the centre of DC. The briefing document she'd been given had done much more than outline the situation on the ground and her personal tasking, which was to work deep undercover as an unacknowledged FBI asset. It had also provided the names and contact details of various people located in and around Washington in various government organisations and had included mugshot-type photographs of most of them. Those images, and her extremely retentive visual memory, had enabled her to walk without a pause directly across the coffee shop and to slip lithely into a corner booth directly opposite a solid, fair-haired man with what she thought were typically American regular features – blue eyes, tanned skin and a wide jaw that seemed to contain far too many teeth, all of them far too white – who looked more like a professional footballer than anything else.

'Hi Grant,' she'd said, extending her hand across the table.

Grant Rogers had immediately stood up, shaken her hand, called over a waitress and ordered her a drink and a snack, all apparently without drawing breath. Then the FBI agent had sat down, formally introduced himself and laid out the immediate problems that American law enforcement, and specifically those involved in Washington D.C., were facing.

'It's a combination of things, really,' he had concluded, as Barbara Simpson finished her coffee. 'As I said, we've been getting whispers from informants and traffic intercepts that seem to suggest some group, most probably with a radical Islamic agenda, is planning on creating a major atrocity right here in DC. But there's been nothing specific, nothing that we could get a proper handle on. And at the same time we've been trying to do a little in-house sanitising, identifying people in the Bureau whose ethnicity or background or anything else might have made them liable to radicalisation, just in case they're a part of it. Whatever it is. If it really exists. Sleepers are a real big problem for us right now and yet no one ever mentions it. Almost every day we find men and woman who slip up somehow and we uncover depths of deception that keep me awake at night. You wouldn't ever know or even suspect that people you've worked with for ten years, people who've served their country with honour and earned medals in combat, harbour a desire to do harm to their communities.'

'Trying to identify the viper in the bosom before it strikes,' Simpson had suggested. 'Treachery has always existed and it always will. The problem is that nobody ever learns the lessons of history. In fact, the one lesson we do learn from history is that nobody ever learns the lessons of history.'

'Exactly. And it's not just us. The Agency – the CIA – and the Secret Service have been doing the same, and probably the NSA as well, but their policy is to never tell anyone anything, so we can't be sure. It's a hellish difficult situation and we have to tread real carefully. If we had any concrete suspicions we'd at least know where we should start looking, but we haven't, so it's all low-key and non-specific.'

'And who checks the checkers?'

Rogers shook his head.

'Don't get me started on that. We're in what James Jesus Angleton called a wilderness of mirrors and we don't know whether we're looking at reality or a reflection.'

'T. S. Eliot,' Simpson had replied.

'What?'

'I know Angleton used the expression, but it comes from "Geron-tion", a poem by T. S. Eliot that he wrote just after the end of the First World War. The title's Greek and it translates as "little old man", and the poem is a dramatic monologue describing the state of Europe after the fighting was over as seen through the eyes of that old man.'

'Literature's not my thing,' Rogers had admitted, 'and I didn't know that. But you can see our problem. What I do know is that the team of people I've got working for me are one hundred per cent straight and loyal. I've picked them myself and I trust every single one of them with my life because that's what you have to do when you're working as a real tight-knit group. Or, to put it another way, if any of my people were actually radicalised closet Muslims, then I have no idea how you could ever trust anybody again.' He looked across at her keenly and shook his head. 'Richard said you specialised in undercover operations and have something of a gift for spotting bad guys.'

'I have. I've spent the last few years down in Colombia trying to identify cartel members on the streets and at the same time trying to work out which of the police officers working with me were also full-time employees of those same cartels. That, let me tell you, was a real wilderness of mirrors, not to mention bloody dangerous with everybody armed to the teeth and just itching to start pulling the trigger. Now, there's not much I can do to help identify people in the Bureau or any other organisation who might be about to switch from being an all-American patriot to a dedicated *shahid* whose latest fashion accessory is a Semtex waistcoat, because that's an in-house problem and you need to be inside the organisation to tackle it. But I should be able to do something on the streets.'

Rogers had waited while the waitress refilled their coffee cups before he'd leaned forward and replied.

'That's where the danger lies, at least in my opinion. But you're brand new here in DC. I've seen your briefing notes, but you don't know the area and you don't know the people, so how do your bosses expect you to be able to help us out?'

'I'm a quick learner, and I have a very good memory. More importantly, people are pretty much the same wherever you go, and in my experience those people who are walking on the wrong side of that thin blue line that separates the law-abiding from the lawless do have certain characteristics. For one thing, they tend to be more aware of their surroundings and that shows. Your average member of Joe Public will travel to work looking straight ahead while he or she thinks about what they'll be doing that day, what meeting they'll be attending, what jobs they need to do, even where they're going to have lunch. They'll take no more notice of their fellow pedestrians or commuters than they need to avoid bumping into them. But the lawless will always be aware of where they are and what's going on because they'll be looking out either for a chance to break the law, to commit some crime like dealing drugs, or for any sign of a police officer who might be looking for them. After a while, you can quite easily spot the bad guys.'

'It's as simple as that?' Grant Rogers had demanded.

'No, of course not. That's just a very basic example of the kind of thing I look out for. Now, I'm going to need some things from you, like a cheap and anonymous place to stay while I'm here in DC. I can't do this from a hotel. I need to be anonymous, just one more face in the crowds on the streets, so that means a small apartment or something.'

'We can sort that. Might take a couple days, but not a problem. What else?'

'Information, really. I'm sure the Bureau has reams of regulations about who can see what, when and why, and as a non-American citizen I've no doubt I wouldn't even be entitled to look at a file cover, far less see what's inside it. But if I'm going to be able to help you I will need an abstract or a summary of whatever leads you're following. Ideally the names, addresses and if possible photographs of anybody your informants have fingered, something like that, just to give me somewhere to start.'

Rogers had nodded, then removed a thumb drive from his pocket, checked that the waitress was out of view and that nobody was paying them any attention. He slid the tiny memory stick across the table and as his fingers released it Simpson had deftly palmed the device.

'You have got a laptop with you, I guess? Okay, I figured you'd need that sort of data so I prepped that thumb drive myself, with the approval of the director of the Counterterrorism Division, the man who's more or less at the top of the FBI tree when it comes to this kind of operation. He's a guy that I trust absolutely. That's pretty much all we have, and it's current as of about two days ago. Everything on it is copy-protected, so don't try moving it onto your laptop because you can't. It's also password-protected.' He'd handed her a thin slip of paper with about a dozen random characters written on it. 'That's it. Please memorise that as soon as you can and certainly before you leave this building. Then eat it. It's rice paper and it doesn't even taste too bad.'

–

Three days later Barbara Simpson had moved into a tiny studio apartment that had somehow been carved out of what had originally been a small two-bedroom flat in the Bloomingdale district in the northern part of Washington, not far from Howard University. It was a long way from the glamour and grandeur of Capitol Hill and the centre of DC, which suited her very well.

And for the next weeks and months she'd walked the streets of Washington, blending in with the crowds and watching. Always watching. She'd followed up the leads Grant Rogers had supplied and built up her own data files on an increasingly long list of persons of interest to her because of their behaviour and actions. She'd also identified links between certain individuals that the FBI hadn't been aware of, and that she'd clarified to Rogers at their regular meetings in coffee shops and cafes.

But there was one particular link that really didn't make sense to her and which she hadn't told him about, simply because she was starting to think that she'd misinterpreted what she'd seen, or rather what she'd heard. In fact, she wondered if she'd seen something that wasn't actually there, and the last thing she wanted to do was to raise it with the FBI only for it to turn out to be completely worthless. Or, worse, it could be a piece of disinformation, something deliberately planted to try to start an investigation designed to divert the Bureau's attention away from the truth.

Trying to clarify that situation, she'd decided, was where she was going to have to concentrate her efforts for the next few weeks.

Her sixth sense had cut in, and she knew better than to ignore it.

Chapter 25

Ben Morgan had been unsurprised to discover that as well as a British Airways ticket to Dulles Airport in Washington – predictably enough in economy class – he was also handed an A4 size manilla envelope emblazoned with a red cross on both sides, his name typed on the front and the flap sealed with wax. He guessed from his previous experience that inside would be a briefing document, most probably with a Secret classification if the envelope was any indicator. He had to produce his passport and sign a classified document register before the unsmiling man in the dark suit, presumably a courier sent out from either Millbank or Vauxhall Cross, would hand it over.

A few seconds later Natasha Black, standing right beside him at the desk, was given an apparently identical envelope in her name and was also required to sign for its receipt.

The anonymous courier nodded at them both, turned and walked away. Morgan and Natasha exchanged glances, both clearly thinking exactly the same thing, and looked at the British Airways official who had witnessed the proceedings.

'I think,' Morgan said, 'that we would be more comfortable in premium economy or business class if that's available, so can you please arrange an upgrade for us? We're on official government business and we'll also need access to a private lounge or office where we can read the documents that we've just signed for.'

The BA man – tall, slim, fair-haired, meticulously shaven and immaculately dressed – looked at their two economy class tickets still sitting on the desk in front of him.

'A business class ticket includes lounge access,' he replied.

'That'll do nicely,' Natasha said, effortlessly taking control of the conversation. 'We'll leave you to sort out the tickets for us and we'll go to the lounge now. We've got a lot of work to do.'

The man from BA didn't look entirely happy at this turn of events, but he probably realised he'd to some extent been backed into a corner.

'You need a business class ticket to get into the lounge.'

'No problem,' Natasha said breezily. 'In that case we'll wait here while you sort them out, but be as quick as you can about it.'

Slightly to Morgan's surprise, about ten minutes later they found themselves seats in a corner of one of the restricted-access lounges. While Natasha used a nail file with a two-inch ceramic blade – an obviously highly dangerous and potentially lethal weapon that would no doubt be confiscated by airport security before they were allowed anywhere near the aircraft – to open up her envelope and extract the contents, Morgan organised coffee and a couple of plates of pastries and biscuits from the counters in the lounge.

'These should plug a small gap until we get fed on the aircraft,' he said. 'Neatly done back there,' he added. 'I was convinced we were going to get the bum's rush and end up sitting in economy with our knees around our ears all the way across the Atlantic.'

Natasha nodded. 'Sometimes turning on the charm does the trick, but usually I find that the steamroller approach works rather better. Just make it perfectly clear that whatever you want to happen is going to happen, and don't take no for an answer. I was half expecting him to refuse the upgrade, in which case I would have demanded an immediate audience with the highest-ranking BA official in the building. I can be very persuasive.'

Morgan pointed at the open envelope on the leather couch beside her. 'So what have our lords and masters given us to keep us awake all the way to the United States?'

'As you probably guessed, it's a briefing document and it's classified Secret, which I frankly think is a bit of a stretch. I reckon it's Confidential at best and it looks like most of the stuff in it is already in the public domain. I've not read it properly yet, but I'm quite good at speed-reading so I've got a good idea about the data. I've scanned the contents list and some of the material that looked interesting. The short version is that the Yanks have seen the same sort of attempted intrusions on the websites of some of their utility companies, but there's very little hard information in the briefing notes about how the attacks were carried out or how successful they were. It'll obviously be your part of the ship to analyse what happened and what needs to be done about it.'

'What authority have we been given to let us do that? We can't just stick our noses into stuff like that in a foreign country.'

'I think,' Natasha said, 'that you've probably been seconded to either the CIA or the FBI – and my guess is to the Fibbies – as a specialist adviser. That's all on the first page of the document. My extensive knowledge of all matters GCHQ-ish is for some reason much in demand at Fort Meade in Maryland, where I am apparently expected to report for duty no later than tomorrow afternoon.'

'You'll be at the National Security Agency?' Morgan asked, sounding surprised. 'But I thought with GCHQ—'

'You thought right,' Natasha interrupted. 'Cheltenham and the wizards at No Such Agency can communicate seamlessly over the NSANet encrypted network, so whatever they want me to do at Fort Meade I could have done just as well sitting in my slightly pokey office at GCHQ. On the other hand, I've got something of a weakness for hamburgers and Coke and steaks the size of a bath mat, and it's nice to get out of the office for a while, so I'm certainly not going to complain.'

While she'd been talking, Morgan had opened his own sealed envelope. He pulled out a red Secret file folder and opened it up.

'You're right,' he said. 'My reporting address is 935 Pennsylvania Avenue, right in the middle of Washington and just along the road from the White House, which means I'll be getting into bed with the FBI. I'm glad I packed a suit and tie.'

Natasha shook her head. 'Not necessarily. I've already checked on the Internet and these days FBI agents are supposed to wear clothing that matches their environment or the crime they're investigating rather than standing out as obvious G-men in their eponymous black suits, white shirts and dark ties, like the original Men in Black. So if you're there to look at white-collar crime you would still need the suit, but for cybercrime and counterterrorism they tend to dress the same way as the people they're after. So as you're probably looking for computer nerds that means torn jeans and a T-shirt with a vulgar message printed on it and pizza stains down the front. Which is more or less what you wear at home, and I know that because I've seen you there.'

'And you?' Morgan asked.

'I'll wear whatever I like, the same as I always do. If somebody doesn't like it, that's their problem not mine. Now shut up, read your briefing notes and then get me another cup of coffee and some more of these rather yumsy shortbreads.'

Chapter 26

The five commonest cars on the roads of America are all Japanese – two of them made by Honda, another two by Toyota and the fifth one by Nissan – which had pleased Mahdi Sadir as he had no wish to contribute to the economy of the United States any more than he had to. In fact, quite the reverse. Because most Americans seem to drive everywhere, one of the first things he had done after he'd arrived in Washington for the first time a few years earlier was to buy a car: a cheap, reliable and anonymous high-mileage ten-year-old Honda Accord that was registered and insured in the name of a trusted local proxy to avoid creating a paper trail. Possession of the car meant that he could get where he needed to be without having to use public transport, at least for journeys outside the city.

That evening he carried out his usual counter-surveillance checks before he went anywhere near the vehicle, and it took him well over an hour before he was satisfied that neither he nor the car was being watched. Then he got in and drove away from DC, heading for a house on the other side of Bel Air.

Bel Air is a primarily residential settlement, shaped something like an inverted letter U and located north-east of Baltimore. It lies outside the main suburban complex around that city which forms a ragged semi-circle, the straight edge created by Chesapeake Bay to the east, and which merges almost seamlessly into the adjoining built-up areas around Gaithersburg, Bowie, Annapolis, Washington D.C., Arlington and Alexandria.

Unlike that sprawling complex, Bel Air feels more like a country town, mainly bordered by farms and open fields. It began its life as a new build back in 1780 when it was constructed by a Baltimore resident named Aquilla Scott on land known as 'Scott's Old Fields'. That wasn't much of a name for a new town and in 1784 it was rebranded as Belle Aire. Over the years, new buildings were constructed and letters were dropped and by 1798 it had acquired its current name and pretty much its present shape.

To the north-west of Bel Air is a much smaller and almost circular settlement called Jarrettsville, and between the two lies a scattering of houses, mainly built on large lots carved from the surrounding farmland, typically on dead-end roads in areas bearing names like Fairview and Forest Hill. Many of these properties are both large – some of them are very large – and expensive, but a few are surprisingly small in relation to the size of the land they occupy.

When Mahdi Sadir had first arrived in America as the various disparate elements of his plan were beginning to come together, he had known more or less where he needed to find a property for the most important part of the final phase of the attack he would be launching against the American capital city. He wanted a detached house – the size and design didn't really matter as long as it had at least two bedrooms – that was not overlooked by any neighbouring properties and was secluded but not completely surrounded by tall trees. That was vital. He had also wanted it to be some distance from the target city, but not so deep in the surrounding countryside that the property wouldn't be able to connect to the fastest possible broadband service. That was something else that was non-negotiable.

The house he'd taken on a long-term rental contract wasn't ideal, but it was certainly good enough. It occupied a corner plot, which meant the garden was a little bigger than most of the adjoining prop-erties. Most of it was grassed, which meant maintenance would be easy, and it was essential that the property was cared for by the tenants to avoid attracting unwanted attention. Quite close to the rear of the house was an area that had perhaps once been a vegetable garden or something of that sort, a smallish level area surrounded on three sides by well-established shrubs and hedges. That was almost ideal for his purpose, because the interior of that space was invisible unless you were actually standing on the property itself. And even if somebody did trespass to take a look, the piece of equipment that Sadir had arranged to be assembled there would not in itself arouse suspicions unless the trespasser had certain specialised knowledge. To a casual observer, it would be immediately recognisable as the kind of object seen close to many properties, especially those located outside a town. But to an expert, there would be one subtle detail that would imply a radically different purpose than its most obvious and harmless apparent function.

Well before he'd reached America, Sadir had already begun recruiting personnel, utilising the substantial finances that Rashid had placed at his disposal, and the two people who had occupied the house for the last three years were in many ways the most important of the dozen or so *jihadists* that he had persuaded to join him. They were the people who would, at the climax of the operation, provide him with the ability to deliver a deathblow to the centre of Washington. But before they could do that, they had been faced with a technological challenge of astonishing complexity that had required the most accomplished and innovative hacking skills. In many ways, the single most difficult task that Sadir had faced was finding people who possessed that kind of ability, and it had taken him the better part of a year to identify and assemble the two-man team that was now operating from the property near Fairview.

The traditional image of a computer hacker, fostered by countless books and films, is of a young man, probably no older than twenty or twenty-five, unshaven and dressed in jeans or shorts and a T-shirt emblazoned with the name of some obscure heavy-metal band, sitting in a darkened room where the only illumination comes from three or four computer screens and keyboards, and surrounded by discarded pizza boxes and empty soft drink cans.

And this image is not necessarily that far from the truth. Hackers tend to be dedicated and committed. Show them a problem, or more likely a target site and a good reason to get inside it, and in most cases they will turn their entire attention to breaching whatever security precautions are in place in order to achieve this. The effort becomes all-consuming, and basic human needs like eating and drinking – along with washing, shaving, showering and the application of deodorant – come a significant distance behind the task at hand. And of course pizzas and soft drinks are not only cheap and readily available but can also be consumed with one hand while the other continues to operate a mouse or keyboard, making them absolutely ideal foodstuffs for a dedicated hacker. And the final bonus is that in most places they can even be delivered, meaning that all the hacker actually has to do to get fed and watered is place his order by phone or through the Internet and then walk across and open the door of his house or apartment in order to take delivery.

Hacking and pizzas really do go together like bread and butter or fish and chips.

And in his darkened room, surrounded by the detritus of fast-food living, the hacker can employ sophisticated tools and software in order to somehow get through whatever firewalls the target site has put in place, or to try to steal log-ins and passwords that would enable him to achieve the same goal. In short, in the popular imagination hacking is seen as an essentially intellectual pursuit, the unshaven but talented renegade male pitting his wits and computing ability against the security protocols and precautions erected by government or big business to keep him out.

And of course it might not just be a single hacker. Teams or collectives of hackers, like the notorious Anonymous, can pool their resources, their knowledge and their software in order to achieve whatever goals they have set themselves. Thanks to the Internet, these groups of hackers may well have no idea of the identities or locations of the people with whom they are collaborating. And that doesn't matter to them, because they're all cut from the same cloth, working together towards what they see as a common purpose or aim.

As the media reports on a regular basis, both individual hackers and loosely organised groups of them have an impressive track record breaching sites in order to steal information, typically a company's customer database containing their log-ins and credit card details, either to commit financial fraud with the data or to sell the information on the Dark Web, or simply to make a political point by defacing a website. Today, cyberattacks of all sorts are a near-constant threat. One recent study claimed that in America alone there is an attempted hack somewhere in the country every thirty-nine seconds on average, though most of these rarely make the news.

But the people that Sadir had found were very different to this image.

Most hackers are amateurs. They have other jobs or ways of earning a living and their forays into the electronic netherworld of the Dark Web or attacks on government or corporate websites are essentially a hobby. All-consuming, in many cases, but still usually a part-time occupation. And because hacking is a dark art and not the kind of course offered by colleges or universities – 'computer science' is about as close as they get – hackers tend to be largely self-taught, learning from other people and downloading and sharing various types of hacking software as their abilities and skill levels increase.

Sadir was neither a programmer nor a hacker, but he knew enough about the subject to avoid trying to recruit the kind of people dismissively known as 'script kiddies', the sort of wannabe hackers who would download software they did not understand and use that to mount extremely amateurish attacks. What he had needed were people who were professionally trained – ideally, government trained – and knew exactly what they were doing. He was looking for the sort of people who had put together the Stuxnet virus that had crippled the Iranian nuclear weapon programme by destroying the centrifuges used for the enrichment of uranium at the Natanz facility in central Iran.

With the increasing importance of cybersecurity to combat various forms of cybercrime, almost all governments have seen the necessity to employ both 'white hat hackers' to combat cyberattacks and also their own teams of 'black hat hackers' who would mount offensive cyber operations. All, of course, completely deniable and off the books. And there was one nation in particular that had refined the art and science of hacking to a high degree and that employed literal armies of highly trained hackers tasked with breaking into websites and intranets and stealing secrets from targeted countries.

One problem was that the ideology of that particular nation was no more in keeping with the aims of radical Islam than it was with the decadent democracies of the West, so an appeal for specialised help on ideological grounds was never going to work. But rather more important than abstract concepts like ideology and philosophy was the appeal of cold hard cash, and that was a weapon Sadir could use to his advantage. And so he had, working through contacts of contacts of contacts until he had finally identified a handful of people with the right qualifications and abilities – they actually had been government trained – and used his financial clout to secure the services of two of them for as long as it took.

And he had offered a bonus: if the scenario played out as Sadir expected it to, as well as the balance of their promised funds, he had told them that at the completion of the operation they would also receive a technological gift that would be of incalculable value to their home country. That wasn't actually going to happen, because Sadir had an entirely different endgame in mind, but the offer was too attractive to be ignored. And so he had obtained access to the specialised skills and abilities that he had needed in the form of two very experienced and professional hackers.

Because what happened at the house in Fairview was the most important part of the plan, he was a fairly frequent visitor, checking on progress and making sure that the two men had everything that they needed. With the implementation date now only a few days away, this visit was the last that he would make to the property before the commencement of the attack.

The area in front of the house had room to park half a dozen cars. Sadir stopped the Honda behind a dark blue SUV and locked it. By the time he got to the main door of the property, it was already open and the two residents were waiting for him on the full-width porch.

Inside, they led him directly through the property to a room at the rear overlooking the garden, a view that had been concealed behind heavy curtains, and which had probably originally been a study or a den but which had been transformed into a computer games room. Or, more accurately, what looked like a computer games room.

Three identical large wood and metal desks had been positioned side by side and touching in the centre of the room. On each was a keyboard, a trackball and a forty-inch flat panel monitor bolted to a kind of frame and being fed by a high specification desktop tower unit. The screens had been arranged in a gentle curve so that a person sitting in any of the black leather chairs behind the desks could easily see everything displayed on all three screens. There were three seats and keyboards primarily to provide redundancy in case one of the computers went down, but also because Sadir intended to be occupying the third seat when the plan came to fruition.

The central workstation differed from the other two in that it was also equipped with a clearly expensive high-end flight simulator yoke control column, rudder pedals, throttle quadrant assembly and a separate modular instrument panel below the flat panel monitor. In that were a compass, altimeter, VSI – vertical speed indicator – and other standard aircraft instruments, clearly making that position the 'hot seat' of the system. The set-up looked like the kind of flight simulator a professional pilot might create in his home to use as both an entertainment console and to help maintain his flying skills.

'Are you ready?' Sadir asked simply. 'In all respects, I mean?'

Both men in front of him nodded, and the taller of the two – Sadir knew him only as 'Michael' because real names were never a good idea in the kind of operation he was involved in – replied.

'We are. We have taken control of the last three flights and altered the course by a few degrees.'

'We only deviated them enough that the pilot would assume it was just the action of the wind,' the other man – Joseph – added. 'Then we immediately severed our connection. They have no idea we are on the frequency. If they notice anything at all, they'll probably assume that because they're using both C-band and Ku-band data links – obviously in the training environment they have to be familiar with both and practise using the two methods of control – there's a brief mismatch between the two of them.'

Both men were remarkably similar in appearance, with almost identical facial features, both clean-shaven and with thick black hair, and even tended to dress in much the same way. Their difference in height, a matter of only two or three inches, was all that Sadir had to distinguish between them.

'What about the routes and the payloads?' Sadir asked.

Michael nodded. 'So far, the information supplied by your contact at the base has been completely accurate in terms of the timing and duration of the flights and their configuration. Sometimes they just do surveillance and at other times they operate on various ranges and inside danger areas, exactly as your source predicted. I presume he has access to the training schedule.'

In fact, the person Michael referred to as Sadir's 'contact' was rather more than just somebody who could glance at a training schedule and then pass on the relevant information. Major Sammy Dawood was an American-born Muslim – his first name was actually spelt 'Sami,' the Arabic word meaning exalted or sublime, but because he both looked and sounded American people automatically assumed it was 'Sammy' – and identifying and recruiting him to the cause had taken Sadir well over a year. That had been one of the first and most important tasks he'd needed to complete once the plan had been finalised.

He'd told two of the hackers he'd recruited in America to begin trawling Islamic websites and social media looking for anybody in any branch of the American military who seemed to be expressing an interest in the activities of ISIS and other radical Islamic groups. What had surprised Sadir was how many people this search had produced. Some could be rejected immediately, for one reason or another, but he'd ended up with a hard core of almost a dozen potential recruits scattered across the continental United States which he had begun cultivating.

From this group, three men had seemed to fit the bill, though one of them was in a branch of the American military machine that Sadir knew almost nothing about – the Air National Guard – and which he had erroneously assumed was some kind of reserve force of ex-military non-combatants using obsolete equipment. When he discovered the reality of the situation, and more importantly about a year earlier had found out that Major Sami Dawood's next posting was to the 174th Attack Wing of the New York Air National Guard, based at Hancock Field at Syracuse, Sadir had concentrated all his efforts on his recruitment and radicalisation.

The process had been lengthy and subtle, beginning with just the occasional exchanged comment about the dislike of Muslims shown by some Americans, and had then escalated through discussions about racist and anti-Islamic treatment being meted out to Muslims in various parts of the Middle East, and had ended with apparently authoritative statements made by an imam about the duty of all Muslims to attack their common enemy, and most specifically about the *jihad*, the holy war against the Great Satan.

Once Dawood had clearly and enthusiastically accepted this premise, the next step was to directly recruit him as an essential part of Sadir's religiously sanctioned operation to visit death and destruction upon Americans in their homeland, in exactly the same way that American soldiers and airmen had rained down mortars and bombs and missiles upon the people of Iraq and Iran, and on the fearless freedom fighters of the Islamic State and ISIS.

In fact, Dawood was the lynchpin of this, the most important single part of the operation, because he was a senior training officer in the team responsible for planning the flight schedule out of Hancock and, crucially, one of his duties was to specify the payload for each mission, which was why Sadir knew exactly what was going to be carried aloft a few hours before he would launch the attack on DC.

A little over two hours later, having thoroughly inspected the equipment, gone over the plan one more time and obtained from both Michael and Joseph the answers he had expected to the questions he had asked, Sadir got back into his Honda for the return drive to Washington.

This, the final component, was in place and ready to be activated on his command. But there were still two other pieces of the overall plan he would need to check. All three different aspects of the attack were separate but complementary, and for the matter to reach the ideal conclusion, all needed to function faultlessly. His next job was to confirm that the weapons they would position within DC itself were also fully prepared, checked and ready to deploy.

Chapter 27

'You don't know me,' the female and clearly English voice in the speaker of Ben Morgan's mobile phone said, 'but we have a mutual friend. Or possibly a mutual friend of a mutual friend.'

'We have?' Morgan replied, his voice sounding somewhat groggy even to his own ears. He'd overslept that morning and had had trouble getting to sleep the night before because he was getting into a different bed in a different city in a different country, and more importantly in a different time zone, to the one that his body clock assumed he was still occupying.

'Are you drunk?' the woman demanded. 'It's not even ten in the morning.'

'No,' Morgan replied, waking up rapidly. 'I flew in last night. I've had about four hours' sleep and I deliberately didn't set an alarm. Your phone call woke me up.'

'Sorry about that,' the voice said, with no particular evidence of sincerity.

'So who are you, and what do you want?'

'First, let me just make sure I'm talking to the right person. I've been given your mobile number, but can you just tell me your name?'

'Ben Morgan. So who gave you my number?'

'Good. I got it from Assistant Chief Constable Richard Boston. You may not know him, but you do know Ian Mitchell. My name's Barbara Simpson. I'm over here in the Wild West as part of a low-level surveillance operation and I need to talk to somebody outside the investigation who knows about cyber and all that crap. Your name popped up at the top of the list. So where and when do you want to meet?'

'Hang on a minute,' Morgan replied. 'I'm not even awake yet. I need to shower and get dressed and then pour some coffee down my throat before I'm even halfway back to being human.'

Morgan was even more confused. What he had assumed was a covert operation involving only him and Natasha Black apparently also involved other people from the eastern side of the Pond. Maybe there was a full UK team on site and all sorts of cogs turning that somebody had decided he had no need to know about.

'I'll make a deal with you. Stop fannying about. Get up, wash the important bits and get dressed and I'll buy you breakfast. Where are you staying?'

A couple of minutes later, Morgan dropped the phone on the bed and pulled himself out of it, still slightly shell-shocked and feeling steamrollered. Barbara Simpson sounded less like a human being and more like an unstoppable force of nature. She'd known exactly where his hotel was located and had told Morgan to meet her in a coffee shop about a block away. He needed to get moving, and quickly, if he was going to make the rendezvous at the time she'd specified.

He headed for the door of the en-suite bathroom then stopped and walked back to the bed. He glanced at his watch then picked up his mobile phone and dialled Ian Mitchell's number back in the UK. Ten thirty Eastern Standard Time meant it was three thirty in the afternoon in London, so Mitchell would certainly be awake and working.

'Do you know a woman called Barbara Simpson?' Morgan asked when his call was connected and they'd exchanged the usual pleasantries.

'I don't know her so much as know of her,' Mitchell replied, 'and I met her exactly once. Why? And where are you?'

'Washington, as in DC rather than Tyne and Wear. She's just called me to arrange a meeting and I know the square root of sod all about who she is or why she wants to talk to me. Is she legit?'

'Definitely. She's a police superintendent who specialises in under-cover work. I ran into her at a briefing here in London about five or six months ago. I gathered she was about to be sent off on some secret squirrel activity, probably in America, but that part of the briefing didn't involve me so I don't know for sure. But if she's in Washington and so are you, it's a fair guess that the faeces are about to impact the air-conditioning system, to coin a phrase. She said – several times, in fact – that she knew nothing at all about cyber, so if she wants to talk to you she's probably run up against something computery that she doesn't understand. But she is kosher.'

'Anything else I need to know about her?'

Morgan heard Mitchell's chuckle from three and a half thousand miles away.

'Oh, yeah. Don't call her a person of colour or try any of that PC crap on her or she'll bite your head off: she told me she's black and proud of it. Her nickname in the Met is "The Nutcracker" because that's slightly more polite than "ball breaker", and that should give you some idea about her personality. And don't for God's sake mention drugs to her. She'll bore the arse off you for the next hour if you do. She hates drugs and she hates drug dealers and she's spent a good part of her working life down in Colombia trying to disrupt the drug trade. But she also thinks we should legalise the lot. To say she's conflicted doesn't really cover it.'

'Thanks,' Morgan said, ended the call and resumed his journey to the bathroom.

–

He stepped into the coffee shop only three minutes late and stood for a moment just inside the doorway looking round. He could see three black women, one by herself in a booth at the back and the other two sitting at tables, all of them alone. But the question of which one was Barbara Simpson was quickly resolved when the woman in the booth stopped looking at her watch, pointed at him, crooked her finger and then gestured at the seat opposite her.

'You'd better be Ben Morgan,' she said as he sat down, 'otherwise you're going to feel a massive spike of pain in your groin, which will be the heel of my shoe crushing your testicles, after which I'll scream rape and run out.'

'I am Ben Morgan, and I'd really appreciate it if you left my wedding tackle alone. Are you going to do me serious bodily harm if I order a coffee?'

Simpson grinned at him and slid a plastic covered menu across the table towards him.

'Good morning, Ben. A deal's a deal. I said I'd buy you breakfast, so why don't you whistle up a waitress, order what you want and get some coffee down your throat. Then we need to talk.'

One of the waitresses cruised by at that moment, poured coffee into the cup that was already on the table and wrote down what Morgan wanted to eat, which was basically an Americanised version of a full English – bacon, sausage, eggs over easy, whatever that meant, and hash browns – then disappeared in the direction of the kitchen.

'How did you know it was me?' Morgan asked, adding milk to his cup and taking a sip.

'I guessed. No new customers had walked in here for the last ten minutes, which is when I arrived, and then you pitched up, a single white male, bit geeky, looking lost and three minutes late. It wasn't particularly difficult to identify you.'

Morgan's breakfast arrived much sooner than he had expected, but America was, after all, the home of fast food, which didn't necessarily just mean burgers and fries. It was hot, tasty and well cooked, and certainly filled the gap left by him not eating dinner the previous evening.

'Finish that,' Simpson ordered, pointing at his plate. 'Then we can talk.'

'So how can I help you?' Morgan asked about five minutes later, cutting the last piece of spicy sausage in half and popping a piece of it into his mouth.

'Do you know why I'm here? In America, I mean, not in this particular coffee shop?'

'I talked to Ian Mitchell,' Morgan replied, glancing around, 'and I gather you're a senior British police officer and you're probably doing something undercover over here. But that's the limit of my knowledge.'

Simpson nodded. 'That's it in a nutshell, yes,' she replied. 'My services, such as they are, were requested by the Americans, specifically by the Feds, because I'm a complete outsider and all the alphabet soup three-digit agencies over here are worried about penetration by people who might have been radicalised. And, more significantly, about the threat of some possible unspecified terrorist attack possibly being planned by a group of possible radical Islamists. There have been whispers in the ether, all kinds of mutterings picked up by low-level informers, but not much in the way of solid information. All possibles but no probables or certainties. My job has been to try to put some flesh on the bones. Either that, or to somehow prove that there is no such threat. I have a knack for spotting bad people hiding in plain sight.

'Now let me answer your obvious first question before you ask it. The Bureau gave me all the relevant information they had, all the whispers, so I knew who they suspected of being involved. That gave me somewhere to start. The reason they thought I might be a useful asset was because they guessed that if there was some terrorist plot being hatched, the people involved would be making sure they weren't observed or followed. And they believed that a black female street person, which is the way I usually dress when I do my surveillance, would be less likely to be spotted than a bunch of white guys in suits with lapel mics and bulges under their left armpits standing about on street corners. Or even the same white guys in casual clothes trying to blend in. My speciality, or specialism as the Americans persist in calling it, is becoming effectively invisible. Just another wino or dropout dressed in rags, wandering the streets or sitting in a doorway. The kind of person that everybody sees but nobody notices.'

Morgan stared across the table at the slim and smartly dressed woman looking at him. He found it difficult to imagine her wandering the streets in rags and begging for coins or drinks or other scraps – what the Americans called panhandling. But that, he supposed, was really the point.

'And is there a viable threat?' he asked.

Just as Morgan had done a couple of minutes earlier, Simpson also glanced round the coffee shop before she replied. 'Yes, there is,' she said, looking troubled. 'At least, I think so.'

As Morgan slid his empty plate to one side, Simpson leaned forward and explained what she'd found. Or thought she'd found.

Grant Rogers, her FBI handler, for want of a better word, had kept her supplied with encrypted thumb drives containing the take from dozens of different data sources, including extracts of passenger flight arrivals at all the major airports from New York down to Charlotte and west as far out as Indianapolis and Detroit. This data catchment initiative was based on two slightly shaky assumptions: first, that any terrorists planning an atrocity in DC wouldn't be home-grown and radicalised in America but would be travelling from the Middle East, so all arrivals with Arabic names or passports issued by any of the countries in that region were being backtracked through airline records to their point of origin to check on their entire route. The second assumption was that if the target was DC itself, the terrorists might try to throw the authorities off the scent by flying to a different destination and then travelling on to Washington by train or car, hence the huge catchment area for the collection of data.

'I figured this was probably a total waste of time and resources,' Simpson admitted, 'but then I noticed something that seemed a bit odd. Not in the current data set, but in one of the historical blocks going back almost three years. Unless you're travelling with somebody you never know who's going to be on an aircraft with you, obviously, and unless you're talking about a popular route with several stops you're unlikely to find the same people on a number of successive flights. I'm quite good at making connections and seeing links that aren't obvious, and I noticed something that didn't really make sense. Or perhaps did make sense, but only in one particular context.

'Just under three years ago, a passenger with an obviously Arabic name and holding a passport issued in Iraq – a genuine passport, as far as I could tell, as it had been scanned at various airports – flew into Baltimore. Nothing unusual about that, obviously. Also on the flight were two Chinese males travelling on PRC passports. Again, so what?

The anomaly was that when the analysts in the Bureau backtracked the Arab's routes over the last few years they didn't make a lot of sense. He'd hopped all round Europe and the Middle East, and even made three flights to Saint Petersburg. 'But what I found interesting was that the one place where he'd stayed for the longest periods of time was Beijing. I also backtracked further. I went back eight years in fact, and I found that the first flight he'd ever made using that passport was from Riyadh to Beijing, but not direct: he made a few stops in Europe first. Again, perhaps a little unusual but not suspicious.

'The real anomaly was that when he flew out of China the last time, three years ago, the same two Chinese males who were on his flight into Baltimore were on the same aircraft. And they were also on all the connecting flights he took in Europe.'

Simpson checked that Morgan was still paying attention, which he was.

'I marked the Arab down as a person of interest to the Fibbies, but he seemed to drop off the radar almost as soon as he landed here. I didn't make a big thing of it because I couldn't find out what he was up to and he was just another name on a very long list. He's popped up a few more times, flying into or out of America, but what he does while he's here we don't know. And the two Chinese males also effectively vanished from sight soon after they arrived. They don't appear to have credit cards or driving licences or any other documentation we could use to track them and nobody seems to know where they are or what they're doing.

'Now, I didn't want to look like a paranoid idiot because I was worried about where a couple of Chinese nationals had got to, so I bypassed the FBI and contacted my boss in the Met. I asked him to try to run a check on them through Five and Six, just in case either of them had ever popped up on their radars. I don't know the source of the data, but Six came back with the information that both men were – and as a matter of fact the man my boss spoke to at Six believes they still are – serving officers in the Chinese People's Liberation Army. And before they climbed onto the aircraft in Beijing to leave the country they were based at Tonggang Road in Pudong on the east side of Shanghai. Does any of that mean anything to you?'

Morgan nodded. 'Definitely. If they were PLA at Pudong that means they were almost certainly serving in Unit 61398. Some people call that the Comment Crew or Byzantine Candor or Threat Group 8223, but whatever name you use, it's one of the most persistent and dangerous cyberattack and hacking units in the PLA. And that does raise an obvious question.'

'Exactly,' Simpson replied. 'Cyber isn't my thing, but I do know that to launch a cyberattack you don't have to be located in the target country. In fact, it's much better if you're somewhere else, somewhere a long way away. So why would they have flown all the way to America?'

Morgan nodded. 'The only reason that makes any sense, assuming that they didn't just pop over to do an extended driving tour of the United States, paying cash for absolutely everything, which seems pretty unlikely, is that they're here to do something that requires their physical presence. And I can tell you that I have no idea what that could possibly be, but I certainly don't like the sound of it.'

Chapter 28

Tysons, Virginia, United States of America

It was both the first meeting of all four of them and also the last, because the deadline was almost upon them. Previously Sadir had just met them on a one-to-one basis so he could explain what he wanted and expected them to do, or they'd communicated using burner phones.

They were meeting on the outside terrace of a popular coffee shop – Sadir knew the value of crowds and the importance of meeting in busy places – on the edge of a shopping mall not far from Greensboro Station in Tysons. The four men sitting around the circular table were casually dressed in jeans and open-necked shirts and appeared unremarkable, except perhaps for their similar dark hair, beards and tanned complexions. But most people probably wouldn't have given them a second glance: they looked just like four people taking a break from work and enjoying some coffee together in the sunshine.

In fact, the three men with Sadir were doing exactly that – taking a break – and had been summoned to that spot at that time by the Iraqi.

Two of them had baulked slightly at the idea of a face-to-face meeting, but Sadir had his reasons, and he was the man with both the plan and the money, so they turned up anyway. And almost the first thing Sadir did once they'd bought their coffee and sat down was to explain his reasoning.

'I know you might have preferred a virtual meeting,' he said, 'but I have a problem with that. If we can all log on to a virtual meeting, then so can other people and organisations, and you don't need me to tell you who I'm referring to. Or they can potentially listen in, anyway.

And if they were sitting there quietly on the Internet monitoring us, we would never have any idea that they were there. But here—' he gestured at the pavement around them '—we would immediately notice if anyone was paying us any attention. So here we can talk freely and securely.'

That sounded reasonable to the other three men, but in fact Sadir had another, and rather different, reason for not wanting to communicate over the Internet, something he would only ever do if there genuinely was no alternative. He was, and always had been, paranoid about the possibility of betrayal, and he didn't believe he could properly gauge a man's responses and reactions by watching the changes in his expression through the small and inadequate lens of a webcam. In the kind of discussions he was involved in, he wanted to be able to look at, listen to and even smell the man in front of him. That way, he knew he should be able to detect the slightest hint of deception in his voice or body language. And that was of crucial importance.

In fact, Sadir doubted if any of the men he had become associated with in America would do anything to betray him, not least because he had made it very clear what would happen to them if they did. They were all totally dedicated to the cause and had enthusiastically welcomed his initial contact, a couple of years earlier, as a validation of their beliefs. They had been told that one day somebody like Sadir would approach them, and they had all known what to do when that happened. But still, it never hurt to check.

'So where are you now, Karim?' he asked the man sitting opposite him. 'And be careful how you answer. No dates or proper names, nothing like that.'

Karim Ganem was the youngest of the four men, tall and slim, with delicate, almost feminine features and long black eyelashes. He had been approached by Sadir because he was a talented hacker and the leader of a group that called itself AnArchy Anonymous that had attacked numerous American government and corporate websites, causing damage and defacing the former and stealing data and commercial information from the latter.

'We have access to three of the locations, Abū Tadmir,' Ganem replied. 'We've created backdoors and we're checking each one at least once a week to ensure our points of access have not been detected or blocked. We're working on the newest site you specified but cracking that is taking longer than we expected. Of course, because they are all high-value sites we had always anticipated that we might encounter some difficulties.'

That was not good news for Sadir, because now they had so little time in hand. He thought for a few moments, then made a decision.

'The deadline is set and cannot be altered. Abandon that site and just ensure that your accesses to the other three aren't compromised.'

Half an hour later, having received similar information, in vague and non-specific language, from the other two men, each of whom had confirmed they had access to the targets he had given them, and discussed the operation, again in general and non-specific language, Sadir issued very specific orders for what they were to do and when they were to do it. Then they stood up, shook hands and walked off in different directions.

It was all, he reflected as he strolled along the street in the general direction of his hotel, coming together neatly and as he had hoped and expected. The men he had recruited were motivated primarily by ideology – just as he was – but the essentially unlimited funds at his disposal meant he could cut corners and purchase equipment like fast, high specification computers to facilitate the tasks they had to perform.

And now the culmination of what he had been planning for the better part of the last decade was only a matter of days away.

Chapter 29

Tysons, Virginia, United States of America

Just like the other three members of the group, Karim Ganem was supremely aware of his surroundings and the people near him as he constantly checked to make sure that he was not being followed. When he reached Greensboro Station, he was certain that he had not picked up a tail and that nobody was paying him anything more than the most casual attention, the same kind of attention anyone would give to a fellow pedestrian on the street.

But in this he was not entirely correct.

Evolution has taught human beings to look at eye level and below because that's where they'll see both predators and prey. Birds were not usually a threat, but bears and sabre-toothed tigers certainly were, so early man naturally concentrated on looking in the most likely threat direction. Millions of years of evolution only reinforced the message and today people rarely look higher than their own eye-line unless there's some object in that area which draws their attention. Or if there's movement, of course. The human eye is particularly well adapted to detecting moving objects, a trait again reinforced by countless millennia of evolution.

Sadir had been right in his belief that they would notice anybody around them paying any special attention, but his belief that they could talk freely at the cafe was badly flawed, because in this case the threat was not anywhere around the table where they had been sitting, but above them and well outside their immediate vicinity.

The FBI team tasked with the surveillance of Karim Ganem had been aware from their initial surveillance of him almost three months earlier that he was always conscious of his surroundings and people in his vicinity.

The Bureau had started taking an interest in the man's activities following a tip-off from the English policewoman Barbara Simpson who, in the process of investigating some of the low-level tips received by the FBI, had got close enough to Ganem in her normal street persona of a penniless vagrant, the kind of person that people saw but didn't notice, to overhear part of a conversation he'd been carrying out on a mobile phone. What she'd heard – references to a sponsored hacking project as part of a much larger and more destructive operation – had been enough for her to convince Grant Rogers to elevate Ganem's status to that of a person of interest. That status and level of surveillance meant that a tap had been placed on his landline, which turned out to be a waste of effort because the target never made or received calls on it.

After several weeks Rogers had begun to have his doubts, because Ganem didn't appear to be involved in any kind of criminal activity, or indeed much activity at all. He spent most of his time in his apartment working on his computer. The techies at the FBI were able to confirm that he had a broadband connection, but as he invariably used a virtual private network, a VPN, whenever he was online they were unable to see what exactly he was doing. All they could establish was that his connection showed data being uploaded and downloaded, just the same as they would expect to see from anybody using the Internet. But they had no idea *what* was being uploaded or downloaded.

The Bureau had been able to get a bug into his apartment by going through the floor of the flat above and positioning the microphone within the structure of the ceiling of Ganem's flat. As a security precaution and also to conserve its battery life, the mic was only switched on when a hidden camera mounted in the hallway on that floor of the building showed that the target was in the flat, and only then after at least an hour had passed, just in case he used some kind of bug detector as a precaution when he returned home. Deactivating the microphone wouldn't prevent a sophisticated detector from locating it, but that technique would be enough to defeat most of the commercial devices on the market.

Simply getting authorisation to position that single microphone had taken longer and required far more form-filling at the Bureau than Rogers had hoped or expected, and he'd realised that trying to obtain permission to conduct video surveillance inside the apartment was unlikely to be granted: they simply hadn't got enough information – or even credible suspicions – to justify it. So they could hear him, but not see him.

Rogers had almost been ready to pull the plug on Ganem's surveillance, until the take from the microphone suggested he was heading out for a meeting, something he hadn't done since the start of the surveillance. All his previous forays out of the apartment had been purely domestic, mainly shopping and visits to one of a handful of restaurants in the area that served Middle Eastern food.

But that morning the target had received a call on his unregistered mobile phone that, from the sound of his responses – because of course they could only hear his side of the conversation – he had been waiting for. Ganem had agreed the time without any apparent attempt to disguise what he was saying and had obligingly repeated it twice so that the microphone was able to pick it up clearly.

But just in case when he'd said 'ten thirty' that was actually code for a quarter to one or half past five or some other time that day, or even a different time on a different day, Rogers had immediately prepped and briefed the team ready to go. He'd positioned one agent with a pair of powerful binoculars, a mobile phone and a two-way radio in a high-rise on the opposite side of the street from Ganem's apartment with orders to make the call the moment the target started doing anything that suggested he was about to leave the building.

But because they had known of the target's preternatural awareness of his surroundings, they weren't going to follow him from his apartment building. Instead, they identified the choke points, the places he would have to pass once he'd left the building, irrespective of where he was going, and positioned a watcher at each of them.

The FBI agent covering the building had used the radio at ten minutes to ten to alert the team that the target was on the move. Then he'd taken the elevator down to street level and walked out onto the pavement at virtually the same moment that Ganem had appeared opposite him. The target had walked down the street and the agent had immediately turned in the opposite direction to head away from him, at the same time again using his radio to warn his team which way Ganem was walking.

As the target had passed the first choke point, the closest watcher had called in the sighting using his mobile phone, which allowed other personnel to re-position to get ahead of him. Using this kind of leapfrog technique they had shadowed him as far as the Metro station. Then they'd risked sending a watcher after him to confirm the direction he was heading and to stay on the train until Ganem got off it, and at the same time they sent a car and a van along the Metro's route to pick him up again when he disembarked. It wasn't the most secure surveillance tactic because it depended on the level of traffic and the speed the vehicles could maintain, but Grant Rogers, as the man running the surveillance operation, had decided he would rather risk losing sight of Ganem than risk the target realising he was being watched.

And in the event, it had worked.

When the target had walked out of Greensboro Station, the car and van were already in position, close enough to positively identify Ganem as he had emerged. Once they were sure of his destination, the men in the van – which was signwritten with the name of a general building company but with a phone number that would be answered by another team member at the J. Edgar Hoover Building on Pennsylvania Avenue should anyone wish to have some construction work done – had swiftly grabbed tool boxes, pulled on white overalls and made their way into the shopping mall.

A very brief discussion with the mall manager, which had mainly involved Grant Rogers telling the bemused man what was about to happen and why he should keep his mouth shut about it, had been followed by the team being given access to the flat roof of the building. They'd made their way up a set of service stairs and across the roof to a position about thirty feet from the coffee shop where Ganem had taken a seat at an outside table and had begun 'inspecting' one of the air-conditioning units mounted on the roof. The mall was only single-storey and an appearance of work was important as they could be seen from the adjacent car park.

One of the pieces of equipment they deployed was a long black tube about the thickness of a broom handle that they mounted near the edge of the roof so that the end of it was pointed at the table occupied by Ganem and the other three men who had appeared at about the same time as the target. This directional microphone, commonly known as a shotgun mic, was intended to record what the four men said and was attached to a small battery-powered digital recorder. Accurate positioning was vital, and one of the agents connected an earpiece to the recorder and minutely adjusted the position of the device until he could hear their voices. Then he had left the mic in place and stepped away from it.

Some seventy yards away in the parking lot opposite, two other FBI agents had stopped their car to use an almost identical mic and recorder, aiming it at their target. The number of pedestrians moving around between them and the coffee shop made it unlikely that they would record much useful conversation, but a belt and braces approach was usually advised in such circumstances. The other thing one of these agents did was to use a Nikon digital camera fitted with variable-power telephoto lens to obtain clear pictures of each of the four men at the table. They needed decent photographs to identify them.

While all this was going on, orders were issued by Rogers for three men to follow each of the unknown contacts when the meeting broke up. He didn't want to risk using larger teams than that because it was important to make sure the targets didn't know they were under surveillance. In the meantime, the images obtained by the agent, known as 'probe photos' because they had been obtained during a current and open FBI investigation, were emailed direct from the surveillance vehicle to FBI headquarters and then forwarded for analysis by FACE.

FACE is the Facial Analysis, Comparison and Evaluation Services Unit, based in the Criminal Justice Information Services Division at Clarksburg, West Virginia, and uses facial recognition technology and software to try to match such surveillance-derived images with pictures already on file with the FBI and with state and other federal databases.

When the meeting broke up it was late morning and both foot and vehicular traffic had increased and, perhaps not surprisingly, all three of the surveillance teams, forced by their orders to keep some distance from and behind their targets, had eventually lost contact with the unidentified men in the crowds albeit, in one case, under slightly peculiar circumstances.

But Grant Rogers still considered the operation a success. They now had photographs of three more of the people within Karim Ganem's circle of acquaintances – or possibly conspirators – and with any luck the recordings of the conversation might produce names for the new faces as well as shed more light on what they were up to.

Because at that moment, the FBI still had no idea why Ganem was in America or what he was trying to do. They only knew that he was a person of interest, and that had been enough to spark the surveillance.

Chapter 30

Washington D.C., United States of America

Hacking is in many ways more of an art than a science, as each company or organisation that is the subject of an attack will offer different challenges. Of course, there are pieces of software that will allow the attacker to do things like check for open ports or run brute force attacks to try to crack passwords, but very often it's the hacker's intuition that leads to the discovery of a chink in the electronic armour, a chink that can then be levered wide open.

But it is also a fact that only in about five per cent of attacks do the successful hackers manage to breach the security systems of a website from the outside solely using different kinds of attack and hacking tools. In the other roughly ninety-five per cent they have help through inadvertent human error, most commonly by people simply not obeying the rules. For example, by users not changing their passwords regularly, by not having strong enough passwords in the first place or by using the same password on different sites, or through arrogance or stupidity.

Hackers targeting a particular company or organisation won't usually waste their time trying to suborn a paid employee because that would be unlikely to work, job security and a regular pay cheque being far more attractive than an extremely dodgy one-off payment, and any such approach would very probably result in increased security being applied to the website. Instead, they'll approach the contract workers on minimum wage, the cleaners, the guards and night watchmen, and ask them to photograph things like post-it notes stuck on the screen of a computer, cards bearing apparently random characters left in unlocked drawers, all that kind of thing, and quite often they will strike gold and identify both a username and password.

Karim Ganem and his fellow hackers in AnArchy Anonymous didn't usually even bother with that sort of messing about, because it was too hit and miss and there was always a chance that the cleaner or whoever they approached would have an unexpected streak of loyalty to the company and report what had happened to a security officer or even to the police, and that would lead to potentially unwelcome consequences. Instead, working with other members of his hacking group, he had devised a fairly simple and virtually foolproof way of achieving exactly the same result, of gaining access to protected company websites through their unwitting employees.

What he relied upon could best be described as a combination of technological snobbery and almost juvenile showiness. He had realised that it was almost a given that the most senior employees of any major company would invariably either be provided with the very latest, fastest and thinnest laptops around and the newest and flashiest mobile phones, or they would purchase the same items for themselves.

Ganem wasn't interested in the laptops, but he knew that the mobile phones could offer a way of getting inside even the most heavily protected computer network. Even if the only call a senior company executive was likely to receive on his mobile at a breakfast meeting was a complaint from his wife about something he had done or equally possibly had failed to do, it was still important to people like that to be seen to be using the very latest mobile when he placed it on the table beside his plate and coffee cup.

And in this Ganem was also helped by the target companies them-selves, which often used publicly available corporate documentation to list the names of their senior executives and other people likely to have seats on the main board, or who would at least be in a position to make decisions. The movers and shakers of the organisation, in other words. Who also, by definition, would be more likely to have much more wide-ranging access to the company website than a normal coalface worker.

So Ganem had decided on a two-pronged approach. Working from readily available information, he would compile a list of the full names of every senior member of the target company that he could identify. Then, using inside sources he had cultivated at the biggest couple of telecommunication companies in America, he would cross-reference the names he had obtained with their customer records. That usually produced several pages of names with linked cell phone numbers, and that was all he had needed to begin his attack.

Using a burner phone to ensure that his message would be untraceable, he would send a very brief piece of text – an SMS – to each number he had identified. It was simple, to the point and most importantly was exactly the kind of message that most businessmen would receive on a daily basis and that would not arouse their suspicions. A typical text would read something like: 'I've got an idea I need to run past you. James.'

The four commonest first names for male children in America are, in order, James, John, Robert and Michael, with William bringing up a distant fifth, and Ganem guessed that almost every recipient of the message would know a 'James' somewhere in their organisation. No doubt some slightly confused conversations would follow within the company when a 'James' would be contacted by a fellow executive and would have not the slightest idea what they were talking about. But that would probably be mentally written off as a misunderstanding and dismissed as unimportant.

In fact the content of the message was the least important part of the entire process. The simple act of opening the message to read the text was all that was required for the breach to be created. That activated a small piece of software that was immediately transferred to the target phone. That software was designed to do three things. First, it remained entirely hidden and covert to avoid being detected by any antivirus program. These worked primarily on virus signatures, by identifying recognisable lines of coding, and Ganem had been careful to ensure that no part of the code he had written resembled any known virus that he was aware of.

Second, almost everybody these days either uses their mobile to handle their emails, or at the very least they have a duplicate mail program running on their mobile so that if they are away from their desk they can still check their messages. So the tiny program was set up to identify and then access their email account, using an algorithm to record the target's email address or addresses – business and private – and crack the password. And, third, once the software had done its job, it then created its own SMS which contained only the relevant email addresses and password in plaintext, and which it sent to Ganem's burner.

This was not a technique that he had developed himself. The basic concept was well over a decade old and had most notoriously been used in 2010 by Chinese government-sponsored hackers who successfully forced their way into Google. This was one of several hacking techniques commonly referred to as brute force attacks, and was both comparatively simple to mount and offered a high probability of success.

The final stage in the operation had been for Ganem to create a suitable internal email, the kind of routine message that every company employee would receive on a daily basis. Many of these were what might be termed housekeeping messages, reminding employees that deep cleaning was scheduled to take place in a particular part of the building or that the parking spaces in the garage were going to be repainted or that the air-conditioning might need to be taken offline to allow it to be serviced. They were the kind of messages that people read and instantly forgot, which was really the point. They were also the kind of messages that employees always opened to read, just in case they were affected by something going on in the company, and also because if they didn't open them they would remain in their email inbox marked as unread.

For each of the target companies, Ganem tailored a different internal email which shared only a single characteristic: each message contained a brief piece of text and an attachment, something that was innocuous, like a not very important survey form about some aspect of the business, or a notification that the company had been entered for some kind of an industry award, or a flyer relating to something an employee was planning to do. Ganem had gone for forgettable but worth reading.

And, again, it wasn't the contents of the attachment that mattered but the left click of the mouse when the executive opened it. As they were then already logged on to the company intranet, another small piece of code that Ganem had created extracted their username from the system along with their password. And as soon that had been completed, his software created an invisible email that would send these details directly to him.

As soon as he had this information to hand, he could log in to the company's intranet pretending to be a particular executive, and once he was inside he could do whatever that executive could do, which could be everything from simply scanning the person's emails and the company website to creating a backdoor to allow him unrestricted low-level access to bypass the normal system security checks.

Obviously not every executive opened his phishing SMS message or the email or the attachment, but enough did to ensure that he was usually successful. The only real variable was how long it took.

The one thing that had puzzled Ganem about the operation was that once he had managed to breach the security systems of one of the target organisations, Sadir had given him very specific instructions that didn't really make sense. In Ganem's experience, once he – or any other hacker he'd spoken to, for that matter – had gained access to an intranet he would always begin looking for information that was saleable on the Dark Web, things like customer names and addresses, credit card details and other financial information. Or alternatively he would create damage of some kind by defacing the site with changed images and altered messages, that kind of thing.

But the Iraqi had told him to navigate to the various system control modules on the intranet and then to begin detailed searches looking for control circuits linked to very specific components. Once he had identified them, he was to analyse the language used to control them and prepare sets of alternate instructions, as specified in detail by Sadir, and hold them ready to implement. Ganem thought he could see the thrust of the Iraqi's plan, what he was trying to achieve, but what he still didn't understand was why.

When he got back to his studio flat early that afternoon, he used his VPN, the virtual private network that he'd found to be both reliable and secure, to access one of the anonymous web-based email addresses that he used for his hacking activities and discovered that his small program had identified a further five sets of log-in details from one of the three companies that Sadir wanted him to attack.

And that was good news, because it meant he had another five ways to access that particular company website. And that, perhaps, meant that they were one step closer to achieving their goal. Whatever it was.

Chapter 31

J. Edgar Hoover Building, Pennsylvania Avenue, Washington D.C., United States of America

'You can't arrest a man for sitting at a cafe and drinking a cup of coffee. Nor for associating with three other men you don't happen to like the look of. It'd make our lives a whole lot easier if we could, but we can't. We're stuck with due process and probable cause and all the rest of that crap.'

It was early afternoon and the debrief was going more or less as Grant Rogers had expected.

The FBI attracts people who want to make a difference to American society, a bigger difference than they could make if they became police officers, and they regard themselves as members of one of the most elite of American law enforcement organisations. Some of them also tend to regard the law as having a certain degree of flexibility when in pursuit of criminals or suspected criminals, their view being that the end in many such cases is more than sufficient to justify the means.

Grant Rogers didn't agree with this attitude, mainly because as the agent in charge of the operation he would be signing off on the case and everything he and every member of his team did would be scrutinised, checked and double-checked by the desk-bound upper hierarchy of the Bureau, the seat-shiners. If any corners were cut or the correct procedures not followed Rogers, as the ASAC, the assistant special agent in charge, would be the one facing a disciplinary hearing. And although he had been told that the operation had to remain entirely covert, he was personally convinced that putting a little pressure on the subjects might actually be a good idea. If a target knows he's attracted the attention of the authorities, he might start making mistakes or do something stupid. But of course he couldn't say that.

Dave Nicholls, one of the more junior agents assigned to the operation, had just echoed Rogers's own private views about the surveillance operation that morning.

'I didn't say we should arrest them,' Nicholls protested, his Texas drawl making him sound like a frontiersman though he looked more like a sharp-suited accountant with somewhat pointed features clustered below a thatch of neatly cut black hair. 'All I said was let's lean on them a little. Let them see the same guy maybe two or three times the same day, that sort of thing. Nothing close up and personal, just enough to spook them a bit, make them jump at shadows.'

Rogers shook his head.

'Can't do that right now,' he said, 'because these guys haven't done anything wrong. About all we can do is take a look at the transcription of whatever the shotgun mics managed to pick up and see if FACE was able to put any names to the three unsubs sitting with the target.'

The operations room they were using had the usual suite of electronic equipment including multiple computers, projection screens, whiteboards, telephones and so on, and Rogers guessed that if any of the three unknown subjects had had their photographs taken for any official purpose while in America, he would have their names within an hour or so. Transcribing the microphone recordings would obviously take a lot longer because of the circumstances.

They had access to voice recognition software that could convert clear speech into a piece of printable text quickly and fairly accurately, but the determining factor was the word 'clear'. A person in a quiet room speaking into a microphone was one thing, but filtering out the extraneous noises like traffic, the comments from people walking past the cafe and all the other factors that would affect the clarity of the recordings they'd made that morning was going to take some time.

'There's something I want to say, Grant.' The speaker was a fair-haired middle-aged man wearing a dark blue suit and standing at the back of the room. William Clark was a very experienced agent and had been the leader of one of the three-man teams assigned to follow the unsubs. His normally cheerful face looked troubled, perhaps even perplexed.

'What is it, Bill?' Grant Rogers asked. 'And before you say anything, nobody blames you for losing the target. In those crowds it would have been amazing if you hadn't. And we have other leads we can follow.'

Clark shook his head.

'I wasn't going to apologise,' he said, 'but I do want to explain what happened, because it didn't make sense.'

'Go ahead.'

'We followed the target easily enough. Because of the pandemic, there are a lot less people out on the streets than usual. It's still crowded, of course, but the target was quite distinctive in his appearance: blue jeans, blue denim jacket and when he left the cafe he put on a light blue disposable face mask. All three of us were keeping pace with him about fifty yards back, but obviously well separated. I'm reasonably certain we hadn't been spotted, not least because all three of us were wearing face masks just like most of the other people on the streets, but he went into a department store, maybe just as a precaution to shake any tails he might have thought he'd picked up. I went in after him and Nick and Ivan covered the other exits. He headed for the lavatories and I decided it was too risky to follow him into such a small space in case he had seen me earlier on. So I found a place where I could see the lavatory door and waited for him to come out. The trouble was, he didn't.'

'What do you mean?' Rogers asked.

'Exactly what I said. The man I'd been following didn't come out, but three other men did. Obviously I checked all three of them very carefully, but none of them looked anything like the target. I used the camera in my phone to take a picture of each one – I can put the images up on the screen if you'd like to see them.'

'Finish the story first.'

'I gave him ten minutes, then went into the lavatory after him. All the stalls were empty and there was nobody else in the room.

There were also no exits apart from a small square window maybe eighteen inches on the side and about eight feet off the ground. It was closed, the glass had wire mesh running through it and the opening was protected by steel bars, so he certainly didn't go out that way.'

Grant Rogers stated the obvious.

'So he must have changed his appearance. Let's see the pictures you took.'

It took a couple of minutes for Clark to connect his mobile to the display system so that he could show the photographs.

'Just to remind you,' he said before he brought up the first image, 'the target has black hair and a black beard, brown eyes and a tanned complexion and he was wearing a denim jacket, blue jeans and a blue face mask. Now check these out.'

The first image showed a man wearing a casual jacket and trousers and with fair hair and fair skin who didn't look unlike Clark himself. He had a light blue face mask in his left hand that he was apparently about to put on.

'There's no way the target could have made himself look like this in about three minutes,' Clark said, 'and that was roughly how long between the target going into the lavatory and this guy coming out.'

The second photograph was of a heavily built white man, the crown of his skull shining in the overhead lights, flanked by the U-shape of his remaining hair and emphasised by the white face mask he was wearing. Again, simply the difference in body size and shape meant that this individual could not possibly have been the target.

'And now we have contestant number three,' Clark said, and all the men in the room leaned forward to look closely at the picture.

The third man was wearing an open-necked shirt and khaki shorts or trousers, the photograph only showing him from about the waist up. Physically, in terms of height, body shape and skin colour the unidentified male resembled the target, but unlike him this man had no mask and was obviously clean-shaven, while the person they had been following had had a black beard. He was wearing large framed tinted glasses and a black beanie cap that covered his entire scalp.

'I don't want to sound like a cracked record,' Clark said, 'but you can't easily go from a full beard to clean-shaven in under five minutes.

And, in any case, I checked the lavatory when I got in there and there was no sign of any hair on the floor or in the sinks and there wasn't enough time for him to shave and flush away the hairs.' He stepped across the briefing room and pointed at the image on the screen for emphasis. 'So that has to be the target that we're looking at, but I've no idea how he did it.'

For a few moments nobody said a word, and then Rogers started to ask the question that every other agent had already formulated in his head.

'So it was probably a fake—'

But Clark immediately shook his head.

'I had eyes on him for over an hour at the cafe and as far as I could tell his beard was the real thing. Fake beards move differently to the real thing when people are talking. And don't forget that all four of the targets have beards. In a lot of countries in the Middle East it's a kind of cultural necessity.'

'Leave the picture on the screen,' Grant said as Clark reached for his mobile phone. He stepped right in front of the screen and stared in silence at the photograph in front of him.

'A couple of questions,' he said, glancing at Clark. 'First, was he carrying anything when he left the cafe?'

'Nothing.'

'Second, was this man—' Rogers pointed at the screen '—carrying anything when you saw him? And were there any discarded clothes in the lavatory?'

Clark shook its head.

'That's three questions, not two,' he pointed out. 'There were no clothes in the lavatory, but he could have had a carrier bag or something in his hand that I wouldn't have seen from where I was standing.'

'Okay. Despite appearances, we have to be looking at the third man, so we'll put this image in the database as well. The change of clothes is fairly obvious. He was probably wearing those shorts or trousers under his jeans, and he's just taken off his jacket, so my guess is when he walked out of the crapper he was carrying a bag with his jacket and jeans in it. How he lost the beard I don't know, but I'll get our photo analysts to take a closer look at this picture and see if they can come up with anything.'

'There's one other thing as well,' Clark added, 'but it's not something definite, more a kind of impression. There were four people sitting at that table in the cafe. We obviously already knew about Karim Ganem, though we still don't know what he's doing over here. So this afternoon we've seen three new faces.'

'Agreed. And your point is?' Rogers asked.

'As I said, it's just my impression, but I noticed that almost every time the more heavily built unsub said anything, the other three seemed to listen very carefully. And none of the other three ever interrupted him. I might be wrong, but that suggests to me that this man, whoever he is, could be the leader of the group. Maybe he's had Ganem and the others working on something for the past year or so and now he's come over to check on what they're doing.'

Rogers shrugged. 'I didn't notice that myself, Bill, but you were better placed to watch them than I was. I don't dispute what you've said and you've been around long enough that your impressions are usually on the money. And that's not necessarily good news.'

'It isn't? Why not?' Dave Nicholls asked.

'Because if Bill's right and this new player is the leader of the cell or whatever, that could mean that whatever they're planning is imminent. Maybe this guy isn't just here to check on their progress. Maybe he's here to kickstart the endgame. And in that case, the clock could already be running.'

A couple of minutes after Rogers had wrapped up the briefing an email arrived from Clarksburg, West Virginia, from the Criminal Justice Information Services Division with the results of the analysis by FACE.

The junior FBI agent sitting at the machine where it arrived glanced at it and immediately sent it to the high-speed laser printer on the console on one side of the room.

Rogers heard the laser starting to spool up and glanced across at the agent.

'That's the stuff from Clarksburg,' the man confirmed. He stood up, collected four sheets of paper from the output tray, handed them to Rogers and resumed his seat.

The senior agent looked at each sheet very briefly, then held up his hand for silence in the room.

'Okay, listen up, all of you,' he said. 'FACE has given us three new names and confirmed the identity of the guy we already knew about, Karim Ganem. The three new players are named Mahdi Sadir – he's the big guy – and the other men are named Talat Wasem and Jamal Halabi. Their photo IDs come from their driving licence applications. Get them and their pictures on the board and start running the usual background checks. I want to know everything about them, from their mobile numbers and addresses to the size of their dicks, by close of business today.'

Chapter 32

Washington D.C. and Damascus, Maryland, United States of America

Damascus is a fairly typical suburb of Washington, although it's actually in Maryland, about thirty miles north of Capitol Hill and with excellent road links. It's far enough out of Washington for the concrete forest of the capital to be replaced by trees and woods, and the town is closer to both Frederick and Baltimore than it is to Washington. By American standards, properties there are expensive, starting at around half a million dollars for anything of a reasonable size, entirely due to the town's location and proximity to Washington.

The problem that Sadir had faced when he'd been looking for a suitable location just over two years earlier was that he needed it to be no more than about an hour's drive, preferably a lot less, from Capitol Hill, and it had to be big enough and sufficiently secluded for the operation he had planned to be undetectable. He also needed either a workshop on the premises or a suitable building where the machinery he needed could be installed, which further limited his choice. And, again because anywhere that close to Washington was prime commuter belt, the houses in every other town he'd looked at had been similarly priced. Eventually, and after an exchange of somewhat testy emails with the sponsoring elders in Iraq, a detached house sitting on about an acre of ground on the northern outskirts of Damascus had been identified and then rented by a proxy, a long-term expatriate Iraqi well known to, and completely trusted by, the elders.

Sadir had taken possession of the property and handed the keys to the three men he had already recruited to carry out the work, made sure that they had all the tools, equipment and raw materials that they needed and left them to it. He'd kept in regular touch with them by email, both parties using draft emails and a web-based account to avoid compromise and detection, but with the deadline now approaching he knew he would have to visit the house in person once again to ensure that absolutely everything was as ready as it could be.

If they'd met a last-minute snag or problem that could delay completion of the weapons it was essential that Sadir knew about it so he could adjust the timetable accordingly.

That afternoon his Honda was on its usual floor in a multi-storey car park on 19th Street and not too far from his hotel, but Sadir certainly wasn't going to walk there and climb into it, because the operation was far too important for that. It was crucial that nobody had any idea of who he was or what he had planned until the moment when everybody would know because their world would be crumbling around them.

Instead, he followed his usual circuitous route to the car park, making his way in what amounted to a couple of rough circles using public transport, which meant several taxi rides and unnecessary visits to hotels and stores where he was able to enter through one door but leave through another. And because the traffic in Washington D.C. was always heavy, the streets were a virtual sea of red-painted cabs, making the task of anybody following him even more problematic.

The colour scheme – a uniform bright red bisected by a curved grey stripe running from the front wheel arch of each vehicle and tapering towards the rear wing, within which the name of the taxi company and its contact number were displayed in black lettering – had been introduced in 2013 by the DC Taxicab Commission to standardise the appearance of the cabs serving America's capital city. The taxis were nothing like as iconic as the ubiquitous yellow cabs that prowled the streets of New York in vast ill-tempered hunting packs, but at least it made identifying a taxi easy enough.

Twice when his chosen vehicle had come to a dead stop in the snarled-up traffic at yet another red light, Sadir had paid the driver what he owed and climbed out of the cab in the road. Then he'd waited on the sidewalk scanning the traffic to make sure that nobody else did the same thing, before finding another cab going in the opposite or at least in a different direction. To further confuse any possible surveillance, Sadir also took one of the Metrobus DC Circulator vehicles for a part of his journey.

The whole of his counter-surveillance checks took over an hour, as usual, and at the end of it he was left with a roughly quarter of a mile stroll to reach the parking garage from where he'd told the last taxi driver to drop him off. Even then, he didn't enter the building but stayed on the opposite side of the road and took a seat at one of the outside tables in the coffee shop almost directly opposite the multi-storey. The fact that there was a cafe with an uninterrupted view of the garage was one of the main reasons why Sadir had chosen that location.

He ordered and paid for a coffee and a pastry and took his mobile and a novel from his pockets. For the next twenty minutes he watched the exit from the multi-storey without at any time appearing to look directly at it, not least because he was more interested in anybody who might be waiting on either side of the street than anyone driving out of the building.

But he saw nobody who raised his suspicions and finally decided that it was safe for him to move. He waited for a gap in the traffic, crossed the road and walked inside the building, but took the stairs rather than the lift as a final check that he was still not being followed. He did a complete circuit of the level where his Honda was parked before approaching the vehicle.

Even then he was cautious. He was very aware that motor vehicles of all sorts had enormous potential as killing machines – the forces of radical Islam had frequently made extensive and lethal use of truck bombs driven by dedicated *shahids* and more recently trucks and large vans had been used to mow down crowds of pedestrians in London and France – but he was more concerned with the possibility that his car might have been targeted with explosive charges if the American authorities had discovered what he was up to. He thought that was unlikely, but he was aware that American law enforcement agencies were perfectly happy to bend the rules when it came to aggressive interrogation of suspects, and in his opinion it was only a fairly short step from sending a rendition flight to Poland to allow suspected Islamic freedom fighters to be tortured in an anonymous black site to eliminating somebody like him with a kilo or two of C4 explosive rather than go through the bother of a lengthy and expensive trial.

In that regard, operating in England was much safer, because the British always obeyed the rules that they themselves had created, something which Sadir had never really understood. But he did know that if he was caught planning some kind of atrocity – the word that the Western media seemed to use with increasing frequency when discussing Islam – in the United Kingdom, the absolute worst that could happen to him would be a long but fairly comfortable incarceration in some prison. In America, the same action would almost certainly see him either strapped to an electric chair waiting for somebody to throw the switch or tied to a purpose-built gurney ready to be given a lethal injection.

In reality, Sadir was still confident that although his presence in Washington might have been noticed by the FBI, they had no idea of the scope of the operation that he was planning. And in the absence of any hard information, the possibility of a booby-trap in his car was fairly remote. But it was still a possibility, so he took precautions.

He used the remote control to unlock the car from as far away as possible, pressing the control into the side of his head as he pressed the button. He had no idea why, but he knew that doing that extended the range of the device by several feet.

When he reached the Honda, he opened the boot and took out an extendable rod with a battery-powered torch and a mirror screwed on to the end of it. He switched it on, slid the mirror underneath the car and carefully examined every part of the underside of the vehicle from the front to the rear bumper. And saw nothing out of place, which was exactly what he had expected.

Then he popped the bonnet and used a different torch to look all around the engine and ancillary equipment. This time, he wasn't only looking for explosives but for any kind of a small box that might conceal a tracker. When he was satisfied, he used the torch and mirror once again to make a final check inside the wheel arches. All his checks were negative, which was what he had both hoped and expected. But checking was never a waste of time, because his life might depend on it.

A couple of minutes later he drove out of the multi-storey and turned south – he had no option about this because that bit of 19th Street was one way – and then followed a somewhat meandering route to the north-east and up into Maryland. He continued as far as Bladensburg before making a left towards Riverdale Park and then continued north towards Damascus.

The cars that stand out in traffic are those that are visually unexpected, like a lime-green Lamborghini or a pink Hummer or something equally exotic or stupid and, on a more mundane level, cars that travel either too fast or too slow. Those are the vehicles that people notice, and more importantly they are also the vehicles that the police notice, and so Sadir ignored the posted speed limits and simply ensured that he was travelling at the same speed as everybody else, maintaining his place in the lines of traffic as he drove out of the built-up area.

He had nothing illegal about his person or in the car, although the mirror and torch on the pole in the boot would probably raise an eyebrow if he were to be stopped, on the grounds that normal law-abiding American citizens do not normally carry purpose-built devices for checking the undersides of their vehicles. But all in all, it was better not to be pulled over for some kind of minor traffic offence to avoid his name becoming known to any branch of American law enforcement, so Sadir simply trundled along in his average and invisible Honda, just one more anonymous vehicle in a line of other anonymous vehicles.

A little over an hour after he'd sat down in the driving seat of the car, he steered it off the road and up the tarmac driveway of the house in Damascus.

He switched off the engine, opened the driver's door and for a few seconds simply stood there beside the vehicle, staring directly towards the property. If he'd arrived by night, he would have been staring into the glare of the two floodlights mounted on the front of the house and fitted with PIR sensors to detect any arrival. His temporary immobility was a simple visual confirmation to the three men in the house of his identity. He knew they were armed, and that at least one of them would have been staring at the car over the sights of a weapon as the vehicle had approached.

He waited until the front door opened and then stepped forward, walking through the porch and into the house.

'*As-salam alaykum*, Abū Tadmir,' the man who'd opened the door said in traditional greeting, and Sadir made a standard response: '*Wa alaykum as-salam*' – meaning 'and peace unto you'.

'You are very welcome here, my brother.'

Although he hadn't seen this man or the other two people in the house for almost a year, Sadir got straight down to business.

'Is everything prepared?' he asked.

The Muslim brother in front of him – he was using the alias Nadeem Ramli – gave a smile and nodded.

'All the devices have been assembled and every component has been checked. We will be running several further final sequences of checks until it is time for the weapons to be deployed.'

'And you are sure that they will work as intended?' Sadir was still acutely aware of the depth of his failure to successfully prosecute the London attack. Ever since the day of the failed attack on the Palace of Westminster, his contact with Rashid had been increasingly tense and strained as he had been reminded time and again of his earlier certainty that both attacks would be not merely successful but devastating. To make matters worse, he still had no idea why it had failed, only that it had. He'd found nothing substantive on social media, the Internet or anywhere else. It was almost as if nothing had happened on the river that afternoon.

The only thing that Sadir could take comfort in was that the Thames attack was a one-shot operation. If the explosive charge had failed to detonate because of a defective blasting cap, or the cabin cruiser had struck some object and been holed or the engine had failed, that would have marked the end of the attack. A single simple glitch that could have ruined everything.

But the DC attack would be very different, with multiple compon-ents and built-in redundancy measures. The failure of a single part of the operation, or even three or four parts, would not derail it. And after London, Sadir was going to check every single factor and event to make absolutely sure that it would succeed and vindicate him in the eyes of the elders in Iraq. This time there would be no mistakes.

Ramli nodded again. 'The technology is fairly simple in both concept and execution and the theory behind it is almost a century old.'

'And they will work?' Sadir asked again.

'They will. I have been told that the Americans themselves have such weapons, though as far as I know they have never deployed them. And a few months ago, as you instructed, we fabricated a miniature version of the device and tested it in a remote location. Apart from its size, it was identical to the full-size weapon. We used the same components and precisely the same design and, as I reported to you after the event, it functioned exactly as we had expected. These devices will work. They will do what we want them to do. And they will be ready on time. In fact, they're ready now.'

Ramli's obvious confidence and his known competence in this field helped Sadir to banish, to some extent, the spectre of his failure in London. And he knew that the test of the miniature device had been successful because he had seen a video of the event and of the effects that it had caused.

'Good, my brother,' Sadir said. 'Now show me the results of your labours.'

Ramli led the way through the property to the rear door and then across the backyard of the house to a substantial concrete outbuilding, which had been one of the main reasons for selecting this particular property: it offered somewhere private and secure where Ramli and the other two technicians could work. The outbuilding was entered through a pair of large doors at one end to allow access for a vehicle, and an extension of the tarmac driveway terminated in front of them. The wooden doors appeared battered and on the point of falling apart, which was quite deliberate, but the wood was securely bolted to new solid steel doors underneath. There was also a separate steel pedestrian door on the side of the building, and Ramli led the way to it.

He knocked twice on the door, paused for a couple of seconds then knocked three times more. Almost immediately, Sadir heard the sound of two heavy bolts being withdrawn and then the door opened outwards, because you can't use a battering ram to force a door that opens that way. Silhouetted against the light, he recognised Rafiq Khayat, and behind him Imran Wardi, both men using aliases that would withstand at least a superficial level of investigation.

'No check to see who was outside?' Sadir asked, quite sharply, as he stepped into the building.

Ramli pointed to a small flatscreen television mounted on the wall beside the door, where four colour images were displayed, one in each quadrant, and showing views of different parts of the property.

'Those are the feeds from four cameras with infrared capability covering the approach to the house, the outside of this building and the path between the two. Installing them was one of the first things we did when we took over the property. Rafiq would not have opened the door to me unless I'd given that specific knock, which meant that I was not under duress with a gun sticking in my back. If I'd just hammered on the door it would have stayed closed but Rafiq would have opened that flap—' Ramli pointed at a steel shutter located in the middle of the door '—and we would have received a very different welcome.'

He gestured to a workbench bolted to the wall beside the door on which was a simple gun rack. Sadir saw that it held three weapons, all pump-action shotguns with cut-down barrels, and an open box of twelve-bore cartridges.

'Much better than pistols in a close quarter fight,' Rafiq Khayat said, 'and a lot easier to buy than any kind of handgun. All three of them are kept fully loaded all the time so all we have to do is click off the safety catch and pull the trigger. Luckily, so far we've never even had to pick one up.'

'Good,' Sadir said, looking around the inside of the building. His attention was immediately drawn to a freestanding bench more or less in the middle of the room, on which was a tubular object about six feet long and over two feet in diameter that appeared to be composed only of tightly wound copper wire. 'Is that it?' he asked.

'That's part of one of them,' Ramli replied. 'As I said to you in the house, all six of these devices have been completed but we are thoroughly examining each of them one last time before they're deployed. That's really only a matter of checking the integrity of the stator winding and making sure that the heavy-duty battery is fully charged. And of course checking that the remote triggering circuitry is intact and functioning properly.'

'And you've confirmed that the mobile phone is synchronised to the trigger?'

'Yes. In some ways, that's the simplest part of the whole thing. We've set up a call cascade system and initiated a five-minute delay within the software on the tablets before the ignition sequence starts. All you have to do is use the mobile phone to call the first number. The call will not be answered, and after three rings the call cascade will dial the second number, and three rings later the third number, and then the fourth, fifth and sixth. The moment each of the mobiles detects the incoming call it will activate the tablet, which will initiate the five-minute countdown and then trigger the ignition. We've been testing it this afternoon so I can show you if you like.'

Sadir nodded and followed Ramli across to another workbench where half a dozen cheap mobile phones lay, each connected to a small tablet computer which was in turn linked to a dry cell battery and a small low-voltage light. Ramli accessed each of the tablets in turn, making a change to something within the program, then stepped back. He picked up a seventh mobile phone from the bench, turned it on and handed it to Sadir.

'There's only one favourite number listed on that mobile, and that's what you need to call to begin the sequence. I've altered the timing in the software to one minute so you can see how it works. Give it a try.'

Sadir pressed the telephone symbol on the screen, then the star symbol to open the favourites menu. He glanced at the six silent mobile phones in front of him, then started the call. Almost immediately the screen on one of the mobiles illuminated and he heard the sound of three rings both from the speaker of the smart phone and the called mobile. Then it fell silent and the second mobile began ringing, followed by the third, then the fourth and the fifth and the sixth. A few moments after that the lamp connected to the first mobile illuminated, followed about five seconds later by the second and then by the others until all six lamps were burning.

'We know the timing is critical on the ignition sequence,' Ramli said, 'and we've worked out that it takes about five seconds for the second mobile to be called after the first one, and we will be building in that slight delay to the timing sequence. So the first tablet will initiate it after five minutes, the second after four minutes and fifty-five seconds and the third after four minutes and fifty seconds, and so on down the cascade, which means all six devices will detonate at almost exactly the same moment.'

'For maximum effect,' Khayat said.

Sadir nodded and looked around the workshop. The other five devices were on the floor of the workshop, their heavy steel jackets removed to reveal the stator winding to allow testing to be done. 'And you've organised transport?' he asked.

'We've already hired six vans and we picked them up yesterday,' Ramli replied. 'They're parked on quiet streets around this house, and we'll prepare each vehicle and weapon today and tomorrow to provide a margin of error in case something goes wrong.' He pointed to a piece of heavy-duty equipment standing in one corner beside the steel double doors. 'That's an engine hoist, designed to lift engines out of cars. It's got wheels so we can use that to move the devices around here in the workshop, and we will also be using it to transfer them into the backs of the vans here in the workshop. We'll have to do it in two stages because the weapons are so heavy. So first we'll transfer the steel cylinder, which is the heaviest and bulkiest part of the device, and bolt that to the floor of the vehicle to make it secure. Then we'll load the core of the device, the part surrounded by the stator winding, into the cylinder and bolt it in place. We'll run final continuity checks on all the circuitry, then position the mobile and the tablet for that weapon on a vertical wooden board that we'll bolt inside the van behind the cab. Finally, we'll secure the heavy-duty battery to the floor of the van, but we won't connect the other components to it until after we've positioned the vehicle.

'And then,' Ramli finished, 'all we'll have to do is drive the vans to the positions we agreed, make our final checks and then leave the vehicles.'

'Will the steel of the vans' bodywork affect the weapons?' Sadir asked.

'No. There's nothing that can affect the output of these devices in that way.' He pointed at a stack of steel sheets resting against the rear wall of the workshop. 'But what we will be doing before we start loading the weapons is welding one of those sheets into the van behind the cab and four other sheets on both sides, the roof and the floor to make a kind of open-ended steel box around the device. That should help channel the force and slightly increase its effectiveness.'

That was something Sadir hadn't thought of, but it did make sense.

'That's a good idea. Just confirm the locations where you'll be leaving the vehicles.'

'The three biggest weapons will be positioned outside the centre of the city. One is probably going to the bend in the road near St Luke's Church, because that's the closest we could get to the base. Because a vehicle stopped there might look suspicious because there's nothing in the area, nowhere for people to walk to, we're going to stage a breakdown. We'll back the vehicle off the road so that the back doors are pointing towards the target, then we'll jack up one side of it and take off one of the wheels. That way anyone who sees it will assume we've just had a flat and taken the wheel away to have a puncture repaired.

'The other two will be a lot easier because there are plenty of car parks in the vicinity of both locations, so we'll just pick one where we can correctly position the van. Then we can just lock it and leave it. The other three slightly smaller weapons we'll be leaving wherever we can find space around the centre of the city. We have got ideal locations already planned, but it will depend upon what's already in the area when we arrive. If something is parked in one of the spots we planned, we'll just find another suitable location as close as possible to it. But the positioning isn't that critical, because the weapons are big enough to do what we want them to do more or less wherever they go.'

Sadir spent about another half hour checking and inspecting what the three men had done for their part of the operation, then confirmed that the final component of this part of the plan, the slightly different seventh weapon, was also fully prepared and ready to go. That was the smallest of all the devices, because Sadir had already identified a suitable detonation point and the weapon would be deployed against a relatively small target at a fairly short distance. And because it was intended to work independently of the other six, it had its own separate detonation system, not linked to the other weapons. It was also different in that Sadir intended to deploy it himself, and also initiate the firing sequence.

'You're a strong man,' Ramli said, looking at the width of Sadir's shoulders, 'so you should be able to manage this without any help.'

He led the way over to another bench in the workshop where a visually similar but significantly smaller device was positioned.

'As with the others, there are three main components: the steel jacket, the stator winding that fits inside it and the battery, and as long as you move them individually it shouldn't be a problem. The steel jacket is the heaviest, so give that a try now.'

Sadir braced his feet slightly apart, got a good grip on the tubular steel jacket and lifted. It was heavier than he expected, but he was able to raise it clear of the bench, walk a few paces with it and then return it to its original location.

'I can manage that,' he said, panting slightly. 'And have you also prepared the cover?'

Ramli nodded and picked a waterproof sheet off a nearby shelf. It bore an obvious camouflage pattern, grey and green and brown random splodges covering it. He also picked up about a dozen steel pegs and a wooden mallet.

'You told us you were positioning this in a woodland setting. My advice would be to hide it in the densest undergrowth you can find, cover it with this sheet and then use these pegs to hold the sheet in place. That way, nobody will have any idea it's there until the moment you trigger it. I suggest you try and drive the pegs home just with your feet, but if you can't, use the wooden mallet. Wood on steel is a lot less noisy than steel on steel.'

About an hour later, Sadir left the house, the seventh weapon separated into its component parts and locked in the back of his Honda, entirely satisfied that everything had proceeded according to plan.

Still he worried all the way back to the parking garage in Washington that something would go wrong, that something he had not foreseen would somehow prevent the crippling attack on the Great Satan from going ahead. But by the time he reached his hotel room he felt better, calmer, and more certain that he was in control of his own destiny and that the operation was going to succeed.

He prepared a draft email using the web-based account he had set up. In it, he explained to the elders back in Iraq who would be reading it later that night exactly what progress he had made in the various phases of the operation and confirmed the date of the attack and the time it would be launched. That was important, because from the start this had been a costly enterprise, and as well as crippling America the elders also intended to reap as large a profit as they could from the event, just as Osama Bin Laden's al-Qaeda had done because of the 9/11 attacks. Back in 2001, al-Qaeda had used proxies to purchase large numbers of put options, mainly on American airline stocks, knowing that their value would fall calamitously once the method and the full extent of the attack had been realised.

This time, proxies would again be used to do the same thing, but not simply on airline stocks. Once this attack had been carried out Sadir expected that there would be massive and prolonged falls across every sector of the market. And not just in America. He guessed that once news of the attack was made public stock markets around the world would go into freefall within a matter of minutes. He had no doubt that the elders would also be buying put options in all of the major exchanges.

Chapter 33

'I'm not entirely sure why you're here,' Grant Rogers said, looking across the table in the small interview room at Ben Morgan's slouching, casually dressed and faintly jet-lagged – though this was not visually apparent – figure.

'Believe it or not,' Morgan responded, 'I don't really know why I'm here either. I received orders from on high and in my experience the best course of action is usually to obey them, as long as they seem to make some kind of sense. Which is not necessarily the case here.'

Rogers, as the man running the investigation into Karim Ganem and the people he appeared to be associating with, had also been the recipient of instructions from above, in his case from a senior seatshiner on one of the more elevated levels in the Federal Bureau of Investigation. His remit, shorn of the usual bureaucratic verbiage, was to see if 'the Limey' had anything useful to contribute to the ongoing investigation and, as something of a secondary issue, to find out why Morgan, as a kind of representative of Her Britannic Majesty's government from the other side of the Pond, and who had apparently been sent to Washington to provide advice and assistance as a cybersecurity expert, had both a stratospheric security clearance and a police record. In Rogers's mind, those two things were mutually exclusive, and he guessed that getting to the bottom of that particular conundrum would probably be quite a good idea.

'According to my briefing notes,' Rogers began, 'what you specialise in is cybersecurity, and because all you need to follow that particular career path is a halfway decent laptop and a fast Internet connection, you could do that job anywhere in the world. Which, as I've already said, makes me wonder why you've been sent over here.'

Morgan shrugged. 'Me too. But let me tell you why I think I'm here. You've obviously heard about the failed boat bomb attack in London, which was a really close call. Luckily, we had a Thames police officer who was prepared to break all the rules and rammed the cabin cruiser carrying the weapon. If he'd been about five seconds slower in his reaction time, the Palace of Westminster would need hundreds of new windows and several months of repair work and the British government would potentially be looking for over a hundred new Members of Parliament. Not that that would necessarily be a bad thing. It was that big a device, and they got that close.'

'I heard about that,' Rogers said, nodding. 'Sometimes the good guys do just get lucky.'

'But what you might not have heard was what happened afterwards.' Morgan explained about the surviving terrorist dying in police custody and the manner of his death, and the questioning of the other two members of the cell once they'd been arrested. 'They were all clearly committed to the attempted bombing, but our interrogations suggested that they regarded it only as a starting point, an attack intended to cripple the British government but which was a precursor to a much bigger event. And that event, at least by inference, is probably going to happen in America.'

Rogers leaned forward across the table. 'Did your people get anything more concrete out of them?'

'Nothing substantive,' Morgan admitted. 'We did establish that all of them were cleanskins and only one of them had ever come to the attention of our intelligence services, and not as a major player. They were all home-grown British citizens nursing a grudge against the West. But it looked like a tight organisation and the man who'd been directing it obviously applied the need-to-know principle. So he'd been prepared to tell them that the London attack was just one step in a much bigger scheme, maybe to keep them onside in the knowledge that they were part of a more ambitious plan to strike at the West, but he apparently never divulged any of the details of that scheme to them.'

'I presume this man wasn't one of the people your guys picked up?'

'No. We know almost nothing about this person, except that he ran the terrorist cell from a distance, never visited the property where they lived as far as we know and just told them what to do and when to do it. The two people we questioned just said he was a brother Muslim who had directed the operation and provided the funding for it, so he's probably acting on behalf of some Islamic organisation in the Middle East. Maybe ISIS, or perhaps some other group. Oddly enough they did name him, though that isn't likely to prove much of a help.'

'Why not?'

'Because the name they used was a teknonym, a thing called a *kunya*, which is an adopted name that Arab parents often use to show their relationship to their eldest child.'

'You're referring to "Abū" and "Umm" meaning "father of" and "mother of" whatever their kid was called, I guess,' Rogers suggested. 'It's not my field, but we get regular threat briefings and radical Islam is pretty much always the main topic. I remember hearing about *kunyas* in one of them. So what name was this guy using?'

'He was calling himself Abū Tadmir, which has to be a *nom de guerre*, not a family name, and chosen for effect, because *tadmir* is an Arabic word meaning "destruction" and not a proper name at all. So he believes he's the "father of destruction", which we think sounds bloody ominous, at best.'

Rogers opened his mouth to reply, then stopped and shook his head. 'Gimme a second,' he muttered, picked up his mobile phone and dialled a number from his contact list.

'Bill?' he said, when the call was answered. 'Can you come down to the interview room and bring the transcript with you.'

Rogers put down his mobile, pointed at the china mug in front of Morgan. 'You want more coffee?'

He pronounced it 'cawfee' and Morgan was already somewhat awash, but he guessed that this meeting wasn't likely to be over any time soon and he would need something to keep him going, so he nodded and at the same time reached for another doughnut. He also knew from his previous visits to the States that the lubricating oil which ensured the smooth running of American law enforcement at all levels was Java.

His mug was slightly chipped and was presumably official issue. Or possibly bought from a giftshop. It bore the letters 'FBI' on one side and the organisation's crest on the other. This comprised the scales of justice in dark blue on a yellow background in a stylised shield above five vertical red-and-white lines flanked by what looked like a laurel wreath with the motto 'Fidelity Bravery Integrity' in a scroll below, all set in a dark blue background inside a circle of yellow stars and surrounded by the legends 'Department of Justice' and 'Federal Bureau of Investigation' in a gold-rimmed circle. Morgan had seen variants of the badge being offered by street sellers on his way to the building that day and he was thinking about buying a couple of 'official' FBI sweatshirts as souvenirs of his visit.

As Rogers topped up both their mugs there was a knock at the door and a smartly dressed middle-aged man walked in carrying a folder in his left hand. Rogers gestured with the coffee pot and the new arrival nodded and extended his hand towards Morgan.

'Bill Clark. Good to meet you.'

'Ben Morgan, from London. More or less.' He didn't think that 'Charlton Kings' – where he actually lived – or even 'Cheltenham' would mean much to either of the two Americans. Or to most residents of the UK, come to that.

Clark sat down opposite him and beside Rogers, then opened up the folder.

'You wanted to see this, Grant.'

Rogers nodded and switched his attention to Morgan. 'We're mounting surveillance at the moment on four Arab males.'

'Let me guess,' Morgan interrupted. 'Did a lady called Barbara Simpson finger them for you?'

Both Rogers and Clark just stared at him.

'I'm not psychic,' Morgan clarified. 'I met her this morning here in DC because she had a few questions about the cyber world and she reckoned I was the right person to answer them. She's quite something, isn't she?'

'You got that right,' Rogers replied. 'And she was the source who identified the first man, yes. Yesterday we had just one suspect in our sights, flagged up by Simpson as a possible person of interest, but because of an operation this afternoon that number's just quadrupled. We believe him to be an accomplished hacker and most probably a member of a known hacking group, an outfit that calls itself AnArchy Anonymous.' He jotted the name down on a piece of paper and slid it across to Morgan. 'I don't know why the hell they can't just spell the words the same way that everybody else does. Anyway, that group's been implicated in a whole bunch of cyberattacks on government websites and what you'd probably describe as hard targets, sites belonging to the government, major organisations and official entities.'

'They're not that hard, most of them, in my experience,' Morgan commented. 'The trouble with websites of that type is that they want and expect members of the public and anybody else to be able to get into them to find information, to download forms or view stuff or to interact with the website in some way. That means that the integrity of those sites is automatically compromised, ever so slightly. And for a talented hacker, any way inside offers potential for an attack. Hard targets are things like very limited access intranets with no public portals.'

'That's your field, not mine,' Rogers said. 'Right, the guy we've been watching is named Karim Ganem. We know where he lives and what he does every day. We have a hidden microphone in his flat, a tap on his landline phone and we've been monitoring his email account, but so far we've picked up nothing incriminating. He's got a burner mobile for phone calls and we also know he uses a VPN whenever he goes on the web.'

Morgan didn't entirely see where this conversation was going, but what Rogers said next clarified the situation.

'We're using Ganem to lead us to other members of his cell, or at least that was the plan sent to us down here at the coalface from our esteemed leaders above.' Rogers pointed a finger at the ceiling of the interview room. 'The hidden mic picked up his half of a short conversation Ganem had on his mobile arranging a meeting. Through the NSA and the phone company we know that the call came from an unregistered mobile that was located here in DC. The meeting went ahead at a coffee shop in a district called Tysons Corner. That's not in Washington but just over the state line in Fairfax County, Virginia, about ten miles from the centre of DC. We followed Ganem there, where he met three other men. We covered the meeting as best we could with video and audio and stills and when it broke up we ran checks through FACE to identify the three new players. Bill, let me have that transcript for a second and tell Ben what happened after the meeting.'

'It turned out that we could identify all three of them,' William Clark said, 'because they'd all made driving licence applications over the last few years and they had to include photographs that were stored in one of our databases. One was a heavily built man named Mahdi Sadir and the other two were called Talat Wasem and Jamal Halabi. Right now, that's about all we know about them, but obviously we've got background checks running. So far, the only new information we've got is that Sadir flew into the States from your London Heathrow a couple days ago.'

Grant Rogers muttered something inaudible under his breath and interrupted.

'This is what I was looking for,' he said, putting the transcript down in front of him. 'What you don't know, Bill, is that our visitor here has some interesting information about those two terrorists who tried to blow up the British Parliament. He has a name for the mastermind behind it, the guy pulling the strings and working the members of the cell to mount the attack. And the name is interesting, because it's not a genuine Arab name but a *kunya*, an adopted name. In this case, more like an adopted title, because he calls himself Abū Tadmir. And that, as Ben explained to me just before you came down, translates as "father of destruction", and that's not good news.'

'That Arabic word is both specific and broad ranging,' Morgan clarified. 'As you said, it translates as "destruction", but it can also mean "demolition", "devastation", "ruin", "wreck" and, potentially the nastiest of all, "annihilation". You really don't want him loose on your streets.'

'The trouble is,' Rogers said, 'I have a feeling he's already here. Okay, the circumstances of the meeting at Tysons weren't ideal from a surveillance point of view. The targets were sitting at a table outside a busy coffee shop in an area with heavy pedestrian traffic. We got some people on the roof of the building with a shotgun mic and another team in a car with a camera and a microphone, but the recordings we've got—' he tapped the pages in front of him '—and that we've now had transcribed are full of gaps and broken sentences caused by people walking past or standing in front of the mics.

'I've listened to the tapes as well as read the transcription and when you said the name Abū Tadmir it rang a kind of distant bell with me. Quite early in the meeting Ganem responds to something that Sadir asked him, something that neither of our mics picked up, but we have got part of what Ganem replied. He said "three of the locations" – which could mean anything but might be a reference to three separate targets if these people are planning some kind of a terror campaign – and then we got a partial name before the mic was blocked again. The transcribers thought that might be Abd or Abdul but it's underlined in the transcript because they weren't sure. When I heard it, it sounded to me like "Aboot", which obviously isn't an Arab name, but if he was actually saying "Abū Tadmir" and we just heard the "Abū T" that would seem to fit.'

'Can I take a look at that transcript?' Morgan asked.

Rogers slid the stapled sheets of paper across the table. 'That's a combination of the feeds from the shotgun mic on the roof of the shopping centre near the cafe and the device used in the car. As you can see, the feeds were blocked a lot more often than we'd hoped.'

In Morgan's opinion, that was something of an understatement. Underneath the FBI logo and other stuff at the top of the first page was a rough diagram comprising a square to represent the cafe table and then the letters G, H, S and W positioned around it. The locations of the two shotgun mics were indicated simply as MIC 1 and MIC 2 together with their approximate distances from the targets. And below that was a decode of the lettering system, obviously based on the later identification of the three new suspects: G was Karim Ganem, H was Jamal Halabi, S was Mahdi Sadir and W was Talat Wasem.

'As you can see from the diagram,' William Clark said, leaning forward over the table and pointing, 'Ganem is facing the shotgun mic on the building roof, Halabi and Wasem are side-on to the mic and Sadir has his back to it. And that's unfortunate, because I think he's the most important of the four men.'

'Why?' Morgan asked.

'It's just my opinion, but I watched almost the entire meeting apart from the first five minutes or so when we were getting into position. I couldn't hear what was being said because we couldn't get a live feed from the shotgun mic on the roof without it being fairly obvious, but I did watch the four men and to me their body language was interesting. When they were in normal conversation they would interrupt each other or make comments and remarks of their own, just like any small group of people talking together. But whenever Sadir spoke, as far as I could tell the other three men stayed silent until he'd finished speaking. To me that suggests that he's the leader of that particular group, and if Grant is right about the Abū Tadmir link Sadir could be the mastermind behind the London attack and the puppet-master for whatever is being planned over here in the States.'

Morgan nodded and looked back at the transcript. It was laid out in three columns, the left-hand one being the time any piece of speech began, the second the identity of the person talking and the third, and by far the biggest column, the transcribed text. The page in front of him was the one Rogers had picked out, and Morgan saw the four words uttered by Ganem about halfway down the sheet.

'There's no point in me listening to the audio,' Morgan said. 'If your techie experts can't identify it for certain, there's no way that I'd be able to be definitive. I think you're making a bit of a jump, and assumptions are always dangerous, but you could well be right. If Sadir is this "father of destruction" that does at least tie in with him flying out of Heathrow after the Thames attack. And if you are going to make an assumption, it always makes sense to assume the worst, and having Abū Tadmir loose on the streets of Washington is definitely a worst-case scenario. So what's your plan? And how do I fit in?'

Rogers glanced at Clark before he replied. 'That's two separate questions and right now I'm not sure they're related. Our plan—' and Rogers unmistakably emphasised the word 'our' '—is to increase surveillance of Sadir and the other three men. Up to now we've been taking a kind of hands-off approach, just watching where they went and what they did, but now there's a suspicion that one of them is a terrorist bomber mastermind, I'll be suggesting we become a whole lot more proactive. Hopefully the senior seat-shiners will see the sense of that and let us get on with it.

'But whether or not we involve you in any of this, Mr Morgan, rather depends on what you say next. Because I have a question that I'd like answering. We occasionally allow members of the public to roam around this building, at least some of the non-sensitive areas, on organised visits, but apart from that we're very choosy about who we let in.

'When we were told you were stopping by for coffee and dough-nuts today we obviously asked who the hell you were, and that raised a red flag, because according to the background checks we did you hold a Top Secret security clearance with a bunch of specific SCI permissions, but you also have a police record back in Britain. And I'd like to know why.'

Chapter 34

The six devices – Sadir mentally referred to them as the 'Peacemakers', a somewhat cynical nickname bearing in mind their actual purpose – that were undergoing final checks and preparations in Damascus were only a part, albeit an important part, of the havoc he intended to visit upon the capital city of the United States of America. In fact, it was the second time the devices had been finally checked, but then the plans for both attacks had ground to a halt.

London had only needed a month's lead time because of the attack mechanism, but Washington was very different and much more complicated. Preparations for that attack had been completed by March 2020, but before they could be implemented the Covid-19 pandemic began hitting the major centres of population around the world. Because of travel restrictions and for other reasons, the plans had to be placed on hold until the global situation improved, which took longer than any of them had expected. As the rate of infection in the United States climbed inexorably towards, and then exceeded, 20 million in the first weeks of 2021, and with a death toll of over a third of a million by the end of 2020, some of the elders began wondering if the attack was necessary at all. After all, even the magnificent events that had occurred in New York on 11 September 2001, the attacks universally referred to as 9/11, had killed fewer than three thousand Americans. But the microscopically small coronavirus labelled Covid-19 was effortlessly laying waste to similar numbers of American citizens on almost a daily basis, decimating the Great Satan. Streets in the cities were empty, road and air traffic had been reduced dramatically, face masks were everywhere and the population was frightened.

But that, as Rashid had pointed out both to his fellow elders and also to Sadir, was irrelevant. The Grim Reaper was working his way very efficiently through the population of the United States of America, as he was in virtually every other country in the world, mainly culling the old and the sick, but a high death toll was not the point. In political and ideological terms, deaths caused by an illness, by any illness, were irrelevant. They simply didn't count. To promote and emphasise the message of radical Islam, deaths in the target country had to be seen to be entirely the work of the planners and the *shahids* of the Islamic movement. The devastation caused by Covid-19 was a bonus, that was all. Even if half the population of America died in the pandemic, the planned attack would still go ahead. Their action would just have to be delayed until an optimum time.

And with the overall improvements in the medical situation, with vaccines on stream and every country in the world moving forward towards normality, there was one obvious date when Rashid decided that the attack should be mounted.

Every year since 1776 the Fourth of July has been a cause for celebration and today is both a public holiday and the national day of the country, marked by a diverse range of celebrations including firework displays, carnivals, political speeches, concerts and the like. And most of the biggest events take place, exactly as would be expected, in and around the capital city of America.

It was arguably the biggest celebration in the country every year, bigger even than Christmas. Sadir was absolutely determined that it would be an Independence Day that nobody ever forgot. But for all the wrong reasons.

Chapter 35

Whatever Morgan had been expecting, it wasn't that, and for a few seconds he didn't respond. Then he took another sip of his cooling coffee and looked over at Rogers.

'That's privileged information,' he said.

'I know. Your police file is sealed, so I know you've got one, but I don't know what's in it. The fact that it exists is a problem: it implies you've had a conviction, and we don't like that here in the US.'

'And why do you need to know anything if my clearances are all current?'

'For exactly the same reason that you would want to know more, probably a hell of a lot more, if you'd been told that you had to work with a convicted felon. Before we take this any further I need to know what happened, what you did and why.'

Morgan didn't reply immediately as he considered his options. He could get up and walk out, and probably have to hop on board the next available flight back to Heathrow, or he could do what Rogers was asking, and talk about an incident in his past that he wasn't particularly proud of. In the circumstances, it wasn't that difficult a decision. He reached into his pocket, took out his mobile phone, put it on the table in front of him and set the audio recorder running.

'Okay,' he finally replied. 'I'm recording this for my benefit so there's no comeback later. This is confidential and privileged information and must not leave this room. Agreed? Both of you?'

Rogers and Clark both nodded.

'No, verbally for the recorder, please. State your names and your positions within the agency and that you agree to what I've just said.'

The two FBI agents did that, both leaning slightly forward and obviously intrigued.

'Right. My background is in computing and IT, and for a few years I was employed by the British police, including a stint with the Metropolitan force in London, to work on the PNC, the Police National Computer, and other computer systems. You may remember hearing about ten years ago that a paedophile had begun operating in the East Midlands area of Britain.'

As he said the word 'paedophile' Morgan could see both the Americans immediately tense in their seats, wondering where this was going.

'That was nothing to do with me, obviously,' he said, 'but because paedophiles tend to inhabit the darker reaches of the Dark Web, the kind of places where British Bobbies not only fear to tread but have absolutely no idea how to access, I ended up tracking one particular guy's footsteps as he swapped images and photographs with other people who shared his tastes. The police knew who he was, but there was no evidence he was doing anything other than looking at pictures and videos as part of this paedophile ring. I was tasked with monitoring his activities and trying to identify as many of his contacts as I could so that when the police did finally roll up that network they could take down as many people as possible. My tasking was just to watch him.'

'I'm guessing something changed,' Roger suggested.

'It did,' Morgan nodded. 'That July a seven-year-old girl named Lizzie French disappeared from the back garden of her family home just outside Lincoln. Her body was found about ten days later. She'd been raped multiple times, then strangled and dumped in a ditch on a quiet side road outside a village around fifteen miles away. That case was followed by the disappearances of three other girls of similar ages over the next six months, all in broadly speaking the same area, within about fifty miles of Lincoln, and all the bodies were later dumped on quiet country roads. Obviously finding this killer became the highest priority of the Lincolnshire police force, but they had very little to go on. No suspects, no DNA – the killer always used a condom and the bodies of the victims were found naked and they all appeared to have been thoroughly washed before they were dumped – no witnesses and no detectable trace evidence.

'Long story short. I wasn't a police officer, so I wasn't involved in the investigation, but obviously I knew what was going on and photographs of the girls were everywhere, on television and in the newspapers, as the police tried to identify anybody who had seen them being abducted or afterwards. And one afternoon I suddenly realised I was looking at a close-up of Lizzie French's face in a Dark Web video.

'Then the camera panned back and I could see that she was naked and spreadeagled on a single bed covered in a plastic sheet with her wrists and ankles roped to the four corners of the metal bed frame, and with a gag stuffed in her mouth. You don't need me to tell you what the rest of that particular video consisted of, but the perpetrator filmed the entire proceedings, first holding the camera in his hand and then putting it on a tripod and pointing it down at the bed to record the main events.

'Police forensic technicians pulled the film apart frame by frame and they found enough clues to suggest that the rapist – who was no doubt also responsible for murdering the girl – was the paedophile I'd been tracking through the Dark Web. There was a very brief shot of part of his face as he turned the camera and that was sufficient to potentially identify him. He was arrested and charged and his house was searched. The room where the rape had occurred was identified, but they couldn't find a single trace of usable forensic evidence that would link him to any of the four dead girls. Everything rested upon the video that the perpetrator had shot himself and on half a dozen other videos we recovered showing him in the same room abusing the other three victims.'

Morgan swallowed the last of his coffee and nodded as Rogers topped up his mug again. The memory still shook him after all this time.

'In the United Kingdom we appear to have a whole flock of senior judges who are very well versed in the law but who don't seem to have any particular regard for justice. When the case came to court, before the proceedings got started there was a long legal discussion between the judge and the prosecuting and defence counsels. It was held in camera, which means everybody else was excluded from the courtroom while it was going on. In fact I think it might even have been held in the judge's chambers. And the conclusion, bizarrely enough, was that the video evidence was inadmissible because all the sequences had been filmed for the man's own private and personal use and the police had had no right to take copies of them without his permission. Which obviously he hadn't given. There was a lot of legalese surrounding the decision but that, as far as I remember it, was the thrust of the argument.'

'So what happened?' Bill Clark asked.

'Exactly what you would expect to happen. The case was dismissed for lack of evidence and this proven paedophile and multiple murderer walked out of the High Court a few minutes later without a stain on his character. There was no doubt about his guilt. He'd actually filmed himself raping all four of the girls and in one video he was clearly strangling his victim, although it wasn't certain that he had killed her on that particular occasion.'

'Shit,' Rogers muttered.

'Couldn't have put it better myself. Of course, the media had been following the case and had been expecting to splurge all the gory details for the delectation of their readers. But suddenly there was no case and they were forbidden from identifying the accused man because in the eyes of the law he was innocent. So none of the families of the victims got their day in court or the satisfaction of seeing the man who'd killed their daughters and ruined their lives sent down for life without possibility of parole, which is what they'd been expecting. They got no kind of closure.

'I was a lot younger then and perhaps a bit too idealistic, and I decided that really wasn't right. It might have been the law, but it bore not even the most tenuous relationship to any kind of justice. A man who'd raped and killed four children and who'd been freed on a point of law, just a technicality, did not, in my opinion, deserve to walk the earth.'

'You mean you killed him?' Rogers asked.

'No. But I had something that neither the media nor the families of the victims possessed. I had videos of the rapes, and I knew the perpetrator's name and address because that information was freely available within the police force. So I put the two things together – copies of the videos and his identity – and sent them anonymously to the fathers of the dead girls, explaining what they were. Then I covered my traces to make sure there was no link between me, the videos and the families. And when, a little over a week later, the perpetrator vanished from his home, a house which was then set ablaze in an obvious arson attack, I pretended to be just as surprised as everybody else. His body was found in a ditch a week or so later. He'd been tied up, severely beaten and castrated – most probably with a saw – and left to bleed to death, and nobody shed so much as a single tear.'

'But somebody rumbled you, I guess,' Clark said.

'That was inevitable. The chain of evidence was clear. I'd burned one copy of each of the videos and given that, with a statement, to the SIO, the senior investigating officer. Every subsequent copy of the video was properly recorded and there were no breaks in the chain, though that obviously didn't mean some officer in the investigation couldn't have burned an illegal copy and then duplicated it. But the obvious conclusion was that if the videos, the only pieces of evidence that unequivocally linked the perpetrator with the murders, had been leaked they could possibly, maybe even probably, have come from me.

'As a matter of routine, when the perpetrator turned up dead members of the families of the four victims were questioned and one of them admitted to having been sent a copy of the video, though of course they denied having had anything to do with the man's death. I was investigated by the police force that I worked for, but there was absolutely nothing that they could do. They had their suspicions, but there was no way to prove that I had done anything other than my job and I made certain that I had rock-solid alibis for the two weeks after I sent out the videos, so there was nothing to link me to the murder. Eventually the investigation was closed, and because of the job I had been doing and the security clearance that I held, the file was sealed.

'And, just between the three of us, right here and right now, I think that even if they could somehow have proved that I had had something to do with those events, I doubt if it would ever have come to a prosecution. The British police don't like stupid blinkered judges any more than anybody else does, and they particularly don't like the idea of violent rapists and multiple murderers walking free.'

Morgan looked from Rogers to Clark and back again. That hadn't sounded too bad to him, and it had the undoubted benefit of being true. Or more or less true.

'So that's why I have a sealed police record, but no conviction. I've had my security clearance since 2005, when I helped prevent a terrorist attack in London and got a new job. Are you happy with that?'

Rogers stood up and leaned across the table, extending his hand. 'Welcome to the team, Ben. I've got a hell of a lot of respect for a guy who does what he knows is right, even if it's wrong, if you see what I mean. I think pretty much anyone else in this building who found themselves in the position you were in would have done the same thing, or something pretty similar, like wasting the guy themselves. You probably won't be surprised to learn that the Bureau is hidebound by regulations governing everything from how often you can take a crap upwards, and they don't exactly encourage free-thinking. Having you around, as a kind of free agent, might be really useful.'

'Thanks. So what's the plan with these four men?'

'So far, we've just done passive surveillance, trying to keep eyes on these guys without them being aware of it, but it's already obvious that they're being careful. They're using counter-surveillance techniques even though we're fairly sure that our men haven't been spotted.'

'I can vouch for that,' Clark said. 'And they're being really inventive. I followed one of the suspects into a department store and watched him walk into the male restroom, but I never saw him come out. Or rather, I watched him come out, but I didn't realise it was him.'

'You mean he put on a disguise?' Morgan asked.

'You could say that. These guys all have a similar appearance – dark tan complexions, black hair and beards. The man who came out of the restroom was wearing different clothes, which most probably meant he'd just taken off his denim jacket and jeans and put them in a carrier bag that I couldn't see or didn't notice, so he was wearing a shirt and khaki trousers or shorts.'

'But you should still have recognised his face,' Morgan said.

'I agree. When I lost sight of him he was wearing a blue face mask: the man who came out of the restroom had a similar complexion but no mask. He was completely clean-shaven. The beard had gone. Before you ask I did check the restroom and there was no sign of him having shaved it off. And in any case he hadn't been in there long enough to do that.'

'So how the hell—'

'Beat the hell out of us too. Our photo technicians solved the problem. I took a picture of him on my mobile when he left the restroom. It wasn't the best picture in the world but it was clear enough for them to work out what he'd done. He *was* wearing a mask, but one he'd obviously had custom made, and it was incredibly effective. It exactly matched his skin tone and it was printed with a nose that was slightly more flared than the subject's nose, different lips and, obviously, no beard. Plus he had on tinted glasses and a beanie cap. It gave him a completely different appearance, and I genuinely never gave him a second glance. He looked just like a guy walking out of the restroom who hadn't yet put on his paper mask.'

'Masks are a real problem,' Rogers pointed out, 'and I don't just mean they're uncomfortable to wear and probably don't work to stop this fucking virus. But look at it from a law enforcement point of view. Before this pandemic got exported from China, if a couple of guys walked into a bank wearing masks you'd have the tellers pressing the panic button and the guards reaching for their weapons. Today, the only people the guards look at closely are those who *aren't* wearing masks when they walk in.

'And as Bill here knows only too well, live surveillance is a nightmare, because people are expected to have their faces covered. Lose sight of somebody for even a minute and in that time they can take off their jacket, lose their hat and change the colour of their mask and they'll look completely different. I mean, if we hadn't already shot him full of holes we could have Osama bin Laden walking around in DC wearing a suit and a mask and nobody would give him a second glance or have any idea who he was.'

Chapter 36

On New Year's Day 1942, just twenty-five days after the Japanese attack on Pearl Harbor, construction began on a military air base at Syracuse, New York, and by August the same year the first military personnel were operating there. Known as the Syracuse Army Air Base or Mattydale Bomber Base – taking this name from the suburb of Syracuse where the airfield was built – it was used as a training facility and for repairing and updating B-17 and B-24 bombers. At the end of the Second World War the military airfield was redesignated for civilian use and became the Clarence E. Hancock Airport. But the military didn't stay away for long, exercising their right of return in 1951.

Back in October 1947 the 138th Fighter Squadron was formed at Hancock Field as part of the New York Air National Guard 174th Fighter Wing, first flying P-47D Thunderbolts and ending up operating F-16A/B Fighting Falcons beginning in 1988. This era of flying fixed wing fighters ended on 6 March 2010 as the final two F-16s made three low passes over a large crowd of visitors and then departed Hancock Field for the last time. Perhaps strangely, following the departure of the last two jet fighters, the number of full-time Air National Guard personnel at Hancock increased as the 174th Fighter Wing morphed into a very different unit and, many people believed, claimed an important place in the future of air combat.

And that was why Mahdi Sadir had spent some time researching the area a couple of years earlier. He'd been looking for a location that was close to the runways and the control facilities and had begun his search online rather than in person, getting a feel for the area from mapping applications and satellite photographs on various Internet sites. But there was obviously no substitute for physically visiting the place himself, and so he'd done that as part of his final checks before implementing the operation. And to his surprise he'd found exactly what he was looking for, an unmade road that was little more than a single track off Stewart Drive, to the north-east of the airfield, a track that ran almost due south towards the airfield boundary through a largely wooded area.

The road was unfenced and unguarded as far as he'd been able to tell, but obviously at some point there would either be a boundary fence or possibly a guard post beyond which unauthorised personnel would not be able to penetrate.

But that wasn't a particular concern because of the calculations that had been done on the weapon's power. He was reasonably certain that even if they had to detonate it anywhere along the unmade road, as long as the orientation was correct the result would be the same.

There was another difference about this weapon. Because of the places where they had to be deployed, the other six heavier and more powerful devices could only be driven to their chosen locations a matter of an hour or so before detonation. But the Syracuse device was going to be concealed in woodland so it could be positioned several days before the attack began. The only limiting factor was battery life, but the people who had built the weapon had calculated that as long as the detonation sequence was initiated within one month, maybe as long as two months, of positioning, the battery should function perfectly.

And that was why, early in the morning after collecting the seventh weapon from the house in Damascus, Sadir drove his old Honda through the streets of Washington D.C., merging in with the start of the morning rush hour. He had a fairly long drive ahead of him, about three hundred and fifty miles, to reach Syracuse, where he'd find a room for the night somewhere on the outskirts. He wouldn't book anything, because that would involve names and credit cards: it would be far easier, and a lot safer, to pick somewhere at random and just pay cash. He was paranoid about not leaving a paper trail. The distance didn't bother him because he knew the roads were good and fast and there should be few hold-ups.

His vehicle was entirely street legal and he would take considerable care not to attract the attention of any patrolling police officers by committing a moving traffic violation. His documentation would obviously raise no questions, but he couldn't afford to let anybody look in the boot of his car because the device he was carrying would be difficult or impossible to explain away.

The motel he picked early that evening was on the northern side of Syracuse – in fact, it was actually in Cicero, the next town and further north than he needed to go – and was somewhat run-down, but the room was clean and the air conditioning worked most of the time. He picked a name at random when he signed in, handed over some dollars in exchange for the room key and received directions to a nearby diner that served meals all day. But Sadir had no intention of leaving the room that night, to eat or for any other purpose. Quite apart from the fact that he needed to keep his eyes on the Honda, which he had secured against theft with a brace across the steering wheel to prevent it turning and by removing the battery fuse from the fuse box, he was not prepared to eat in any American diner because of the danger of inadvertently eating pork.

Islamic law absolutely forbids any Muslim to consume pork, the meat being considered *haram*, meaning both a religious and a cultural taboo. He was aware that Americans enjoyed eating bacon and in his opinion there was too much chance of bacon fat or – a most disgusting thought – even small pieces of that meat being served in other dishes simply because they would be cooked in the same kitchen. Instead, he had prepared a number of cold snacks made with *halal* meat and vegetables – that Arabic word meaning lawful or permissible, almost the exact opposite of *haram* both practically and linguistically – which he would eat in his room.

And the following morning he would position the weapon that would trigger the start of almost the final act in the attack on America.

Chapter 37

Washington D.C., United States of America

'There's something else you need to know. Barbara Simpson's uncovered something peculiar that's relevant to this problem. She was checking back through some of the historic data you'd supplied and she noticed an anomaly. Nearly three years ago an Arab male with an Iraqi passport arrived in Baltimore on a flight from the UK. Also on the flight were two Chinese nationals, and the odd thing is that the Arab passenger's ultimate point of departure was Beijing, and those two Chinese men were also passengers on every flight he took from China all the way to Baltimore.'

'That could just be a coincidence,' Rogers suggested, not sounding entirely convinced.

'It could be, but Simpson thought it looked odd, so she did a bit more checking through her contacts back in the UK. The people at Six – James Bond-land in London – discovered that the two Chinese passengers were officers in the Chinese People's Liberation Army, and they'd almost certainly been working at Unit 61398 in Shanghai. That's one of the most persistent and dangerous of all the Chinese hacking outfits. Then she checked some of the details over here in the States and found that the two Chinese men had dropped off the grid almost as soon as they'd arrived.'

Roger shook his head. 'That doesn't make sense. Cyber's more your thing than mine but I do know that these hackers can run their attacks from anywhere in the world, so why would they travel to America if that was their target? They could have stayed in Shanghai and done everything from there.'

'That,' Morgan agreed, 'is the anomaly. What could they be doing here that they couldn't be doing just as well from the other side of the world? But the fact that according to your records they haven't used credit cards or driving licences or any other kind of document that could identify them suggests that they've gone to ground somewhere and somebody has been providing them with cash for their living expenses.'

'So why do you think they could somehow be involved in this attack?'

'The thing about passports is that the days when you could just wave a reasonable facsimile at an immigration officer and hope that that would do the trick are long gone. These days, at least in the developed world, every passport is scanned electronically and if it doesn't match what's in the linked databases it won't be accepted. So the passports the two Chinese men produced were the real thing, or at least they were genuine People's Republic of China passports, and the document produced by the Arab was also genuine. Whether or not the names given in those passports match with the actual birth certificates of the three individuals is another question altogether.

'What I'm getting at is that these days even an international terrorist needs to use genuine travel documentation, and it's difficult to obtain multiple genuine passports. So we do know that for at least the last three years the Arab male who flew out of Beijing with the two Chinese hackers has been travelling on the same passport. And the important thing is the name inside that document.'

Rogers looked interested. 'And the name is?'

'Mahdi Sadir. The same name as the man Bill Clark here thinks is the leader of this bunch of four terrorists here in DC. The one calling himself Abū Tadmir.'

Chapter 38

The following morning Sadir didn't get on the road until three hours after he had knelt down to face Mecca and said his dawn prayers, the *salat al-fajr*, because he wanted to wait until the level of traffic increased, when he would become just another anonymous commuter or shopper. Following the directions on his windscreen-mounted satnav, he headed south along US-11 rather than the interstate because of where he was going. When he reached North Syracuse, he drove down Brewerton Road and turned left onto E Taft Road at the busy intersection to track east. That would take him just to the north of the Syracuse Hancock International Airport, his target.

Once he drove east of the interstate, the level of traffic diminished considerably, and by the time he reached the right turn he needed to take – William Barry Boulevard – there was only one vehicle on the road in front of him and two cars heading in the opposite direction. He took the turn and drove south on a country road dotted with industrial units. At the T-junction at the end of the road he turned left onto Stewart Drive and about a hundred metres further on he swung right down the unmade road, checking his mirrors and looking in both directions as he did so. But at that moment, Stewart Drive was deserted.

He reduced his speed on the narrow road, which ran straight as far as he could see. The left-hand side of the road was bordered by trees and undergrowth, with an open field to his right beyond which he could see another industrial unit, this one a distribution company.

Ahead of him the road, which bore no name but which he had learnt from one website was called Presque Isle Road, a somewhat exotic name for what amounted to a gravel track, climbed gently and was bordered by more trees, making it almost ideal for his purposes.

He passed a turning on his left – another unmarked road which he thought was called 2nd Street – and slowed the car as he approached what he thought was a good location, about as close to the airfield boundary as he wanted to risk going. He was surrounded by trees and undergrowth with plenty of places to pull off the road where his car would be out of sight unless somebody actually stopped and looked into the treeline.

Sadir steered the Honda off the road and stopped it behind a patch of heavy undergrowth that rendered it completely invisible. He got out and walked back towards the tarmac road, checking for tyre marks. But the ground was dry and solid and although he could see a few patches of crushed vegetation there was really nothing to suggest to anyone that a vehicle had driven that way.

He stood beside the car and for a few moments just listened. The only sound he could hear, apart from the slow ticking noise as the Honda engine cooled, was birdsong and the distant sound of automobile engines from the roads that more or less surrounded him. Satisfied, he opened the boot of the car and lifted out the steel casing of the weapon and placed it on the ground. He'd fashioned a sling which went around his shoulders to help him carry the object and he quickly assembled it and then stood up. With most of the weight now being carried by his shoulders rather than his arms he found it much easier to manoeuvre it.

He walked deeper into the woods, looking for a suitable location to assemble and prime the weapon. In less than two minutes he found a spot that seemed ideal, away from most of the larger trees but with undergrowth so thick that he doubted if anybody had even tried to walk through there in the past decade. He lowered the casing to the ground, released the sling so that he could use it to carry the stator, and retraced his steps to the car.

In less than ten minutes, all the components were laid out on the ground in front of him. He listened again for any noise that could indicate a human presence nearby, then quickly began the assembly, which was simply a matter of bolting the stator into the steel casing and making sure it was pointing in the correct direction. Then he connected the wiring to the heavy-duty twelve-volt battery that would supply the current for the detonation when he rang the mobile phone that formed part of the circuit Ramli had constructed. It was an old Nokia from the days when a mobile phone only needed charging about once a month and he had no doubt that the battery would hold more than enough charge to ensure that the explosion would take place exactly when he wanted it.

He checked the wiring and all the other components to ensure that he had missed nothing and had made no mistakes in the assembly, then took the camouflaged tarpaulin and laid it over the top of the device, pulling it tight so that it wouldn't flap if the wind started blowing because that noise might attract attention. Finally, he forced the steel pegs into the ground to hold the tarpaulin securely in place, the strength of his legs being enough to drive them all the way home so he didn't have to use the wooden mallet.

Then he stood back and looked at what he'd done. Not only was the device completely invisible, but because of the shrubs and undergrowth and leaf litter the camouflaged tarpaulin was an almost exact match for the ground around it. Sadir turned away for a few seconds, then looked back and chuckled. Even knowing the shape of the shrouded device, and knowing exactly where it was, he still couldn't see it. And that meant the chances of somebody else finding it were effectively nil.

Twenty minutes later, he was again sitting in the driving seat of the Honda, steering the car back north along Presque Isle Road on his way back to Washington. He wouldn't get there until late in the evening, but that didn't matter.

In the glade in the woods behind him, the device was absolutely silent. For now, the only part of it that functioned was the mobile phone. That was on standby waiting to receive the single call that would allow the circuit to be completed and the detonation to take place.

Chapter 39

For the forty-eight hours after his meeting with Grant Rogers, Ben Morgan stayed in contact with Barbara Simpson, meeting her in various cafes when she wasn't dressed in rags and panhandling her way around DC, and remained in the FBI loop as well, attending some briefings and updates in the Hoover building – as in John Edgar, rather than a vacuum cleaner factory – as a specialist observer.

He also had a longish telephone conversation with Natasha Black, who was still wearing her GCHQ hat in the monolithic black slab of a building that was the home of the NSA out at Fort George G. Meade in Anne Arundel County in Maryland. It was basically a catch-up and 'how are you doing out there?' call, but Morgan did have one idea, and a fairly obvious related question, that he wanted to run by her.

'The Fibbies have eyes on four Arab suspects here in DC,' he began, 'and there's a strong possibility that one of them might be this Abū Tadmir character. The problem is that they have four names for these guys based on photographic ID but they only have an address for one of them. They tried following the other three suspects after a meeting but lost them in the crowds.'

Morgan could hear what sounded like a snort of disgust from the other end of the call.

'Typical Bureau incompetence,' Black said. 'Most of the FBI agents I've met couldn't follow a cow across an empty field in broad daylight without stepping in a pile of shit and managing to lose sight of the animal. Look, if these really are bad guys, the chances of them using a registered mobile are about the same as my chance of becoming the next American President. That's nil, by the way. They'll have burners, obviously, and they'll have given false names and paid in cash at whatever hotel or apartment building they're living in. They'll be way under the radar.'

'I had kind of worked that out for myself, Natasha,' Morgan replied. 'But I was wondering if there was a way we could at least use their mobiles to try and track them through the resources you're sitting on out at Fort Meade.'

He outlined what he had in mind, but as usual Natasha Black saw exactly where he was going well before he'd finished.

'The answer to that's fairly obvious,' she said. 'It's yes and no. Yes, we have the resources and ability to do what you've suggested and no, the NSA can't legally do that. There are laws and rules in place, even when you're turning over stones trying to find a bunch of scabby terrorists hiding under them while they plan to blow up the White House or whatever, and what the NSA can't legally do is spy on American citizens or anyone living in the country.'

'So that's that, then?'

'Of course it isn't, Ben. Do try and keep up. We just do it through the back door. The NSA can't spy on American citizens, just as GCHQ can't spy on British citizens. So what we do is tell the NSA which people in Britain we'd like them to watch and let them get on with it, and they tell us which American citizens we need to keep an eye on. And then we just swap the data. That way, both the NSA and GCHQ are obeying the letter of our respective laws rather than their spirit, and that keeps the lawyers happy. Or at least quiet. We've been doing that for years. I'll set it up through Cheltenham, but I will need whatever data you've got because we'll have to have somewhere to start.'

'I've got a date and a time and a confirmed location in DC for the receiving mobile.'

'That'll do nicely. Lay it on me.'

For the remainder of those two days nothing appeared to happen. The Bureau had teams of agents out on the streets monitoring the movements of Karim Ganem, the only suspected terrorist whose address they knew, but he never left the building except for domestic purposes such as food shopping, on each occasion trailing a full team of FBI watchers behind him like the straggly tail of an unlikely comet.

The single microphone the FBI had installed in his apartment hadn't produced any useful intelligence. They suspected he was waiting for something, but at no point did he say anything in his infrequent telephone calls that gave any indication of what he was planning to do or when he was planning to do it. He never used his landline so the Bureau had to rely upon their electronic eavesdropping device to hear what he was saying, and even then they could only hear his side of the conversation.

The first useful clue, in fact, came not from anything organised by the FBI but in a long-distance telephone call to Morgan's mobile from another UK-registered mobile, a call that – perhaps predictably – woke him from a confused and confusing dream at a little after four in the morning. At least he wasn't still jet-lagged.

'Who is it?'

'For God's sake, Morgan, you sound about as sharp as a sponge. Where's your get up and go? In the SBS we were trained to react in under a second from being sound asleep.'

'It got up and went,' Morgan replied, immediately recognising the caller's voice. 'It's four in the morning, Cam, and I need my beauty sleep, so I hope you didn't call me just so we could swap clichés.'

Three and a half thousand miles away, Cameron Riley sounded irritatingly chirpy and buoyant, probably just to annoy Morgan.

'Not exactly, no. This is your early morning early warning call. The London Exchange has seen an unusually high level of well out-of-the-money index put options traded this morning, and that's been mirrored in most of the European exchanges and the Far East as well. My guess is that when Wall Street opens you'll see the same pattern on your side of the Pond. It's time to circle the wagons. If your deduction is right, that means whatever these people have got planned is pretty imminent, so best you put on your boots and spurs, grab a six-gun and a Winchester rifle and sort it out.'

'Washington these days isn't quite like that, Cam, so enough of the Wild West stuff, okay. Anything else?'

'Only that I assume you've checked the calendar?'

'Why? Is it your birthday or something?'

'Not *my* birthday, no, but you could say that tomorrow was and is the birthday of an entire nation, so I do just wonder if these guys are planning their own personal form of celebration. Something to remember them by, that kind of thing.'

Morgan didn't need to check the date, because Washington was already abuzz with preparations for the parties and concerts that would dominate the city the next day.

'Shit,' he said. 'I see what you mean. Thanks for the heads-up. I'll try to get the wheels turning.'

Morgan glanced at the illuminated digits of the bedside clock in the hotel room and made an instant decision. There was nothing he could usefully do at that time in the morning, so he reset the alarm for six, switched off the light and closed his eyes again.

But sleep proved elusive. By six he was up, showered and dressed and on his way down to the coffee shop to buy himself a double-shot caffeine kick-starter to complete the waking up process. An hour after that, he'd called both Barbara Simpson and Natasha Black on their mobiles to bring them up to speed and was sitting in the back of a cab on his way to 935 Pennsylvania Avenue to talk to Grant Rogers.

It was probably, Morgan reflected as the taxi driver carved his way through the early morning traffic, going to be a fairly short briefing. The single piece of new information he had, which was in fact merely a logical deduction based on a certain kind of activity in the stock markets, suggested that the terrorist attack – assuming that they weren't seeing something that wasn't there – was imminent.

He still had absolutely no idea what form the attack would take, where it would happen – except most probably somewhere in DC – when it would be launched, though sometime the following day looked favourite, and, crucially, he had no clue what the hell they could do to stop it.

Chapter 40

'How sure are you about this?' Grant Rogers asked, looking quizzically at Ben Morgan. 'Say on a scale of one to ten.'

'I suppose about a seven or eight would more or less cover it. It's faintly possible that we could just be looking at a major change in the global market sentiment, the bulls all turning into bears, something like that, but I genuinely don't think that's very likely, not least because it seems to be worldwide. You always get fluctuations in the types of options being traded, but those tend to affect a single company or perhaps one specific sector of the market because the traders are expecting either very good or very bad news. But what my contact back in the UK is telling me – his name is Cameron Riley – is that all the markets he's looked at are experiencing the same thing, all the way from Hong Kong to London.'

'Look, finance isn't really my thing,' Rogers said, 'so just assume I'm an idiot and I know nothing about options. Can you tell me what the hell is going on?'

Morgan knew that was a simple question with a complicated answer. Warfare in the twenty-first century was about controlling economic markets and who owned what, rather than trying to make territorial gains using armies and tanks and bombers. The Russians, the Chinese and even terrorist groups like IS had realised that misinformation, fake news and cyberattacks were low cost but high impact ways of becoming wealthier. They didn't want to destroy companies, just to control them or make money from them. Globally, governments were less important than the big tech firms, banks and critical infrastructure, and all nations were beginning to realise this. In the UK there's now a National Cyber Force that's predicted eventually to absorb over 50 per cent of Britain's annual military budget.

Explaining all that could take the rest of the day, so Morgan just answered the question Rogers had asked, sticking to the specifics.

'Look, I'm not an absolute expert, but for a short period I was involved in banking in Britain so I do know how the markets work. In simple terms, buying an option is the same as placing a bet. Just assume that the share price of a company is ten dollars but you think the price is going to rise. If you want to make money out of it, you've got two choices. You can go out and buy shares, but each one will cost you ten dollars, so if you buy a hundred you'll be laying out a grand. If you haven't got that money available you can buy a call option on the stock at, say ten dollars and fifty cents. That will give you the right, but not the obligation, to buy that stock at ten and a half dollars – that's called the strike price – and the option will only cost you a small percentage of the price of the underlying stock, say one dollar. It's not quite that simple, because the cost of the option depends upon the strike price you've selected and the time before the option expires, but I still haven't really woken up yet so I need to keep the figures really simple to allow my brain to keep up.

'So the cost of buying a call option that gives you the right to purchase one hundred shares in the company will only cost you one hundred dollars, not one thousand. If the stock then goes up to, say, twelve dollars, if you'd actually bought the shares you'd have made a two hundred dollar paper profit, because you'd have bought at ten dollars but you could sell at twelve dollars. That's a two dollar profit per share and you'd bought one hundred of them. Simple arithmetic.

'But if you bought the option instead, your outlay would have been one hundred dollars, but because you can now buy shares in the company for ten dollars fifty cents and then sell each share for twelve dollars, each option is now worth the one dollar you paid for it plus one dollar fifty. That's the original price of the option and the increase in value of the underlying stock. So your one hundred dollar investment is now worth two hundred and fifty dollars, that's a one hundred and fifty per cent profit. Of course, if you guessed wrong and the stock value falls, your option will expire worthless so you'd have lost the one hundred dollars. That's the risk you always take when you buy an option. If you buy the shares and they then fall in value you've obviously made a paper loss but you still own the stock, so you can just hang on for the ride until the price recovers.

'Put options work exactly the same but the other way round. If you assume that the price of the stock is going to fall, you'd buy a put option at, say, nine dollars, and if the stock value fell to eight you would have the right to sell shares at nine dollars so your profit would be one dollar per share. The attraction of options is that they're much cheaper to buy than the underlying stock, the financial risk is minimal, just whatever the option costs to buy, and if that stock rises or falls a long way the profit potential is virtually unlimited. A lot of investors use them to hedge their bets, so if they own stock in a company and they're uncertain about its future they might buy a chunk of put options just in case the stock value falls, things like that. And investors who like a gamble might buy both call and put options on the same company – that's called a butterfly – if the share price looks really volatile. If its value goes up, they can exercise the call options, and if it goes they down exercise the puts. They'll only lose their money if the share price remains exactly the same, which means both options will expire worthless. Does that make any kind of sense?'

'My head is beginning to hurt and I think my ears are starting to bleed, but I more or less follow what you've said. And you said that index options don't relate to individual shares or sectors of the economy but to the index as a whole. The Dow Jones or whatever. And these guys are expecting it to fall.'

Morgan nodded. 'You've got it. The other thing about the trading Cameron reported is that the options being bought are well out-of-the-money so they're cheap. The closer any option is to the actual price of the stock or index the more expensive it is. So if the Dow Jones is at 30,000, for example, and somebody buys a put option at 29,000 they won't pay very much for it because nobody expects it to fall that far, but if they bought one at 29,990 it would cost them a lot more money. Again, rough and ready figures only. But from what Cameron was telling me these option purchases are way below the normal spread, and that alone is suspicious. It implies, at the very least, that the people buying these options are expecting the market to fall through the floor. In fact, it looks as if they're expecting almost every market to fall through the floor.'

'Can we identify the people doing the buying?'

Morgan shook his head. 'I haven't investigated this myself because I can't, but Cameron – he's the top security guy at the Bank of England and the Treasury – did run some initial tracing action and the purchasers are almost all proxies, and most probably proxies acting for other proxies. Unpicking the trail all the way back to the guy who actually speculated the money would be possible, but difficult and time-consuming. And at the end of it you'd probably find some person who knows nothing about options trading or anything else to do with finance but who's just been given a wodge of money by some third party and told exactly what to do and how and when to do it, so that would be where the paper trail would stop, a long way from the principal involved.'

Rogers nodded. 'So if your man in London is right,' he said, 'when New York opens we should also see a whole bunch of options trading on the value of the Dow Jones, the S&P, the NASDAQ and all the others?'

'Yes, but I think most of it will be concentrating on the NYSE Composite, because that covers all the stocks traded on the New York Stock Exchange. If there's no activity, or only the normal level and types of trades, I'd be really happy because that would mean we've got it wrong.'

Sometimes the timing of events just seems to work out almost perfectly. As Rogers finished talking he glanced at his watch and opened his mouth to say something else, but right then his mobile phone rang. The conversation was short, probably less than a minute in length, and Rogers said hardly a word, just listened. When he'd finished he looked over at Morgan.

'New York's been open about twenty minutes,' he said, 'and they're already reporting unusually heavy trading on the Composite index, most of the purchases being well out-of-the-money put options.'

'Bugger,' Morgan muttered. 'So we need to decide—' He broke off as his own mobile rang.

His conversation was also short and largely monosyllabic.

'That,' he said when he'd finished, 'was the NSA. Or to be more exact, a friend of mine who's been seconded to Fort Meade. Just like before nine eleven, the NSA is picking up significantly increased Internet traffic, particularly in and around the Middle East and also from that region to destinations worldwide including here in the States. They've also intercepted a handful of encrypted emails, some of which your NSA analysts and our guys over at GCHQ in England have managed to decrypt.'

'And they say what?'

'Pretty much what you'd expect them to say, which means nothing specific, and what they do say needs to be interpreted because of the nuances in the Arabic language and the possible different translations into English. They include general and non-specific statements like "Death from the skies," "Vengeance is coming" and "America will pay" – which is exactly the same expression that those attempted boat bombers in London used – but much of it is the kind of doubletalk that we're used to from radical Islam and Arabic terrorists generally. Messages where they substitute innocuous words for what they really mean. Bicycle instead of bomb, that kind of thing.'

'Like al-Qaeda weddings, you mean? Which are actually planned bombings.'

'Exactly. Trying to decide which emails and stuff on the Internet relate to a real wedding rather than a planned al-Qaeda attack is almost impossible, and they can even send them in clear. But these messages were encrypted, so at least we can be reasonably sure we're looking at the right stuff. Even so, there are no mentions of the kind of attack being planned, but at least we know when. It'll be tomorrow. Independence Day. Several of the emails encode the date rather like Mohamed Atta did before the nine eleven attack, with his message

243

about two sticks and a cake with one stick down, representing the numbers eleven and nine. These messages use different imagery, but the numbers four and seven are fairly obvious and consistent, and April has come and gone so it looks like the Fourth of July is the target date.'

Grant Rogers looked like a man bearing the weight of the world on his shoulders. He slumped down in his seat, shoulders sagging. Then he appeared to mentally strengthen himself and straightened up.

'Okay. We've got one suspected terrorist identified and under surveillance. Everything we found out so far suggests that the attack will happen tomorrow, so what do we do with him? Pick him up and sweat him, or let him run?'

Morgan wasn't sure if those were rhetorical questions, but he did have some ideas of his own.

'I'm not sure that picking up that one man would be particularly helpful,' he said. 'There's no way that those four people could carry out any kind of catastrophic attack on a city this size by themselves unless they've got a suitcase nuke or something equally devastating tucked away somewhere. There must be more of them involved than that, and if you arrest him the other three will still be out there and we'll have no idea how to identify and locate any of them. So if it was up to me I'd let him run and hope he leads us to whoever else is involved so we can seize whatever weapons they're planning on using. You'd just have to make sure your people didn't lose him, because that could be a disaster.'

Rogers nodded. 'That would make sense to me as well, but it won't be my decision. At the very least my SAC will have to sign off on it, and he'll probably take some convincing because he's more of a bureaucrat than a streetwise agent, plus he'll want top cover from the high-level seat-shiners. For now I'll leave the surveillance team in place and make sure there are no holes in the net he can slip through. Then I'll kick the problem upstairs and wait for guidance from on high.'

'Before you do that,' Morgan said, 'I was told back in the UK that you had cyberattacks on some of your utility companies, and we were experiencing the same kind of thing. Is that still going on over here?'

'It is, but as far as I know there haven't been any successful breaches. The agent giving one of our threat briefings said it was possible the intention was to hack into the local electricity companies and shut down their systems to try to create a blackout, but there's a whole lot of redundancy here, just like you'd expect around the capital, and even if they did manage to disable one provider – and the briefer didn't know exactly how that could be done because their systems are really robust – there are other companies that could take over the demand. So at worst you might get a blackout lasting a few seconds, or maybe a few minutes.'

'Not exactly "Death from the skies" then?'

'No. We did look at the radar and radio links at Andrews and Ronald Reagan International and Dulles in case these terrorists thought disabling power on the ground would cause aircraft to crash, like a sort of nine eleven for DC, but there's no way it could happen. All the airports have backup generators and uninterruptible power supplies for critical systems, but even if somehow everything was completely shut down all the aircraft in the air could simply divert. So that didn't make sense as a terror attack, unless their plan is just to mildly inconvenience us.'

Morgan nodded. 'I hear what you say, but I still don't like the look of the pattern that seems to be emerging, the hacking attacks on utility companies. There must be a reason for it, but right now I don't know what it could be. And the "Death from the skies" phrase does worry me. It has echoes of nine eleven and definitely suggests some sort of aerial assault. But the terrorists don't have any bomber aircraft, unless they've cobbled together some kind of IED, an improvised explosive device, that they're going to try and drop from a hijacked light aircraft on the crowds that will gather here tomorrow for Independence Day. And I guess you have defences here that would take care of something like that really easily.'

'You got that right,' Rogers said. 'This is the capital of the country and we've got the air defence side of things screwed down pretty tight. There's a thing called the Washington D.C. Air Defense Identification Zone, the ADIZ, that surrounds the capital. Inside that is a Special Flight Rules Area that's got a radius of about thirty miles and a Flight-Restricted Zone that extends out to about fifteen miles. And then there's a prohibited area around the White House. All that airspace is covered by a whole arsenal of sensors, not just radar but also infrared and electro-optical cameras and various types of passive sensors. And if any unidentified aircraft do approach the area, we won't just detect them. We can also shoot them down.

'We've got Alert 5 and Alert 15 F16s sitting on the ground at Andrews just waiting for the go command, plus helicopters operated by Homeland Security fitted with fifty cal weapons amongst other stuff, and if anything manages to get through that lot we've got a bunch of Norwegian NASAMS waiting to knock them out of the sky.'

'I presume that's a kind of surface-to-air missile,' Morgan suggested.

'Yup. The acronym stands for National Advanced Surface to Air Missile System. That was developed from the old AIM-120 AMRAAM air-to-air missile, which was a really effective weapon. That's our intermediate range defensive system, which gives cover out to about twenty miles. And if anything somehow manages to get past that we've also got the Avenger system using FIM-92 Stinger missiles and fifty cal machine guns for real short range defence. That system's mounted in turrets on the tops of buildings dotted around the city, one of them covering the White House. The whole system's fully integrated and even if all the radar systems went down, which they wouldn't, the Stingers are infrared guided so they would still work.'

'So if some rogue airliner headed for DC these guys would bring it down? They would pull the trigger?'

'Definitely. Our view is that if an airliner's been hijacked, it's going to end up in a smoking hole in the ground somewhere anyway, and if we can make sure that hole in the ground is well outside Washington or any other urban area we're going to save a lot of innocent lives. So if we did have a nine eleven or something like that here, I can pretty much guarantee that what we wouldn't have is thousands of people dead because it crashed into a building. The fighter jocks, who'd probably be the guys doing the intercept, would make sure it came down somewhere in the countryside. And, yes, everybody on board the aircraft would be killed, but they would hopefully be the only casualties. So a few hundred lives would be lost rather than a few thousand. We think that's a reasonable trade-off.'

'I can't argue with any of that,' Morgan said.

Chapter 41

4 July – Independence Day

Washington D.C., United States of America

The very first thing that happened that morning was that all four of
the suspected terrorists – Mahdi Sadir, Karim Ganem, Talat Wasem
and Jamal Halabi – only one of whom was under close surveillance by
teams of FBI surveillance specialists, all slipped the net at exactly the
same time.

Sadir triggered one of the fire alarms in the large hotel where he
was staying and slipped away in the ensuing confusion, Wasem left by
way of the roof of his apartment building, stepping onto the adjoining
structure and making his way out from there, while Ganem and Halabi
both left their apartment buildings and climbed onto pedal cycles. The
FBI team had been ready to follow Ganem on foot or on to public
transport, or by car, but bicycles could go faster than pedestrians and
slip through spaces that cars simply could not. Within fifteen minutes
of Ganem's appearance – and then almost immediate disappearance
about a quarter of a mile further down the road – none of the watchers
had the slightest idea where their quarry might be except, obviously,
still somewhere in Washington D.C.

–

Mahdi Sadir had had no idea whether or not he and the other three
men had been under surveillance, but it was obviously prudent to
assume that they were, hence his instructions, given at their meeting
in Tysons, for them to simultaneously scatter on the morning of the

attack. If they had acquired unwelcome followers it was essential for them to leave their properties at exactly the same time, because if they were under surveillance the moment one of them slipped the net the authorities would certainly order the other three men to be picked up immediately.

So he'd precisely timed it for 0838, and by 1100 that morning the three hackers Sadir had recruited were established in their alternate locations, places that they had prepared well ahead of the operation but had not visited for the last six months. They were in locations well outside DC, one of them in Woodstock and the other two at opposite ends of Harrisonburg, out to the west of Washington.

Sadir hadn't followed the same path as the others because his function in the final part of the operation was very different. Instead, he had headed in virtually the opposite direction, north-east towards Bel Air, and was at that moment sitting in his Honda outside the house in Fairview between Bel Air and Jarrettsville, using his burner phone to contact each of the other three men in turn.

Once he was satisfied that they were all in place and ready to act, he checked the local weather forecast through the Internet. It probably wasn't going to be the hottest day of the year but it was certainly going to be very warm, which was exactly what he had hoped and expected.

Then he glanced at his watch. He was waiting for one very specific piece of information that would determine what he did next, or to be precise *when* he would do it, because the plan was in every other respect ready to implement. He did nothing for a few seconds, then composed a brief text message that he sent to a mobile phone number that he rarely called.

The message read: 'Estimate?'

About half a minute later his mobile emitted a double tone to indicate receipt of a message and the equally brief reply he was waiting for.

The SMS text read: 'ETD 1330.'

That was later than he had hoped, and later than he had originally planned, but because he was in overall control of the operation he could still make it work. In fact, there was no reason for there to be any delay in starting the attack. Once the operation was in progress it would be unstoppable, and the longer the first phase lasted the more confusion and chaos would be caused in Washington, and in some ways the longer that went on the better because it would ensure the highest possible death toll.

Rather than calling the other three men he composed another text message and sent it to each of their phones simultaneously.

That simple and unambiguous message read: 'Implement immediately. Acknowledge.'

He didn't need to say any more than that, because each of them knew exactly what they had to do. Less than a minute later he'd received confirmation messages from all three of the men.

The operation, the product of nearly a decade of research, recruitment, planning and scheming, was finally running.

Karim Ganem sent the acknowledgement text on his burner and looked at his watch. Then he opened up the laptop computer that he had brought with him in his backpack, plugged it in, switched it on and logged on to the building's Wi-Fi network. He opened up his VPN to hide his traces, then opened TOR, The Onion Router, which would provide a further layer of protection against people trying to identify his location. Then, using the backdoor access that he had created, he entered the intranet of the first target company.

There's a standard tradition in the world of computer science that the software engineers who build systems, and especially those who design the security protocols, will frequently include a backdoor, a way of getting into the system in the future without having to go through all the tiresome business of being an authorised user and then using verified log-in details to gain access. It's much simpler, quicker and more efficient to sneak in without anybody noticing and particularly without leaving a trace on the access register. These backdoors are not used for nefarious purposes but simply provide a way for the engineer to gain access to the source code of the system to find and fix some problem. But of course, this form of access is also the Holy Grail for a hacker, and Ganem had created several of them.

As he began his work, he knew that his actions were being mirrored by Talat Wasem and Jamal Halabi in their separate locations, their targets different power companies. Ganem's first task was to insert a software patch into the master control program in the operations room of the first of his three targeted electricity-generating companies. Its presence would not be detected easily because all it did was to disable one of the alarm circuits, which would ensure that the staff on duty would be unaware of a particular fault.

Then he accessed one of the utility programs and adjusted settings that would begin disabling certain air-conditioning circuits at the times he specified. He also accessed the circuits controlling various thermo-stats and coolant pumps and changed the timing and parameters of the cooling equipment. Those actions, Sadir had explained to him, would inevitably cause overheating on certain generators. That, in turn, would cause circuit breakers to trip and generators to shut down, failures that the operators would initially be unaware of from their instrumentation because of the patch he'd created and installed. They'd only realise something was wrong when the calls started coming in, and that would just serve to increase the confusion.

Load shedding would begin but as his manufactured faults would affect most of the generators, the likely outcome would be a cascade effect as one generator after another failed, either because of the manufactured internal faults or because the demands of load shedding would exceed its capacity.

And then, as surely and as appositely as night follows day, blackouts would begin spreading across much of Washington D.C.

Of course, turning out the lights and the air-conditioning units in America's capital city by day could hardly be classed as a terrorist attack, but it was only intended as a precursor, as an enabler. The blackouts would begin in about half an hour and certainly create chaos. Things that people take for granted on a daily basis, things like escalators, lifts, traffic lights and all the way down to kettles and cookers would stop working, depending upon the availability of backup power supplies. There would be road accidents, people would be trapped inside buildings, perhaps inside lifts, and the emergency services would be out in force responding to calls. Office and shop workers, faced with failed lighting inside buildings, would probably end up standing out on the streets as their places of work were forced to shut down without power.

And that was exactly where Mahdi Sadir wanted them.

Chapter 42

Washington D.C., United States of America

Imran Wardi steered the hired van down Old Branch Avenue, the road running parallel to US-5 to the west of Joint Base Andrews, the sound of the traffic on the busy highway audible but the vehicles themselves invisible behind the long line of trees and undergrowth that separated the two roads. Just north of the Shoppers Supermarket, the roads started to diverge, US-5 bearing south-east while Old Branch Avenue continued on a southerly heading.

At the crossroads in Clinton, Wardi turned left onto Woodyard Road, MD-223, crossed over US-5 at the cloverleaf and continued north-east towards Woodyard itself. At the traffic light-controlled crossroads, he turned left, continuing along Woodyard Road as far as the next crossroads, where he again turned left, this time into Dower House Road. It was a pleasant street, bordered by large detached houses and then, as he drove further north, by industrial units. The further he drove the less traffic he saw until, as the road narrowed significantly as it approached the boundary of Joint Base Andrews, he could see nobody ahead of him or behind him. The road didn't end, simply turned left through about one hundred degrees and became Leapley Road, and that sharp bend was his destination.

Wardi stopped the van right beside the bend, then reversed it off the road onto a patch of scrubby grass and gravel on which was a tall wooden pole carrying electrical cables, two road signs, each displaying an arrow and pointing in opposite directions, and a short length of metal barrier presumably intended to bring to a stop any careless drivers who failed to make it around the bend. The barrier would also prevent them driving through the wooden fence which terminated at the apex of the corner, beyond which lay Pearl Harbor Drive, the name itself a clue: it was one of the roads within Joint Base Andrews itself.

He manoeuvred the vehicle so that the rear of it was pointing in the optimum direction for their purposes. Working quickly, he opened the rear doors, checked the battery, the mobile phone and the wiring of the weapon and everything else, then jumped out carrying a wheel-brace and the van's jack. He loosened the wheel nuts on the left front wheel, jacked up that side of the van, removed the wheel and placed it, along with the wheel-brace and the nuts, inside the back of the vehicle.

Then he locked the van and, as a final touch, scribbled a note on a scrap of paper and tucked it under one of the windshield wipers. The note read: 'Gone to garage' and was obviously self-explanatory. Hopefully, any police patrol or inquisitive local seeing the van would assume it had had a puncture and that the driver was attending to it and no steps would be taken to remove the vehicle because the matter was in hand. He didn't think anybody would try to remove it because it was clearly not causing any kind of obstruction.

They'd picked that spot because it was the nearest they could get to Andrews, and also because the closest local residents were all dead and lying under the ground in the graveyard of what was marked on the map as St Luke's Church, though the church building itself was conspicuous by its absence, unless it was lurking somewhere within the treeline. But the only thing Wardi had seen in there was what looked like a yard full of old cars and trucks, presumably waiting to be broken up for spare parts.

Less than five minutes after he'd immobilised the van, a Chevrolet Cavalier nosed its way down the road, Nadeem Ramli behind the wheel. Wardi sat down in the passenger seat and Ramli accelerated away.

'Any problems?' he asked, in Arabic.

Wardi shook his head and replied in the same tongue. 'None. Traffic was light and I made good time. I checked the weapon thoroughly and everything is correct. What about the other vans?'

'All in position, more or less. DC is busy because of the celebrations but we'd allowed for that and we will have no trouble meeting Abū Tadmir's deadline. Your journey was the longest, and when Rafiq contacted me about half an hour ago he said he would be able to park the last van within the hour. Obviously one of the problems has been that we had six vans to position and only the three of us to do it, so I've been acting as a taxi driver all morning ferrying you and Rafiq around, but it's worked out as we expected.'

'And once that last vehicle is in position we can leave,' Wardi stated. 'And watch the fireworks from a safe distance.'

'That's right,' Ramli said, grinning wolfishly. 'It should be quite an interesting afternoon. As long as you're a long way from Washington, of course.'

Chapter 43

'I didn't want you here in the first place, Morgan,' Charles Bouchier – you could just tell that he had never been known as 'Charlie' in his entire working life – ground out through gritted teeth. 'The very last thing I want to see in this building is someone like you, an Englishman with a sense of entitlement and an extremely shady past, if what Rogers told me is correct. Let me make myself perfectly clear. I do not want to see you in this building ever again. I forbid you from contacting Rogers or any other member of the Bureau, and the moment this meeting is over I will have you escorted out into the street.'

Morgan didn't respond immediately, just glanced slightly sideways at Grant Rogers, who replied with the faintest possible shrug of his shoulders and a facial expression that somehow seemed to convey irritation, an apology and a sense of resignation all at the same time. Charles Bouchier, a black haired, somewhat jowly and thick-set man, particularly around the waist, an indication that he was more of a seat-shiner than a front-line agent, a man who probably spent most of his time attending committee meetings and consuming large working lunches rather than chasing down bad guys on the streets, was Rogers's immediate boss. He was the SAC, the special agent in charge, of the operation designed to provide continuing surveillance of Ganem and to locate the other three suspects. He had been incandescent with rage when Rogers had admitted that Ganem had slipped the leash and was on the loose somewhere in DC or maybe even further afield, and the man he apparently blamed for this situation was, bizarrely enough, Ben

Morgan, who at no time had had anything to do with the surveillance operation.

And Bouchier was really just getting started, his loud and hectoring voice filling the briefing room where the three men were standing, Morgan on one side of the table and the two FBI officers on the other.

'And what evidence have you brought us to support this preposterous claim that a disorganised ragtag band of Arab terrorists are intending to launch an attack on Washington D.C. today? Hmm? An attack that you can't even describe because you have no idea what form it might take. We're well aware that the streets of the city will be full of people today, all celebrating the day this country finally achieved independence from the likes of you. We have ample police and security forces out on the streets with them to ensure that the chances of anybody being able to plant a bomb or drive a truck into a crowd of pedestrians or do anything else are nil.'

Morgan nodded. 'Are you interested in what I've got to say, or do you want to just throw me out into the street right now and have done with it?'

'Don't be impertinent.'

'I'll be as impertinent as I fucking well please. I don't answer to you or anybody else out here in the colonies. I was sent over the Pond to try to help you, get that, to *help you* attempt to stop this attack. It was only thanks to a colleague of mine, who's also British, by the way, that you even know about these four Arab comedians who might – or who might not – be planning to mount some kind of an attack here.'

Bouchier's face had flushed dangerously red and Morgan guessed it had been a long time since anybody in the Bureau had actually stood up to his bully boy tactics. Before the SAC could respond, Morgan ploughed on. He, after all, had nothing to lose.

'Now we can sit here and trade insults for the rest of the day if you want, but I've got things I need to do and you've probably got a big lunch heading your way, so let me just say this. This isn't some ragtag bunch of terrorists. This operation, whatever the hell it is, has been planned for years, maybe as long as a decade, and the last thing these guys are going to do is try and mow down a few pedestrians in a stolen truck or plant an IED on Capitol Hill or anything like that. Planning that kind of attack would take about twenty seconds. Based on what we found out from the surviving *jihadists* who carried out the failed attack in London, this will be much bigger and much more subtle than anything like that.

'My guess is that it'll come in stages, and very probably start with attempts to shut down your utility providers, your electricity-generating companies and distributors, based on what Grant has told me about the cyberattacks you've had over here. I don't know what the next stage is likely to be, or what they hope to achieve by creating a temporary blackout in DC, but I do think that will only be the first step. But the attack, the real attack, will come from the air. And it will happen today. So you do whatever the hell you want, but I want on record that I'm here to try and help, not hinder. That's why the mobile phone in front of me is recording everything said in this room and uploading it to the cloud.'

'You have absolutely no right—'

'Oh, give it a rest, Charlie. You've said your piece. Now it's time to let people like Grant here, people who actually give a shit, do what they can to find these guys and stop whatever they've got planned.'

Before Bouchier could respond, the lights in the briefing room flickered twice, then went out completely for a couple of seconds before switching on again.

'I told you so,' Morgan said with impeccable timing and a straight face. 'That's it. It's started. I'm doing no good sitting here listening to this brain-dead sack of shit, Grant, so I'll get back out on the streets and see if I can find out what's going on. I'll call you.'

Chapter 44

'I sure hope you've got a nice easy one for us today, Sammy, bearing in mind it's Independence Day and we've all got families to get back to.'

Major Sami Dawood, a stocky, solid-looking man a little under six feet tall with black hair, a tanned complexion and a somewhat bulbous nose centred in his otherwise regular features, looked up from his notes and grinned at the speaker, one of the 138th Attack Squadron's MQ-9 pilots and part of the 174th Attack Wing based at Hancock Field.

'All my exercises and evolutions are easy,' Dawood replied, 'as you know.'

'Actually, they're not,' the lieutenant responded, 'so give me a clue.'

'Okay. Full tanks, full weapons load, half surveillance and half weapons delivery for a bit of variety, and most of the flight in daylight. Does that sound easy enough for you?'

There's a kind of tradition in the armed forces of all countries that most exercises and activities should begin at a time usually described as something like 'crikey o'clock', before even the earliest of the early birds are awake and prepping for the dawn chorus, but many drone sorties were flown during daylight hours, to the relief of those involved.

'Depends on when and where, I guess,' Lieutenant Nagell said, 'but at least I won't get bored looking through my straw.'

Predator and Reaper pilots have often described controlling their drones as like flying a normal aircraft while looking through a straw.

'Okay. You ready for the briefing?'

Nagell nodded and sat down in the front row of seats in the aircrew briefing room. A slim and wiry man with closely cropped blond hair and an air of relaxed competence about him, Nagell was a former F-16 jockey who'd transferred to the slightly less frenetic world of remotely piloted aircraft a couple of years earlier. As he would explain to anyone prepared to listen to him, he'd had a successful flying career, basing this statement on the somewhat shaky premise that he'd had the same number of take-offs as landings, meaning that he'd never crashed an aircraft. In fact, he had been regarded not simply as a very competent pilot but also as a man who never got flustered. His nickname, and the name printed on his flying helmet, had been a testament to this: No Sweat.

No Sweat Nagell had entirely embraced the idea of remotely controlled air combat on the grounds that it was just as effective as riding a Fighting Falcon in reheat but a hell of a lot quieter and more comfortable because he could sip a cup of coffee, eat a sandwich or even take a trip to the crapper mid-mission. And he could sleep in his own bed every night instead of sharing a two-berth hut in Kandahar or Baghdad or somewhere surrounded by mosquitoes out for blood and alternately listening out for the whine of incoming mortars or the sound of his hut companion farting. For Nagell, it was no contest.

He wasn't the only man to take a seat as three other officers, two of them responsible for the drone's sensors and the third the second pilot for the day's flight, strolled in moments later and also sat down. The controlling team for each Reaper comprised a pilot and a sensor operator, backed up by a Mission Intelligence Coordinator for operational sorties, and it was normal operating procedure to brief the relief team at the same time as those who'd be controlling the Reaper for the first part of the mission.

'Met, please,' Dawood ordered, and a slim, bespectacled man stepped forward and used a handheld remote to display a single schematic map of the local area on the projection screen.

'I'll give you the real short version: it's a beautiful day for flying. Winds light and variable, unlimited visibility and sod all in the way of clouds. Eight eighths blue, in a nutshell. No change expected before tomorrow, roughly mid-morning.'

Cloud cover is reported by meteorological officers and air traffic controllers to aircrew in octas, meaning one eighth, so four octas means that half the sky is obscured by cloud. 'Eight eighths blue' is a common military shorthand term to indicate a sky devoid of all cloud cover.

There were no questions about that, predictably enough, and Sami Dawood cracked on with the operational part of the briefing. The Reaper was to get airborne and climb to its assigned cruising altitude of 30,500 feet, flight level 305, well below its operational ceiling of 50,000 feet. Flight levels are a kind of verbal shorthand, the altitude of an aircraft in thousands of feet with the last two zeros knocked off, and above about 25,000 feet are based on whole thousands. So, strictly speaking, flight level 305 didn't exist, which was why it had been chosen.

The allocation of flight levels worldwide is based on a very simple rule. If the aircraft's track is between 0° and 179° the flight level must be an odd number – 190 or 230, for example – and if it's between 180° and 359° an even flight level must be chosen, like 180 or 220. This provides the most basic possible separation so that aircraft flying in opposite directions will always be vertically separated by at least one thousand feet. Selecting an intermediate flight level, in this case between flight level 300 and flight level 310, meant that no civilian aircraft would be at that altitude, so that no matter what happened the drone would always be at least five hundred feet clear of all air traffic. Of course, the Reaper would be under control from the ground control station, the GCS, and its on-board radar would alert the remote pilot to any conflicting traffic, but it provided an additional margin of safety because of the drone's relatively slow speed: even at its maximum velocity it would be travelling less than half as quickly as most civilian airliners.

It was to maintain a cruising speed of 150 knots to conserve fuel – flat-out, the Reaper could reach 240 knots – and proceed north-west to Lake Ontario, where it would descend to 15,500 feet and carry out a series of surveillance runs aimed at identifying ground-based and waterborne targets along the southern shore. That phase completed, the pilot was to turn the Reaper east, climb to high level again and transit the short distance to the Adirondacks air-to-ground range at Fort Drum, near Watertown in Jefferson County at the eastern end of Lake Ontario. The attack headings, altitudes, targets and the weapons to be used there would be specified on arrival overhead to increase operational flexibility.

It was the kind of briefing that Nagell and the other men had sat through on countless previous occasions, and the mission profile was in no way unusual. It wouldn't be especially challenging for a pilot of his experience, and the first part of the mission, over Lake Ontario, was going to be far more of a test for the sensor operator than for him. He would just be the taxi driver, following whatever route he was told to take while the cameras in the drone were used to record the surveillance data and allow the images to be analysed.

'No sweat,' Nagell muttered as the briefing ended, living up to his nickname.

Chapter 45

Washington D.C., United States of America

The J. Edgar Hoover FBI Building occupies an entire trapezoid-shaped city block between the wide eight-lane dual carriageway that is Pennsylvania Avenue to the south, E Street NW to the north and 9th and 10th Streets NW to the east and west respectively. The southern entrance of the vast structure lies on the wide and imposing Pennsylvania Avenue which leads directly to the White House a few hundred metres further west, or to the Capitol to the east, but Morgan stepped out of the northern end of the building onto E Street, somewhat in the manner of a person leaving by the tradesman's entrance.

A sudden cacophony of blaring horns drew his attention to the E Street and 10th Street traffic light-controlled intersection. Only the traffic lights weren't controlling the junction, because power to them had obviously failed, resulting in a snarl-up of angry drivers trying to make their way across the intersection, none willing to give way and most of them, by the sound of it, venting their obvious fury through the audible medium of their car horns. He looked the other way, to the 9th Street junction, and saw a similar, but not quite so noisy, exchange of views taking place.

He already knew that that area of Washington D.C. was usually busy with cars and tour coaches rather than pedestrians, most Americans being reluctant to walk more than a few hundred yards if there was some form of motorised vehicle they could use instead, but there were far more people on the sidewalks than he had previously seen in that vicinity. They might reasonably have been described as pedestrians, but most of them weren't walking anywhere, just standing around in small groups, talking and gesticulating. He guessed that they probably worked in some of the nearby buildings and had moved outside because whatever electric or electronic equipment they were using had ceased functioning. As he watched, the E Street and 10th Street traffic lights flickered back into life and then almost immediately shut down again, presumably as another generator came online and then almost as quickly some breaker somewhere tripped because of an overload and the feed was shut down.

In 2003, what became known as the North-east Blackout, which began because of a software bug in a computerised alarm system in a power company in Akron, Ohio, progressed to surges and outages and then cascaded into a loss of power in parts of eight American states. The blackout directly affected some 45 million Americans and about a further 10 million people in Ontario. The lack of power contributed to roughly one hundred fatalities and affected everything from mains water systems when the pumping system power supplies were cut, to rail services, oil refineries, gas station forecourts where petrol and diesel pumps stopped working and led to long queues of vehicles, television systems and general communications, as well as domestic heating, lighting, air conditioning and other utilities, all of which either shut down or suffered outages. Even industries and businesses which had backup generators suffered, because although the blackout only lasted about eight hours some of those generators ran out of fuel within that time.

Morgan guessed that what DC was experiencing was far more localised than that event, with a much smaller affected area and population. But it was, he was sure, only the start of the threat. Looking at the gathering crowds, he also wondered if whatever attack was planned involved something like napalm or some other chemical that would have a bigger effect on an exposed population rather than people still inside buildings. Maybe that was the reason for the blackouts.

He shivered slightly at that thought and almost unconsciously looked up to stare at the sky, or what he could see of it from the bottom of the concrete canyon in which he was standing, searching for danger or anything that shouldn't be there. Then he pulled out his mobile phone, checked the screen to confirm that the network was up – during the North-east Blackout mobile providers had suffered outages – then dialled a number that he knew almost as well as his own.

'I'm just about to pour my second cup of coffee of the morning, Ben, so you've caught me at a good time. What's on your mind?'

'Good morning, Natasha. Everything okay at your end?'

'My end is fine, if you're talking about where I'm working, rather than something more personal. Why are you asking?'

'DC is getting hit with power outages,' Morgan replied. 'How about Maryland?'

'As far as I know, the No Such Agency hasn't had a problem, so maybe our supplier is unaffected. On the other hand, this place has massive backup generators and if there was a power cut it's quite possible we wouldn't even notice. Are you thinking this is enemy action?'

'I'd be amazed if it wasn't. But obviously there must be more to it than just a few lights going out. Any joy with the tracking idea we talked about?'

'Oddly enough, yes, because we both know how rare it is for one of your ideas to actually pan out. You gave me a specific location where an unregistered mobile was located and the date and time when another unregistered mobile called it. So I gave one of my guys back at Cheltenham the job of identifying and tracking the calling mobile, because you figured that was the one being used by the person in charge, and to start a tally of its activity and its location and to monitor the calls and messages. You probably won't be entirely surprised to hear that most of the time that mobile has been switched off, which suggests to me that you were right: the person using it is the one giving the orders rather than receiving them. He only switches it on when he needs to tell somebody something.

'As far as locations are concerned, it pops up all over the place and at very different times, usually in and around DC, but we've also had hits in Damascus – that's the one just north of DC, not the city half a world away in Syria, before you ask, a district called Bel Air near Baltimore and one out at a city called Syracuse up in New York State. My man also did historical checking, running back through the records of the service provider to see if it was used before making that call to the mobile. It was, but again the results were the same: only occasional usage in DC, Damascus, Bel Air and Syracuse.'

'And did your man also—' Morgan interrupted.

'I hadn't finished. Whoever this person is, he doesn't seem to have many friends, because he's only ever called six other numbers, and to save you exercising your limited allocation of brain cells, I'll tell you where they were located. They were all mobiles, three of them in DC, one in Damascus, one in Bel Air and one in Syracuse. To me, that makes it look like we're dealing with a small number of people located in different places and probably tasked with doing different jobs as part of a single operation. Significantly, none of those mobiles are registered and all of them have been switched on almost all the time, only going off the network between late evening and early in the morning. If you give me a few minutes, I'll bung the data file over to you now.'

'Thanks,' Morgan said. 'Can you also run a check in real time and find out if those mobiles are switched on right now and where they are? And if your man back in Cheltenham managed to run an active intercept I'd like to hear anything he recorded from any of the target numbers.'

'I'll see what he's got and you'll have it pretty much immediately.'

'Now, I've also managed to fall out with the hierarchy of the Bureau in a fairly big way, so I'm kind of on my own and this is getting urgent.'

'Another set of official toes you've trodden on, eh?'

'More like stamped on, really, repeatedly and wearing hobnail boots. I'm definitely not on their Christmas card list any more. Not that I was in the first place.'

'Typical of you, Ben. Right, you should have the file in the next couple of minutes. Keep me in the loop and try not to piss off any other branches of American law enforcement. If we're going to wrap this up, we're going to need help. Lots of help. And it'll need to be help with badges, body armour and big guns.'

Chapter 46

A little under ninety minutes after the briefing had ended, the fully prepped General Atomics MQ-9 Reaper was towed by an army 4x4 utility vehicle out of its purpose-built beige-painted hangar, the structure bearing the legend '174th ATKW' painted in black above the white doors. It was accompanied by two airmen walking beside its wings and carrying chocks that could be used to stop the drone if required, and which would be used to keep it stationary on a hardstanding while the pre-start and other checks were carried out before it taxied for take-off.

All the underwing weapons pylons were occupied, carrying the maximum load of four AGM-114 Hellfire missiles, two 500-pound GBU-12 Paveway II laser-guided bombs and one 500-pound GBU-38 JDAM – Joint Direct Attack Munition – precision-guided bomb. The missile's 'AGM' designation simply meant 'air-to-ground missile' while 'GBU' stood for 'guided bomb unit'.

That particular Reaper was, as American pilots are so fond of saying, 'loaded for bear'.

On the hardstanding, with the two main wheels chocked and the brakes engaged, the engine was started and the various systems, like the rotatable camera mounted under the Reaper's nose, were tested to ensure they were in correct working order. The power lead and telemetry lead were unplugged, the final safety pin, marked by a prominent red flag, was removed, and the drone was ready to taxi.

As the Reaper headed towards the runway, just as on a conventional aircraft a series of pre-take-off checks were carried out to ensure that it was in a flyable condition, the most visually obvious of which was a test of the brakes, the nose of the drone dipping as Nagell applied them. Then the UAV proceeded steadily to the threshold of the active runway. Once the local controller was certain that the runway was clear of turbulence – wide-body passenger jets, in particular, create vortices on landing that are powerful enough to flip a light aircraft onto its back – take-off clearance was granted. The drone accelerated down the runway, lifting off at what was obviously a much slower speed than the passenger jets that had preceded it, and after a much shorter take-off run, thanks to its light weight and straight, glider-like wings.

Until 2019, all Reapers launching from Syracuse Hancock International Airport were required to be escorted by a piloted aircraft to ensure separation from other air traffic, the concern being that the comparatively small UAVs would be difficult for commercial pilots to see and avoid. The rule was that a Civil Air Patrol jet would follow the Reaper from the airfield up to a height of 18,000 feet and act as the eyes and ears of the UAV pilot on the ground. This system also meant that the Reapers were not permitted to fly in marginal weather conditions, because it would not be possible for the pilot of the chase plane to reliably maintain visual contact with the drone.

All that changed in 2019 when a company based in Cicero, just outside Syracuse, developed a ground-based radar known as LSTAR that could accurately detect all aircraft, including drones, and determine a contact's altitude even if it didn't have a functioning transponder. The new radar had been created for an entirely different purpose – to detect and track incoming mortar rounds as fast as possible in a battle situation to allow retaliatory fire – but despite its comparatively short range it had proved to be capable of monitoring air traffic around Syracuse both accurately and reliably.

In the thirty-foot-long air-conditioned ground control station, No Sweat Nagell sat in a comfortable chair that looked more like the kind of seat to be found in an upmarket airport lounge than in a military establishment, but with Predator and Reaper drones routinely able to remain aloft for twenty-four hours, and with even longer duration

UAVs on the drawing board, the comfort of the remote pilot was a paramount consideration.

In front of him was a control panel, the most important element of which was a fairly standard flight stick, a multipurpose vertical lever that could control most aspects of the Reaper's flight path. The pilot would use that just as if he were sitting in the cockpit of a conventional aircraft, the main difference being that the inputs he made were transmitted to the UAV initially using a C-band line-of-sight data link. The other difference was that all the pilot had to rely on, his eyes, as it were, were the video screens in front of him that displayed the feeds from the Reaper's on-board radars and cameras and provided a limited view of what was in front of the UAV. This was nothing like the all-round vision experienced by a pilot flying any kind of an aircraft, hence the 'looking through a straw' analogy.

Once the drone moved outside line-of-sight range, as was the case when the pilot was sitting in a GCS in Montana or Nevada or somewhere, but the Reaper was taking off from an airfield near Mosul or Kabul, almost literally on the other side of the world, the routine was somewhat different in that a local pilot would handle the taxiing, take-off and initial climb out of the vehicle and then hand over control to the remote pilot once the drone had reached a safe altitude. Control from then on, until the mission had been completed and the drone was returning to its base, would be handled via a Ku-band L-3 Com satellite data link system. Recovery was the reverse of take-off, the local pilot again taking control as the drone approached its home airfield and then handling the landing and taxiing to its hangar or shelter.

For this flight, Nagell would be both the local pilot and the remote pilot and would be using both the line of sight and satellite communication systems to control the drone at different stages and locations. He levelled the Reaper at 30,500 feet, adjusted the speed and heading and then relaxed as the drone continued on its planned track towards the southern shore of Lake Ontario. The on-board radar showed no contacts close enough to be a problem and even the limited view through the cameras confirmed that it was a lovely day out there.

With a bit of luck, Nagell thought, the weather might hold until he could hand over to the second pilot in a few hours and head off home to enjoy what was left of Independence Day.

Chapter 47

Ben Morgan picked up a filter coffee from the counter of the Hard Rock Cafe on the corner of 10th Street and E Street, almost opposite but just out of sight of the FBI building. That was the only hot – or in this case still very warm – drink the staff could offer because all of their machines had shut down due to the blackout. Then he took a seat at an outside table. As he did so his mobile beeped. He opened it up to see he'd received a message containing a longish piece of text, a big data file and several audio files, all from Natasha Black.

He read the message and scanned the data file but didn't bother listening to the audio files because of what he read in the message. The audio files, Natasha explained, were the original take from the GCHQ intercepts, but the participants only spoke in Arabic, knowledge of which, she pointed out in her usual slightly acerbic manner, was not part of Ben Morgan's very limited skill set. The analyst at Cheltenham, or more likely one of the linguists on the staff there, had translated the Arabic messages into English and included the results within the data file, as well as the contents of a handful of SMS messages, all of which had been written in English.

By the time he'd finished his coffee he'd read the entire file. He knew nothing more about the putative attack than he had done before he'd started, but he did have several pieces of potentially vital information, none of which were the slightest bit of use to him personally, but which he knew that the FBI – or at least Grant Rogers – could, and should, be able to act on. Just as a precaution, he took out a notebook and pen from his pocket and made a written note of the most important data.

You can always rely on a pen and paper when everything else fails and, looking up and down the street at the noisy chaos being caused by the non-functioning traffic lights and the increasing number of people now wandering along the sidewalks, Morgan reckoned the situation in DC was probably going to get a lot worse before it got any better. His phone was almost fully charged and was still working, but he had no idea how long it would be before the service provider shut down the system because of the power outages.

Morgan decided not to call the FBI agent in case he was still being bellowed at by Charles Bouchier and simply sent him a five-word text message: 'I know where they are.' That should, he thought, provoke the reaction he expected.

His mobile rang less than a minute later.

'Where are you?' Rogers asked.

'Sitting outside the Hard Rock. Fancy a drink?'

'Yes, but not there. That's far too close to your new best friend in the Bureau. Meet me at The Smith on the corner of Ninth and F Street. Ten minutes.'

'I'll be there.'

Morgan headed north on 10th, then turned east on F Street before crossing the road to the opposite side where the restaurant was located, taking his life slightly in his hands because none of the traffic lights there were working either and the cop standing in the middle of the intersection clearly had his hands full just trying to unravel the angry automotive jigsaw surrounding him. He obviously had no time at all to help pedestrians get where they needed to go.

Rogers walked into the restaurant a few minutes after Morgan had taken a seat, plopped himself down in the chair opposite him and nodded his thanks for the can of Coke that was already on the table. Just like the Hard Rock, the interior of the restaurant was a confusion of shadows barely illuminated by wall-mounted emergency lighting, but the staff were doing their best, serving cold drinks and salads and only taking payments in cash. American 'can do' in action.

'Did Bouchier give you any trouble?' Morgan asked. 'I don't think he and I got off to the best of starts, somehow.'

'You got that right. I don't think anybody ever called him a brain-dead sack of shit before, but I know quite a few people who wouldn't disagree with that description. He's typical of the kind of desk-bound bureaucrats who clamber over everybody else to get to the upper floors of the Bureau where they can sit and pass judgement on the guys who actually do the work, who get out on the streets and mix it with the bad guys. Anyway, he can't ban me from talking to you. The FBI is there to serve the public and as far as I'm concerned you're a member the public, so fuck him. Okay, what have you got?'

Morgan quickly explained about the trace and intercept program that the analyst at GCHQ had been running on Natasha Black's orders, and the results that had been obtained.

'This woman a friend of yours?' Rogers asked, when he'd finished.

'She's both a friend and a colleague,' Morgan replied. 'We move in different circles and different disciplines but our paths often cross. And she's definitely a wheel, not a cog, in the GCHQ machine.'

'Well, it looks as if she's managed to do some stuff that I didn't even know you could do. So these intercepts can pin down the locations of these guys – Ganem, Halabi, Sadir and Wasem – or at least the locations of the mobiles they've been using, plus another three potential suspects whose names and involvement we don't know. Not that knowing their names would help much, because they'll probably all be using aliases.'

'Exactly,' Morgan said, leaning closer and showing Rogers the screen of his mobile phone, on which he'd brought up a map of DC. Overlaid on that were four locations each marked with a capital letter: G, S, X and Y.

'Those are the places where the four suspects were staying in DC,' he said. 'The letter G, obviously, is Ganem, the suspect you first identified, and you already had his address. But the important thing is that they're not there any more. The trace shows that at exactly eight thirty-eight this morning all four of them – not just Ganem – started moving, and I don't believe that was a coincidence. That was a pre-planned and timed move designed to throw off any surveillance they might have picked up.'

Morgan used his finger and thumb to change the scale of the map display and then pointed over to the west of DC where the letters G, X and Y were showing.

'That's where Ganem's now located,' he said. 'He's in an apartment building in Woodstock, and if he's there for the music he's half a century too late and in the wrong Woodstock. X and Y are Halabi and Wasem, but I don't know which one is which, and they're out here, at opposite ends of Harrisonburg, but the one we should be concentrating on is Sadir, because he's way up here in Fairview, north-east of Baltimore.' He altered the display again to show the area around Bel Air. 'The rats are scattering, abandoning the ship they're trying to sink.'

'So you think Sadir is the one pulling the strings?'

Morgan nodded. 'He's the only one who switches his mobile off and on at irregular intervals. The other three – in fact the other six people involved, if we include the people he's got lurking out at Damascus, Fairview and Syracuse – have their phones on all the time. So they're the ones waiting for orders and instructions, and Sadir is the person giving those orders. He only turns his phone on when he's got something to tell them. And what he's doing is issuing orders. You can see that from the translations of some of his calls and what he's said in his text messages. Sadir is definitely the one we need to nail.'

'If we take him down, do you think that will stop the attack?'

'I still don't know what the attack is, or how they're going to do it, but if we can take Sadir out of the loop that might be all we need to do. If he can't issue his orders then maybe the others involved will stop whatever they're doing. My guess is that they won't, because of the mindset of the kind of people we're dealing with. But whatever you decide to do, I think you need to do it quickly, before the cell phone system dies.'

Rogers nodded, pulled out his own mobile, opened his contacts list and selected William Clark's mobile number. 'Bill, we've got a good solid lead on these suspects but we need to move real fast. First, get onto the Baltimore Field Office and tell them to prep their SWAT team to take out a confirmed target in a district called Fairview. The type of property and number of hostiles is unknown, so we'll need overkill, probably double whatever number of agents they'd normally use. Tell them this is an unfolding emergency situation in response to the blackouts in DC and proper authorisations will follow. Any problems, give them my number.'

There are 56 FBI field offices, and each one has its own Special Weapons and Tactics team. The Baltimore Field Office is located at 2600 Lord Baltimore Drive in the city and is also responsible for eight smaller offices, known as resident agencies, located at Annapolis, Bel Air, Frederick, Rockville, Salisbury, Dover and Wilmington.

'We'll need a chopper on standby just in case the suspects run, but the SWAT team should prepare to approach by road, no sirens, no lights, until we know what we're dealing with. We'll need a chopper to pick us up in DC ASAP and fly us out to somewhere in Bel Air. We can use the resident agency there to brief the SWAT guys and decide on tactics. What? No, the chopper will have to pick up you and me, along with Ben Morgan, because he's the guy who unravelled this particular ball of string. Bring a couple of satellite phones along with you just in case the mobile network goes down. And don't tell Bouchier, obviously. I'll sort that out when this lot's over.'

Morgan's mobile rang at that moment. 'Yes, Natasha?' he said.

'Two things you need to be aware of. First, the mobile out at this Fairview place has been switched on all morning, which is not typical of the way it's been used up to now, so I think the user was waiting for a message or messages. Second, about an hour ago he sent a one word SMS to the mobile up in Syracuse, just asking for the 'Estimate', and the response was 'ETD 1330'. Our intercept system put the Syracuse mobile at the Hancock International Airport there, so maybe he's just waiting for some associate of his to fly out of the country. What we can assume is that whatever flight he's talking about is not one that Sadir plans on catching, because there's no way he can get to Syracuse and go through the shuffling horror of check-in within the time he has left. So that's a minor mystery.

'Third, in the last twenty minutes he's had one call from each of the three mobiles out to the west of DC. Each conversation was more or less the same, again in Arabic, and each caller just told him that they'd completed their task. More significantly, each caller also finished their message with just two words.'

'The *Takbir*?' Morgan suggested.

'I'm pleased you've been paying attention,' Natasha said. 'Exactly. Each of them said *Allāhu akbar* – 'God is great' – and the man they were talking to repeated it before ending the call. And a few seconds after each of these three men had finished the conversation he switched off his phone and it's been off ever since.'

'Got it, Natasha, and thanks.'

Morgan looked across at Rogers, who was waiting expectantly. Morgan explained what Natasha Black had told him. 'At the end of the call they each said *Allāhu akbar* and then they switched off their mobiles. I don't like the sound of that. The obvious implication is that they've done their bit in this attack, and the obvious conclusion is that these are the three guys who've been orchestrating the blackouts and outages here in DC. So they might well be packing up ready to leave any time now.'

Rogers nodded. 'I'll get Dave Nicholls – he's another member of the team I've been using for this – to get the wheels turning. The fastest way to reel them in is to let the police out at Woodstock and Harrisonburg handle it. If these three perps aren't in the wind yet the local boys in blue should get them.'

He dialled another number on his mobile and crisply issued a series of instructions, including the precise lat and long figures the GCHQ tracking had provided.

'Get them moving immediately, Dave,' Rogers instructed, 'and as soon as you can send them ID photos and the best of the pictures we took when these four guys met out at Tysons. And keep me in the loop.'

'Where do we pick up the chopper?' Morgan asked, when Rogers finished his conversation and stood up. 'The roof of the Hoover building?'

Rogers shook his head. 'Only in *The X-Files*,' he replied. 'These days you need a whole bunch of top-level senior seat-shiners to approve something like that, plus there'd be the problem of sorting out permissions and getting you into the building and up to the roof while Bouchier is on the war path. We'll use the South Capitol Street Heliport. Much more discreet and a lot fewer questions will get asked.

'We'll get a cab and fight our way through this gridlock. Bill will meet us there and by the time we arrive the chopper should be ready.'

Chapter 48

'Is there somewhere you need to be, Sammy?' Nagell asked, glancing behind him at the training officer, who was pacing about behind the control position. 'You keep looking at your watch.'

Major Dawood shook his head. 'Just wondering how much longer you're going to take with this fairly simple exercise,' he replied.

'As long as it takes, Sammy. You know I always do a good job.'

In fact, Sami Dawood was keeping a very close eye on the time, but also on the progress of the exercise, which he did as a matter of routine for every training mission that he planned and supervised.

But on that day he was working to a rather different deadline, one that he knew would explosively mark the end of his military career in America, as well as end the lives of an extraordinarily large number of citizens in Washington D.C.

And what he was waiting for right then was a call or maybe a text message from the Iraqi freedom fighter he knew only as Abū Tadmir. A message that would tell him the final preparation, the final link, was now in place and that he could move on to his own personal endgame. What he would do then would ensure that his name would be revered throughout Islamic history as one of the greatest *shahids* of all time.

Chapter 49

The drive to the heliport, which on a normal day and in normal traffic conditions would have taken about ten minutes, maybe even less depending on how you caught the traffic lights, took them almost half an hour. The taxi Rogers had hailed on the street got jammed almost as soon as they moved off, and after remaining stationary for about five minutes, the two men got out and walked.

Then Morgan spotted a police car with an officer at the wheel, half on and half off the pavement at the end of D Street, and they jogged over to it. Rogers produced his FBI credentials and a few seconds later they were on the move, the driver clearing a path with its lights and siren. Even so, they had to double back a couple of times and take to the side roads to avoid streets that were completely jammed with stationary vehicles.

And all the way Morgan fretted that they were losing too much time as the unknown and unknowable deadline drew invisibly closer. He wondered if the blackouts and the inevitable chaos that had followed as the traffic lights stopped working had been specifically intended to frustrate the movement of law enforcement personnel trying to locate and arrest Sadir. But realistically, he knew that there had to be much more to the blackouts than that.

As the police car pulled up on the street outside the heliport, the growl of its siren dying away to a whimper, a black painted helicopter dropped out of the sky and settled onto one of the parking spots, its metal skids separating slightly as the weight came off the rotor.

'That's our ride,' Rogers said. He thanked the police officer for getting them to the heliport about as fast as anybody could have done in the circumstances, and then they strode quickly to the entrance.

Inside, William Clark was already waiting for them, holding what looked like a sports bag but which he opened to reveal a couple of Iridium satellite phones, two Glock 23s in .40 S&W calibre with belt holsters and an unopened box of .40 cal ammunition. Although the 9mm Glock 17 and 19 are extremely popular personal weapons in America, the FBI and many American police forces have opted for the heavier calibre Glock 23 because the .40 calibre S&W ammunition offers much better stopping power than the smaller round. No law enforcement officer ever wants to shoot a suspect, but every law enforcement officer also wants to be certain that if he does have to fire, the person he's shooting at will be taking no further part in the proceedings after being hit. The 9mm round simply does not possess sufficient kinetic energy to always ensure that this will happen.

Rogers glanced in the bag and nodded. 'Good thinking. I'm a big fan of redundancy, and you can never have too many guns.'

Clark had grabbed a Bureau car and caught a break with the traffic, getting down as far as the junction of 4th Street with M Street in the Southwest Waterfront district before he reached the end of another jam, and even then the lights and siren fitted to the FBI Suburban meant that he had been able to keep moving, albeit slowly.

As soon as the pilot of the Bell 407 gave the appropriate signal to the ground marshaller, the three men ducked involuntarily under the rotor disc, as everybody approaching a running helicopter always does, and then climbed into the back of the THU chopper. They sat down, strapped in and pulled on headsets so they could hear each other above the roar of the Allison turboshaft.

The Tactical Helicopter Unit is the FBI's elite rotary wing division, attached to the equally elite HRT, the Hostage Rescue Team, and employs some of the most highly skilled helicopter pilots in the world, trained to fly in all weathers, in all conditions, and in all possible locations including tight spots that most regular chopper pilots wouldn't even consider landing in. The hop from the heliport to Bel Air was hardly going to be the most taxing flight that particular pilot had ever made.

'No news yet from Woodstock or Harrisonburg,' William Clark said to Grant Rogers.

'But the local police are mobile, yes?' Rogers asked.

'Yes. I think the biggest problem is that while, thanks to Mr Morgan here, we've had triangulation of their locations, that only indicates the buildings they were in, not the actual apartments, and checking the map it looks to me as if they probably are in apartment buildings. It'll just take time to look at everyone in each block and haul out the suspects. And from what you said, they might already have headed for the hills, so we may already be too late.'

'We might still get them,' Rogers replied, 'even if they have already run. We have their names – maybe their real names but more likely aliases – and we have their pictures. We can stick them on the website in the Most Wanted Fugitives rogues' gallery and wait for some citizen to spot them. And because of what's happening in DC, we can probably put them right at the top of the top ten and add a juicy price tag to each one. That's something else that seems to work.'

The Bell lifted off as soon as the pilot had checked that his three passengers were properly strapped in, and Morgan was treated to a view of Washington D.C. that he'd never seen before as the helicopter flew north-east in the general direction of Baltimore, more or less following the course of the Anacostia River. The most obvious landmark was the Washington Monument and behind that the unmistakable shape of the White House and, closer and further to the east, the Capitol Building. What surprised him was the number of green and open spaces there were once they'd cleared the centre of DC. It seemed to only take a few minutes before they were over more or less open countryside.

'That's where your girlfriend's working,' Rogers said, pointing out of the right-hand side window of the Bell at a brutal lump of a building entirely surrounded by acres of car parking, most spaces apparently occupied.

'No Such Agency,' Clark confirmed. 'Famous for never telling anybody anything, even if you ask them really nicely. I'm really surprised that they let an Englishwoman in there, allowed her to cross the hallowed portal.'

Morgan nodded. 'She works at GCHQ out at Cheltenham, back in England, and a lot of the stuff she does – which she also won't tell me about, by the way – means tapping into the NSA's databanks pretty much on a daily basis. So I suppose you could argue she's kind of an honorary NSA employee, just with a different accent and a different colour passport. And she's not my girlfriend, only a colleague.'

'Whatever you say, Ben, whatever you say.'

The Bell continued heading north-east, the pilot maintaining a track that would take it to the north-west of the sprawling urban-isation of Baltimore and also keep them well clear, both laterally and vertically, of the traffic patterns at the busy Baltimore/Washington International Thurgood Marshall Airport, commonly known as BWI, which was rather less of a mouthful. Once the helicopter had passed abeam of the Liberty Reservoir, the pilot altered course to an easterly heading to track almost directly towards Bel Air.

The FBI resident agency in the town was a low, two- and three-storey brown brick building located at 2107 Laurel Bush Road, opposite a warehouse selling building supplies and in an area marked by industrial units of one sort or another. There was limited parking outside the building for cars and no spaces at all for helicopters, but that wasn't a problem. A short distance to the west was a U-shaped development of businesses and retail units and in the centre of the U was a large car park, the centre of which had been cleared of vehicles and fenced off to allow space for the Bell to touch down.

'Takes all the fun out of it when they make it so easy,' the pilot – he'd introduced himself as 'Richard Muldoon, and you can call me Rich but not Dick' – muttered as he flared the helicopter and brought it in for a gentle landing on the tarmac surface. 'I'm sticking around in case you need top cover for this op,' he added as he started shutting down the aircraft, 'and when you've blown away the bad guys or whatever the hell it is you're doing out here in the sticks, I can give you a ride back to DC if you want.'

'We might just take you up on that,' Rogers said, 'but we'll definitely need you in the air, or at least ready to take off, once we hit the target.'

'Which is where? Presumably not here in Bel Air?'

'No. It's near a place called Fairview, which is four or five miles north-west of here. A couple minutes in the air if you're already turning and burning.'

'Yeah. No sweat. I'll stay here with the chopper. Don't want some country boy getting inside and trying to hot-wire it.'

Waiting outside the cordoned off area which was marked by linked steel barriers were two men, both looking fit and well built, around six feet tall and wearing dark suits, white shirts and dark ties. One of them even had on a pair of sunglasses, making both of them look like the archetypal Men in Black, but these two weren't looking for aliens. Or at least, not aliens from another planet.

'ASAC Rogers?' the one without sunglasses asked, extending his hand.

'That's me,' Rogers replied, shaking his hand, and quickly made the introductions. 'This is Senior Special Agent William Clark and the third member of our group is Ben Morgan, who's on secondment to the Bureau for just this one operation.'

That was close enough to the truth, Morgan hoped, to avoid too many awkward questions being asked.

'Understood. I'm Special Agent John Baker and this is Special Agent David Crawford, both of us out of the Baltimore Field Office. Our SAC is here as well, and he's waiting for you at the resident agency. Our SWAT team is already in the area and on its way to Fairview. But everybody involved has a whole bunch of questions and they'd really like some answers.'

'I'll bet they have.'

Despite the distance from the car park to the resident agency only being perhaps two hundred yards, the two special agents had arrived by car. In fact, they'd arrived in two cars, if two black Chevrolet Suburbans could actually be classed as cars. To Morgan's English eyes, used to the much more compact vehicles found in the UK and Europe, they looked vast, more like small coaches than cars.

'We weren't sure how many of you there'd be,' Baker said in partial explanation as he steered the Suburban down the street, 'or if you'd have a bunch of equipment with you.'

Inside the resident agency a heavily built black man wearing an impeccable light grey suit, white shirt, silver tie and an almost palpable air of authority was waiting when Special Agent Crawford led the way through the door.

'Rogers?' he asked, staring at the new arrivals.

Grant Rogers nodded and stepped towards him.

'Follow me. Now.' And with that the man turned away and strode down a short corridor to an open door, Rogers trailing a few feet behind him. Inside, the man sat down in a large leather swivel chair behind a mahogany desk and stared across it towards Rogers.

'I'm the Baltimore SAC, Lewis Gordon,' he said, 'and I'm here at this resident agency because I want to know what the hell's going on. I've just spent a very unpleasant five minutes on the phone listening to your SAC, Charles Bouchier, tell me exactly why he wants you to be suspended and some guy called Ben Morgan, who I presume you brought with you, to be arrested immediately. The last thing I want or need is some guy from the Hoover building I've never heard of telling me to prep my SWAT team, to clear a space for a helicopter to land right here in Bel Air, and to make plans for carrying out an assault without authorisation or justification or even giving me the faintest fucking clue who's going to be assaulted, where they are or why they've suddenly become a target.

'So if you don't want an awesome shower of shit to descend upon your head from a hell of a height, Rogers, then I suggest you start talking and give me one good reason why I shouldn't do what Bouchier wants, right now.'

Chapter 50

Sami Dawood's attention was divided between three different things: the Reaper's training flight, which he had devised and was personally supervising; his wristwatch, where the minute hand seemed to be rotating around the dial at ever-increasing speed; and his mobile phone, which was remaining ominously silent.

Of those three things, it was the seemingly far more rapid than usual passage of time allied to the absence of any contact from the person he was expecting to hear from that was causing him the most mental distress and anguish. At this, almost literally the fifty-ninth minute of the eleventh hour, after months and years of planning, surely they could not fail. Surely Allah would not permit it.

What should he do if the call didn't come? If there was no contact? If that nightmare became a reality? He had come so far in his personal and spiritual development, thanks to the imam who had recognised and acknowledged his anguish and inner turmoil as a senior member of the selfsame military machine that had been slaughtering hundreds and thousands of his brother Muslims in Syria, Iraq and Afghanistan, delivering death by remote control using their fighter and bomber aircraft and their infernal, devilish drones, invisible, inaudible and impersonal killing machines.

When he had first contacted the imam, he had been seeking guidance, an explanation, not absolution or anything of that sort. His dilemma was as obvious as it was apparently irreconcilable: how could he remain a devout and practising Muslim if the job he was doing involved training people in the safest, easiest and most efficient and cost-effective methods of going out there and killing Muslims on behalf of the United States of America?

Praying hadn't helped, and nor had the conflicting voices in his head. He was trying to do the impossible, to balance the exhortations of Allah, the acknowledged reality that all Muslims on every continent were brothers and brothers didn't kill brothers because family, whether local or global, was sacrosanct, with the comradeship and profession-alism of the American military, the organisation that he had pledged allegiance to, just as he had pledged allegiance to America itself. How could he reconcile that, and how could he accept and cope with the knowledge that his country of birth was now at war with radical Islam and, at least by implication, with the whole of the Muslim world?

Until he had talked with the imam, he had almost felt as if his very soul was being torn apart. But eventually his prayers and the imam's guidance had shown him where his true destiny lay: he was first, last and always, a Muslim, and the conduct of the West, and particularly of the Americans in the Middle East, had shown beyond all doubt that they were godless polluters of the planet, a radicalised Christian nation that would not rest until every other religion had been crushed beneath their steel-shod feet. And the imam had shown him that he was in a unique position, a Muslim able to help redress the balance, to even the scores, and able to do it from the inside, from the very bowels of the American war machine.

When he had grasped that essential – and in retrospect, entirely obvious – truth Dawood had managed to quiet his inner demons and was able to worship Allah with a clear conscience, while at the same time carrying out his military duties with his usual quiet profession-alism while he waited for further guidance. And that guidance had been provided sooner than he had expected.

He had been contacted by a man who had understood his inner conflict, sympathised with his dilemma, and had finally been able to show him the way forward, to specify the precise route that he would have to take to retain his Islamic purity and at the same time help to strike a blow for Muslims everywhere. A route that would also, as a *shahid*, ensure his eternal life in the beatific presence of Allah himself.

That man had called himself Abū Tadmir, and Dawood neither knew nor cared what his real name was, only that his wisdom and certainty of purpose served to further quell his doubts and reinforce the path that he knew in his heart was the correct one to follow.

And now, when the retaliatory strike against America's capital city was about to begin, the contact, the instruction, that he had been waiting for simply hadn't arrived. He could only assume, and hope, that Abū Tadmir had encountered some kind of technical difficulty that was hampering the changeover. At least, that was what he was silently praying was the reason.

'Surveillance run complete,' Nagell reported. 'The Reaper's in the climb for the transit to Fort Drum. We'll need briefing on targets and weapons pretty soon, Sammy.'

Dawood stopped beside the control console and nodded. 'You'll get them in a couple minutes. Let me know when you're at cruising altitude.'

The surveillance operator who been operating the sensors for the runs over the south coast of Lake Ontario stood up, stretched, announced that he needed a comfort break and walked out of the room.

And at that moment, just when Sami Dawood was convinced that the whole operation had failed for some unknown reason, his mobile phone finally displayed a message on its screen. It read: 'Log-on problems. Contact now established. Execute.'

Dawood breathed a sigh of relief that his deduction about the delay had been correct. He could now carry out the actions that he had been mentally rehearsing for weeks. His lips curled in a slight smile as he looked again at the final word on the SMS message Abū Tadmir had sent him. It was more than just appropriate: it was an executive instruction with two separate but intimately linked meanings.

He walked across to the door of the control room and locked it, then strolled back to where Lieutenant Nagell was concentrating on steering the Reaper towards the Adirondacks air-to-ground range at Fort Drum. As he approached the seated man, Dawood reached into his uniform jacket pocket and took out the weapon that he had purchased perfectly legally, as a senior military officer, almost a year earlier.

It was a Walther Arms PPQ M2 pistol in 9mm calibre, with a fully loaded fifteen-round magazine inserted and one round already in the chamber, because Dawood hadn't known how many people would be in the control room when the time came for him to fulfil his destiny. Like the more common Glock handgun range, the PPQ has no external manual safety catch and instead relies upon various internal safeties.

He stepped across to Nagell, held the pistol about six inches behind the seated man's head and squeezed the trigger twice, the unsuppressed gunshots explosively loud in the confined space.

The effect upon the seated man was instant and terminal. Most of his face and forehead were blown forward onto the control panel in front of him and he tumbled forward, collapsing sideways half out of the seat and onto the floor, a spreading pool of crimson blood expanding around his shattered head. It had at least been quick. No Sweat Nagell had been a popular man on the base, and despite his intentions, Dawood had seen no particular reason to make him suffer unduly or even to make him aware that he would be dead in a matter of seconds.

Dawood stepped back and looked down critically at the corpse of the man he had just killed, alert for any indication that against the odds Nagell was still alive. But there was no movement.

Dawood replaced the pistol in his pocket, took out his phone and tapped out an instant reply to the SMS message: 'Execution complete. *Allāhu akbar.*' Then he dropped the mobile to the floor, aimed his pistol at it and fired a single round. The bullet blew the phone apart, permanently ending his conversation with Abū Tadmir and eliminating his link with the man.

He looked around, then knelt on the floor of the control room facing east, the approximate direction of Mecca, and said his brief final prayers.

Then he walked over to the other side of the room where he had a temporary desk and chair and sat down. He placed the Walther pistol on the table in front of him where it was within easy reach, and then just waited.

The sounds of the gunshots would have carried a considerable distance even outside the GCS and he knew that the locked door of the control room wouldn't keep anybody out for very long. Even as he sat there listening, he could already hear the sound of running footsteps from somewhere outside, and an unidentified voice bellowed, 'Shots fired!'

Somebody tried the door of the control room, and then hammered on it, shouting something unintelligible, though the meaning was clear.

They would be inside in minutes, perhaps even in seconds, and although Dawood knew he could take some of them with him with the rounds he had left in the pistol, the outcome was obviously never going to be in any doubt.

At least it would then all be over. Within a matter of minutes, at the most, he would know the essential truth of *Jannah*, the Garden of Paradise where, like all true Islamic believers, he would spend the rest of eternity accompanied by seventy-two *houris* – beautiful, full-breasted and utterly compliant virgins – to attend to his every wish and desire.

Three minutes later, the door to the control room crashed open and two soldiers dressed in full battle gear, one toting a Colt M4A1 carbine, the standard weapon of the American infantry, and the other a Remington M870 12-gauge pump-action shotgun, kicked their way inside and immediately separated.

Dawood stood up, picked the target on his left and fired two rounds from his Walther. One missed and the other hit the soldier on his body armour but did no lasting damage to him. The other soldier was the one with the shotgun, and before Dawood could pull the trigger again he had loosed off his first round.

At that range, the shotgun was by far the most lethal weapon in the room. The three-inch magnum charge of buckshot ploughed into Dawood's right side, almost tearing his arm from his body, and about a second later the second charge of buckshot tore through his stomach and lower abdomen, virtually ripping his body in half.

Dawood was clearly well beyond any kind of medical help, but he was still going to take time to die. With the room secured by the two soldiers, several officers from the unit entered to inspect it. Two of them walked over to look down at Dawood, one of whom almost immediately vomited noisily over the fallen man's legs. They were easily able to reconstruct in their heads what had actually happened in there, though what they couldn't possibly know was why.

None of them felt much like interrogating Dawood, who lay twitching and moaning on one side of the control room in his own spreading pool of blood, vomit covering his legs and most of his intestines splattered across the wall behind him.

And none of them felt like ending his agony, either.

Chapter 51

About five minutes after he'd received the final, triumphant, message from Sami Dawood, Sadir had set the next part of his operational plan in motion, using his mobile phone to dial the first of two numbers he had recorded within the contacts list on his burner. That was the number of the Nokia that he had hidden in the woodland adjoining Hancock Field. That phone emitted no sound, because the ringer was set to silent, but that had no effect upon what happened next.

Ringing the Nokia completed the circuit between the heavy-duty twelve-volt battery and the device, a specialised kind of bomb known as a non-nuclear electromagnetic pulse weapon, or NNEMP, which was designed to do far more than just explode. The weapon had been fabricated by the three electrical engineers in the house at Damascus, the men using the names Rafiq Khayat, Nadeem Ramli and Imran Wardi, following Sadir's most precise, detailed and specific instructions. Three men who would even then be assuming new identities and putting a safe distance between themselves and Washington D.C.

Initially in complete silence, a series of actions then took place with extraordinary rapidity under the camouflage-patterned tarpaulin. First, the entire current from the heavy-duty battery was fed down a pair of high-capacity insulated copper cables to the stator winding. This sent an immediate electric current through the stator which, as anyone with a knowledge of basic physics would be aware, generated a magnetic field. Electricity and magnetism are inextricably linked within the force known as electromagnetism: the passage of an electric current generates a magnetic field and the reverse is also true, a moving magnetic field producing an electric current. In this case, the design of the stator, the tight winding of the mass of copper coils from which it had been constructed and the sheer size of the device meant that the magnetic field generated was both intense and enormously powerful.

After a predetermined interval – an interval so short that it was to all intents instantaneous – a separate electrical circuit triggered a blasting cap within the core of C4 – Composition 4 – plastic explosive packed into a steel cylinder, the armature, around which the copper wire forming the stator had been wound, the cylinder and the stator separated by an airgap. Far too fast for any eye to see, the explosion blasted through the armature as a wave, expanding with incredible rapidity, the sound of the detonation crashing through the woods beside the base.

That sudden expansion forced the metal of the cylinder into contact with the winding of the stator, producing an immediate short-circuit and disrupting the current from the battery. The forward motion of the short circuit, in its turn, compressed the magnetic field, resulting in a massive burst of electromagnetic energy, an electromagnetic pulse or EMP, which travelled across the comparatively short distance between the weapon's location and the control facilities for the airfield.

A few fractions of a second after the explosion, the electro-magnetic pulse, containing a confusion of powerful electric and magnetic fields, ploughed into its target, wreaking havoc on every electrical system that it reached, causing voltage surges, current spikes, short-circuits and electrical fires, fusing circuit boards and destroying every electronic circuit that it reached. The result was immediate and instantly catastrophic. Cars and lorries stopped moving as their engine control systems were fried. Battery-powered watches stopped working, mobile phones burnt out, and virtually everything else, every electrical device from power points and lighting to control circuits, air-conditioning systems, radios and radars, simply shut down.

The weapon that Sadir had envisaged as functioning as the second phase of his attack on Washington D.C., albeit indirectly in the case of the device located at Syracuse, had worked perfectly.

Everybody in the control room heard the bang at the same instant as every light went out. The screens, illuminated instruments and controls on the drone pilot's position instantly turned black and the all-pervading hum of the air-conditioning system, a sound that hardly any of the people there ever really heard because it was a permanent part of the background noise, immediately ceased. In some ways, that was the most alarming thing of all because it meant there'd been a total and complete shutdown of power, not just the simple tripping of a breaker somewhere in the electrical system.

A couple of the officers pulled out their mobile phones to try to find out from somebody what was going on, but in both cases their handsets were not only warm to the touch, but also completely dead. It wasn't just a case of the failure of the mobile phone system: their phones had simply become small and slim electronic paperweights, neither useful nor ornamental. The landline phones in the GCS were also completely dead. The most senior officer there, another major, posted one of the armed soldiers outside the door as a guard while the rest of them dispersed to try to find out what had gone wrong.

Within minutes, it was clear that virtually all the electrical systems in that section of Hancock Field had suffered catastrophic burnout. Almost nothing was working, not even cars and jeeps, and there was no obvious way of recovering the situation. A team of electrical engineers from the base began examining the circuits and equipment and rapidly came to the conclusion that fixing it was going to require replacement of virtually everything, including many sections of wiring, rather than attempting any kind of repair.

Hancock Field, and more specifically the GCS used to control the Reaper drones, was blind and deaf and dumb, without radios, satellite links, data links or even raw radar.

And that was a problem, because somewhere, probably about thirty thousand feet above their heads and some miles away, was a fully armed MQ-9 Predator drone that nobody was actually controlling.

Not only was nobody controlling it, but none of the people who were now standing around in the dark and windowless GCS, aiming torches pointlessly at the silent banks of equipment, had the slightest idea how to rectify the situation.

'It'll keep flying,' a voice said out of the darkness. 'So at least we've got time to find it.'

'How?' another and more senior-sounding voice snapped. 'With binoculars? And then what do we do?'

'I don't think we've got any choice. We need to get a fighter airborne out of Andrews or somewhere and shoot it down.'

'That sounds easy if you say it quickly,' the base commanding officer replied. 'But there are a few tiny problems, like we don't know where it is, we don't know how high it is, we don't know which direction it was flying and we don't know what transponder code it was using, so how the hell is anybody going to identify it? The only two people who knew any of that are lying dead on the floor right here. Even the surveillance systems operator only knew that the camera run at Lake Ontario had been completed and that the drone was on its way towards Fort Drum, because then he decided he needed a leak and left the room. I suppose we're lucky he did that, because if he hadn't there might be another corpse lying on the floor over there, and we wouldn't even know that much.'

'That was probably deliberate,' another senior officer suggested.

'Deliberate? What the hell do you mean? Of course it was deliberate.'

'The reason for the killing, I mean. That bastard Dawood had to shoot Nagell because he was the pilot. He would have known where the drone was, and the squawk, and we would have been able to get another radar unit to track it. At least, we could have done that, until all the lights went out.'

The CO looked around at the dark figures – they were most of his senior officers – clustered around him in the lightless and silent control room.

'And there's something else none of you might have thought of,' he added, 'and that's the professional suicide angle. I, personally, am not entirely happy about the idea of authorising the destruction of a perfectly serviceable fourteen-million-dollar Reaper and having that put on my military record.'

'I think they're closer to sixteen million these days.'

'Whatever. So before we start calling up fighter support we need to do what we can to find it. Whoever said it was still in the air got that right. With no control inputs, it should keep on flying at the same height, at the same speed and in the same direction, but what worries me is that it's probably not doing that.'

Nobody responded.

'What I mean,' the CO clarified, 'is that we've been hit by some kind of EMP weapon, and whoever did that didn't do it just to fuck up our aircon units and trucks and phones. Building a weapon like that takes knowledge and skills that most people don't have, so I think we're looking at terrorist activity here. I think that Reaper's been hijacked, though I'm damned if I know how, and right now it could be heading straight for New York City or somewhere to try to finish what nine eleven started.'

'Shit,' somebody said.

'You got that right, and we're neck-deep in it. So we need to get out of here and find somewhere on this base where there's a working telephone. Then we contact Fort Drum and see if their systems are working, because if they can use their radios or satellite link we might be able to regain control of this thing and bring it down at an airfield somewhere, maybe up at Wheeler-Sack.

'The other thing we do is let our command structure know what's happened, because we're not looking at any kind of an accident here. This was enemy action. So we pass the buck up the line and suggest mounting combat air patrols near high-value targets like New York in case the Reaper is heading that way. Then if it does get shot down it won't be on my chitty. Short term, I want armed patrols covering the perimeter until further notice. And get a team together to locate the source of the explosion that kicked off this shitstorm. Right, let's get moving.'

Chapter 52

For whatever reason, establishing control of the Reaper drone out of Hancock Field through the satellite data link had taken far longer than Sadir had expected, and for a few minutes he wondered if they would have to abort the attack that day. But the significance of the date and what they were trying to achieve was so important to him that he shoved that idea to the back of his mind. Completing the operation on that most important day of the year for almost every American was essential to drive home the message of radical Islam.

Michael and Joseph had been sitting alongside him ever since he'd arrived that morning and ever since they had identified the data feeds to and from the drone they'd been doing their best to intercept and monitor it. That had caused the delays, because for some reason they had been unable to establish a secure link to the drone as quickly as they had hoped and had previously managed.

But finally they had done so, and the moment they had both confirmed that they were happy with it Sadir had made the call to Sami Dawood to set the operation in motion, and he'd followed that a few minutes later with the mobile call to trigger the detonation of the NNEMP he'd hidden in the woods alongside Hancock Field.

As a precaution, Sadir had waited about half a minute more and then called the same mobile number again. That had come back with a number unobtainable message, which he knew meant that the mobile phone must have been destroyed in the explosion and that the Reaper GCS at the airfield had been rendered permanently incommunicado, which was the object of the exercise.

Acting on Sadir's instructions, Michael climbed the drone to almost fifty thousand feet to get it well above all civilian traffic and at the same time switched off the Reaper's transponder. That wouldn't make the drone invisible, as it would still generate a small primary radar return, but it would almost guarantee that civilian controllers would simply ignore it and military controllers might see it but wouldn't do anything about it because they would probably assume it was a small, low-flying aircraft below controlled airspace or even an angel, an atmospheric phenomenon, a bit of anomalous propagation that generates intermittent returns on radar displays.

'Now start tracking south-west towards the airfield,' Sadir ordered, 'and keep the speed down so it doesn't trigger alarms anywhere.'

He glanced at the two young Chinese men sitting in the seats on either side of him and smiled.

'We've done well,' he said. 'I hope your country will be appreciative of the work you've done here and with the prize that you'll be able to ship to Beijing or Shanghai, in the diplomatic bag, of course. In fact,' he added, 'I think you probably deserve a drink to keep you going, because it's still a long flight to where we'll land the drone. Stay here, and keep the Reaper heading in the same direction.'

'There are Cokes in the fridge,' Joseph said, as Sadir stood up to leave the room.

In the kitchen, he opened the refrigerator, took out two cans of Coke, half filled a couple of glasses and then, with a surreptitious glance back towards the door of the room, he took two small vials of colourless liquid out of his pocket, snapped off the tops and poured the contents into each of the glasses, and used a teaspoon to mix the contents, being careful not to rattle the steel spoon against the glass.

He walked back into the room they were calling the control suite, handed over the glasses and then returned to the kitchen to pour his own drink, which he would consume neat, without any extras.

Sadir had only been able to obtain the services of the two professional, Chinese government-trained, hackers – their range of techniques and abilities went way beyond the level that Ganem and the other two men had reached – by agreeing with their employer that his plan would deliver not simply a current and state-of-the-art Reaper drone, but also a full weapons fit, intact and undamaged. He had agreed to fund the entire process of stealing the drone on the understanding that on delivery he would receive substantial remuneration for conducting the operation. That was his stated motive, though his real agenda was of course entirely different, and he had managed to convince the senior officers running Unit 61398 of that.

As the two Chinese men sipped the drinks and imbibed the nanobot cocktail that would kill them both in under half an hour, Sadir began to quietly celebrate in his mind. His two companions had had no idea what had happened at Hancock Field, except that Sadir had somehow managed to disable the ground control station. They believed that all they then had to do was land the drone at the small private airfield they had identified as a suitable location, and where a small delegation of Chinese diplomats was probably already waiting to see the drone descend from the sky. He wondered how long they would stay there before it dawned on them that something had gone wrong and that the Reaper, the enticing high-tech prize that Sadir had dangled in front of them, wasn't going to appear.

He had calculated that Joseph and Michael would collapse at least twenty minutes before he would need to swing the Reaper onto a southerly heading to track directly towards Washington D.C., where he would unleash the entirety of the weapons load carried by the drone into the soft underbelly of the people of the capital, the crowds that he was certain would already be out in the streets in response to the series of blackouts Ganem and the other two hackers had engineered. The kind of crowds that a typically cynical American military pilot would probably describe as 'a target-rich environment' if the Reaper was overhead somewhere like Baghdad. Well, they were about to find out that the same mentality could also exist over Washington D.C.

Sadir's final act would be to plunge the Reaper directly into the portico of the White House, where the substantial quantity of fuel remaining in the tanks – it should still be carrying almost half of its initial fuel load – would create an impressive, and hopefully fatal, fireball. He wouldn't be able to kill the President because the bulletproof glass and thick reinforced walls of the building would prevent that happening, but he should certainly be able to take out several of the Secret Service bodyguards and anybody else within range. And the sight of the front of the White House apparently bursting into flames, an image which he was certain would travel around the world in a matter of seconds thanks to the power of social media and, almost incidentally, send most of the stock markets into free fall, would be the culmination of the attack that he and his associates in Iraq had been working on and planning for most of the last decade.

He sipped his own, uncontaminated, Coke with a feeling of quiet satisfaction as he waited patiently for his two companions to die.

Chapter 53

Grant Rogers stared back at the clearly angry Lewis Gordon. The Baltimore SAC's reaction had not been entirely unanticipated, because obviously Charles Bouchier would have discovered fairly quickly that one of his ASACs and a senior special agent had left the Hoover building unexpectedly and he would probably have been informed about the flight of the Bell helicopter out of DC up to Bel Air carrying three passengers and requested by somebody at the Bureau. Putting two and two together to make four is not a particularly difficult trick.

'We have an unfolding situation in DC,' Rogers began, but Gordon interrupted him immediately.

'I know. A few blackouts. Perhaps you can tell me what the hell that has got to do with the FBI. Or has the Bureau now started working for the power companies?'

'Sorry, but you've been badly misinformed,' Rogers replied. 'There haven't just been a few blackouts in DC, as you put it. The information I received from the electrical engineers who were trying to restore power was that they were facing a cascade situation where circuits would overload, trip and shed the load onto other circuits which would then do exactly the same thing. And the reason they were doing this wasn't because half the residents of DC suddenly decided to hike their air-conditioners up another notch or two or turn on their ovens. It was because some hackers had created artificial faults inside the networks, shutting down generator cooling systems, fiddling with thermostats and altering settings. And they managed to affect virtually every power company that supplies DC and the surrounding areas.

Unravelling it and finding and fixing all of these faults is probably going to take them at the very least the rest of the day, maybe longer.'

Somewhat to Roger's surprise, Gordon had listened to what he said attentively and without interrupting.

'Okay, maybe I was misinformed. Maybe there are a lot of blackouts. But my question still stands: what has that got to do with the FBI? And while you're at it, maybe you can tell me exactly what the hell you're doing here in Bel Air and why you needed my SWAT team activated?'

Rogers nodded. At least Gordon was listening to him, something that Bouchier only very rarely did, and even then he had a habit of constantly interrupting whoever was talking, like the kind of unpleasant, biased and aggressive interviewers seemingly favoured by many satellite television news channels. He'd never met the Baltimore SAC before but he knew of him, the FBI being just as gossipy as any other large organisation, and Gordon had a reputation for being exceptionally bright and with a very low tolerance for both bullshit and fools. And the fact that he had made it as far as he had in the Bureau's hierarchy not only as a comparatively young man, but also as a comparatively young black man, was a clear testament to his abilities.

'The short version is that DC is under attack, and the information that we've obtained suggests that the blackouts are simply the first stage in what's going to happen. We've had help from the NSA and the British GCHQ and what we know is based primarily on mobile phone intercepts and the triangulation of those same mobiles. That's why we're here, and also why we requested the activation of your SWAT team – because we believe the mastermind behind these attacks is located just a few miles from here, in Fairview, and right now he's probably making his final preparations to launch his strike against DC. Time's passing and the longer we just talk, the more chance there is of that attack happening. And what we certainly can't do is hang around waiting for somebody like Charles Bouchier back in the Hoover building to decide there really is a problem and start issuing orders. Our information suggests we don't have days. We might not even have hours. Right now we might be looking at just a few minutes before the attack commences.'

'Okay, Rogers, you've got my attention, and I agree that if we waited for Bouchier to make a decision we'd probably be sitting around here for the rest of the week. To set your mind at rest, the SWAT team is fully kitted out and on its way to Fairview right now, as your man requested, with no lights or sirens, just a couple of black Suburbans driving nice and quietly through the suburbs. I know those SUVs just scream "Bureau" or "Secret Service" but they're all we've got. They'll park up somewhere and wait for the go signal, and I guarantee they will be ready when we need them.'

'Thank you for that.'

'So what's the target?'

Rogers outlined the information they had obtained from the GCHQ intercepts, the translations of the Arabic speech used in the phone calls, and the content of the SMS messages.

'So you hope the local cops have picked up those three hackers, or the people you think are hackers, and you believe this man Sadir, this "father of destruction" as he calls himself, is out at Fairview right now, presumably with his finger on the trigger. What you don't know is what pressing the trigger will do. And these other two contacts, one at Damascus and the other at Syracuse. What are we doing about them?'

'There's not a lot we can do, as far as I can see. We had enough evidence to move against the three suspected hackers – or just about, anyway – and we've established Sadir's role. But we have no idea who the other two people are or what they're doing, and we certainly don't have probable cause to do anything more than interview them. Maybe we'll get around to doing that when this is all over. But right now, I'm certain the danger is Sadir and whatever nasty little plan he's concocted, and that's what we need to get sorted.'

'Okay,' Gordon said, standing up, 'let's move it.'

Chapter 54

Joseph, sitting on Sadir's left, suddenly stood up, emitted a kind of strangled gasp and fell backwards, bouncing off the arm of the swivel chair he'd been sitting in and sending it sliding across the carpeted floor towards the back wall of the room. Sadir had seen the effect of his lethal nanobot cocktail numerous times and knew beyond doubt that Joseph was already dead. That just left Michael to deal with.

'Joseph!' Michael called out, springing from his own chair and stepping over to try to assist his friend and colleague.

Sadir also stood up, glanced across at Michael's half-empty glass and realised he would need to assist the process of the Chinese man's imminent death, and that he needed to act immediately.

As Michael bent over and tried in vain to revive his friend, Sadir reached into the inside pocket of his jacket and pulled out a fully loaded Glock 19 semi-automatic pistol fitted with an Obsidian9 suppressor, an expensive unit optimised, as its name suggested, for the 9mm Parabellum round, the most popular handgun and submachinegun cartridge in the world.

It was a point-blank range shot.

Michael turned his head slightly to look at Sadir and opened his mouth, perhaps to call for help, and at that moment the Iraqi pulled the trigger. The sound of the shot was like a hard slap, completely inaudible outside that room, but the effect on Michael was instant, dramatic and terminal.

The 9mm Parabellum bullet is not renowned for its stopping power, but at that range it didn't matter. The copper-jacketed slug tore into the upper left-hand side of the man's back at around nine hundred miles an hour, missing the spinal column by a couple of inches. It passed between two of his ribs and ploughed through his heart and right lung.

Michael slumped to the floor, not quite dead but fatally wounded, a hoarse scream erupting from his throat. His agony was short lived as Sadir pulled the trigger a second time, the bullet hitting his back only a couple of inches away from the first wound, and then a third time. But for that final shot, the Iraqi altered his aim and shot Michael in the side of the head. That's when he finally stopped moaning and stopped moving.

Sadir stared down for a few seconds, looking dispassionately at his two victims. They were not the first people who had died at his hands, and as the events of this day were going to prove, they were certainly not going to be the last.

Chapter 55

When they stepped back into the foyer, Ben Morgan was using his mobile, and held up his hand to Rogers as he ended the call.

'I've had Natasha Black on the horn again,' he said. 'Something's been happening up at Syracuse. The GCHQ monitoring system reports that Sadir sent his contact there a message in English about twenty minutes ago. The message read: "Log-on problems. Contact now established. Execute." Three minutes later his contact at Syracuse texted him back. That message read: "Execution complete. *Allāhu akbar*", and then that mobile shut down. So something's going on there.'

'What?' Rogers asked.

'I have no idea. About two minutes after that, Sadir rang another mobile number, but his call wasn't answered because that phone went off the air almost immediately, and not long enough for GCHQ to get a confirmed location. But the initial trace suggested it was somewhere near Syracuse, certainly within about a fifty-mile radius. That mobile is also still off the air. All that sounds to me like other parts of the plan falling into place, though I still don't know what the plan actually is.'

Morgan's clearly English voice immediately attracted Gordon's attention.

'I presume you're this Ben Morgan character who's managed to stick a burr a couple feet up Charles Bouchier's ass?'

'Guilty as charged,' Morgan admitted. 'But right now Bouchier is the least of my worries. That second call Sadir made worries me because he could have been activating a bomb or something by ringing a mobile attached to an IED. I can't think of any other reason why a mobile would shut down virtually as soon as it received a call. But I have no idea why a bomb or something at Syracuse would be part of an attack on Washington. It must be three hundred miles away.'

'Morgan is the man who's been getting the intercepts from GCHQ through a woman called Natasha Black who's now working at the NSA,' Rogers clarified.

'I kind of guessed that bit,' Gordon said. 'You told me that this guy out at Syracuse sent another SMS today about a flight departure, or did I get that wrong?'

Morgan responded before Rogers could answer. 'Exactly. He quoted an ETD, an estimated time of departure, and I've no idea how that links to Sadir's message about log-on problems and establishing contact. Look, I don't know this country, obviously, but I do know there's an airfield at Syracuse and that ETD comment must refer to an aircraft. You don't say ETD if you're talking about catching a bus or a train or even driving a car somewhere.'

'Unless he was just using it as a form of shorthand,' Gordon pointed out. 'I mean, using ETD rather than saying "the train leaves at two" or something. You've just said that your whizz-kids over GCHQ could accurately triangulate the location of these mobile phones as long as they stayed connected. So where exactly at Syracuse was the first mobile before it went off the air?'

Morgan fished his notebook out of his pocket and found the correct page. He ringed a pair of geographical coordinates with his pen, the latest triangulation update Natasha Black had sent him, and handed the book to Special Agent Crawford. The FBI man sat down at a computer terminal, pulled up a mapping application and fed in the information. Then he leaned back in the chair and pointed at the screen.

'The mobile's position was at the Syracuse Airport,' he said, 'so I don't think that piece of data gets us any further forward.' Then he paused for a moment and looked more closely at the mapping display.

'What is it, David?' Gordon asked.

'Well, that position *is* on the airfield, but not where I would have expected to see it on the airfield. The passenger terminals and customs and all that stuff are on the north side of the runway, but the location Mr Morgan has given me is to the south of the runway, so maybe our mystery man wasn't waiting for a flight to depart.'

'What buildings are near that location?' Rogers asked.

'It's pretty close to the southern edge of the airfield so there are a bunch of utility companies there, offering stuff like hydraulic and pneumatic repair, batteries, a distribution hub and even a medical centre. I guess they're all outside the airfield boundary fence and the location I've been given is pretty much in the middle of that lot.'

'The accuracy of the triangulation depends on a bunch of different factors,' Morgan said, 'but mainly the number of masts in communication with the cell phone. Don't just focus on the coordinates I gave you. Is there anything else in the area that's more interesting than a battery shop?'

Crawford studied the map again, then shook his head. 'Not really,' he replied. 'The only thing marked inside the airfield boundary near there is the Hancock Field ANGB, and I don't know what that is.'

'I do,' John Baker said, 'but I don't think it helps us any. Syracuse Airport is a joint civil and military airfield, and on the southern side of the runway is the Air National Guard Base. They call that bit Hancock Field.'

That simple statement and the transcription of the penultimate call that the GCHQ intercept had picked up struck a chord in Morgan's brain. The expression 'Contact now established' could mean that Sadir had been talking to a military pilot. Maybe he had suborned a fighter jockey and intended to have the pilot run strafing runs over Washington D.C. That would certainly count as 'death from the skies'. In his head, it was all beginning to make a bit more sense.

'What aircraft does the Air National Guard fly?' he asked, expecting Baker or somebody to reel off a collection of numbers beginning with the letter 'F' for 'fighter', but instead the special agent shook his head.

'They used to fly Fighting Falcons, F-16s,' he said, 'but the last one left back in 2010. Since then they've only operated MQ-9 Reapers. You know, like a Predator drone but with teeth. Loaded with missiles and bombs and stuff.'

That wasn't what Morgan had expected him to say, but at that moment several disparate and apparently unconnected facts – the blackout in DC that had forced people out onto the streets, the two Chinese government-trained hackers who had flown to America on the same aircraft as Sadir had done about three years earlier, and perhaps most significantly of all the 'Contact now established' SMS that GCHQ had picked up – all started to make sense. And it painted a picture that Morgan really didn't like the look of.

'I think Sadir has hijacked a Reaper,' he said into the silence that followed Baker's remarks.

Chapter 56

Sadir replaced the pistol in his jacket then turned his attention back to the flight control console and checked the position of the hijacked Reaper. In a few minutes, he would need to alter its course to the south-east to begin the attack run towards Washington D.C. At the moment, it was still at high level to the north-west of his target and would be painting as a faint primary return on any surveillance radar set with coverage of that area, but it should not be attracting any attention because of its non-threatening heading.

He had done most of his research at a very early stage of the planning for this mission, and he knew that the moment he altered course towards the capital city of the United States of America, alarm bells would start ringing and hands would hover over telephone handsets, precisely because the UAV was not wearing a transponder squawk and so would be considered to be potentially or actually hostile.

So first, he had to do something about that. It was time to begin the third act of this particular play.

He picked up his mobile phone, scrolled down his list of contact numbers until he found the one he was looking for, and dialled it. He listened to make sure that the recipient number was ringing, and heard the faint difference in sound as the cascade system Nadeem Ramli had devised shifted to call the second mobile number.

He ended the call when he heard the sixth mobile start to ring.

Chapter 57

Gordon smiled, then laughed out loud.

'That's another one of those things that probably sounds easy until you try it. All the communications with those UAVs are encrypted, scrambled like you wouldn't believe. There's no way some terrorist could break into that system.'

'I specialise in cybersecurity and cyber warfare,' Morgan said quietly, 'and if I had a hundred pounds for every time some security officer had told me that their intranet or computer system or website or whatever was unbreachable, I'd be a millionaire by now. There's no system ever devised that can't be breached if somebody has the time and the talent and the will to do it. Whatever this plan is, what we do know about it is that it's been a long time in the gestation stage.

'And there's something else,' he went on. 'Hacking can be done from anywhere on the planet, obviously, but we've established that two professional Chinese military hackers travelled all the way from China to America with Sadir about three years ago and then immediately dropped out of sight. Why would they have needed to physically travel to America? Why did they have to be on the spot? To me,' he concluded, 'the only answer that makes sense is that there was something they had to do over here that they could not have done from back in Beijing. And I think that something was to design a system and work out a way of hacking into a Reaper's control systems so they could use it to attack Washington D.C.'

'That wouldn't work,' Gordon insisted. 'This isn't my field, but it makes sense that if the guys on the ground at Hancock Field suddenly lost control of a Reaper and couldn't get it back, about the first thing they'd do would be to whistle up a couple of F-15s or F-16s or something and blow it out of the sky. End of problem.'

Rogers's mobile rang. As he listened to what the caller was saying, his face seemed to turn pale.

'That was one of my guys back at the Hoover building,' he said. 'We've just been notified about an emergency situation up at Syracuse, called in by somebody from outside the airfield. All inbound and outbound flights have been cancelled because the airfield's radar and radio systems have stopped working and nobody seems to know why. There have also been reports about a bomb blast to the north-east of the airfield but very close to the boundary. What there aren't, at least so far, are any reports about bomb damage, which again doesn't really make sense because the two events – the bomb explosion and the radar and communications failure – pretty much have to be linked.'

Nobody in the room responded for a few moments, and then Morgan nodded briskly as another unspoken question that had been on his mind was suddenly answered.

'That might be the last piece of the puzzle,' he said. 'A bomb that doesn't cause major damage but results in the failure of electrical and electronic systems more or less has to be an EMP device. The bomb wouldn't have been designed to do much physical damage, just to generate big enough electric charges and magnetic fields to shut down various systems at the airfield, like the radars and radios. And that's why nobody's punched a fighter into the air to shoot down the Reaper, because they've got no idea where it is now that Sadir's controlling it. In fact, they probably don't have any communications out of the base at all at the moment because an EMP blast is really good at frying mobiles and even landlines.'

'That's pure speculation,' Gordon said, but there was little conviction in his voice.

'I'm a simple soul,' Morgan said, 'I follow William of Occam so I always choose the simplest explanation for any sequence of events. If you've got a better idea, now would be the time to explain it to us. If you haven't – if nobody has – then we need to get over to

Fairview right now. And if we find Sadir sitting in a lawn chair, reading a magazine, drinking a cup of coffee, looking at the view on this lovely afternoon or doing something else completely innocent then I'll apologise to him and I'll apologise to you because that would mean I've got it completely wrong. But I don't think I'll be saying sorry any time soon.'

'Fair enough,' Gordon said. 'We'll take your chopper and I can brief the SWAT team en route.'

Chapter 58

A couple of locals in a flatbed Ford had driven past the van parked on the corner of Dower House Road W and Leapley Road about twenty minutes after Imran Wardi had stepped away from it and climbed into the passenger seat of the Chevrolet Cavalier Nadeem Ramli had been driving.

The Ford's driver had pointed ahead through the windscreen as they'd approached the van and given a brief laugh.

'Hell of a place to get a flat,' he said. 'Funny he didn't have a spare with him.'

'Maybe he had,' his passenger suggested, 'but maybe that was flat as well. Whatever, he'll have had a real long walk to find a garage. I think the closest is probably back in Woodyard, and that's maybe three miles away. Let's hope somebody gave him a ride.'

Two other local drivers passed the vehicle over the next couple of hours, and their reactions mirrored those of the first two men. None of them saw the van as anything other than a bit of bad news for its driver.

An hour or so later a Washington D.C. police patrol car drove along the same road. Colloquially referred to in America as 'black-and-whites', the DC cars are anything but. This cruiser was a Dodge Charger, and its bodywork was almost entirely white, with the word 'POLICE' in large light blue letters signwritten on each side and embellished with short horizontal red stripes overlaid by a thin, sinuous, curving horizontal blue stripe. Apart from the word written on both sides of the vehicle, and the inevitable lightbar on the roof, it could almost have been an upmarket company car wearing a corporate logo.

Inside it was much the same in terms of equipment as any other police patrol car in America, as were the two men sitting in the front seats. They were trained to look out for anything unusual, and an abandoned van missing one wheel and left on a quiet country road certainly fitted that description. So unlike the locals, the two cops in the Charger didn't simply drive past but stopped on the apex of the bend where the driver switched on his roof bar lights.

'You run the plates, Dick,' he said, pushing open his door, 'and I'll take a quick look around.'

What he found was exactly what he had expected to find when he'd first seen the abandoned vehicle: it was fairly new, the driving compartment appeared clean and tidy and all the doors were locked. He pulled the note out from under the wiper, read what was written on it, shrugged and replaced it.

'Anything?' he asked as he sat down again in the driving seat.

'Nope,' his partner replied. 'It's a rental from a DC company and the insurance and everything else checks out. And at least the guy driving it managed to get it off the road so it's not causing an obstruction. I'll just log it and get the late shift guys to check if it's still here tonight.'

'Sounds like a plan,' the driver said, switching off his roof bar lights as he accelerated away.

Nobody else went anywhere near it on the public roads for the next ninety minutes, though a handful of vehicles passed it on the other side of the fence, on the roads within Joint Base Andrews.

And then, seconds after Sadir had dialled the number of the first mobile, the screen of the Nokia burner phone clipped to the board in the back of the van illuminated when it received what would be its last ever call.

Chapter 59

'You got coordinates for where this Sadir guy's at?' Gordon asked, his voice clear enough through the headset Morgan was wearing in the back of the Bell helicopter.

'Yes,' he replied, and tore another sheet from his notebook after checking that he'd copied the numbers correctly from Angela Black's message on his mobile phone.

'Thanks.'

Gordon had a handheld two-way radio, pre-set to the same frequency that the SWAT team was using. He lifted one half of the headset from his right ear so that he could use the radio, and he quickly passed the coordinates to whoever he was talking to at the other end. He listened to the reply, then ended the transmission and replaced his headset.

'The team leader's already scouted the area and he thinks he knows which property those coordinates refer to, but he'll check it out on his map to make sure. Then he's going to put a drone up – not a Predator or Reaper, obviously, just a small camera-equipped quad-copter – to do a surveillance run around the property, keeping it high enough to be invisible and inaudible. When we know what we're facing, we can go in and sort this.'

'Got a question for you,' the Bell's pilot asked.

'Go ahead, Rich.'

'This is all covert, right? Landing a chopper ain't what you might call discreet, especially if I'm putting it down in some guy's back garden. So how about we do what aircraft are supposed to do and land at an airport?'

315

'There's an airport here?' Morgan demanded, staring through the windscreen at the patchwork of woods and fields and occasional houses that lay directly ahead of and below the helicopter.

'It's not quite like LaGuardia or JFK,' Richard Muldoon confirmed, 'but there is an airport, right here in Forest Hill.' He briefly pointed ahead of the aircraft towards a thin strip of tarmac lying to the south of the road they were just approaching and which was bracketed on both sides by what looked like rows of industrial units.

'That's Forest Hill Airport,' Gordon confirmed. 'Not so much an airport as a right-of-way in a field, according to a pilot friend of mine, but it does have a tarmac runway and a helicopter landing there isn't going to attract very much attention, so that's a good call. Put us down, Rich, and I'll tell the SWAT team to pick us up from there.'

Muldoon tried to raise the airfield on VHF 122.7, the only frequency published in his aeronautical information guide, but got no response.

'That's only a UNICOM frequency,' he said on the intercom, 'and that's like a small handheld VHF set, so I don't think there's anyone home. It's a private airport and you need permission to land so I'll just park this bird on the grass by the undershoot to runway one three. There's plenty of room there and your SWAT guys can drive straight in off the Jarrettsville Road to pick you up. If anyone turns up to complain I'll just tell them we're on FBI business and to send the bill for landing fees to the Hoover building.'

Something had been niggling away at Morgan's subconscious, something that didn't quite fit with the attack scenario that he was almost certain Sadir had planned, and as Rich Muldoon settled the Bell down smoothly a few yards north of the western end of the thin and short tarmac runway – it was only a little under 3,300 feet long – at the Forest Hill Airport, it suddenly came to him.

'Oh, shit,' he muttered.

Chapter 60

In complete silence, the screen of the last linked mobile illuminated, completing the automated cascade system that Ramli had devised. That action initiated the small program on the tablet computer, which then in its turn triggered the first step of the firing sequence, at virtually the same moment as the other five tablets in their dispersed locations did precisely the same thing.

The NNEMP weapon bolted to the floor of the rented van parked beside the boundary fence on the eastern side of Joint Base Andrews was several orders of magnitude larger – in all respects – than the device that Sadir had manhandled into the woods adjoining Hancock Field. It was so heavy that its total weight was very close to the maximum permitted load in the back of the van, and the three engineers working at the house in Damascus had had to use the engine hoist to manoeuvre its component parts into the vehicle, and then manhandle a collapsible steel frame and a chain hoist into the van as well as use long levers and pry bars to assemble it.

It was one of the three biggest weapons because of the job that it was going to have to do: to send the largest possible pulse of electromagnetic energy surging across Andrews. The other two maximum-size weapons would carry out precisely the same function at Ronald Reagan Washington National Airport, just south of the centre of DC, and at Dulles Airport out to the west of the city, while the three remaining, very slightly smaller devices, would cripple the central part of Washington.

The full current from the heavy-duty battery began flowing through the tightly wound copper coils of the stator for the briefest of instants before the C4 plastic explosive charge tightly packed inside the steel armature detonated, causing the short circuit that initiated the electromagnetic pulse.

That NNEMP weapon had been the last to be positioned and was also the last of the group to explode, but only by a barely measurable fraction of a second. The epicentre of the detonation was roughly the midpoint of the vehicle, and the device was aimed directly at the rear doors.

No airfield that stays open 24/7, least of all one as big as Joint Base Andrews with its plethora of different military and civil units, is ever silent. Activity of one sort or another goes on around the clock, everything from aircraft taking off and landing to service and maintenance vehicles, and even private cars, moving around the airfield. That afternoon it was comparatively quiet, precisely because of the date, with very little air traffic and just a handful of vehicles driving along the roads and taxiways.

This relative peace was ripped apart by the detonation of the charge of plastic explosive in the centre of the stator of the fabricated weapon, the noise a deafening assault upon the ears. The sound rolled and crashed across the largely open space around the epicentre of the explosion and echoed off the buildings in its path.

The detonation reduced the van to its component parts, flinging the engine and transmission across the road and a couple of dozen yards beyond it. The engine itself smashed into the trunk of the solitary tree that marked the apex of the triangle of grassed land on the other side of the road.

The rest of the van was blown into torn and twisted slivers of steel. One second the van was disabled but intact and a few milliseconds later virtually nothing of it remained, or at least nothing immediately recognisable. The explosion also demolished dozens of yards of the airfield boundary fence, flattened the short length of crash barrier and toppled the pole carrying power cables. They tumbled down to land in an untidy tangle around the wreckage of the van.

The blast reduced the NNEMP weapon to millions of scattered and shattered pieces, just as it was supposed to do to launch the payload.

A huge, devastating and completely invisible charge of electromagnetic energy expanded across the airfield. It destroyed everything electrical that it touched, blowing or fusing circuits, melting wires, frying components and wrecking electric and especially electronic equipment. And these days, virtually everything, almost every machine that performs a useful function, contains at least one electronic circuit.

Moving cars and lorries within range of the blast simply stopped working, their electrical circuits fried. Because it was Independence Day, most of the aircraft were on the ground, and the EMP did a very efficient job of disabling them, the surging currents destroying electronic components, melting wires and creating myriad short-circuits. In the control tower the lights went out, radios fused and fell silent and radar screens instantly shut down.

For probably the first time since the airfield had begun operating as Camp Springs Air Base back in 1942, all activity at Andrews stopped and a total and utterly unnatural silence fell.

Of course, it wasn't just Andrews that was affected.

At Ronald Reagan, a civilian airliner taxiing to the threshold of the active runway simply stopped when every instrument in the cockpit ceased operating and two small electrical fires broke out behind the instrument panel. When the pilot tried to radio the ground controller, he discovered that all the radios, too, had ceased operating. But even if somehow that particular piece of equipment had been spared, the ground controller was looking at a blank screen in the now entirely unlit, dead and lifeless radar room. And the tow truck that would normally be sent out to recover an aircraft suffering such a catastrophic failure was itself unable to move because its ignition circuit and almost every other piece of wiring on it had been burnt out.

Throughout much of DC itself, those electrical devices that were still operating despite the blackouts ceased functioning, permanently, as the electromagnetic surges from the three NNEMP weapons ravaged their circuitry. The various additional sensors that had been installed to protect the capital city against air attack were fried, meaning that any airborne incursion would not be detected. And, even if such an attack were to be detected, the last line of defence, the Stinger surface-to-air missiles, were also neutralised by that same EMP, their circuits destroyed.

Washington lay defenceless against the assault that was to come, but not silent. Gathering crowds of people thronged the streets, asking questions and looking for explanations for what had happened to their city. Explanations that nobody could give, because nobody there had any idea what was going on. About the only thing most of the population knew was that there had been a truck bomb, or maybe more than one, in the city. There had been casualties, but because the vehicles hadn't been left in crowded areas, not that many. But that, of course, didn't explain why nothing, not phones or tablets or computers or cars or buses or ambulances or fire trucks or even some wristwatches, still worked.

The third phase, or the third act, as Sadir was mentally calling it, had been completed exactly as he had planned, expected and hoped.

Of course, he himself had no way of telling whether or not the devices had worked, but he had no reason to suppose that they hadn't. One way or the other, he would find out soon enough when the Reaper began its final approach towards Washington D.C.

Because now it was time to raise the curtain for the grand finale.

Chapter 61

'We're missing something here, Grant,' Morgan said. 'Sadir had to use an EMP weapon at Syracuse to permanently knock out the ground communications with the Reaper so he could take control of it. But that's only half the story. You told me that DC is well protected, with layered defences from fighter jets on standby all the way down to half-inch machine guns mounted in turrets on the tops of buildings, so well before that drone gets anywhere near the city somebody sitting at a radar set will notice, hit the panic button and punch a fighter or two into the air.'

'Shit,' Rogers muttered, immediately seeing what Morgan was driving at. 'He must have planted another electromagnetic bomb back in DC.'

'Not bomb,' Morgan said, 'but bombs. These devices have a fairly limited radius of action so he'd need several to take out enough of the city's defences to give him a clear run for his attack. At the very least, he'd need to hit Andrews and Ronald Reagan and maybe Dulles as well to take out their radar systems, and to cripple any fighters on the ground.'

Rogers nodded, picked a name from the contact list on his mobile and rang the number. Then he shook his head, tried another, and then a third.

'Number unobtainable,' he said. 'That's the Hoover building and the base operator and the command post out at Andrews. This bastard's already done it, hasn't he? He's already triggered the weapons.'

'Which means the Reaper is probably already on its attack run,' Gordon said, his earlier doubts about Morgan's hypothesis clearly dispelled. 'We need to move now.'

Chapter 62

Mahdi Sadir had trained as a private pilot at an airfield in Spain where the weather could be guaranteed and had been awarded a EASA – European Aviation Safety Agency – private pilot's licence, a PPL, allowing him to fly SEP – single engine piston – aircraft. That had been almost five years earlier, and since then he had hired aircraft on an irregular basis depending upon where he was in the world, just to keep his licence current and, much more importantly, to keep his piloting skills as sharp as possible. He now had over a hundred flying hours under his belt and could confidently follow the somewhat clichéd but vital axiom drilled into every pilot, to aviate, navigate and communicate, actions that applied to routine flying as well as what to do in an emergency. That meant he could take off, fly a route and land most fixed wing aircraft powered by a single piston engine and talk intelligibly to air traffic controllers while he did so.

But despite his familiarity with aircraft not dissimilar in size, shape and performance to the Reaper, he was finding controlling the UAV to be a far from easy task. In something like a Piper PA-28 Cherokee, an aircraft he had flown many times, he had unrivalled visibility and controls that responded to the slightest touch. And, more importantly, whenever he moved the control column or the rudder pedals he would actually be able to feel the effect of his actions through the seat: the changes in the effect of gravity when climbing or descending and of centrifugal and centripetal force when turning or manoeuvring. Somebody had once told him that that was where the expression 'flying by the seat of your pants' had come from.

But on the Reaper, there were obviously no physical sensations at all, no matter what he did with the controls, and his view forward was extremely restricted, limited to what the camera in the nose of the drone could see and display on the screen in front of him. So while he'd been sitting in the middle seat of the control suite that the two Chinese hackers had designed and built, for most of the time he'd been content to leave the UAV on autopilot, flying in a straight line at a steady speed and maintaining the same height, while he made his preparations for the attack.

He was able to plot the drone's progress thanks to its GPS and INS – inertial navigation system – feeds displayed on a second computer screen, on which he had also overlaid the track that he wanted the Reaper to follow. The other thing he had done since he had shot Michael in the back was to access the weapon control module on the UAV to make sure that he had control over the Hellfire missiles and the bombs. He wouldn't, of course, need to do any specific targeting – any old street full of people in Washington D.C. would do nicely – but he did need to make sure he could release the weapons when he needed to do so. And as far as he could see, that would be no problem. The now deceased Michael and Joseph had obviously done a very professional and comprehensive job, giving him control of all the functions of the fully-armed UAV.

Sadir switched his attention back to the mapping screen, where the symbol representing the Reaper's position was still following the original straight-line track towards the private airfield where the Chinese delegation was waiting to receive it. The symbol was approaching the alternative track that he had input himself, the track that terminated in the heart of Washington D.C. He waited a few more seconds, then adjusted the autopilot, moving the desired heading through ninety degrees to track south-east.

Within a matter of minutes, the drone would be in a position to release the first of its bombs. And then the carnage would begin.

Sadir felt his mouth go dry in anticipation and took another sip of his Coke. This truly was the endgame. Nothing could stop him now.

Chapter 63

Morgan, Rogers, Gordon and the special agent commanding the SWAT team crowded around the Panasonic Toughbook rugged computer, all staring intently at the screen which was displaying the live video feed from the surveillance drone, thanks to a Bluetooth connection. The device was being controlled by another SWAT team member, using a small panel fitted with a CCTV screen which was supported on a nylon harness around his shoulders. He was steering the drone in a wide circle above the target property, keeping it at a height of around a hundred feet where it should be inaudible to anybody on the ground below, and using the zoom feature on its camera to closely inspect the exterior of the building.

They'd been picked up by one of the SWAT team's Suburbans and driven the short distance from Forest Hill to Fairview, where they'd parked on a patch of open ground about a hundred yards from the target house. When they'd arrived, the drone was already in the air and in transit, the team having been briefed by Gordon even before the Bell helicopter had landed.

What was puzzling all four of the men was the fact that the building appeared to be completely deserted, although there were two vehicles parked outside it. The SWAT team had already run the plates and the local DMV, the Maryland Department of Motor Vehicles in Glen Burnie, not far from Fort Meade, had supplied the names and addresses of the registered owners. Neither of the names on the titles was Sadir, and neither listed address was the property that was under surveillance.

'You quite sure that's the right place?' Gordon asked, saying exactly what the others were thinking.

'That's the closest property to the geographical coordinates that the GCHQ intercept flagged up of the target mobile,' Morgan said, trying to inject his voice with more confidence than he was actually feeling. 'The problem is that we're kind of out in the sticks here, so the triangulation is based upon a smaller number of cell phone towers, so the location can't be quite as accurate as it would be in a built-up urban area.'

The drone passed behind the property and overflew the rear yard. An oblong area came into view, largely surrounded by what appeared to be established hedges. For a brief moment, Morgan thought it looked like a vegetable patch, though he had no idea whether or not American properties would incorporate such a feature, but then his attention was drawn to a roundish white object at one end of it.

'We need to take a closer look at that,' he said.

'It's a satellite dish,' Rogers said, stating the obvious.

'I know what it is,' Morgan replied, 'but what I want to know is where it's pointing.'

'Gotcha,' Gordon said, and told the SWAT team leader to zoom in on the dish.

On the screen of the Toughbook, the picture wobbled slightly and then seemed to accelerate directly towards the dish. Then it stabilised so that they were looking down at it from above, the tripod of metal arms holding the LNB, the low-noise block downconverter, at the apex.

Morgan looked at the compass heading on the screen, showing the direction that the drone was pointing, and then quickly worked out the approximate direction that the satellite dish was facing.

'Most of your American satellite television companies use birds that are located down to the south-west,' he said, gesturing at the screen. 'That dish is pointing somewhere east of south, and that's the bit of sky where most of the communication satellites are located, birds like the Intelsat and Inmarsat vehicles. So whoever's in that house isn't sitting there surrounded by empty beer cans and watching old reruns of *Bonanza* or *I Love Lucy*. He'll have something very different on the screen in front of him.'

'That's good enough for me,' Gordon said. 'Time to kick the door down.'

Chapter 64

'Can I assume this is not some kind of a joke?' Major Oscar Paulson asked.

'Damn right you can.' The caller had introduced himself as Colonel David Moore and had stated he was calling from Hancock Field at Syracuse, and that was the first problem the major had had with the conversation.

'Then why, sir—' the man had sounded official and senior and angry, and so Paulson was hedging his bets until he found out more '—are you not calling on an official line?'

'I say again, Major, and please listen carefully, because we have very little time, I cannot call on an official line because the fucking things have all been fried. Some terrorist detonated an EMP weapon on the airfield boundary and we lost the lot: radios, radar and telephone lines, including mobiles. But none of that's important. What is important is that we had a fully armed MQ-9 Reaper airborne when this happened, and we've got reason to believe that a terrorist group has hijacked it.'

Major Paulson opened his mouth to say something, then thought better of it and instead said: 'Please go on.'

'We don't know where it is or what these terrorists intend to do with it, but it's got bombs and Hellfire missiles on it so they could do a hell of a lot of damage in New York or Washington or wherever. We could be looking at another nine eleven, in spades. So what I'm ordering you to do is get your GCS manned like right now and find this fucking drone. And when you do, just get the thing on the ground, anywhere. Preferably at Fort Drum or Syracuse, but any airfield would do at a pinch. Any questions?'

Paulson had been suggesting and rejecting scenarios in his mind while he listened to what the caller was saying, and in the end he decided that manning the GCS was probably the easiest and safest thing to do, just in case he wasn't being spun a yarn. 'I'll get on that now, sir,' he replied. 'Can I call you on this mobile number once we're up and running?'

'Yes, yes. Just get on with it.'

Before Paulson did anything else, he dialled the number for the Air National Guard base at Syracuse. It came back as number unobtainable, and that single result was more convincing to him than anything that the man calling himself Colonel Moore had said.

Ten minutes later, Paulson led his team into the ground control station and explained briefly what little he knew. He didn't mention terrorists or hijacking because that idea was stretching his own credulity, and instead described the incident as involving a 'rogue' drone caused by a massive equipment malfunction at Hancock Field.

'We need to find this Reaper,' he said, 'and that won't be easy, because we have no idea where it is. In fact, when they lost contact with it, the UAV was on its way to the air-to-ground range here at Fort Drum, but where it is now nobody has any idea. It probably isn't squawking so we need to start looking out for primary contacts. Check with all the local radar units and try all our usual contact frequencies, including the Ku-band links through the satellite. I'll try and get some more information from Syracuse.

'Right, let's get to it.'

329

Chapter 65

Fairview, Harford County, Maryland, United States of America

But before they could formulate a plan, far less move, Morgan's phone rang and the screen told him the caller was Natasha Black.

'Yes, Natasha,' he said.

'Chummy's been on the horn again,' she told him. 'He made a call to another mobile number that hasn't been flagged up before. The peculiar thing is that he just rang it, but there was no conversation, and that mobile is now off the air.'

'We think he's triggered several EMP weapons in DC to knock out the radars and radios,' Morgan said, 'and that call could have been the activation signal. Our best guess is that he's steering an armed Reaper drone towards the city. We're just about to try to take him down. Just to confirm, you haven't got a more accurate set of coordinates for the location of his phone than you supplied before?'

'No,' she replied, 'but maybe I can help you identify the property.'

'How?'

'His mobile is still switched on. I don't know if that means he's expecting another call from somebody or if he just forgot to turn it off, but when you get outside the house or wherever he is, text me and I'll call him up. I can be a phone company executive with an offer that he simply can't afford not to take. You should be able to hear the phone ringing from inside the building.'

'Good idea. We'll do that. Now we've got to move.'

The target house was located on a large corner plot, and the area was sufficiently rural that the SWAT team members were able to get to within about twenty yards of the front door without any possibility of being seen by the occupants. But that was as far as they could go, because as soon as the special agent in charge – the fabric nametag on his black combat clothing read 'Wayne' – scanned the front of the property with his binoculars he spotted two small cameras covering the road and the short driveway.

'If we get any nearer,' he said, 'we might as well walk over there and ring on the doorbell. Let's try round the back. There might be cameras there as well, but because of the trees and shrubs we should be able to get a whole lot closer to the building without being spotted.'

They left two of the team members to cover the front of the house with their sniper rifles and the rest of them retraced their path until they were able to step into the open ground behind the property.

Wayne had been right: there was a camera aimed at the lawned area to the rear of the house, but the sides of the property appeared to have no surveillance devices in place, and that omission allowed them to get close without being detected.

'We need to lose that single camera,' he said, and moments later two of his men flattened themselves against the back wall of the property and walked sideways until the camera was directly above them. One of the men crouched down, braced himself and used his linked hands and shoulders as stepping stones for his partner to climb up high enough to reach not the camera, but the cable that fed it. He took a pair of insulated wire cutters, in case the camera was fed by mains power, and briskly snipped the cable in two.

Chapter 66

Inside the improvised control suite they'd constructed at the back of the house, Mahdi Sadir was suddenly aware of a change in the room, or more specifically of a change in the ambient lighting, but for a few moments he wasn't aware of what had caused it.

He checked the screens and controls in front of him, but they all appeared to be normal. Then he looked up towards the ceiling, at the three small flatscreens which displayed images from the CCTV cameras on the property. Strangely, only two of them still showed the feeds from the area around the house. The rear camera, the one that covered the yard, was no longer working. Sadir stood up in order to see better and carefully checked the pictures being produced by the two front cameras. Everything in front of the house appeared to be perfectly normal, exactly as it had been all day. No pedestrians and no new vehicles were visible.

It was probably, he rationalised, a defective camera, or possibly a problem with the wiring, and of no consequence to him – not when he was so close to the end of the operation.

Chapter 67

The two CCTV cameras mounted at the front of the detached property meant that the SWAT team would have to go in at the back, but Morgan was wondering if there was another option.

'Maybe we should do a bit of divide and conquer,' he suggested.

'Meaning?' Rogers asked.

'There are two cars outside, and my guess is there are at least two people inside the building, maybe more than that. Before your people kick in the back door, let me go and knock at the front. If one of the occupants comes to the door, that's one less person for your SWAT guys to cope with at the back. I can just be a lost Englishman wondering how to get to Bel Air.'

'Why you?'

'Because, Grant, I'm the only person here who isn't wearing a full set of combat gear or who doesn't look like an FBI agent.'

'That's true, but I don't think—'

'Good idea,' Gordon interrupted, and handed Morgan a beige-coloured ballistic vest. 'Put this on under your jacket. It's a Modular Tactical Vest, or MTV, and it should stop anything up to a nine millimetre.'

'That's encouraging. Suppose he aims a forty-four magnum at me?'

'Then I guess this isn't your lucky day.' Gordon's wide grin showed a lot of very white teeth. 'Seriously, the two guys covering the front of the house will cover you as well. If somebody carrying a bazooka opens it, they'll take him out before he can pull the trigger. Just remember to stand well away from the door once you've knocked on it.'

Morgan shrugged his jacket back on over the heavy ballistic vest, nodded to Rogers and Gordon and strolled off down the road towards the target property. As he stepped off the street and started walking towards the house, he pulled out his phone and sent a text to Angela Black. It just said: 'Call now.'

He heard the mobile ringing as he reached the house and stepped onto the porch.

He gave three sharp knocks on the door and stepped half a dozen paces to one side, to make sure he was out of the firing line of the two SWAT team snipers.

Chapter 68

Sadir sat down again, and almost immediately his mobile phone began to ring. He stared at it for a few seconds in surprise, because he had thought he'd switched it off after activating the electromagnetic bombs located across DC, then shrugged and answered the call.

'Hello?'

'Good afternoon, sir,' a chirpy female voice with an unusual accent said, 'I wonder if you've considered changing your long-distance provider. We have some spectacular deals this month, with some of our rates slashed to less than half the normal cost. If you're interested in seeing our tariffs we can—'

Sadir powered down his mobile and tossed it to one side. He'd received enough marketing and cold calls in the past to know that listening to them was a complete waste of time, even if you were a genuine customer, and he was a long way from being that.

A sudden movement caught his eye and he looked up at the CCTV screens on the wall. A figure was walking straight towards the front door of the house. A man, quite smartly dressed as far as he could tell from the tiny image. Probably a salesman of some sort, parking his car on the street and then going door-to-door with a pocketful of brochures and a smart line of chatter. The man rapped three times on the door and then stepped to one side, waiting expectantly.

Sadir ignored him. He switched his attention to the navigation screen for the Reaper. It showed that the drone was just inside twenty miles from the centre of Washington, and that meant it was time to initiate the final phase.

He accessed the autopilot settings and set the UAV into a powered descent to 15,000 feet, high enough to keep it out of range of the heavy machine guns that he knew were scattered on the tops of buildings throughout Washington, but low enough for him to identify suitable targets for the laser-guided bombs and Hellfire missiles hanging on the stores' pylons below the Reaper's wings. In point of fact, he had no specific targets in mind. He would simply aim the bombs and the missiles at the largest crowds he could see on the ground and then release them.

American weapons of war would be unleashed upon the civilian population of the capital city to devastating effect.

Chapter 69

Special Agent Vernon Wayne had identified the ideal way in as the French doors at the back of the house which gave access to the garden. They were an obvious weak point in the property and were almost certainly where any prospective burglar would have wanted to try his luck, which was probably why the rear camera had been positioned above them. But whereas a burglar would have tried to open the doors, perhaps with a lock pick or a pry bar of some sort, the SWAT team had a rather noisier, but infinitely more effective, way of getting inside.

In fact, they had a couple of options. They could wrap plastic explosive around the lock on the doors and detonate it, which would allow them entry but might still require the doors to be pulled open and would add precious seconds to the time it would take them to get inside. So they picked the second option, to remove the glass from the doors to allow them to step straight through them.

Working as quietly as they could, two of the SWAT team taped a double length of orange Primaline 5 detonating cord, a thin, flexible plastic-covered tube of pentaerythritol tetranitrate (PETN) – high explosive – around the edges of the glass of the French doors. Detcord is a high-speed fuse normally used to trigger other explosive charges, but unlike other fuses it explodes rather than burns, so it can be used as an explosive in its own right. And the speed at which it does this is around 23,000 feet per second, or a little over 15,650 miles per hour, so the effect is as near instantaneous as makes no difference.

With the charge in place, one of the team inserted a pyrotechnic blasting cap with a short fuse to act as the detonator, waited for Wayne to give them the okay, then lit it and stepped well clear. Unlike shaped charges, when detcord explodes the force blows in all directions.

Ten seconds later, the Primaline exploded.

Chapter 70

Fairview, Harford County, Maryland, United States of America

It was all going to work. If any radar sets had still been tracking the drone, he knew that by this stage and this close to Washington the UAV should have been intercepted and brought down. But it hadn't been, which meant that the EMP weapons must have done their work and taken out the radars and probably the fighters as well.

Suddenly Sadir switched his attention from the controls in front of him to the house itself. He had heard something, a scratching sound and a faint muffled thump, like a large object falling a short distance onto a wooden floor. The failure of the rear surveillance camera on the house suddenly took on a new and sinister significance. Perhaps that hadn't just been some kind of random electrical fault in the camera or cabling. And maybe the man at the front door wasn't a salesman.

It might be nothing, or it might mean that somebody had finally put the pieces together.

Sadir smiled.

Whatever had caused the sounds he'd heard, it didn't matter. He had never expected to walk away from this operation, but he was determined to see it through to the end. He turned back to the controls and altered the autopilot setting as a precaution, specifying a new final altitude for the descent of ground level and opening the throttle of the Reaper's engine, hiking its speed to 200 miles per hour. He also slightly altered the heading to aim the drone directly at the White House.

He picked up his Glock pistol, took the magazine out of the butt and inserted a full one. Then he turned round to stare at the door of the room, which was where he was sure the danger lay. If there really was a threat, if he wasn't just hearing the normal, innocent sounds of the house.

He took a final glance over his shoulder at the instrumentation and control panel, checking that the UAV was still on course, then picked up his pistol and aimed it at the door, ready for whatever or whoever came through it.

Chapter 71

The twin double-glazed units of the French doors instantly shattered, driving lethally sharp spears of glass into the heavy drapes that covered the opening, ripping holes in the fabric and smashing into the walls.

Immediately, two members of the SWAT team, closely followed by two others, crashed their way in through the remains of the shattered French doors, thrusting the heavy drapes to one side and looking for a target.

Wayne would have preferred to lob in a couple of flash-bangs – stun grenades – to disorient the occupants of the room before his men entered, but the obviously thick and heavy floor-to-ceiling drapes had prevented that being an option. What he was hoping was that the unexpected explosion of the detcord would have had a similar effect upon whoever was in the room.

Chapter 72

Fairview, Harford County, Maryland, United States of America

Sadir had been looking in the wrong direction when the blasting cap triggered the detcord. The explosion was both deafening and shockingly unexpected. The drapes were blown inwards and the area of the room beside the French doors was suddenly filled with exploding glass.

He swung round to face the threat and even before the echoes of the explosion had died away he was confronted by two strongly built and heavily armed men wearing full combat gear. Both were pointing Heckler & Koch MP5 submachineguns straight at him, and both were yelling.

His ears still ringing from the blast, for a second or two he couldn't make out their words. Then, as two more bulky figures stormed into the room, all wearing the same green combat clothing with FBI patches on their shoulders and 'HRT' on their chests, he finally understood the words they were bellowing: 'Drop the weapon. Drop the weapon.'

But that was the last thing he was going to do, quite literally.

Sadir smiled slightly, still holding the pistol in his right hand, and stared at his attackers. 'You're too late,' he said. 'Much, much too late.'

Then he took rapid aim with his Glock and squeezed the trigger three times, even as two of the FBI SWAT team opened up with their MP5s, the 10mm bullets smashing into Sadir's torso and driving him backwards and down to the floor.

One of the SWAT team stepped slightly sideways so that he could cover the fallen man with his submachinegun, while another member approached him cautiously. He kicked the Glock well out of reach, then knelt down beside Sadir's body, checked for a pulse in his neck and stood up.

'He's dead,' he said. 'Check the rest of the house and get Wayne and that English guy in here ASAP.'

Morgan stepped into the room about half a minute later from the front of the house, as Rogers and Gordon crunched their way in from the back over the carpet of glass shards. They took in the three corpses lying on the floor, but Morgan's attention was immediately seized by the improvised control suite that dominated the room.

'There were three of them?' Gordon asked, the house echoing to shouts of 'Clear' as the SWAT team checked every room.

'It looks to me like they had a falling-out,' the SWAT officer said. 'When we came in, the only one standing was that guy on the floor over there, the one who looks like an Arab. The other two, the two Chinese here, were already dead. The Arab fired three times and so we returned the favour.'

'But none of you are hurt?'

'No, because he didn't fire at us. He fired at that.' He pointed at the control suite, where Morgan was just sitting down.

'I think Unit 61398 of the Chinese People's Liberation Army is now permanently down by two of its most experienced hackers,' Morgan said, glancing at the two bodies on the floor behind him. 'Which is no bad thing, in my opinion. But that doesn't help us right here and right now.'

'What you mean?' Gordon asked.

'Sadir knew that once the SWAT team guys were in the house, he was only going to leave here in a body bag. So he didn't fire at them: he fired at the control panel to try and disable it. The reason he did that must be because he's already got the Reaper inbound to DC on quite literally a crash course, and by disabling these controls he knew there would be nothing we could do to stop it.'

'Knew, or hoped?' Rogers asked.

'I don't know yet.'

Chapter 73

Fairview, Harford County, Maryland, United States of America

Sadir's bullets had smashed the flatscreen monitor directly in front of the central seat on the console, ripped through the control column mounted on the desk and ploughed through a black plastic box containing several circuit boards. On what was left of the front of the box Morgan could see various analogue-type, but obviously digitally powered, flight instruments. He presumed that was a device running in tandem with the Reaper's instrumentation circuits that he expected to see displayed on the flat-panel monitors. A throttle quadrant was clamped on the right-hand side of the desk and below it he could see a set of rudder pedals. A standard computer keyboard and a trackball completed the set-up. It looked very like some of the other much-modified home flight simulators he'd seen.

He knew time was running out, and he also knew that he was the only person in that room and in that house with anything like sufficient knowledge of computer systems to recover the situation. And that depended upon him getting the control console up and running again, soonest.

The control column was way beyond repair, just a shattered collection of plastic and wires, but Morgan knew the way that computer programmers thought and worked, and he was absolutely convinced that somewhere in the room, in one of the cupboards or drawers or somewhere, there would be spare components. No serious computer user ever just has one machine or one screen or one mouse or one keyboard because people like that are always looking for faster or more responsive equipment, and so inevitably they accumulate bits and pieces that are perfectly functional and usable but not quite the newest or highest-spec.

All they had to do was find them.

'Grant,' he said, 'can you see if you can find a spare control column somewhere, as fast as you can, please.'

'Got it.'

Morgan stepped around to the back of the control console, unplugged the ruined screen and connected the undamaged one on the right-hand side, then walked back to the seat. Behind him, one of the SWAT team members was photographing the room and the three bodies lying on the floor, hopefully to allow the corpses to be moved somewhere else.

As he sat down the screen came to life and displayed the view from the Reaper's main forward-facing camera in the upper portion – the view was simply sky and clouds with nothing at all to indicate the drone's location – and below that, in a separate window, the flight instruments of the UAV.

He looked to his left, at the other undamaged flat-panel monitor, and realised it was showing the location of what could only be the Reaper, a tiny blue triangular symbol following a red vector and over-laid on a map of the local area. What immediately worried him was how close it was to Washington D.C. He checked the scale displayed at the bottom right of the screen and mentally applied that to the distance the UAV still had to run.

'Shit,' he muttered. 'That's fifteen miles, eighteen at the most.'

He switched his gaze to the other screen and to the flight instruments displayed there. The ASI, the air speed indicator, was showing 175 and he knew that the speed of an aircraft was normally given in knots, so that meant 200 miles an hour. Or just under twenty seconds to travel one mile.

The altimeter was unwinding at a frightening rate, and as he looked it passed 20,000 feet in the descent. He did some very rough and ready calculations in his head and estimated that the drone would reach ground level at about the same time as it would be over the centre of Washington.

Which was obviously the point.

Sadir must've heard something or guessed that he wasn't going to get the chance to drop whatever weapons the Reaper was carrying and instead had set it up to crash into the city centre, relying on the explosive power of the fuel still in the drone's tanks to cause as much mayhem as possible.

'I found this,' Rogers said, handing Morgan a complex-looking control column studded with buttons and switches.

'Great.' Morgan grabbed it, dived under the desk, identified the sockets on the system unit that the destroyed control column was plugged into, ripped them out and plugged in the new device.

He sat in the chair again and looked at the screen. At the bottom right-hand side a notification had just popped up: 'New device found. Driver loading.'

'It this going to work?' Rogers asked.

'Buggered if I know,' Morgan replied. 'But if I don't get this control column to function, and bloody fast, we are comprehensively screwed, and so's a hefty chunk of the population of DC. The only difference is that we'll get to walk away.'

The notification cleared from the screen. He rested his feet on the rudder pedals and began easing the control column back. He wasn't a qualified pilot, but he knew enough about aircraft to know that that would stop the drone's descent.

But it didn't.

The view from the camera now showed the unmistakable shape of the city in front of the UAV, the buildings becoming clearer with every passing second, and the altimeter still showed an unaltered rate of descent.

Morgan shifted his gaze to the mapping screen. The Reaper was down to 10,000 feet and on the map had roughly five miles to run. At that rate, he guessed that impact would occur in just over one and a half minutes.

And he was going to have a bird's eye view when it happened.

Chapter 74

Ben Morgan watched helplessly as the unmistakable skyline of Washington D.C. came into view on the screen in front of him. He could see the Washington Monument and the Capitol Building and the White House. He was still using the control column, or trying to, but none of the inputs he applied had the slightest effect upon the Reaper's course.

Maybe the control column was defective. Maybe that was why it had been put away. Then a new dialogue box appeared on the screen: 'Device installed'. Loading the driver had just taken a lot longer than he'd expected. Or maybe it just felt that way.

He again eased back on the control column. But again what he did had no effect on the flight of the Reaper.

Morgan slumped back in the seat, despair on his face as he tried to work out what was wrong. He again ducked under the desk and checked the control column connections, even though he knew if they were wrong the system wouldn't have detected it and loaded the device driver.

The image from the drone's camera showed exactly where the UAV was heading. Filling the screen and getting closer with every second that passed was perhaps the most potent and evocative symbol of the United States of America.

The Reaper, its fuel tanks half full and with a full load of lethal high-explosive ordnance, was less than a mile from the White House and on a definite collision course.

Chapter 75

'I can't stop this,' Morgan said. 'It's not responding.'

On the screen, the individual figures of pedestrians were rapidly becoming visible, as were stationary vehicles positioned at odd angles on the streets where they'd presumably ended up when their engines died. Directly in front of the Reaper, the unmistakable shape of the White House was growing bigger by the second, and Morgan unconsciously pushed the chair back to try to distance himself from the inevitable impact.

He kept on pulling the control column, and moving it from side to side, but nothing he did had the slightest effect. The Reaper just continued its inexorable powered descent to oblivion.

'Ten seconds,' Morgan said. 'Maybe less.'

Chapter 76

One of the SWAT team pushed Morgan to one side and stared at the displays on the two monitors for a moment. Then he reached out a hand to the trackball, span the wheel to move the mouse pointer on the screen showing the flight controls, selected one particular switch and clicked the left mouse button.

Then he reached for the control column and eased it back.

And instantly, as if by magic, the camera view changed. The streets and buildings, which had seemed close enough to touch, were suddenly replaced by the solid blue of the sky above Washington. Morgan could have cried with relief.

'How did you do that?' he demanded, recognising the man as the agent who'd been piloting the quad-copter drone around the target house before they made their approach.

'You had the autopilot locked on,' the special agent replied, as Morgan reached out for the control column again. 'Don't climb it too steeply. If you stall it, we'll be even deeper in the shit than we were before. Do you want me to do it? I've got lots of experience with drones. Not Reapers, but a drone is still a drone.'

'Oh, God. Yes, please,' Morgan said, stood up and backed away as the agent took his seat.

He watched the navigation screen that showed the Reaper's location and the agent steered it north-east, away from the capital, and checked the altimeter display, which confirmed the UAV was climbing steadily.

'We've still got a problem,' Gordon said, stepping over to him. 'Well done for gaining control of that UAV, but it can't stay in the

349

air indefinitely, and you can't just land it with the controls we have here. I don't know too much about these devices, but I do know that the take-off and landing have to be handled by a pilot at whatever airfield is being used.'

'If we can't land it,' Morgan said, 'I suppose we could fly it out over the Atlantic and just ditch it.'

'We could,' Gordon replied, 'but these things come with a multi-million-dollar price tag and it's bound to be carrying weapons as well, so that has to be our option of last resort. We do know that it took off from Hancock Field, up at Syracuse, so I suggest we turn it round and head it in that direction. Maybe there's a way of getting a military controller up there to find it on his radar and for another remote pilot to take control of it.'

The SWAT special agent now controlling the Reaper listened to the exchange and then turned round to look at Gordon.

'I've got it heading north-east right now,' he said, 'and I'm climbing it to forty thousand feet or thereabouts to keep it well above any civilian traffic. Hancock Field isn't the only unit up that way that flies these things. There's a military base called Fort Drum at the eastern end of Lake Ontario, and they operate drones as well. Maybe we should try calling them and find out if they've got any bright ideas. And there'll be no problem with the identification. I can just set the Reaper's transponder to squawk emergency, 7700, and that'll make it stand out like a dog's balls on any radar set that can see it.'

'Do it,' Gordon said, pulling out his mobile phone. 'Do it right now.'

Chapter 77

The so-called 'rogue' Reaper touched down entirely without drama on runway 21 at Fort Drum's Wheeler-Sack Army Airfield a little over three hours later, its weapons payload intact and undamaged.

The emergency squawk had allowed a completely faultless and easy identification of the UAV while it was still as far south as Baltimore. The handover had involved a prolonged telephone conversation between Lewis Gordon and Major Oscar Paulson. It was a most unusual situation, and the worst-case scenario would have seen the handover to the GCS at Fort Drum failing and the Predator continuing, entirely out of control, before crashing somewhere in a ball of flame. Eventually, the best solution they could come up with was to engage the drone's autopilot again, keep it at 45,000 feet and steer it due east. That way, if Fort Drum couldn't establish control, the UAV would simply fly out over the Atlantic Ocean and continue heading east until it finally ran out of fuel.

When Morgan shut down the computers in the improvised control suite, an action that would sever their communication with the Reaper, there followed an anxious three or four minutes while Paulson's men attempted to establish a link with it.

And when Paulson came back on the line and uttered a simple three-word sentence: 'We have control,' the house at Fairview erupted into cheers and clapping.

Chapter 78

Ben Morgan acquired something of a souvenir from the house at Fairview. The FBI team had searched the bodies of Mahdi Sadir and the two anonymous Chinese males and had recovered what appeared to be insulin vials and testing and injection equipment from Sadir's corpse. None of them actually believed the Iraqi had been a diabetic and, even if he had been, he certainly wasn't going to need insulin now.

'This could be important,' Morgan had said to Lewis Gordon, and explained what had happened back in the UK with the deaths of the SAS soldiers and the terrorist while in custody. 'I think this is probably what Sadir used to poison those men, and I'd like to take some of these vials back with me. Porton Down might find the contents interesting.'

'Fine with me,' Gordon had replied. 'I'll send a couple to the CDC, the Centers for Disease Control, out in Atlanta, and maybe a couple to Fort Detrick right here in Maryland. They're both in the dangerous bugs business, one way or the other.'

–

The damage in Washington was both extensive and expensive to rectify, the high-powered NNEMP devices working with remarkable efficiency. Something like half the cars and other vehicles on the streets had ground to a halt as their electrical systems burnt out, buildings suffered failures of lighting, air conditioning and elevators, and the vast majority of computerised systems and almost anything that incorporated electronic circuits were severely damaged or destroyed. The clean-up would take a long time and cost a lot of money.

But on the plus side, the loss of life had been minimal, less than twenty people having been killed by the explosions of the devices and another thirty-five or so injured, while a further dozen had died in related traffic accidents and the like. All in all, fewer than one hundred citizens of Washington had died or been injured as a result of the NNEMP attack. Of course, that didn't stop the papers and the media savaging the police, the armed forces, the government and anybody else they could think of to blame for what had happened. But no details of the so nearly successful but ultimately aborted Predator attack were released, or ever would be.

The three hackers whose actions had caused the initial blackouts in DC – Karim Ganem, Jamal Halabi and Talat Wasem – were all arrested by American police officers and charged with numerous offences relating to cybercrime and held in custody pending their trials. All would eventually be found guilty and receive a combined total of 187 years behind bars.

The identities of the people who had fabricated the NNEMP weapons were never established, and no arrests were made.

Ben Morgan, Natasha Black and Barbara Simpson received the grateful thanks of the American government for what they had done, individually and collectively, to help thwart the attack. The only tangible benefits they received were three upgrades to first class for their flights across the Atlantic back to London Heathrow and home.

Chapter 79

Two months later

Southern Iraq

Rashid had weathered the storm caused by the failure of Mahdi Sadir's ambitious attempt to strike back at America, but only just.

It wasn't the fact that the attack had failed that had caused such despair in the hierarchy of the Islamic State. It was the fact that they had committed the bulk of their treasury to the purchase of hundreds of thousands of put options, all of which had expired worthless when the stock markets around the world had failed to collapse. Because he had been so certain that the attack would succeed, Rashid was blamed publicly and privately for what had happened, his judgement had been called into question and his position in the hierarchy hotly disputed.

But he had survived. And he knew there would be other attacks, and other *shahids*, and other opportunities to bloody the arrogant face of the Great Satan. It was just a matter of picking a suitable target and devising a method – a simple one, with few opportunities for it to fail – and a date to carry it out. Recruiting the *shahids* would probably be the easiest part of the entire operation.

In the meantime, Rashid decided that he would maintain a low profile, and not get involved too deeply with any other operations being considered by the Islamic State, at least until the organisation had started to replenish its coffers and people had begun to forget what had happened.

He had a small farm on the outskirts of Karbala, not far from the Holy Shrine of Al-Abbas, some fifty miles to the south of Baghdad, where he would be close enough to the action to know what was going on and for people to remember him when decisions needed to be taken, but far enough away that people wouldn't see him on a daily basis and be reminded of what had happened. But he was determined to remain in touch with the organisation that he had served for so many years.

He fairly quickly settled into the routine, tending his sheep and goats, but always keeping a wary eye for danger. As far as he knew, the Americans had no idea who he was, far less what involvement he might have had in what had happened – or rather hadn't happened – in America's capital city.

In this belief, he was sadly mistaken.

With the situation in Washington under control, the NSA and their partner the GCHQ began picking apart the actions and particularly the communications that Mahdi Sadir had employed, not only while he was in America but also in the years leading up to that, when he was visiting places in Europe and China and even further afield. It is amazing what information can be collected by a careful examination of anybody's mobile phone usage, and although Sadir had been careful, he had still left behind near-invisible traces that could be detected by dedicated analysts.

Piece by piece, a picture began to emerge of who Sadir had been and who his contacts were. And from this amorphous data map the number-crunchers at GCHQ utilised Venn diagrams, 3-D graphs and other analytical tools to make sense of the connections. As they had expected, certain names and certain numbers began to surface, some repeatedly, as the entire picture started to emerge.

One of these was a man named Rashid who, along with certain other senior Islamic State officials, was clearly identified as being behind the linked plots in London and Washington. It was soon confirmed that Rashid, as the most senior member of this group, had apparently been the driving force behind the attacks.

And that meant his life was forfeit.

The Americans decided that retribution would come from the skies, but not as a random bombing or anything as imprecise as that. Instead, they obtained pictures of Rashid's face and the location of his smallholding and bided their time.

As a kind of poetic twist, they also decided that their weapon of choice would be a Reaper, and the man controlling it would be operating from the GCS at Hancock Field, the seat – or to be exact an identical replacement seat – that No Sweat Nagell had been sitting in when Major Sami Dawood had executed him.

–

Late on a Saturday afternoon, Rashid was walking along a country road, returning to his smallholding, when he heard an unusual sound in the sky. He stopped and looked up, shading his eyes against the harsh sun over Iraq, and watched as an unusual-looking aircraft with a long nose and straight wings overflew him at an unusually low altitude. When it had passed, the aircraft began climbing away and was quickly lost to sight.

–

'That's a match,' the sensor operator said, comparing the frozen image the Reaper's camera had recorded with a colour photograph of the man they were seeking. The low pass had allowed them to obtain excellent quality pictures.

'That's good enough for me,' the pilot replied, already arming one of the UAV's Hellfire missiles. 'We'll attack from the west, out of the sun.'

'Just a shame he won't hear it coming.'

–

The AGM-114 Hellfire missile was originally designed as a Mach 1.3 supersonic tank-buster but has proved to be equally adept at the elimination of selected high-value targets. People like Rashid, in fact.

This particular Reaper was carrying a Hellfire variant, the AGM-114R9X. Commonly known as the Ninja Bomb or the Flying Ginsu, the high explosive has been replaced by a kinetic warhead comprising a one-hundred-pound lump of material and six high-speed blades to slice and dice the target. It is specifically intended as an anti-personnel weapon and designed to reduce collateral damage and has been successfully deployed in the trouble spots of the world since 2017.

The man who masterminded the bombing of the USS *Cole* in 2000, Jamal Ahmad Mohammad Al Badawi, was eliminated by a R9X, as was Abu Khayr al-Masri, one of the most senior members of al-Qaeda. It has also been used against al-Qaeda members in Syria and senior Taliban fighters in Afghanistan. It's a precision assassination weapon against which there is almost no defence.

–

Rashid resumed his walk along the dusty track, wondering briefly about the aircraft he had seen. And then, perhaps gripped by some kind of subconscious premonition, he stopped and looked back, towards the west and the slowly sinking sun. At a greyish dot, very high and moving slowly.

And then he saw something else, below the grey dot, something that seemed to glint, high in the sky. Something small and fast moving. Very fast moving. Something that seemed to be heading towards him.

And in that instant he knew they'd made the connection. His last conscious thought was that he'd heard that the Americans didn't either forgive or forget.

Author's Note

SINCGARS

SINCGARS stands for Single Channel Ground and Airborne Radio System. It's a piece of standard military equipment and comes in various flavours, including the AN/PRC-119 manpack radio, which permits communication with airborne units. Typically, each patrol would include a soldier carrying one of these units.

Another is the AN/PRC-148 MBITR handheld unit. The designation MBITR stands for Multiband Inter/Intra Team Radio and is a personal combat radio system developed to address the requirement for individual communications on the battlefield. This is reflected in the designation AN/PRC, which stands for Army/Navy Portable Radio used for two-way Communications.

The SINCGARS system operates in the VHF – Very High Frequency – FM radio band and employs frequency hopping, changing 111 times every second, to ensure secure communications.

Fairchild Republic A-10 Thunderbolt and the GAU-8/A Avenger

When combat aircraft are designed, the provision of weapon mounting points is of crucial importance. Usually, pylons are fitted on the underside of the wings or occasionally on the base of the fuselage. The obvious exceptions are heavy bombers like the American B-52, which carry their payload inside the fuselage in bomb bays, and stealth aircraft like the Lockheed F-117 Nighthawk and the Northrop Grumman B-2 Spirit, which have to carry their weapons internally to preserve their extremely low radar cross-section and avoid compromising their stealth capability.

But there is one aircraft that breaks all the rules. It doesn't so much *carry* a weapon as is *built around* a weapon. The Fairchild Republic A-10 Thunderbolt, affectionately known as the Warthog, or just the Hog, and rather less affectionately as the ULF, or Ugly Little Fucker, is essentially an airframe constructed around a cannon. It's effectively a flying gun.

The GAU-8/A Avenger is a Gatling-type gun as big and heavy as a large family car, tipping the scales at over four thousand pounds when fully loaded, representing over 15 per cent of the unladen weight of the A-10. What that means in practice is that if it ever has to be removed from the aircraft the tail of the Thunderbolt has to be supported first – otherwise the aircraft will tip backwards when the gun is taken out.

The weapon is mounted very slightly towards the port side of the A-10 to allow the firing barrel of the Avenger – it has seven rotating barrels – to be aligned precisely with the centreline of the aircraft to avoid the massive recoil from shifting the aircraft off the attack line. This is essential because the recoil generated by the weapon firing is 10,000 pounds-force, slightly more than the 9,000 pounds-force output generated by each of the A-10's jet engines.

It fires 30mm projectiles fitted with plastic driving bands, to help preserve barrel life, from cartridges nearly a foot long, at a rate of 3,900 rounds per minute, meaning that the entire standard magazine load of 1,150 rounds would be exhausted in just eighteen seconds of continuous firing. To preserve barrel life and conserve ammunition the weapon is normally limited to one- or two-second bursts.

Accurate up to 4,000 feet or about three-quarters of a mile, the shells pour out of the rotating barrels at the rate of sixty-five every second, delivering a virtually solid stream of ordnance, more like a hose pipe than a machine gun. It's an enormously effective tank-buster, typically employing a five-to-one mixture of PGU-14/B API (Armour-Piercing and Incendiary) rounds and PGU-13/B HEI (High Explosive Incendiary) rounds. The PGU-14/B rounds are slightly the heavier of the two, mainly because each shell has a penetrating core of depleted uranium and titanium inside an aluminium outer body, which delivers enormous kinetic energy on impact. 'PGU' stands, rather boringly, for 'Projectile Gun Unit', a kind of military confusion-speak for 'cartridge' or 'bullet'.

Abū Omar al-Qurashi al-Baghdadi

Hamid Dawud Muhammad Khalil al-Zawi was born in 1959 in a village called Al-Zawiyah (hence his name) near Haditha in western Iraq and had an almost entirely undistinguished career as a police officer before working in an electronics repair shop and becoming the imam of a local mosque. Things changed for him, and for tens of thousands of other people, when coalition forces led by the United States of America invaded Iraq in 2003.

Al-Zawi responded by starting his own small terrorist gang and then became a major figure in the militant opposition group known as the Mujahideen Shura Council. This was formed in January 2006 and was an umbrella organisation that contained half a dozen Sunni Muslim insurgent groups including the Tanzim Qaidat al-Jihad fi Bilad al-Rafidayn, far better and more concisely known as 'al-Qaeda in Iraq'. The council didn't last long, being disbanded in October of the same year, and was replaced by ISI, the Islamic State of Iraq, essentially a rebranded al-Qaeda in Iraq. Al-Zawi became one of the three leaders of the new insurgent organisation, taking the position of the First Emir of the Islamic State of Iraq.

Not only did al-Zawi change his profession radically, switching from being an imam responsible for the religious education, welfare and guidance of his congregation to acting as a Kalashnikov-toting terrorist leading an insurgent group that specialised in slowly beheading people in front of video cameras, but he also changed his name.

A kunya

Names can be confusing and, in the Arab world, somewhat flexible. Given names can be replaced by a *kunya*, a teknonym or paedonymic that identifies the individual by reference to their offspring. So a man, irrespective of his actual name, may become known as Abū Waleed, meaning 'father of Waleed', while a woman can be called Umm Muhammad as the 'mother of Muhammad'. But a *kunya* can also have an entirely different and less innocent meaning, being used as a *nom de guerre* by Arab terrorists and unconventional or clandestine warriors. Osama bin Laden, for example, used the *kunya* 'Abū Abdullah'.

Hamid al-Zawi first adopted the *kunya* Abū Mahmud, but then adopted the *noms de guerre* Abū Omar al-Qurashi al-Baghdadi and Abū Hamza al-Baghdadi. The 'al-Baghdadi' suffixes literally translate as 'the one from Baghdad' or 'who came from Baghdad', meaning that his origin was either Baghdad city or the Baghdad Governorate, which of course it wasn't: the village of Al-Zawiyah is located in the Al-Anbar Governorate. Presumably he deliberately chose the name as part of his *nom de guerre* to try to associate himself with the capital of the country.

The name Abū Omar appeared on the radar of the coalition forces at a fairly early stage as a spokesman for the Mujahideen Shura Council, but his very existence was persistently questioned. In July 2007 an American military spokesman stated definitively that he did not exist and that the various verbal statements attributed to him were actually spoken by an Iraqi actor. A terrorist captured by the coalition forces also claimed that Abū Omar was a fiction and had been created simply so that a man of Iraqi origin could be perceived as the leader of an insurgent group run by foreigners, meaning al-Qaeda. This story was reinforced in March 2008 by another terrorist group – Hamas-Iraq – which claimed the same thing, that the Abū Omar character had been created by al-Qaeda as the Iraqi face of the insurgent organisation.

There was further confusion when the Iraqi Interior Minister stated that Abū Omar – or al-Baghdadi as he was commonly known – had been captured in Baghdad in March 2007. That was apparently somebody else who looked a bit like him. Then the same source claimed al-Baghdadi had been killed during a joint American–Iraqi operation north of the capital. That was followed by another report that the man had been arrested by the Iraqi military in April 2009, with photographs released to prove it. ISI denied this claim as well as all the others in a statement made by al-Baghdadi himself, and he continued to release audio statements and recordings throughout 2009 and 2010.

He was finally and definitively identified as one of the people killed in the raid on the safe house near Tikrit in April 2010.

Vektor, Gosudarstvennyy Nauchnyy Tsentr Virusologii I Biotekhnologii
(Vector, Russian State Centre for Research on Virology and Biotechnology)

Koltsovo Naukograd, Novosibirsk Oblast, Siberia, Russia

Koltsovo – Кольцо́во in the Cyrillic alphabet – was created in 1974 around Vektor, the Russian State Centre for Research on Virology and Biotechnology, an institute that studies particularly dangerous viruses. Named after Nikolai Koltsov, a respected Russian biologist, the settlement was granted *naukograd* or science town status on 17 January 2003 and is part of the group of Russian laboratories known as the *Biopreparat*.

Vektor itself is located a short distance to the east of the main town of Koltsovo as part of a scattered cluster of buildings encircled by a boundary road. The location is relatively secluded and has a permanent garrison of Russian Army soldiers because of what's held in the building. The six-storey structure contains samples of some of the most lethal bugs on the planet, including the Ebola, Marburg, Lassa, dengue and yellow fever viruses, and secure biosafety level 4 – BSL4 – laboratories where work on these deadly pathogens can be carried out in safety. Safety in this case is something of a relative term: in 2004 a female researcher at Vektor died after pricking herself with a needle contaminated with Ebola. The establishment is one of only two locations in the world, the other one being the Centers for Disease Control in Atlanta, Georgia, that are official repositories for samples of the smallpox virus.

During the Cold War Vektor was heavily involved in the development of biological weapons, but today it's an important research centre concentrating on creating antiviral vaccines and drugs, and on developing diagnostic tools and protocols for the treatment of infectious diseases.

Officially, that is. In fact, the unit's remit is far wider than that and includes a number of other, largely unrelated disciplines linked only by the two facts that the materials involved in the research are both extremely small and are dangerous or lethal to human beings. But lethal viruses and bacteria are not the only sub-microscopic entities that require specialised handling and storage.

After the collapse of the Soviet Union, the Vektor management found that although its diminished client base still included the Russian government and various organs of the state, many of the approaches it received were from outside, often from well outside, the boundaries of the new Commonwealth of Independent States. But a research project was a research project no matter where the principals were located, and Vektor had no particular difficulty in accommodating requests, as long as those requests were backed by a sufficiently attractive offer of remuneration. And one of the defining characteristics of many of its new customers was that they had very substantial, in some cases effectively unlimited, sources of funding.

Theory of flight

The most commonly accepted explanation of why aircraft fly is based on a theorem worked out by a Swiss mathematician named Daniel Bernoulli in 1738, when the only things in the air were birds, bats and insects, none of which bore much resemblance to an aircraft. Bernoulli calculated that if the upper surface of an aerofoil section is curved, like a modern aircraft's wing, air will have to travel faster over it compared to the speed of the air along the underside. That means the air over the upper surface will be at a lower pressure than the lower, so the wing will be 'sucked' or lifted upwards. This is known as lift.

But there's a problem. If the theory is right, then an aircraft should not be able to fly if it is upside-down, because then the effect of lift would be to force the aircraft down towards the ground. But display aircraft at air shows and the like routinely fly upside-down for prolonged distances, so Bernoulli can't be entirely correct.

It also doesn't explain why aircraft with flat, non-aerofoil wings, like some modern fighters, still manage to get into the air.

The other main contender is the Newtonian principle, based on his Third Law, which suggests that an aircraft's wing is forced upwards by the pressure of the air on its lower surface as the speed increases. The argument is that air has mass, and so the downward pressure of the lower surface of a wing should result in an equal and opposite force from the air to push the wing upwards.

This theory is more comprehensive because it can be applied to wings of any shape and is equally valid when an aircraft is flying inverted. However, the theory does not explain why there is a measurable area of low pressure above an aerofoil wing when an aircraft is in flight.

Joint Special Forces Aviation Wing (JSFAW)

One of the newest units in the military, the JSFAW was only created in April 2001 as a somewhat unlikely marriage of 7 Squadron of the Royal Air Force, flying Chinook HC2 heavy-lift helicopters, and 658 Squadron of the Army Air Corps, which operates the much smaller Eurocopter AS365N3 Dauphin II. The latter aircraft is often referred to by the British press as 'Blue Thunder', presumably on the reasonable if rather dull grounds that it's painted blue and makes a lot of noise.

A front-line helicopter base and specifically the home base of the British Chinook force, RAF Odiham at Hook in Hampshire, not far from Basingstoke, is home to 7 Squadron RAF of the JSFAW while 658 Squadron AAC is based at Stirling Lines, home of the Special Air Service (SAS) at Credenhill, near Hereford.

The JSFAW is nothing if not flexible, certainly in terms of what it comprises, with at least two sub-units no longer a part of it. 657 Squadron AAC was a part of the JSFAW, flying Lynx AH9A helicopters and based at RAF Odiham until the squadron was disbanded in 2018, while 651 Squadron AAC was based at Aldergrove in Northern Ireland at the Joint Helicopter Command Flying Station and originally operated Lynx and Apache helicopters before being disbanded in 2003. Three years later it was reformed as a part of the JSFAW, flying Defender AL1 and AL2 fixed-wing turboprop aircraft, better known in civilian commercial use as the Britten Norman BN-2T-4S Defender 4000, originally the Britten Norman Islander.

But although 651 Squadron is still operational, it's no longer a part of the JSFAW. The squadron's function was to provide UK special forces in Iraq and Afghanistan with ISTAR, meaning Intelligence, Surveillance, Target Acquisition and Reconnaissance. In Iraq the squadron was based at Al Amara, and in Afghanistan at Basra, and in both countries it was primarily involved in detecting and monitoring movements by insurgent groups. In Iraq, it also provided ISTAR support to the SAS Task Force Black, and more recently supplied airborne surveillance over East London during the Olympic Games in 2012.

Hawala

The *hawala* value transfer concept arose in India as early as the eighth century and differs from all modern financial systems in that funds are not physically transferred from the sender to the recipient. Instead, the sender deposits a sum with a *hawaladar* together with a password or other means of verification and another *hawaladar* in the destination city is informed about the transaction. The recipient approaches that *hawaladar*, provides the necessary verification and is given the agreed sum less a small commission.

But the funds are never actually transferred during the transaction: the system is based upon, and relies totally on, honour and the belief that the debt owed by the sending *hawaladar* will be repaid. In practice, each *hawaladar* maintains careful records of all transactions and the settlement of debts may not necessarily take the form of cash but can involve the provision of services, the supply of goods or other options.

Allāhu akbar

This Arabic expression is known as the *Takbir*, meaning the 'magnification of God', and it translates into English as 'God is great'. It's a very common expression used on a daily basis by Muslims in a wide variety of different contexts, including within the calls to prayer uttered by the *muezzin* – the *adhān* – as well as in normal conversation to express feelings or emotions like happiness or sadness, or just as a simple statement of faith.

It is one of the most used and religiously significant expressions in Islam, and not just as part of a spoken language. The expression *Allāhu akbar* can be found in the middle of the Iraqi flag, repeated multiple times on the flag of Iran and, since 2004, on the flag of Afghanistan as well. It has also been used as a battle-cry during conflict and more recently during terrorist attacks.

The Federal Bureau of Investigation (FBI) Criminal Justice Information Services (CJIS) Division

In October 1991 building work began on a nearly one thousand acre site in Clarksburg, West Virginia. The client was the FBI, and in July 1995 the structure was completed both on time and under budget – somewhat strangely for a government contract of any sort. The main building occupies half a million square feet and includes a cafeteria with seating for 600 people, an auditorium with seats for 500 and a computer centre that extends to some 100,000 square feet.

This was designed to be the home of the Criminal Justice Information Services Division, a high-technology arm of the FBI. Numerous technology-based programmes were either incorporated within it at its inception or were later transferred to it. These included IAFIS (Integrated Automated Fingerprint Identification System), NCIC (National Crime Information Centre), NIBRS (National Incident-Based Reporting System) and UCR (Uniform Crime Reporting).

FACE (the Facial Analysis, Comparison and Evaluation Services Unit) is also based there. The database available through FACE is vast: it comprises over 400 million images culled from numerous sources and including almost 200 million photos from driving licences and ID pictures, nearly 150 million visa photos and, inevitably, over 25 million police mug shots.

The defeat of Saddam Hussein's dictatorship was a beginning rather than an end for covert operations in Iraq. Although Hussein was about the only leader who'd managed to keep al-Qaeda out of his country while he was in power, after the campaign ended the terrorist organisation moved in. Fighting a group like al-Qaeda is akin to fighting smoke: the enemy is insubstantial and elusive, and it was recognised that using conventional military forces and tactics wasn't going to be enough.

Accordingly, in 2003 a squadron from the SAS was sent out to join a combined US/UK force to conduct operations against senior figures in al-Qaeda. Originally called Task Force 145 (TF-145), it was briefly renamed Task Force Knight and later TF-88. It included Task Force Black, a Sabre squadron from the SAS that was rotated every six months, supported by Task Force Maroon, a company from the Special Forces Support Group (SFSG), men drawn from the 1st Battalion, Parachute Regiment (1 PARA), the Royal Marines and the RAF Regiment. Task Force Black operated from the so-called 'Green Zone' in Baghdad at a base known simply as 'the Station'.

The three other units in TF-88 were Task Force Green, a contingent from the American 1st Special Forces Operational Detachment (Delta Force); Task Force Blue, US Navy SEALs from the Naval Special Warfare Development Group (DEVGRU), more commonly known as SEAL Team 6, and Task Force Orange, a team of signal intelligence analysts from the United States Army Intelligence Support Activity (USAISA or just ISA), part of the Joint Special Operations Command (JSOC).

TF-88 had air support provided by the American 24th Special Tactics Squadron, the 160th Special Operations Aviation Regiment (SOAR) and UK aircraft from both 7 and 47 Royal Air Force Squadrons. Intelligence collection was the responsibility of the American military, working with the British Joint Support Group (JSG – see *Cyberstrike: London*), the Secret Intelligence Service (SIS or MI6) and the Special Reconnaissance Regiment (SRR – see *Cyberstrike:*

London) as well as specialist operators from 18 UK Special Forces Signals Regiment.

Task Force Black left Iraq in 2009 when British forces withdrew from the country and was later redeployed to Afghanistan.

Anonymous

This loose but highly coordinated hacker collective – for want of a better term – has been around for about two decades, but first came to public attention in 2007 when the Canadian media announced that a fifty-three-year-old suspected paedophile had been arrested by the police after having been identified and located by a so-called 'Internet vigilante group' named Anonymous.

The group is unusual in that it is both unstructured and decentralised but highly coordinated. It is also very open and public about its plans and uses social media to invite anybody interested to join in and help carry them out. There is no leader or central control, just a widely dispersed collective of people who jointly decide what to do and how and when to do it, and then get on with the job. One of the members of Anonymous described what they did in the pithy – but undeniably accurate – phrase 'ultra-coordinated motherfuckery'. Anonymous tends to pick targets that it sees as acting against the interests of the general public, of repressing freedom of speech, of trying to control the Internet and, especially more recently, of political 'Big Brother' measures.

This is far from a comprehensive list, but since 2007 the group has been involved in attacks on, in no particular order, the Church of Scientology, the Motion Picture Association of America, the Recording Industry Association of America, the Bank of America, PayPal, Mastercard, Visa, the Government of Zimbabwe, the Government of Tunisia, the Los Zetas drug cartel and an American computer security firm named HBGary Federal.

In February 2011 a man named Aaron Barr, the CEO of HBGary Federal, made a catastrophic mistake. He told the media that his company had successfully infiltrated the loose collective of hackers known as Anonymous and would publicly promulgate the information that had been obtained. He had absolutely no idea what he was getting himself into.

In response, Anonymous very quickly hacked into and took over the HBGary Federal website, posting an explicit message that refuted Barr's claims of infiltration and mocked the ability and professionalism of the alleged 'computer security' experts the firm claimed to employ.

That's the polite way of putting it. Anonymous actually described them as a 'pathetic gathering of media-whoring money-grabbing sycophants', which seemed to express the group's opinion clearly enough. And then Anonymous used the Internet to publish almost 70,000 messages, memoranda and other private and sensitive material from the company files.

This caused more than just severe embarrassment, because the information included offers by HBGary Federal to illegally target journalists and other people for the firm's clients and, most embarrassing of all, Aaron Barr's suggestion that he might log into various teen-centric Internet chat rooms while posing as 'Naughty Vicky', a highly sexed sixteen-year-old girl. Anonymous also hacked into Barr's Twitter account, which allowed them to publish his home address and Social Security number.

Within a month, HBGary Federal's credibility had been utterly destroyed, a congressional committee had been tasked with mounting an investigation into what were seen as inappropriate and potentially illegal contracts entered into by the company, and Barr himself had been forced to resign.

The final message from Anonymous on the hacked company website seemed a reasonable summary of what had happened. It said: 'It would seem the security experts are not expertly secured. We are Anonymous. We are Legion. We do not forgive. We do not forget. Expect us.'

Donald Trump and the US Federal Depository Library website

In January 2020 the home page of the website of the US Federal Depository Library Program was defaced by a face. In this case, it was the bloodied face of Donald Trump being punched by a fist emerging from the green sleeve of a jacket that bore what looked like the insignia of the Islamic Revolutionary Guards. The image also included two gold-coloured missiles, each marked with the Iranian flag, and photographs of Ayatollah Ali Khamenei, the country's supreme leader. Text left on the site claimed that the 'Iran Cyber Security Group Hackers' had been responsible for the hack and stated that what they had achieved was 'only a small part of Iran's cyber ability'.

This hack occurred after an important Iranian military figure and leader of the Islamic Revolutionary Guards, Major General Qasem Soleimani, had been killed in Baghdad by an American drone strike. The defaced site also warned that 'severe revenge awaits those criminals who have tainted their filthy hands with (Soleimani's) blood and the blood of the other martyrs'.

In hacking terms, this website was a soft target as it allowed free and unrestricted access for the American public to view federal government information, so getting inside wouldn't have been difficult, though breaching the internal security systems to access the code running the site certainly should have been.

According to an official statement from the Cybersecurity and Infrastructure Security Agency, a part of the Department of Homeland Security, 'a misconfiguration with the content management system allowed a malicious actor to deface the website', the short version of which would read 'we were hacked'. The website was taken offline for about twenty-four hours while the damage was repaired and, hopefully and presumably, better security protocols were put in place.

Nanotechnology

Three events – a talk in 1959 by physicist Richard Feynman, the invention in 1981 of the STM, the scanning tunnelling microscope, and the discovery of fullerenes, an unusual allotrope of carbon that formed a closed or semi-closed mesh, in 1985 – sparked the creation of an entirely new kind of technology: the manipulation of matter at the molecular level. In fact, nanotechnology already existed in nature and in certain manufactured substances like colloids, combinations of chemicals where one substance is evenly dispersed throughout another, although the nanotechnology element wasn't understood.

There are millions of examples of nanotechnology in nature, like the feet of a gecko, a kind of lizard, which can hang upside down without using any kind of chemical adhesive to maintain its grip, and the colours on the wings of some butterflies and beetles. These colours aren't pigments but are caused by the spaces in an arrangement of microscopically tiny pillars made from sugars or proteins. These gaps actually manipulate the light that falls on them to produce certain colours or iridescent sheens.

Panhandler/panhandling

This is a unique Americanism used to describe a beggar or begging, and there are two possible derivations of the word. It could be a reference to the typical stance of a beggar standing with his or her hand held horizontally away from their body and hoping for somebody to put money on their palm. Using a bit of poetic licence, this stance could be considered to look something like a saucepan with a handle.

Perhaps the more likely explanation is that it comes from the days of the American gold rushes, when miners would sift through pebbles and stones in a pan looking for gold nuggets, because these days many panhandlers hold out pans or cups rather than their bare hand.

Security clearances and SCI – Special Compartmented Intelligence/Information

Most officers in the British Armed Forces hold a basic security clearance which allows them to occasionally see documents classified up to and including Secret. Until fairly recently, this was known as 'Negative Vetting' or NV and was intended to weed out obvious security risks like card-carrying members of the Communist Party or people who walked around with photographs of Stalin or Hitler or, these days, some radical Islamic preacher, in their wallets. To be allowed access to higher classification documents, individuals were subjected to a much more thorough and invasive procedure known as 'Positive Vetting'

(PV), which essentially began at the moment of conception and finished the day before the vetting started.

This was a simple and in most cases an effective system, as long as you ignored the obvious anomalies like Kim Philby, Anthony Blunt, Guy Burgess, Donald Maclean and John Cairncross, all of whom should have been detected well before they entered British – rather than Russian – government service. Burgess, for example, actually joined the British Communist Party while he was a student at Cambridge, which should have raised something of a red flag to any halfway competent checker. But in those days there was a peculiar belief that as long as a man had been to the 'right' school and the 'right' university and came from the 'right' family background, that somehow outweighed any completely obvious and totally unambiguous indications that he might be described as less than entirely patriotic.

These days, the security clearance system is much more complicated but the changes were not, oddly enough, sparked by the damage done by groups such as the 'Cambridge Five' but far more likely by the inevitable need for the British government to complicate everything it touches. What they have managed to do, reduced to its most basic level, is replace the simple and obvious NV and PV system with something that's virtually the same thing but much more difficult to understand.

Negative Vetting has been supplanted by an almost identical procedure with the clumsy and cumbersome title of Baseline Personnel Security Standard, or BPSS.

Then they've added a couple of extra checks, the Counter Terrorist Check or CTC, intended for people appointed to certain posts, and the Security Check or SC, which allows the holder access to Secret material and occasionally to Top Secret documents. Just in case you thought that was all a bit too simple, there's also a check called the 'enhanced Security Check' or eSC, which means they also want to see how much money you've got in the bank and where it came from.

At the top of the tree is Developed Vetting (DV), which is by far the most comprehensive check and is intended for people whose jobs require them to have regular and uncontrolled access to documents classified Top Secret. It's also exactly the same as the old and much easier to understand Positive Vetting. Oh, and there's also 'enhanced Developed Vetting' or eDV, which, just like eSC, allows a bunch of nosy bureaucrats to root about in your various bank accounts and ask impertinent questions.

Special Compartmented Intelligence or Information (SCI) is a kind of refinement and embodies the need to know principle. Just because somebody holds a DV clearance, for example, does not mean that they are entitled to see any Top Secret document that they want. Specific operations or documents are frequently restricted to that small number of people who have an absolute and obvious need to know the contents, which may not even be classified as Top Secret but which are so sensitive that a restricted clearance list is essential. To gain access to that particular material, somebody with a DV clearance would also need to be on the approved SCI list.

There are also several established restricted access categories, such as ATOMAL (meaning UK atomic data released to NATO) and Cosmic Top Secret or CTS, which again have restricted access even to people holding a DV clearance. 'Cosmic' in this instance has nothing to do with space or anything of that sort and is simply a sexy sounding acronym that decodes as 'Control of Secret Material in an International Command'. There's more than a sneaking suspicion that the bureaucrat who thought up that one decided that somehow he simply had to use the word 'COSMIC' because it sounded so steely and James Bond-y, and then spent hours or days trying to work out what the letters might stand for to justify his choice.

Independence Day and the Declaration of Independence

On 4 July 1776 the Declaration of Independence was adopted by the Second Continental Congress, the fledgling government of the thirteen colonies that made up the fledgling nation. In what was then legally an act of treason, the Declaration permanently broke the ties between America and Great Britain and established the country as a free and independent nation, no longer subordinate to or a subject of the British monarch.

The American Revolutionary War, also known as the American War of Independence, had started in April the previous year, and the preparation and signing of the Declaration did nothing to end the hostilities: the tide only turned decisively against the British with their defeat at the end of the Siege of Yorktown in October 1781, and the final peace accord, the Treaty of Paris, wasn't signed until September 1783.

In point of fact, Americans actually celebrate the wrong date: the decision to declare independence had been voted on and passed by Congress two days earlier, on 2 July, but the Declaration itself was not made until 4 July 1776. And it's almost certain that not all the members of Congress signed the document on 4 July, or indeed at any time that month: it's far more likely that many of the fifty-six delegates only put pen to paper as much as a month later, on 2 August.

The morning of 4 July 1777 was marked by a thirteen-gun salute – one for each of the thirteen colonies – at Bristol in Rhode Island, a celebration repeated as dusk fell that evening. Ever since then Independence Day has been celebrated across America. Interestingly, it wasn't until 1870, almost a century after the Declaration of Independence, that the date became a holiday for federal employees – unpaid, of course. They had to wait for another sixty-eight years, until 1938, for it to become a paid holiday.

Unmanned Aerial Vehicles (UAVs) or drones

One of the defining characteristics of warfare in the first two decades of the twenty-first century has been the increasing reliance upon RPAs and UAVs – remotely piloted aircraft and unmanned aerial vehicles – of various types, ranging from intelligence-gathering platforms to armed devices the size of a small aircraft, all types now universally known as drones. And it's not difficult to see why.

Drones cost much less than a military aircraft designed to do the same job and can be both lighter and have a far longer endurance than a conventional aircraft, largely because they're not having to lug around the deadweight of the pilot or pilots in the cockpit. And, if something catastrophic happens in the air or the drone is hit by a missile or anti-aircraft fire, the end result is a smallish crater on the ground filled with torn and twisted aluminium but, crucially, no living pilot to be captured and paraded in front of the world's press. Or, if the ground troops are a part of ISIS, to be doused in petrol and then burnt alive in front of a flock of video cameras and a crowd of radical Islamic thugs baying for blood.

These days, people are familiar with the occasional image on the evening news showing the aftermath of a drone strike – a new word that has now entered the vocabulary of the English language – that has targeted a wanted terrorist in a remote area of the Middle East where conventional forces would find it extremely difficult or impossible to operate. Such attacks typically involve a Hellfire missile fired from a drone known as a Reaper, an extremely efficient airborne killing machine that frankly does its job much more effectively than any pilot in a manned aircraft could ever do.

What many people don't realise is that although drones like the MQ-1 Predator and the MQ-9 Reaper are unmanned, they do have a man at the controls, a trained military pilot usually sitting in an air-conditioned bunker on an air base in Nevada or Montana, half a world away from the scene of the action, who communicates with the UAV through satellite links and who can see what is in front of or below the drone through high-resolution camera systems. It is almost as if the pilot is actually in the aircraft, but without the inherent danger that his physical presence would pose.

The figures are unambiguous. How long a UAV can remain in the air is largely determined by its weapons fit, and the Reaper can carry a maximum payload of 3,750 pounds of munitions, primarily a mix of Hellfire missiles and GBU-12 and GBU-30 bombs. With a full fuel load and that payload the Reaper's radius of action is 1,150 miles and it can stay aloft for between sixteen and twenty hours. Some drones are now achieving airborne endurance times in excess of forty hours. To manage anything like the same endurance with a typical fighter or ground attack aircraft would require multiple air-to-air refuelling missions and exactly how sharp any fighter pilot would be after sitting in a cramped cockpit at the controls for sixteen hours, desperate for a drink and a visit to the loo, is something of a moot point. But the pilot of a Reaper can hand over control to another pilot whenever he feels in need of a coffee, something to eat, a lavatory break or some sleep. It's undeniably a safer, cheaper, more effective, and much more efficient way of going to war.

And the pilot in America doesn't even get involved with arguably the two most difficult phases of any flight – take-off and landing. Because both of these require instant responses to potential obstacles, the ability to steer the drone along a particular sequence of taxiways, to take account of the prevailing wind and to obtain clearance from the local controlling authority, these two parts of the operation are handled by a local pilot at whatever airfield or air base the drone is operating from. The pilot in America only takes over control once the aircraft is clear of the airfield and at altitude, and he hands back control well before the drone approaches the runway for landing.

The general consensus is that these devices are an extremely useful addition to the armoury of the United States of America, and the use of UAVs and UASs – unmanned aerial systems, a generic term usually applied to unarmed reconnaissance vehicles – has been increasing in recent years. In fact, it's been increasing a lot.

It's been established that there are over a thousand American military bases worldwide, and for a drone to operate from one doesn't require anything like the infrastructure that would be needed to operate conventional manned aircraft. A fairly short concrete or tarmac runway, a small hangar or other building in which the drone can be kept and where maintenance work, refuelling and re-arming can take place, a handful of qualified pilots and maintainers and suitable communications, and that's about it.

But as well as bases overseas located in or near potential or actual trouble spots, there are drone bases in at least thirty-nine of America's fifty states and UAVs are an increasingly common sight to observers on the ground and an even more common sight to air traffic controllers sitting in front of radar displays. Not all of these drones are operated by the American military. American Customs and Border Protection use Predators to monitor the borders of the country, the Central Intelligence Agency operates a small fleet of UAVs for classified purposes – almost everything the CIA does is classified, obviously – and the Defense Advanced Research Projects Agency – DARPA – frequently flies drones over the continental United States.

What is perhaps more surprising is the range of organisations that possess Certificates of Authorizations or COAs that allow them to operate drones over America. These include police departments, colleges, universities and even a few towns and small cities. What characterises these UAVs, however, is the fact that they are unarmed and are normally used for tasks like surveillance, photographic reconnaissance and mapping missions.

Drones operated in the airspace above continental America by the military, on the other hand, are normally armed, and some of the bases used are in surprising locations. As is stated in this novel, two of them are in New York State. Syracuse, New York is the location of the Hancock Field Air National Guard Base, which operates Reapers, and fairly recently the American Army base at Fort Drum, also located in New York State, began training missions using Reapers, initially operated by qualified drone pilots from Hancock Field.

SSR Secondary Surveillance Radar

One common factor relating to drones flying in either military or civilian airspace is the requirement that they be identifiable, both to ground-based radar operators and to other aircraft. And, just like manned military and civilian aircraft, this identification is achieved by means of SSR – secondary surveillance radar – transponders. This word is an example of a portmanteau, a word made up from two other words, in this case 'transmitter' and 'responder', which is precisely how it functions.

The transponder receives an interrogation message on 1030 MHz and sends a reply on 1090 MHz. What it replies depends upon the type of aircraft it is fitted to. Military aircraft can transmit an IFF – identification friend or foe – signal, a coded message that can be read by military radar operators and fighter aircraft, while both military and civilian aircraft can transmit a code comprising 4,096 different options in the form of four digits that use the numbers 0 to 7, so 0000 to 7777. This code can be converted by a radar station using a system called code/callsign conversion to display the aircraft's callsign, speed, and altitude if a Mode C transponder is fitted, along with its rate of climb or descent.

Within this allocation are certain reserved codes used to silently indicate the status of the aircraft, the most important of which are 7500 (hijacking), 7600 (radio failure) and 7700 (emergency), all of which are shown as enhanced returns on radar displays.

For drones, the carriage of SSR transponders is essential because many of these devices are too small to be seen with the naked eye until a mid-air collision might be unavoidable. The other side of the coin, obviously, is that flying a Reaper or a Predator over the badlands of Afghanistan with its SSR transponder unambiguously announcing its presence to any hostile unit equipped with a suitable radar and a truckload of SAMs is clearly a recipe for disaster, so the ability to remotely turn the transponder off and on is essential.

Hijacking or taking over a drone

It would be reasonable to expect that as the Predator and Reaper drones and their lethal kin are as well armed as a modern ground-attack aircraft, the designers and engineers would have ensured that their software was impossible to hack and made certain that their transmissions could not be intercepted or compromised. That expectation, sadly, has proved to be somewhat optimistic. The reality is that data transmitted from any device can be intercepted or jammed or disrupted in some way and this applies equally to an airborne drone and to its base station.

In December 2009 the *Wall Street Journal* published a headline that probably sent shivers down the collective spines of the American government and much of the US military machine. The headline read: 'Insurgents hack US drones: $26 software is used to breach key weapons in Iraq; Iranian backing suspected'.

The suggested implications were frightening. If the Iranians genuinely had hacked their way into the control systems of the then $4 million Predator UAVs and were able to redirect the drones to release their missiles and bombs against Western targets, none of the Allied forces in Iraq and Afghanistan would ever be safe again.

Fortunately, like most claims of this sort made by the media, the headline was both hysterical and factually inaccurate in almost every single respect. There had been no hack, nor had there been a breach and as far as it could be established the Iranians weren't involved in any way, though the Russians were, albeit indirectly. In fact, the only thing the headline actually got right was the price of the software involved: it cost $26 in the shady backstreet black markets of Baghdad.

What had actually happened was that an insurgent with a fair degree of technical know-how had obtained a piece of software produced in Russia called SkyGrabber, a program that was not designed to assist hackers in any way or to be used by them. In fact, it's specifically intended to allow users to download televised football matches and movies and other stuff from satellite television channels without the inconvenience and expense of actually paying for them.

The insurgent loaded the software onto a computer, hitched the computer to a satellite dish and then began scanning the skies until he locked into a stream of video data being transmitted by a Predator drone. Unlike the transmissions and responses used in controlling the UAV, the video feeds from its cameras were not encrypted, so all that had actually happened was that an unauthorised individual had managed to log on to and record a transmission he wasn't supposed to see.

So no breach, no hack and no Iranian involvement. All good news.

Unfortunately, almost exactly two years later the Iranians certainly did become involved with an American drone.

On 4 December 2011 American CIA operators lost contact with a Lockheed Martin RQ-170 Sentinel unarmed UAV, allegedly while over the airspace of Afghanistan though the Iranians claimed they had detected it some 140 miles inside their borders. The following day the Iranian government announced that its cyber warfare unit located in north-eastern Iran at Kashmar had taken control of the drone and had successfully landed it.

Western news sources initially stated that the Sentinel had been shot down, but this was obviously not the case as the Iranians quickly displayed the apparently intact UAV: if it had been hit by a missile or gunfire and had then crashed there would have been little left to put on show. Clearly, the Iranians had somehow taken control of the drone and managed to make it do a soft landing. The obvious question was how?

According to an unidentified Iranian engineer, they had successfully jammed both the satellite and ground-based control signals and then carried out a GPS spoofing attack that sent incorrect GPS data into the UAV's navigation system. This data suggested to the drone's navigation system that it was near its home base in Afghanistan and instructed it to land. The obvious problem with this suggestion is that the primary navigation aid on almost all of America's manned and unmanned military vehicles, including the TLAM (Tomahawk Land Attack Missile), the MQ-1 Predator, the MQ-9 Reaper and the RQ-170, isn't GPS but inertial navigation. This is the case because GPS signal jamming and spoofing is a fairly simple technique to employ, whereas the INS, the inertial navigation system, is internal to the craft and cannot be compromised.

But however they had done it, it was obvious that the Iranians had somehow managed to establish control over the Lockheed Martin drone at least to the extent necessary to persuade it do to a soft landing. Or soft-ish, anyway. If they did manage to feed incorrect GPS data into its system and had been able to generate a landing instruction, the drone's controlling software would have assumed that it was landing on its home-base runway rather than some anonymous stretch of desert near Kashmar. There were some suggestions that the drone had suffered some damage, presumably on landing, which the Iranians had hastily patched up before putting it on display.

What is beyond dispute is that the Iranian government did take possession of the Lockheed Martin RQ-170 Sentinel, a fact unofficially acknowledged by the Americans on 6 December 2011. A somewhat optimistic request for the return of the drone by President Obama was haughtily rebuffed by the Iranian government, along with a complaint to the UN Security Council about the American violation of Iranian airspace by the UAV.

Having obtained the intact or largely intact and undamaged RQ-170, the Iranians then set about reverse engineering it to produce their own version. This was shown on Iranian television in May 2014 but was widely dismissed by Western observers as a mock-up rather than a working UAV. This was followed in November 2014 by claims by the Iranians that it had made a successful test flight and in September 2016 a statement that a UAV called *Sa'egheh* had entered service with the Iranian military.

Critics and disbelievers of these claims were silenced in February 2018 when Israeli forces shot down a *Sa'egheh* UAV. Examination of the drone showed conclusively that it was primarily derived from the RQ-170 UAV and that the design was both advanced and embodied Western technology.

Non-nuclear electromagnetic pulse weapon (NNEMP)

Known as an explosively pumped flux compression generator bomb, or more commonly as a non-nuclear electromagnetic pulse or NNEMP, or even just as an E-bomb, the weapon had its roots in a suggestion by theoretical physicist Arthur Compton back in 1925. Compton believed that the high energy photons generated by electromagnetic energy would be capable of freeing electrons from lighter elements, those with low atomic numbers, and that those freed electrons could then interact with the Earth's magnetic field. That would produce a fluctuating electric current, which would in turn induce a very powerful magnetic field. This became known as the Compton Effect.

Nearly three decades later, in 1951, a Soviet physicist named Andrei Sakharov came up with a variant of this idea. He suggested that a non-nuclear electromagnetic pulse could be produced by using an explosively pumped flux compression generator, basically employing an explosive charge as part of a weapon to create fluctuating electric and magnetic fields. His work, and all parallel work on NNEMPs, remained classified for some years.

The idea surfaced again in September 2001 in an article in *Popular Mechanics* magazine which covered the design and concept of a flux compression generator bomb or FCG, a relatively simple but potentially devastating weapon that wouldn't even be particularly expensive to manufacture. Such devices would be short-range weapons, with only about one millionth of the power of the EMP produced by a nuclear blast, but because of their comparatively small size they could be positioned close enough to their intended targets to ensure that they were effective.

It is known that the American military includes certain types of EMP weapons in its arsenal, and of course it is well known that very powerful EMPs are associated with the detonation of nuclear weapons. However, it is also well established that for some years the United States has concentrated on what are known as HPMs, high-power microwaves, weapons that have a similar effect to a NNEMP but use a different mechanism to achieve the same result.

The HPM, as its name suggests, is essentially a kind of hugely scaled up and focused microwave oven, the idea being that the device could be carried as part of the weapon load of a drone or cruise missile and the beam of microwave energy could be focused on ground targets, again disrupting or completely destroying electrical and electronic systems. This would allow the weapon to be reused, whereas an E-bomb only produces its EMP when it explodes, so it's a one-shot device.

Acknowledgements

With thanks to Dame Janet Trotter CVO, Nicola Whiting MBE, Richard Berry, Cameron Rogers, Hal Evans, Angela Edwards and Barbara Spooner MBE.